S0-ABZ-298

Purgatory

Purgatory

MONTY MICKELSON

St. Martin's Press
NEW YORK

For Anastasia

The author wishes to express his appreciation to the Bush Foundation for its support.

 For information, address St. Martin's Press, 175 Fifth Avenue, New York, N.Y. 10010.

Library of Congress Cataloging-in-Publication Data

Mickelson, Monty.
Purgatory / Monty Mickelson.
p. cm.
ISBN 0-312-08877-9
I. Title.
PS3563.I352P87 1993
813'.54—dc20 92-43887
CIP

First Edition: April 1993

10 9 8 7 6 5 4 3 2

Part One

◆

Sanctuary

There is no fate that cannot be surmounted by scorn.
—Albert Camus, *The Myth of Sisyphus*

Chapter One

◆

The road is the best part of this job, if you want my opinion. I see road tripping as a little dividend, a little celebration. It comes at the end of a score when everybody's happy and nobody's busted or dead. I usually leave at night. I head up to Barstow and then across the desert; set the cruise on some gas-hog rental, pop a tape in the deck, and relax. I don't sing along; I hardly even listen. I just let the breeze blow out all that dead air and open up every pore, man, every valve. By the time I reach Kingman, I'm hollow—I'm so ripped and reamed that you could play me like a flute. By that time, I've got to go to work. If you can call it that.

The younger guys all think the business is nickel bags and silk shirts and pinky rings. They want high profile and they get it. They get their faces in every post office lobby. They get their phones tapped, their mail read. The DEA kicks their doors in and the feds audit their taxes. "Retail chickenshit" is what Luis calls it. But Luis started carrying a sword cane—a *sword cane*! Like he's going to play Zorro when some punk whips out an Uzi. And Luis flashes his money as bad as the rest. I've got 350 K in the trunk of this car, and I never flash more than a twenty.

And that's why I've never been stopped, never spotted on a laundering trip. I sell the fake, the small business transaction thing because that's what it means to me. The money is just goods, just inventory that I've got to move. I dress down; I don't wear jewelry. I'm polite as hell. And when I leave the bank, I'm the last face that teller would recall. Look at me and you might believe that, but it's not as easy as it sounds. Lots of banks don't see seven, eight grand very often, so they want to chat. You've got to blow some convincing smoke. You don't want them calling over the head teller. The best story I ever had was following Bob Parson's Show, "The World's Cleanest Midway." In every town where they set up, I told the bank I was carrying receipts. *All that money from circus games! I s'pose those quarters add up!* They certainly do. Got to get back to the fairgrounds. Bye.

It's just that simple, and just that hard. You've got to know which bank would be suspicious, which town would never see that kind of cash. I walk through lots of banks without even batting an eye. Sometimes I'll book after I meet the teller. It's all acting and vibes. And instinct. You trust your instincts and you don't blow a score that started six months ago just for one cashier's check.

Luis trusts my instincts and—so far—he's trusted me. He treats me well because he knows how a man can be tempted. I get fifty bucks on every thousand I wash, plus a bonus, plus expenses. Other than that, it's just me, the money, and the car out there. All that road and time to think. Of course, we set an itinerary and I've got to call in. Luis almost never picks up. I just leave the town and the motel on his answering machine: Best Western, Needles; TraveLodge, Flagstaff; Flamingo Hilton, Vegas. He gets rattled when I miss. I got stranded once in the Mojave because nobody would call me a truck. People wanted to take me to a station, but I can't leave the car with the money. So I sat all night with a broken tie-rod. Then, while I was getting towed, a car skidded out of the other lane, pulled a U-turn, and followed us. It was Luis and a couple of friends. They drove straight through from L.A. when I missed my call. Real Samaritans.

But usually we don't talk until I get back with the checks. That's why I was kind of shocked when he picked up the phone last Friday. Hello Carson City, he says. And Luis doesn't ask about how much I've done or if I've got any problems. All he says is that he wants me to pick up a friend of his down in Scotty's Junction. I think hard. I get out my map. Scotty's Junction . . . Scotty's Junction. It's out by the nuclear testing range, halfway to Las Vegas. End of civilization, man. Edge of the universe. What kind of friend could this be? I wonder. Some nuclear mutant?

An old friend, is all Luis says. He used to carry the money. If he's still a dusky, we might bring him back in, Luis says. Dusky my ass, I say. Have you talked to this guy? Have we gone fraternal? Are we the Salvation Army? This ain't no vacation, I remind him. *I'm carrying the friggin' money.*

You pick him up and you get along, Luis says. We already got him some I.D. so he can earn his keep.

I don't like it, I don't like any of it, and I give that spic bastard an earful. *What's this about? Are you fucking with me? I earn my own goddamn keep.* I never miss a call; I never cheat you a dime, I say. Three years now and I need a baby-sitter? *What's this about, Luis?*

He's a stand-up guy, balls to the wall, Luis tells me. You're the best, Danny. Nobody wants to take away your job. (I can hear him tapping the floor with that silly cane—*bratta-dat-dat.*) Listen, we owe this guy and we take care of our own. You might even like him; he's a real character.

Scotty's Junction is stranded in the 1950s—a period piece right down to the thermometer on the Coca-Cola sign. Everything is coated with this fine fallout dust, and at night it all takes on this red glow from the neon out by the road. Just gas pumps, a diner, and a toy casino. Hardly worth a piss break. But that's mostly what blows people in the door; collect a key on a block of wood and amble around the corner. The urinals have these little plastic targets. The HOT knob is gone from the faucet. No hand towels. No soap. You figure they're conserving water because it hasn't rained here in two hundred years. They're also scrimping on payroll. The same girl who deals blackjack checks your oil. She's also the postmaster, notary, and chef. Ask her name and you'll get a look that would freeze the Panama Canal.

Cowboy truckers spread their asses over the counter stools. GIs pass out on their duffels while they wait for the Greyhound. Frowzy girls swing past you with a load of breakfast platters. Everybody's chain-smoking and picking their teeth and pumping the slot machines. It's the kind of place that does a roaring business in Tums and clip-on shades. They sell *Racing Form, National Enquirer,* and those air-freshener cards with pictures of topless babes. Every desert state has a Scotty's Junction or two. Their whole scam is based on the human bladder—they're exactly one piss break from Vegas, or Phoenix, or San Bernardino. That third cup of coffee served two hundred miles ago is all that keeps them afloat.

So I buy a few shorted gallons of gas and play some blackjack against the short house deck. I walk through the diner, trying to guess which greaseball is Luis's new recruit. I figure Luis gave the guy my picture, but nobody gives me a second look. I decide to play pinball, and I've just fed in the quarters when I glance out the window at the car. The fabled dusky is leaning on my fender, picking tar off his boot with a stick. *Too much hair,* is my first thought. He can't move money looking like that. He's got this wild curly crop growing every which way. A beard, too. Chino pants and one of those tuxedo shirts with the pleats; then a wool blazer with dark rings where the elbow patches used to be. *A character,* Luis said. Got that right, I say to myself as I walk out into the neon as bright as day.

Three days, and I'm so tired of asking questions that I give up and listen to the tapes. We cover almost six hundred miles. We get the kid a haircut, a shave (he keeps the mustache), and some different clothes. We move a lot of money in Vegas and he works the exchange just fine. I talk about how I plan the itinerary, how I pick the banks. I tell him how I met Alonzo in Phoenix, how I linked up with Luis and moved to L.A. I talk about women, about cars, about the Lakers, the Kings, and the Rams. I talk about the Raiders and about the point spread I beat in the Rose Bowl. I talk myself hoarse and this character doesn't say shit.

He does tell me his real name is Tommy. He says he grew up in Wisconsin but that everybody in his family is dead. When I really put the screws to him, I find out that he carried money for Luis six years ago when he was going to school in L.A. He doesn't say what he was studying, or why he got out of the business. All the rest I get from what I see—that he doesn't smoke or drink or read anything except a menu. He's got this real menu fetish. He'll agonize over the menu in some podunk sandwich shop, bugging the waitress about ingredients and stuff. It's like he's at "21" and wants to know what's in all those sauces.

So he likes reading menus, and the billboards that go ticking by. We'll pass some sign and he'll go a few miles and ask something about the product. The sign talks about copiers, and old Tommy will jump on the topic. *I didn't know Canon made copiers,* he'll say. *How long have they done that?*

Who knows and who cares, I say. When they make one that prints money, then I'm interested.

Tommy gets real interested in clothes shopping. I figure he should look a little more cowboy, a little less Venice Beach. I take him to that mall on the Vegas strip that has Saks and Nieman Marcus, but he says he doesn't want new. If you ride the range in the Southwest, he says, you don't wear designer jeans. He finds a Goodwill in the city where the welfare witches shop. He sorts through pipe racks and digs through barrels for two hours. He gets real authentic. He gets jeans with the seat pocket worn in the shape of a snuff can. He gets a frayed western shirt and a Stetson with a sweat stain on the brim. He gets a tooled belt that says NED on the back. He buys himself a buckle the size of a pie plate. He squints and frowns and fusses with that hat. And when he leaves that store, Tommy is all cowboy. But back in the car, he is the billboard addict again; the silent partner.

I even try to get him going on Twenty Questions. We're heading to Kingman on U.S. 40. I can't find a decent radio station. So I ask Tommy if he ever did any of those riding games—like

Twenty Questions. He says no, he's got a better one. It's a fantasy game, he says. You use your imagination.

Uh-huh, I say. Does this game have a name?

Sure, he says. It's called Beach or Buffet. Those are the categories, sort of like "animal, vegetable, or mineral." The way you play, he says, is that you choose a category—beach or buffet—and I describe it. Well more than that, he says, I *re-create* it. I populate the beach. I describe the ultimate buffet. Uh-huh, is all I can say. Then I ask how you score points, how you win.

It's not really *competitive*, Tommy says. It's more like an exercise. And then he's talking a mile a minute, saying how you have to make it as vivid as life. For instance, he says, you choose beach as a category. I give you Daytona Beach in March. It's the first day of the first week of college break. It's dawn. You get a low surf, really gentle, carrying those little crests of foam. And when it pulls you back, you feel the sand eroding under your feet. It caves under your heels and then slaps your calves with the next wave. And that sensation is new and exotic because maybe you drove all night from Ohio or Indiana, where they don't have oceans or waves.

Maybe, I say.

And you look up to see the sun on the horizon, and pelicans floating about fifty yards out. It's still too early for the cars to come down, for the guys to lug in their coolers and stake out a spot in the sand. You've almost got that beach to yourself.

Almost?

Just ahead of you, walking in the same surf, feeling the same sensations, is a girl, Tommy says. The first thing you notice is her great posture—shoulders back, walking on her toes so that her calves stay nice and tight. She's wearing one of those low-back one-piece suits that show every notch in her spine. And maybe she just arrived yesterday, he says, with her sorority friends from UVA. She's got a little color on her shoulders and the backs of her legs. The suit is brand-new, Tommy says, and she's self-conscious about whether it covers her ass. She reaches back every few steps to tug it back when it rides up over one of her cheeks.

Firm cheeks? I wonder.

The best, he replies. So good that you're afraid to have her turn around, afraid that the front won't stack up. But it does, Tommy says, with this huge grin. You see her profile when she stoops over to pick up a shell. Strong chin, full lips, nice bones, Tommy says. The breeze is just cool enough to perk up her nipples.

Blond hair, blue eyes? I ask.

Why not? he says. Cut in kind of a page boy that she tucks behind her ears. She pulls back some hair and sees you as she turns. You smile. She smiles back. You keep walking, but then she makes some comment about a shell. She holds it for your inspection. And all of the sudden, you're close enough to catch her scent, to look down the rim of her bathing suit. She's laying on that sweet Virginia accent, and you're lapping it up. She smiles again and your stomach drops as the waves keep pulling the sand from under your feet. It's like she's sapped out all the winter chill and the hangover you've been fighting all morning. You've got this incredible clarity of mind, enough to pitch some story about fossil coral, he says.

And she buys it?

Absolutely, Tommy says. But more important, she likes you, likes the way you look, and even likes the way your eyes take in her hips, her thighs, her ankles. Because while you're doing that, she's done her own little survey and you pass with flying colors. Pretty soon, you're walking the beach together. Then you're sunbathing on the same towel.

I ask him if we ever leave the beach. How far does this fantasy go?

As far as you like, Tommy says. As far as your motel room. Far enough to smear a little lotion on each other, to draw down the straps of that new swimsuit while she slips you a little tongue. Far enough to see those perfect brown fingers working on the drawstring knot of your trunks. Busy fingers. Real busy. Lips, too. You never quite finish applying that lotion, Tommy says. At least not until after.

I clear my throat and shift a little. I decide to ask about the buffet. And I get more of the same—a food fantasy with all that lurid detail. He's amazing—switching gears from banging that goddess to stuffing his face. He starts with every fruit you can name—half I've never heard of. Then come the egg dishes, the meats and cheeses, the triple-layer cakes. And while he's describing this incredible spread, it finally dawns on me: The whole connection with Tommy and Luis comes clear. This is just glorified jailhouse bull. I heard it in Quentin all the time. At night, after lockdown, when there's no drugs, no TV, you talk yourself to sleep. You talk food or gash. Some guys talk sports and criminal law. But mostly it's about what you miss the most. Jailhouse bull. It explains the menu fetish. Tommy got caught on a run for Luis. Six years in stir gave him that dusky status. Beach or buffet—that's choice. He's a real character, all right.

Tommy's driving; I'm sleeping in the back when I hear the tires hit gravel. It's supposed to be paved roads all the way to Flagstaff, so I sit up and ask what the hell.

I can get us to Phoenix quicker, Tommy replies. We cut southeast through these mountains and make up at least a hundred miles.

What about my bed and shower? I ask. We had a bank stop in Flagstaff; we're supposed to call in from there.

I know a little town you're going to love, Tommy says. Little funky mining town, got a great bed-and-breakfast. And you can pass nine grand at the local bank tomorrow morning. He doesn't name the town. He eyeballs me in the rearview mirror.

Right off, I'm getting these red flags, but I try not to let on that I'm suspicious. *Balls to the wall,* Luis said. *A stand-up guy.* Well, if he's such a righteous dusky, why does he wait until I'm asleep to change the program? I reach under the seat for my gun, slip it into my jacket pocket. I climb back into the front with the jacket heaped up in my lap.

I don't like funky mining towns, I say. And I told you about podunk banks. Everybody knows everybody. Nine thousand dollars would make them shit tacks. You might as well try to pass *nine hundred grand*—sell some drugs while you're at it.

Tommy glances over with these red, red eyes. The air is bluish and it's obvious he's smoked a bowl while I was sleeping. He sees my expression and the smirk fades away. I never get stoned on the road and he knows better. Maybe he senses something with the jacket.

I'm sorry, Dan, he says. I forgot about calling in. I was just sick of the motel scene. Thought you'd like the surprise.

I hate surprises, I tell him. I like motels.

We won't stay; we'll just call Luis and keep driving, Tommy says. You're probably right about the bank.

You bet your ass I'm right, I say. You got to learn to trust guys who are smart enough to stay out of the joint.

That one hits home. I know I'm right about the menu fetish when he cuts me a hard look and flicks on the radio.

A couple of hours and we pass the sign for Jerome: ARIZONA'S FINE ARTS COMMUNITY. The Lincoln really has to work to climb the mountain—lots of hairpin turns that make the power steering groan while half the car hangs over the ledge. I'm wondering how many pipes Tommy smoked, how good his depth perception can be. The headlights fall on some old stucco buildings and a gas station with pumps that look like chess pieces. We pass a stairway coming out of the embankment, chopped off and leading nowhere. A few more swings of the wheel and we're on the main street of a ghost town. Funky, real funky.

The whole town is on this severe tilt, just clinging to that mountain. It's part Dodge City, part shantytown. You can see how the main drag was a real promenade—all these connecting verandas and storefronts. One building was maybe the sundries store, another one hardware or feed. There's squat little houses and big crumbly hotels with trees grown through cracks in the courtyard. And everything that isn't boarded up or derelict is all painted and frilled for the tourists. The main street is an artist's ghetto—rock hounds and potters and shops that sell coffee tables made out of stumps. Real funky. All of these jewelers and candy stores and art galleries—a bunch of old hippies hustling their *dreck*. See one arts colony and you've seen them all. Of course, Tommy thinks he's died and gone to heaven. Jerome is a wet dream for him.

Man, I wish I had lived here in the thirties, he says as he climbs out of the car. You could just see this street on payday, when the shift comes down from the mine. They get a beer, a bath, then go up there—he points to this ruin of a hotel—for a piece of ass. Fifty cents a throw, he says, two bucks for an all-nighter.

Two bucks. I whistle. In Vegas, the meter runs at a C note an hour. And you pay for the drinks and the show.

That clapboard house was probably the sheriff's office, Tommy says as we walk along. That one had to be a bank; he points to a realty office on the corner. Maybe that was the livery stable.

On and on like that he goes. We're wandering down these angled streets, past hippie houses with all kinds of crap in the yards. The place looks bombed out—no glass in the windows, no screens on the doors. The curtains are tie-dyed, or made from American flags. All kinds of desert junk on the porches: cow skulls, steer horns, cactus skeletons. The gear-heads have cars on blocks at the curb; whole engines stripped out in the yard. It's hillbilly hick, right down to the humping dogs and cats oozing out from under everything. There's cats on the cars, and cats in doorways, and cats on the roofs. It's like cats have eaten all the hippies and taken over the place. We don't see another soul, not a face in the window, but Tommy doesn't mind.

I glance over while we're walking and I can see Tommy's eyes getting wider, more excited every step.

Look at that old rooming house, he says. Hasn't changed in eighty years, I'll bet.

I'll bet. Listen, Tommy, I say. I've seen enough of this shit. My shoes are killing me. Let's call in and get out of here.

Right, right, he says. I know there's a phone booth just off the main drag. Follow me.

Tommy doesn't say how he knows this place, when he was here before. But he's walking so fast, I got no choice but to follow. I take a last look back at the car as we turn off the street and walk through a gravel lot. You can see some lights from ranches below us in the valley. There's other parts of the town scattered down the mountain. I can see an old stucco church that some bikers have taken over; hogs parked outside in a row twenty deep. I can't wait to get the hell out, but Tommy's ducked into this cluster of scrub oak and he's calling me over. Here's where all the drunks ended up, he says, stepping out of the bushes.

The Jerome jail broke apart some years back and rode the erosion down the hill. Parts of the floor and one wall are still there. Even a window with bars inside. Tommy steps down on the section of floor and walks over to the window. In the dark, with his floppy old hat, Tommy looks like the typical inmate.

You've got to see this view, he says.

So where's the phone booth? I say.

We'll find it, Tommy says. Lighten up, Danny. Check out this view. Best damn view of any jail I've seen.

I've seen the view, I say. I'm thinking about a sign I saw on the old hotel that said: BEWARE: RATTLESNAKES. And Tommy's Hardy Boys attitude is sending up flags again. He's led me around for an hour like he's running from something. We don't find a phone in two minutes and I'm leaving him here. I tap the pocket that holds my gun. I step down onto the floor of the cell and walk up to the broken-down wall. Tommy takes this angular tilt against the wall and motions me over. He nods his head at the window and grins. I hate grins. I look out through these rusted bars at the desert.

All right, I've seen it. Let's go.

When I turn back, Tommy's arm is coming around and I can't duck fast enough. He catches me above the ear with some iron—a tire iron he's carried in his sleeve. He's had it ever since we left the car, and this is his big moment.

My head kicks back and I get a little woozy, but I've still got a hand on the gun. My arm comes up on his second swing and I fire as the iron pops me again. Then I'm on my back and feel him over me, twisting my hand back and up. I'm dizzy, but I'm still thinking. I'm thinking that I caught him with that first shot. I'm thinking that I will kill this son of a bitch, and then I will kill Luis. *A stand-up guy*, my ass. That spic set me up.

I can feel him tugging my arm as I pump the trigger and the sky flashes with the shots. I'm kicking at his legs and twisting away, but then I feel my elbow pop. Then the gun is gone. I can't see his face under that hat, but I hear him breathing hard. Then he lifts the iron and lets it fly. Once, twice, three times. It hits my arms, my shoulder, and then he lands one on my neck. I can't see, but I feel him coil up to swing again. Then everything goes black and I don't feel anything at all.

Chapter Two

I don't remember any fire. I don't remember the car, or any sensation of falling—but they tell me I took a quarter-mile ride down a mountain face and there was fire everywhere. I rouse myself from this Tijuana hangover, this anesthetic nap. And I only wake up because I itch. My nose itches; so do my back and my hands and even the family jewels. My stones feel like they're getting diddled by a peacock feather, so I guess I'm probably dreaming.

So I try to scratch, and find myself all manacled to this S and M bar above the bed. The first thing I see when I open my eyes are these two gauze boxing gloves that used to be my hands. They're chained to the little trapeze above me, and somewhere under all that wrap is the kind of itch that makes you wish for an ice pick. So I wish myself back to sleep with the idea that this is just as much a dream as the peacock feather. And I wake up to this piercing white light and some fingers prodding my face. It's some doctor flipping my eyelids, poking around with a penlight.

Can you hear me? he says. Can you see the light, Mr. Delorme?

What's this Delorme shit? I'm thinking. The name is Danny Castellano, depending on who's asking.

If you can see the light, he says, follow it with your eyes.

There, I followed it. Happy? I can fetch and roll over, too.

Tell me if you can hear my voice, the doc says. Try to say your name, *Tommy*.

I'm still seeing penlights swirling around and thinking, Who the hell is Tommy? *Tommy Delorme.* For some reason, I'm thinking of a desert truck stop. I get this image of a guy with a beard, then he's lost the beard and he's riding next to me in a car. The *car,* I'm thinking, Jesus, where is the *car?* I never let it out of my sight in three years of working. Working . . . I was working banks in Arizona and somehow I lost track of the car. When I start catching on to what I do for a living, who I am, then the rest of it follows. Tommy Delorme, the new dusky . . . menu fetish . . . Arizona's Fine Arts Community . . . the whole act at the ruined jail . . . Come look-see. . . . Wham! And instead of thinking about itching or following lights with my eyes, I've got a whole new headache. I'm in some podunk hospital and Luis is out 350 K.

Don't try to get up, Mr. Delorme. Please don't, they're saying, and I feel some hands pressing me down. When I move, my head throbs like mad. They can't begin to know; they can't have a fucking clue what it feels like. I'm trying to speak, but it's like my whole face is spinning and my brain can't find the gear. The words are back there, way back. You think you've got them and they slip back. You try and they come closer next time. Then you can feel your throat moving with your mouth. Closer. Closer again. I open my eyes and there's this huge woolly head in my face. Some black nurse has her ear bent down to catch what I'm saying. I can smell the activator on her hair. I can see the little bobby pins that tack her wedgie hat in place, and I can feel her weight over me.

Slower honey, she's saying. Take your time.

I get some kind of croaky, burpy noise. Once more and the words finally come. *I itch. . . . I itch like a son of a bitch.*

That's 'cause you healin' like a son of a bitch, she tells me. I could kiss her for that one, and for not calling me Tommy Delorme. That's when I get the story about rolling down a mountain in a burning car. She tells me I've been out for three days. I have a fractured skull. There's a splint on my nose and some ribs are cracked. My head took something like fifty stitches—she promises to count them if I want. The nurse says they did grafts on both hands—which is why they itch so much. And they peeled about half an acre of skin off my stomach, what they call a "donor site." You're going to be pretty uncomfortable, she says. You'd almost wish you was still unconscious, but we'll do what we can.

You think I got trouble staying comfortable; I got problems staying alive. I couldn't give a shit about my aching head, my burns, and even that plumbing extension they jammed up my wang. Do it to me, I thought, do your best. You're still going to lose this patient.

I don't know how much of this is self-induced, what with all the pain and the drugs. But what I felt kind of relates to the trouble I had speaking. In fact, the whole sensation existed *in place of* the ability to speak. It's like there's this whole other person drifting around out there in the fog, absorbing everything with incredible clarity. And for those few floating moments, I could predict the future.

For instance, I knew when my roommate was dying. I knew it even before his joy buzzer alerted the nurses. His name was Gary or Jerry, and he was in because of angina. Ever since I was aware of him, he's been the picture of health. He eats three full trays of food a day. He takes long walks and does stretch exercises in bed. He gets about sixty visitors a night. The rest of the time, he's on the phone. He tried to chat me up, but I was too far down on sedatives to hold his interest. *Buck up,* he kept telling me. *Buck you, Jerry.* I can't say I miss the vital bastard. It was like rooming with Jack LaLanne.

Anyway, I wake up out of a sound sleep one night because I'm sure Jerry's dying. I've got cold sweats and my pulse is nuts and it could be me—but it's him. Again, I've got that sense that something's happening. And I mean, I was *convinced.* By this time, I'm free of the trapeze and I have one of those multicontrols. My hands are still bandaged knobs, so it's hit or miss on the buttons. I miss the light button and get the television. David Letterman flashes on and the light plays over Jerry. He's asleep, breathing regular, with this buck-up-buddy grin on his face. But like I said, I was sure. So I move the control to my face and hit the call button with my nose. Some nurse wanders in and asks if I have discomfort.

No, I just have this premonition that Jerry's buying the farm. Humor me and check him out.

He's on a monitor, the nurse says. We'd know if he coded on us. So she leaves and Jerry proceeds to code about thirty seconds later. I watch this whole transformation: He stops breathing and his face pinches down so tight that I can't recognize him. He fights to get his hands from under the blankets as the nurses come swarming in. They hit the panic button and then the room is full of residents and interns and God knows who. The board goes under his back and they're pounding away on his chest. Somebody shoves my bed aside to make room for that shocker unit. Stand clear! they yell, and then *boom*! Jerry takes a few thousand volts. *Zap!* They keep charging him as his lips get real chalky.

I'm watching this whole ordeal, and yet I'm not. I'm completely aware of the bedlam scene, the frenzy among the staff. But I'm also doing a circuit of the room, moving out and away from the activity until I can look down on it. And by the time I can will myself back down, back into a sharper consciousness, I see that Jerry is not responding. I have returned, and he is gone.

As soon as I'm cognizant enough to speak, I get a visit from the sheriff. A tall, rangy-looking bastard with the Ray-Bans hanging in the shirt pocket; the Sam Browne belt so full of weapons and toys that he can't even fit in the little guest chair. So he parks it on the bed, and Josephine—she's the head nurse with the wedgie hat—kicks him off. Tells him those sheets are sterile. I love that gal. So Marlboro Man relocates to the windowsill and stares at me. I'd been trying to compose my story, and he is giving me plenty of time.

He introduces himself as Yavapai County Sheriff Lloyd Peters. Asks how I'm feeling, if I can answer some questions. *I been better. Sure, why not?* Wants to know if my name is Thomas Winton Delorme.

No sir, I'm Tony Granato, I say. (That's my alias for banks—I always use Italian.) From Trenton, New Jersey. Why does everybody think I'm this Thomas Delorme?

Because we found this. He pulls a wallet out of an envelope and tosses it on my stomach. Then he realizes I've got no finger control, so he opens it and shows me that cheese eater's California driver's license. There's nothing else in the wallet except some postage stamps and a package of rolling papers. Since I'm all bandaged and taped, I guess I can look like anybody, even Tommy Delorme.

That was the driver who picked me up in Vegas, I say. I tapped out at Caesar's and he seemed like a Samaritan. I'd cashed in my plane ticket, so he offered to take me down to Phoenix. I was sleeping on the drive down. I woke up and we're parked in some ghost town and he's going through my pockets. We fought for awhile, but he brained me with a tire iron. I woke up here, man. That's all I remember.

Why would this Delorme try to rob you if you were tapped out from gambling? Lloyd wants to know.

I had all kinds of plastic, I tell him. Which reminds me—I'd better cancel all my cards.

I'll do that for you, he says. But we've got a few other discrepancies. For instance, that car was deliberately torched—somebody lit a rag in the gas tank. If this Tommy put out your lights, why didn't he just chuck you in the ditch? That's quite a gesture, torching the car and pushing it over the side.

He panicked, who knows? I say. This was a kid who did lots of drugs. He freaked. Maybe he likes to hitchhike.

Lloyd scratches his buzz-cut hair and says, I don't think so, *Tony*. I think he torched that rented Lincoln because it was yours. He knew how it was obtained and he didn't want the hassle.

Obtained? I ask, and my head begins throbbing. I'm ready for another pill, but I try to play indignant.

Sheriff Lloyd says the Lincoln was rented in L.A. by an Angelo

Musante and secured with a MasterCard. (He's reading crib notes out of his envelope, holding it about six feet from his face.) This Musante is an *extremely regular* rental customer, always taking luxury cars and paying cash. The cash is the reason they never found Musante to be an alias, Lloyd says. But after we reported your accident, they ran the card. It was part of a stolen batch of blanks from Nebraska, he says. They'd been processed through the I.D. black market in L.A., sold as a package set for people who need to be other people.

That was Tommy's car, I insist. And you'll be glad to know he didn't call himself Tommy. He called himself Angel in Vegas.

The sheriff takes back the wallet and says, That's mighty lame, Mr. Granato. We're a long ways from Miami, but we see plenty of drugs up here.

What's that supposed to mean?

It means you were set up and you were hit and it wasn't over no credit cards. And when you got roasted in the crash, you were supposed to be Tommy Delorme, he says.

I was what?

The sheriff looks around for old Josephine and then he sits right down on my bed. We found the wallet inside one of those asbestos bank deposit bags, inside the glove compartment, he says.

B.F.D., I say.

Some strange piece of luck, he continues, that wallet surviving the fire. All the luggage burned, the seats, the interior. But there was the wallet, zipped in asbestos, as far from the gas tank as possible. I knew you weren't Tommy Delorme before I ever met you. Somebody wanted the world to think Tommy Delorme is a dead french fry. In the insurance trade, it's called body substitution. But you screwed that up by getting thrown clear. Now I want to know what you were carrying and what this kid had in mind.

Am I under arrest? I say. Maybe I should refer you to a lawyer.

I won't arrest you until I know who the hell you are, *Tony*, he says. Then the sadist prick slaps me with the wallet on my donor site.

And how do you plan to do that? I'm wheezing with pain.

I'll get that rental clerk up from L.A., the one who gave Angelo Musante the car. I figure we can make a good case for credit-card fraud.

I don't quite look like myself, I say. That won't stand up in court and you know it.

The sheriff gives me another tap, then stands up and grabs his hat. You just keep cooking up them aliases, he says. I'll worry about what flies in court. You might also think about who else would like to finish what Tommy started. I can be mighty accommodating; I could even post a guard. Can't have people shooting up the hospital.

Fuck you, I tell him. You want to arrest my ass, do it. Otherwise, get the hell out.

Don't you want me to cancel your credit cards? he asks.

Eat shit and die, I tell him, but it comes out as a cough while he's laughing his way down the hall.

As if that visit wasn't enough, the geek from the business office drops by next. How will you be paying for your treatment, *Mr. Delorme*? My Blue Cross card burned up in the crash, I tell him. I'll make a couple of calls. I'll take care of it. Of course, the guy has already cross-referenced Thomas Winton Delorme and didn't find any coverage. I think about faking some convulsions right then, but I know Josephine would never buy it. So I tell the twerp, I'm indigent, okay? I can't pay and I can't be discharged, so sit on your pencil and spin. So he gets all prissy and miffed and beats it down the hall.

The next morning, old Josephine is changing the dressing on my hands. We're yukking it up about something or other—she thinks I'm hilarious—when she drops the bomb. I always enjoy the feisty ones, she says. Too bad you leavin' us. Who's leavin' us? I ask. Have I been upgraded or something?

Chief of surgery says they shippin' you out to the prison hospital in Tempe, Josephine says. *Tomorrow*. I hear her, but I get away from myself again. I'm out in that same fog, except this time it's not a happy place.

That's not soon enough, I say.

Soon enough for what? she wonders.

I'm going to die here, I tell her—just like that. Like saying, I'm going to park the car. It was fact. You remember how I predicted Jerry-the-Mouth? I tell her. I'm just as sure, Josie. They're going to kill me tonight.

Keep talkin' like that and we're gonna cut back your meds, she tells me. But she sees this big tear roll out of my eye and over the tape on my nose. I'm crying for the first time in years and I feel like a classic ass. Josie wipes my eyes and gives me this frown of hers.

You got some kind of business, don't you, Tommy? Some kind of trouble in your life, she says.

The name's Danny Castellano, I tell her. You remember it. I'd like people to know who I really was.

Josie frowns some more while she clips my bandage in place, then she takes her kit and stands. I'll look in on you tonight, Danny, she says. Don't you worry about nothin'.

She almost had me convinced until I saw Hector Lupino in the hall. Luis's top toady, yes-man, goon. I bring Hector the checks after a laundering trip. He takes about six hours to run the numbers—the man is hopeless for anything but grunt work. Which is what brought him to the hospital. It's the middle of the afternoon and there's Hector strolling by, carrying a bouquet of ragged-looking flowers. That's his big disguise—flowers and a satin disco shirt right out of Luis's closet. He passes out of view and I'm up in a second, holding my ribs and shuffling after him. Hector! Hector, it's me. It's Danny!

He hears, but he doesn't turn. He doesn't want to believe I spotted him. I'm wheezing and saying, I'm in three-oh-one, *cabrone*. Hey, are those flowers for me?

Hector stops at the elevator, punches a button, and then turns. He's about two feet shorter than me, and he looks up, shaking his swarthy little head.

Fucked yourself up pretty good, he says. You look like hell, Danny.

I feel like hell, and I've been waiting for someone to show up,

I say. We're right at the nurses' station, so I move in and whisper, We've got to talk about that dusky friend of yours. We've got to talk about the money, I say. You know Tommy hit me and took it all, Hector. He's laughing at all of us. I'm not the one you're after. I want to talk to Luis.

Hector's eyes are roving around. Maybe he's checking the line of fire, figuring the hall is a bad idea. Luis got indicted on an income-tax rap, he tells me. I'm running things for awhile. The elevator arrives and he steps in. Hector says, Oh, these are for you. He tosses me the flowers he dug out of the trash, says, See you around, *cabrone*. And he points with his finger as the doors close, dropping his thumb and making a popping noise with his mouth.

I turn around and Josie is behind me. She watched the whole thing. Now do you believe me? I ask her. She tells me to get my ass back in bed, but I can see that it's shaken her up.

Somebody is trying a doorknob, shaking a latch when I wake up. I'm so far down that I can't figure what door and where the hell I am. More shaking, then some scraping through the wafer lock. I'm hearing this and I'm only just getting focused. You're in a hospital, I think. You're in a shower stall. You fell asleep even though you're cramped up like a fetus. You fell asleep even though you rolled your sedative back on your tongue and spit it out when the nurse had gone. You were going to flex your fingers all night, let the pain keep you alert. But it doesn't work, because the only thing that wakes you up is Hector Lupino working the lock.

Hiding out was my last resort. I had the option of calling up Sheriff Lloyd and rolling over like a two-dollar whore. If I played the tease, I could maybe get him to put a guard on, just one night. But that meant giving that smirking son of a bitch the satisfaction of being right. No, I figured if I made it into the prison hospital, I could get a decent attorney. The right lawyer could grease the pole for me. That left either skipping out or hiding. Since I don't have a dime to my name or the ability to stand for more than five minutes, I chose hiding.

So I trail the control unit into the john, turn out the lights, and hide in the shower. Some plan, huh? Three hours later, somebody's jimmying the lock and saying, *Danny? Hey, Danny, you in there?*

I've got the same problem with the console—too many buttons and no fingers. I'm mashing my bandage into the buttons and I hear the television go on and off; I see the lights flicking under the door. Old Hector probably thinks the room is possessed. But he gets through, anyway. I see a form step in from the light. He flicks on the bathroom light and I crouch against the tile and wait for the bullets. Then I hear the voice saying, What the hell have we got here?

I squint up and see that it isn't Hector Lupino. It's some big bald-headed guy in surgical scrubs. I don't place him at first.

That ain't very dignified, Danny, he says. Stop playin' hide-and-seek.

It's Charlie Cadeaux, that's who it is. A dirty cop from the DEA that I knew when I was bagman for payoffs. Special agent Cadeaux. I used to bring him his money in Vegas, then I'd stay and help him spend some. We played the sports book at Caesar's once a month for almost two years. He retired to a place in Phoenix, and now all of a sudden he's back, dressed up like a male nurse.

Charlie, Jesus, I say. You come to kill me, too?

No way, *compadre*, he says. I'm your ride out of here. Get your ass in this chair; I'll explain later.

I get in the wheelchair and he throws a blanket over me and then we're rolling down the hall. I'm still not convinced that he's a dusky. I could be headed for the bottom of a reservoir. *Can't have people shooting up the hospital.* But Charlie seems totally at ease, whistling as he pushes me along.

Hector Lupino paid me a visit, I say. I figure he'll be back.

He is, Cadeaux says. He's in a car out front with a couple of buddies. I called the local dick on them to see if I could slow them up.

Charlie reaches the fire exit at the end of the hall and backs me in. He says it's the only way to avoid the nurses' station. So he leads and I'm bouncing behind; dropping each step with a *bam!* that shakes my head, my aching ribs. *Bam-bam-bam:* We're jouncing down until I look up and see the door above us open. Not Hector; no, this time it's Josephine.

Hold it up right there, she says. She's carrying a cardboard box for latex gloves and shaking her head.

Got yourself a private nurse, Danny?

He's a friend, I say.

Not a friend like them guys out front? she asks.

Oh you saw them, too? I say. No, Charlie's a *niño.*

Maybe, but he ain't a therapist, is he? she says. You want to avoid infection, you want to use them hands, you listen to old Josephine.

She walks down to us and hands me the box. It's a little care kit she threw together. She gives a little five-minute dissertation, pulling out each item I need: This is your analgesic, Percocet; take two a day. These are sedatives, Serax; one at night with food. You've seen me change your dressing—here's gauze and Ace bandages. And a couple tubes of the ointment. Keep them hands elevated to reduce edema, honey. And you keep the scarring down by wearing these gloves. Get yourself some nice tight driving gloves in a month or so. Don't expose them grafts to the sun, and honey—you got to move them digits no matter how it hurts. Squeeze a tennis ball; play the piano.

Josie, you're the best, I say.

I may be the stupidest, darlin'. But maybe your luck will change. Now that you got your own nurse and all. She pats my gauzy head and starts back up the stairs.

And thanks for the stuff, I tell her.

What stuff? she says.

Chapter Three

◆

Like I said, I first met Charlie Cadeaux when I was a bagman for payoffs. Luis moved a lot of money through Las Vegas then, cashing in chips for a big casino check. We had to grease nearly every moe in the hotels, from bellhop to G.M. And when you've got that many thumbs on the scale, the DEA will get wind of it. So I flew up there once a month on the Lost Wages red-eye. Before I left one Friday, Luis passed me an extra five K, told me to meet a Mr. Cadeaux at the Flamingo Hilton pool.

If you've been to the Hilton, you know what a snipe hunt I was in for. These casino architects create this kind of spiral deal where everybody gets sucked into the tables no matter where you want to go. Nothing's marked; there's no aisles. You just wander and hope that you find an exit, an elevator, a toilet. The slots players piss in those paper coin cups because they can't find the johns—I swear to God. I didn't resort to that, but *damn near*. I saw some family all dressed in beachwear, carrying the inflatable toys and the towels. I figured they knew the layout. I followed them for ten minutes and it turned out *they* were lost.

The net result was I missed the payoff to Charlie Cadeaux. So the next afternoon, I was at Caesar's Palace. I stood on this balcony level over the back casino—they call it the Romulus Room or something. So I was up there staring down some keno queen's dress, minding my own business, when two guys joined me at the railing. One looked like a fed in his Brooks Brothers suit. The other one looked real greasy and hip. They knew my name. They asked if I would please follow them. They led me downstairs to the little corral reserved for high-stakes poker. We stood at the fence for awhile, watching six guys play a few hands. Finally, this big, burly bald-headed guy with a little ring of red fuzz above his ears stood up and came over. He didn't acknowledge the escorts; he just looked at me.

You're exactly the person I need to see, Charlie said. You get lost yesterday?

Matter of fact, I did, I told him.

You have something for me?

I nodded, and he said to give it to Richard. Then Charlie asked Richard to turn it all in for chips. The goons left just as this corny waitress arrived. She had this toga thing going and this dunce-cap hair extender and fake eyelashes out to here. There's nothing scarier-looking than a Vegas barmaid. What's your drink? Charlie asked me. He sent her off with the order and said, *What's your game?* Casino game, he meant.

I told him sports book.

Mine too, Charlie said. I never win at stud poker. But I have to circulate among the tables so it looks like I'm working. He asked if I had a pick for the U.S. Open golf—it was starting the next day.

I told him golf is a sucker bet, *especially* the U.S. Open. The favorites almost never win. It's alphabet soup. If you bet the Open, ignore the names and take the field. You take the entire field against the celebrities and you get six-to-one odds.

I was kind of pulling for Watson, Charlie said.

So's his mother. That doesn't mean he'll win it.

Charlie gave me this big grin and said, Why should I believe a guy who can't even find the pool at the Hilton? We finished our drinks, and he walked over and put one hundred on a field bet in the Open. Larry Nelson came out of nowhere that year and took it all. Charlie bought dinner and it was the beginning of a regular habit. *Work hard, play hard* was Charlie's motto. He'd fly into Vegas after testifying for a solid week at some trial. Other times, he'd work a bust with the Border Patrol; spend the night flicking off scorpions and waiting for some pot plane to land.

Charlie worked in L.A. and he worked in Phoenix, but we always met in Vegas. He said, That's because it's the only city in the world where I can hang out with *dregs like you.* He called me Danny Gator, because of my alligator shoes. And Charlie was real generous with Luis's grease, blowing it on meals and shows and sports book. He told me half the payoff went back into bribes for DEA snitches. (I think his term was *positive amortization.*) Whatever Charlie managed to save went into his retirement home. Old golfers never die, he told me, they just move to Scottsdale. And that's where he took me after he sprang me from the hospital up in Cottonwood, Arizona.

Charlie rags on Luis for most of the drive down. My head is killing me. I'm trying to listen and work the child-guard cap on my pills with my big bandaged mitts.

Luis gets a little federal scrutiny and he feels like the whole empire is crashing down, Charlie says. The spic panicked, let's face it.

What scrutiny? I say. This tax rap that Hector was talking about?

Yeah, he and Alonzo were under indictment. Did you hear? Charlie says. They skipped bail. But that's not all: The feds were moving on a laundering rap. Here, I'll get that. Take the wheel.

We're going about ninety-five and I can't grip the wheel. He lets go and snatches the pill bottle out of my lap. So I'm driving with my wrist, trying to keep us out of the ditch. Charlie is talking and working on the bottle cap.

I should never have opened my mouth, but the truth is, I was worried about you, Gator. About a month ago, I golfed with some old DEA chums, and they described this little sting they've got going with South-Central Bankshares—shit, you need a hand grenade to open these. Whoa, Danny—try not to weave so much.

I'm trying, I say. What's this Bankshares stuff?

After all this restructuring and mergers, South-Central owns nearly every bank east of the Sierra Madres. There, I got the fucker. Just don't put the lid back on, he says, handing me the bottle and taking the wheel. I inhale a couple of capsules.

And since all these banks got acquired, they all get a centralized data base, standardized practices, right?

Right, I say, feeling two dry lumps working their way just below my collarbone. And I'll bet I patronized a few of those banks.

Fuckin'-a you did, Charlie says. You keep deposits below ten thousand, that clears you from Currency Transaction Reports. However, the dicks at Bankshares decided to do some internal tracking of cash deposits above three grand.

Three grand, I say. That's every grandma with a nest egg. What could they hope to find?

They find patterns, Charlie explains. They found *you, compadre.* It's like somebody had too much free time. Bankshares was getting all these random transactions for cashier's checks. The DEA wondered if they could track the deposits with the surveillance film. You know, the spy cameras for robberies? They wanted to see if the same guy was making a series of large cash transactions.

And I was that guy?

Read 'em and weep, Charlie says. You transact nine thousand in Barstow on Monday and you're fine. You pass six grand in Needles on Tuesday and you're interesting. You show up with eight grand on Wednesday in Flagstaff and now you're a suspect. They had your face. They had your MO. They were just waiting for you to go out again. They figured to tail you back to the source.

You told Luis about this sting? I ask.

Sorry, *compadre,* Charlie says. I didn't think it through. I figured he'd take you off the road, give up on cashier's checks for awhile. But Luis is already indicted, so he freaks.

And has me hit? I say.

He must've been afraid that you'd flip, spill out the whole story, Charlie says. That's the nature of the business, Gator. All that loyalty-dusky-*niño* stuff gets forgotten when the indictments come down. For every major bust in Miami, there's ten guys waiting in line to flip and make a deal. Luis knows human nature. And I know Luis, which gave me this real bad feeling about your prospects, Gator. More I thought about it, the more I figured *you* were the guy I should've warned.

I can't say much for your judgment, I tell Charlie, but your timing is perfect. How did you find me?

Well, I figured if anyone was going to do a hit for Luis, it was going to be Hector Lupino, Charlie says. I do a little PI work on my own, find out he's got an address in L.A.

Westwood. You called Hector?

Oh no; no, I didn't want to tip my hand, Charlie says. I called my old colleague in the L.A. DEA and had a tail put on Hector. Gave them a cock-and-bull story about how he only flies out to collect major shipments.

And by the way, call me if he *does* fly out . . . ?

Exactly, Charlie replies. I even arranged a diversion while I absconded with you. See, Hector was camped in a car across from the hospital. I found some kid at the arcade who's willing to hand him this suspicious-looking sack of doughnuts. The stakeout jumped Hector after that—strip search, the whole bit. At the very least, they got him on a weapons charge. They're probably giving him the third degree even as we speak.

And this surgical costume?

Maternity ward, Charlie replies. They always leave scrubs around for dads to wear during delivery.

Nothing to chance. I sigh. Just pray that kid with the doughnuts doesn't pick you out of a mug book.

Charlie gets a good laugh out of that. We drive a long stretch while he hums along with the radio, then he asks, Luis has given up on the pot trade, hasn't he? All the best people are in coke now, or crystal meth. He still flying it in?

No, I reply. Luis calls that Cessna shit Colombian roulette. Colombians send out three planes and two get caught—the third one still pays the overhead. But Mexicans like the land routes, shipping lanes. Take their chances at the border. Getting bailed out of jail is lots easier than bailing out of an airplane.

Amen to that, Charlie says. So it's body cavities and luggage compartments for Luis?

You understand that shipping isn't my department—I handle cash flow, I tell him. But I know Luis pays his taxes through an electronics company. Place down in Covina makes parts for clock radios. They ship the parts to Chihuahua, Mexico. Pay workers some scum wage to put it all together.

This is legit? Charlie asks as he shields his eyes from some oncoming headlights. He sells real clocks?

Snooze alarm, warranty, the whole bit, I say. But this new digital technology gives you smaller components—takes almost no room in this big clock box. Leaves a nice cavity inside.

So you make up the space with high-grade blow, Charlie says.

Sometimes yes, sometimes no—depends on the border vibes, who's been greased this week, I reply. But the clock plant covers Luis's tax problems—at least it used to. I got a paycheck, withholding, the whole bit. Of course, there's plenty of bonuses off the books.

You're riding in some of that action, Charlie says. Don't tell me about bonuses.

And that's how I wound up convalescing among the Stucco People. Stucco People live in little mission-style homes behind stucco walls in stucco Scottsdale. These developers are trying to be very *villa ranchero hacienda,* but they end up with something between Taos and Disney World. Charlie says it all starts with some forsaken hunk of desert between Paradise Valley and the McDowell Mountains. The developers get a star like Jack Nicklaus to lend his name as a "course design consultant." They fit eighteen holes in amid the boulders and saguaros and horned toads. They partition the rest for lots. Put up a wall, build a little guardhouse, and you've got a community. Golfside sanctuaries are the wave of the future, Charlie says.

To me, the future looks an awful lot like tract homes with tile roofs, like Orange County with fancier cactus. Call it Valhalla Acres, call it Sundial Estates; I call it Land of the Living Dead. Talk about Cadillacs and cataracts: Charlie Cadeaux is the youngest guy on his street by an easy twenty years. Half the people on the golf course look like they should be trailing IVs. They order home nursing and oxygen here like other people order pizza. At dawn, the walkers clog the streets, but afternoon siesta makes the town look like nuclear winter.

Of course I'd rather be in Stuccodale than in the Yavapai County morgue all ventilated by Hector Lupino. The low-slung buildings give you a nice clear shot at the sunsets over the ridges in Paradise Valley. The sunsets kind of win you over. It was a few days before I was willing to look at one. Charlie lures me out to his deck, saying how I miss the best part of the day. I'm still real leery about being seen outside. I get real spooked at strangers now, being a fugitive and all. Charlie did a little checking and learned that Hector was indeed caught with a concealed weapon but was sprung on bail. And you can bet he won't show up for jury selection.

Charlie lives on the first tee, "just a wedge shot away" from the clubhouse. The codgers drive their carts right past his lot. Charlie says, Bring your drink and get your ass out here. They wouldn't let Hector past the guardhouse, Charlie says. This is Anglo City. So I put a hat over my stitches and pull up a chair under his big umbrella.

The sky is all lit up pink and reddish and sort of russety at the horizon. It coats everything with this goldish glow. It's a nice way to feel, all gold while you're pounding the gin and tonics, squeezing that tennis ball. But the sunset isn't the only reason Charlie lures me out there. He's puffing himself up for a speech. He's got himself an agenda.

Do you know where I'd be, he begins, if I tried to chase down every double-cross, every punk who yanked my chain?

I don't know, I say. Busy?

I'd be flying fifty-two weeks a year, he says. I'd be out of money, out of my mind, probably dead. It doesn't bother my golf swing to know that shit still walks the earth. Doesn't affect my sleep. Vengeance is one of the few luxuries that I've denied myself, Gator.

I call it a necessity, I reply. I call it survival.

So you plan to go after all of them? he asks. Luis, Alonzo, this guy in the desert?

I'll start at the top and work my way down, I tell him. Whoever I can find. They crawl out from under a rock, I'll be waiting.

So the bagman turns vigilante. Charlie smiles. Do you know guns, Gator? Do you know all about killing?

Enough, I say, but the bluff doesn't fly with Charlie, and his grin spreads into those hammy red cheeks. It's like he can see that I never killed squat, that I haven't been in a street fight for years, that the closest I've come is shooting holes in the sky while Tommy Delorme worked me over in Jerome. I hate seeing it, thinking of it all just when I was enjoying that gold-filtered sunset buzz. If you think of one hundred ways to avoid that tire iron, I've thought of one hundred thousand. I've refought that prick more than you can imagine. It's sick, I know. But all I want is another shot. I'm convinced it's the only reason I lived, the only way I got out of that car. It's the reason I'm healing this fast. Hate power, baby. Hate cures. Touch me and heal thyself.

So I gave you back your life, and this is how you plan to spend it? Charlie asks.

Don't get all high and holy on me, I tell him. You're also the one who got me hit, so I figure we're even there. I'm running a little deficit on groceries and booze—

Forget it, Charlie says. You been picking enough winners with my sports book to cover your overhead. Man, I can't wait for football season. If you stay through the fall, I'll be able to pay off my mortgage. You're hotter than ever, Gator. And it shows where your talents lie. Some of us are lovers, some of us are fighters, and some of us are clairvoyant. We can't waste this gift on bookies in Phoenix. When your head gets better, we're flying up to Vegas and driving back in a Brinks truck. No prisoners this time. We don't quit until we own the hotel.

I'll keep at it just long enough to stake myself, I say. What do I need with hotels? What I need is a new identity, and I start on that tomorrow. I'm going down to the Hall of Records to find me a birth certificate. Got to take my driver's test; open a checking account. And I'll need plastic so I can rent cars.

Charlie doesn't respond for awhile. He is watching some four-some of grandmas veer off the fairway and park at the edge of his lot. This little gnome of a granny slides out of the cart and marches straight into Charlie's cactus garden like some kind of health inspector.

And after you get your I.D. and your money, I can guess what you'll be asking me for, Charlie says. A MAC-Ten maybe? A Baretta? Perhaps one of those Street Sweeper shotguns with a magazine the size of New Jersey?

Can't fly with guns, I tell him. They screw up too many travel plans. I was thinking maybe a tire iron. Tit for tat. No, I say, the favor I want from you, Charlie, is information. You've got contacts in L.A. People who can get into those data bases.

Maybe the NCIC, Charlie says. FBI and Treasury both have huge mainframes. But I don't have access.

Somebody does, I tell him. They're tracking Luis's assets; I'm sure they're working up a family tree. I want files on the whole gang—Alonzo, Hector, Tommy Delorme. I want it all.

Sure you do, Charlie replies. But that's calling in more favors than I've got out. I'm retired, remember?

I tell him if he wanted it for himself, he could get it. We'll do that Vegas trip, I say. You name it. Just get it.

Charlie drains off his glass. Then he stands up and takes a golf ball out of his bag against the rail. He nods his head at the old lady rutting in his yard and says, Here's a little lesson about the real world, Gator. Mrs. Ranheim there is as blind as a rat, but she can't admit it to herself. About once a week, she gets convinced that her ball is in my cactus. And she'll climb in there and root until her fingers bleed. If I let her go, I lose ten plants easy—but mostly it's painful to watch. And she won't take my word that the ball didn't drop here. She's fucking obsessed.

Charlie leans in, holding the golf ball like a diamond, pinning me with his bloodshot eyes. In an ideal world, I could maybe persuade her, he says. Or I could exercise property rights and kick her ass onto the fairway. But trust me; the former is impossible and the latter carries a dear penalty with the Homeowners' Association. And since I function in the real world, I find a compromise. I'm going to take this Max-Fli down there, put it in her pruny little hand, and say, Look, Mrs. Ranheim, I found your ball.

So you give up a ball, what's the point? I ask.

The point is, she doesn't know it's a gift, but I do it because she's painful to watch, Charlie says. That's you, Danny Gator. You've been given your life and you don't even know it. And whatever happens now is going to be painful to watch.

So Charlie takes his ball and clomps down the stairs to put the old lady out of her misery.

Chapter Four

◆

A week of scamming around Phoenix and I've turned myself into Darrel Fuller. I get this third-hand car and make all the stops on the I.D. circuit. Darrel was a year older than me and a lot more careless behind the wheel. He had the same kind of accident as me, but they carried him out in a sack. But as they say on sportscasts, his legacy endures. I've resurrected his whole paper trail and even got the passport that he never had. I look like a jar-head on my driver's license—Josephine trimmed pretty close around my stitches—but what the hell. You look at the photo, think maybe I'm behind the times and a few bricks shy of a load. I look a little dangerous and that's just fine. My days of playing Marvin Merchant are over. I'm out of the business of being invisible.

The first checks I write from Darrel's new account are for a whole new wardrobe. I used to like really nice shirts, double starch and all that. They all burned in the crash, along with my dress pants, belts, and shoes. Good riddance. My new look is heavy on the Ralph Lauren khakis, with Banana Republic stirred in. I bought hiking boots and a fedora and those sweaters they wore in the RAF. I stopped short of buying camouflage fatigues—leave that shit to the weekend mercenaries. It's really kind of fun to recreate Darrel Fuller, not that he knows the difference.

I remember how Tommy renovated himself at the Salvation Army. That whole excursion paid off for him after the hit. He probably knew, even then, that he'd be hitchhiking away from a car wreck with a duffel bag of coca bucks. The perfect chameleon act. You want to vanish in the great Southwest, you got to dress western. I can't say where he'll lead me, but it won't be anyplace where I need starched shirts.

I figure that I will need plenty of stamina, a little more muscle on the frame. I lost my paunch in the hospital and I intend to keep it off. I do fifty sit-ups every morning and night. I use Charlie's exercise machine in the basement, the kind with the resistance bar. My hands still can't grip enough to pull it down, so I hook it the other way and do bench presses. My evening walk turns into a jog, and I quit smoking—mostly because I can't open the pack with my hands wrapped. I view this whole recovery as a monastic thing, like basic training for the soul. And I can't stop thinking about how weak-ass slow I was when Tommy started swinging. The fucker had reflexes like a cat, and I'm going to have them, too.

Charlie takes all of these changes in stride. I'm so painful to watch, remember? I'll be pressing the weight and he'll park himself on the pool table with a beer and the sports section. He reads from the pitching rosters and gets my picks between repetitions. Oakland at Boston, Dave Stewart versus Harris. *Wheeze. Pant. Groan.* Boston favored, seven-to-eight. *Boston's home record stinks—pant, pant.* Oakland's on a five-game slide. *My point exactly, groooaaannn! Fenway is a hitter's park; how many homers does Boggs have this year?* My point exactly. Boston by two. *Oakland by two; McGuire will go three-for-five—puff, puff. Stewart's slider is on and the Sox might get two hits. Mark my words.* I always do, Danny Gator.

We're doing our pick-and-pant routine one night when Charlie tells me my stitches are slipping. He peers over the weight bench and says it's time they came out. So we adjourn to the living room for minor surgery. Charlie moves a chair in front of his big-ass television so we can watch an NFL preseason game. He dabs my head with alcohol, gets out his manicure kit, and goes to work snipping and yanking sutures. You'd be pleased to know that I got a call from a friend today, he says.

Yeah? Which friend is that?

DEA pal, based in L.A., Charlie says.

Can he get those files? Any news on the hunt for Luis? I ask.

Times are tight, Charlie replies. He's got a new commander and they can't pull files willy-nilly.

I don't want willy-nilly, I say. I want Luis, Alonzo, Tommy—

Charlie gives one stitch a little punitive tug and says, Very funny. My friend took a chance even calling back.

Why is that?

I'm persona non grata, Charlie says. I got no markers around there. I was lucky to get what I got. This new honcho, Max Kohler, associates me with the times when the agency was steeped in graft. His words, Gator; *steeped in graft.*

Sounds fair, I tell him. You didn't buy this golfside sanctuary on a government pension.

Charlie takes special offense and yanks up with his tweezers. You want to hear this or no? he asks. Maybe you'd rather go broke touring the country without any leads?

No, no, I need to hear it. I need whatever you got.

Turns out that Delorme was one of the bones that Luis used to throw us, he begins. See, we couldn't turn the other cheek forever. Luis had to serve something up every six months or so—almost always Mexicans carrying pot that he recruited out of Guadalajara. We'd bust them. They'd do maybe two years and then get deported.

He never mentioned it, I tell him. But it doesn't surprise me a bit. Luis never got upset over a pot bust for less than twenty keys.

This was three keys of coke, Charlie says, six years ago up in Reno. Just a routine setup buy in the parking lot of a ski area. We swooped in, got a nice headline. Got the powder on the table at the press conference. The only twist was that Luis served up a gringo—your friend Tommy Delorme. He was released two months ago from Carson City.

I'm watching the football, but I'm hearing my last conversation with Luis, on the phone in a motel room in Carson City. *An old friend. He used to carry the money. If he's still a dusky, we might bring him back in.* Tommy did his time; he paid his dues, I say. And Luis thought Tommy never figured out that he was disposable bust bait, a one-time bonus. Luis tried to recycle Tommy and pretend he was grateful.

That's how I see it, Charlie agrees. It's hard to tell if Delorme had a contract on your life. But he saw his chance to screw Luis and disappear. It's just like your buddy the sheriff said—body substitution. Put his wallet in the glove compartment, your body in the car, and burned it to a crisp. That gives him the money and leaves Luis chasing your ghost. The only problem came when you survived. That's a problem for Luis and for Tommy.

You bet your ass, I say. A terminal problem. What else did you get?

Something interesting from Tommy's stay in Carson, Charlie replies. It seems the DA planted a snitch in his cell. Fella named Carl Dupree. Petty criminal, in for b and e. Anyway, he works out a suspended sentence in exchange for sucking up to your man Tommy.

I'm thinking, Poor Carl played hundreds of hours of Beach or Buffet and what did he learn? Names of all the French sauces? Positions of the Kama Sutra demonstrated on Daytona Beach? I envision Carl's mouth watering, his dick rocketing through his pants while Tommy dishes the detail. *Carl, you should've done the time,* I think. *Snitching can be slow torture when you have to listen to that.*

And what did Carl learn? I ask.

That wasn't in the file, Charlie says. That was Reno DA material and it never came out in court. What the file did say is that Carl got Federal Witness Protection status, Charlie says. He persuaded them that his participation was life-threatening, the old Mafia lament. Anyway, he went under last spring.

Where? I say. You didn't get that?

Federal Witness Protection is a data base out of Washington, Charlie says as he snips at the seam in my head. I don't have the codes, and I couldn't ask.

Well, if that's all you've got, then that's where I start, I say. Roommates in stir know everything. Charlie, you've got to link me up with this Dupree.

He doesn't say anything, but he reaches in his pocket and hands a scrap of paper down to me.

I thought you'd key on that snitch, he says. So I copied down his phone number. I swear to God, Gator, that's all that was there. It's an Alaska area code, by the way.

That doesn't even tell me his new name, I say. I'm supposed to call him up out of Witness Protection and say let's chat about your checkered past? Charlie gives my scalp a solid yank, and I cry out and look down at the scrap of paper and see little blood flecks. *You've opened the cut!* I yell at him. *I was only kidding.* I reach up, and the blood is oozing over my whole head, clear down my neck. I turn just as Charlie heaves over on top of my chair and sends us both crashing to the rug. It's Charlie's blood, pouring out from a chest wound, from a bullet neither of us heard.

A second shot comes just as we fall. It hits the little cable-selector unit on top of the TV and sends it flying in several pieces. Probably where my head was, I'm thinking. We're drawing fire though the patio doors, and the only thing that saved me was my dead, dead friend. Charlie's draped over me, but I twist around enough to see the shattered panes in the door. Another one punches in while I watch; glass shards fall away from a tiny hole. Across the room, some books jump on a shelf. There's no report—he's too far away. I figure the sniper has a clear line of vision—probably up higher than the rail of the deck. He can see the exit to the kitchen, the telephone on the counter, and most of the furniture. I'm behind a stuffed chair, crushed by Charlie and a prisoner of all the light in the room.

When I get my legs free and roll Charlie away, I can see his wound. There's no breathing bubbles, no pulse forcing out all that blood. I'm slick with the mess; feel it caking up on my hair and my back. But mostly I'm thinking about the lights. Charlie wanted lots of light to work on my head. I can't reach any switches. I can't get down the hall. If I don't make it dark, I'm dead too.

I see the cord for the reading lamp. I reach out, yank the plug, and draw another shot. One down. I throw this metal ashtray at the lamp on the opposite side of the sofa. It falls, but the goddamned bulb stays lit. I reach the cord with my foot, reel it in, and shut it off. That leaves the television and the overhead fixture. I kill the television with the remote control, but I don't have another ashtray for the light. Charlie's got a conch shell on the coffee table. I heave it up at the ceiling, and two more quick shots come. Semiautomatic, I'm thinking. Or a second shooter. The bullets strike this framed print on the wall and send it crashing down. The conch shell breaks the ceiling fixture but misses the bulb.

For some reason, that last, mocking bulb sends me over the edge. I start screaming: FUCK YOU! FUCK YOUR MOTHER, HECTOR LUPINO! YOU'RE DEAD, YOU PIECE OF SPIC SHIT! And when I finish, I'm thinking, Where are Charlie's nosy neighbors? Can't anyone hear the shots, see the muzzle flare? They complain about dogs barking, about cars without mufflers. A little gunplay, a firefight is no big deal. The whole town turns off its hearing aids at 9:00 P.M. I'm on my own here. Me and Hector, *mano a mano*. So I lift up the chair and pull off a caster. It's solid brass, just the right heft, and I break the ceiling bulb on my first toss.

It's about ten feet of open floor to the kitchen counter, and while I'm doing the four-legged sprint I'm thinking, Darkness isn't going to save me. He's locked in on the spot and he's going to take a few Hail Mary shots. But the shots don't come, and I'm in the kitchen pulling the phone into my lap. Of course it's dead. Where was the stupid security guard when Hector was cutting the lines? No doubt talking on the phone and listening to Guns N' Roses. Some deterrent.

So I get some paper towels and sit back against the cabinets, mopping my head and catching my breath. And that's when I get the sense again, this fog outside of myself. I hadn't had it since the hospital. And I hadn't been *sure* of anything like that until the shooting started. But now I'm out there again, sharing that air with somebody else, and it isn't Charlie. Charlie is gone, but I'm seeing Hector approach the house. He's crossing that crushed rock that passes for lawns around here and carrying a stubby rifle. Come to finish business. He's coming straight in, and me with no gun. Schmuck! I think. You should've gone for a gun instead of the phone.

I follow the wall past the kitchen to the entry. The living room is on this landing above the stair, and I can see out a long window beside the front door. The house throws a shadow across the yard, straight and vertical. But the line breaks with this lumpy silhouette. Hector, against the exterior wall, ready to storm the place. And me with no weapon.

I move off the landing and down the hall toward the bedrooms, thinking, Where would Charlie keep his gun? I duck into Charlie's room first and try the closet. I'm frantic now, whipping aside all of Charlie's western-style jackets and finding nothing else. Nothing in the shoe boxes on the shelves except bank statements and canceled checks. Next I try the dresser, tossing his shorts and golf shirts and black little gooseneck socks on the floor. Five drawers and no pistol. Come on, Charlie, I'm thinking. All those guns you confiscated and you never kept one?

I'm rooting through the nightstand when I get another sensation. He's coming inside. Not the door, not in front. Charlie always opens the basement windows at night. Hector is sliding through one of these—all tangled and pinched and helpless. The perfect angle for a shot, but I got nothing to shoot him with. All I find in the nightstand are paperback novels and Sominex. I give up and pop back into the hall, try the den, which is next to the stairs. For the second that I'm in the hall, I can hear a wheezing, like Hector's got his groin hung up on the windowsill. Hang away, sweetheart.

I find Charlie's riot gun leaning behind a coatrack in the den.

I pump it and find the chamber empty, but it's sweet consolation. Give me three shells and it's a fair fight. Hell, give me *one.* So it's back to shoe boxes and rooting drawers. I'm sorting through another closet and I strike on something strangely heavy. It's a hunting vest. It's got shell pouches and shell slots, all jammed full. I take the vest and the gun and slide down against the wall in the den. It's a bitch handling the shells with driving gloves on (Josephine's prescription), but I manage. I'm loading the gun and thinking, All I need is one little sound, Hector. Trip on something; stub your toe. *Give me a sign.*

Of course, Hector is operating on sounds, too. He's slinking around like an alley cat. I've got to work the pump, chamber a shell without alerting him. And just when I'm ready to pump anyway, I hear this incredible clatter out of the basement. Hector has tripped over the billiard rack, spilling cues all over the floor. It's perfect cover for the dull snapping sound of me chambering a round. Thank you, sir; may I have another?

But Hector doesn't give me another sound. He's learned his lesson and probably shed his shoes. If he's on the stairs, I can't tell. I'm pointing the gun at the door, trying to slow my breathing. The sweat streams off my face and into my mouth with the metallic taste of Charlie's blood. I can't spit, can't shift an inch out of fear of being heard.

Then it's like all of the fear falls away. I'm back in the knowing mode, okay? I'm real calm all of a sudden and I get a perspective on the whole house. I'm seeing Hector and his rifle on the first flight of stairs. He turns, moves a step, and listens. He steps again and in three more steps he will be adjacent to the den wall. Better still, adjacent to a spot of wall between the closet and a bookcase. I know the construction is prefab; the wall is Sheetrock and R-19 fluff. Buckshot would pass through like hot piss in a snowbank. I level the gun and close my eyes and see Hector mount that third step. I squeeze ever so lightly and squeeze some more. Hector lifts his foot and then the shotgun kicks and flashes. The explosion comes like I'm firing inside a culvert. The flash just keeps spewing and spreading toward that wall and then it's swallowed by plaster dust and powder smoke. There is a *crack!* in there somewhere of a rifle report. Not answering fire, more the reflexive jerk on a trigger. When I look out past the hole, into the dim stairwell floating in powder haze, I know. I'm so sure that I don't even pump the shotgun again.

I caught Hector right below the armpit and the force carried him over the rail and down the stairs to the basement. When I go down to check, I nearly shoot him again because his eyes are wide, wide open. His fingers are still gripping a carbine with a scope and a big banana clip. He looks like he could lift the muzzle and dust me from beyond the grave. But Hector has flinched his last. He's so pathetic and squirrely-small-looking; his little stocking feet propped on the stairs. I sit there with the shotgun in my lap, thinking that maybe it's different if you blow away some big, formidable fucker. The only thing formidable about Hector is the gun. Without it, he's just a kid dressed up in disco clothes.

I'm almost sorry until I remember that he just killed the only friend I had in the world. Shot Charlie in the back, and only because he was standing in front of me. So you're not running things anymore, I tell Hector, right out loud. Don't fuck with the man who can see through walls, who can leap tall buildings in a single bound. I point my finger and drop the thumb, make that little-Hector popping noise. I wish Josephine could see you now, could be here to draw the zipper on your body bag, *cabrone*.

I've got no time to dance around Hector or get all dewy-eyed about Charlie Cadeaux. There's an excellent chance that somebody heard the shotgun blast. If they come knocking at the door, I've got to finesse them away. If they call the cops, I've got to be gone. I figure I won't get far all soaked down with Charlie's blood, so I begin with a shower. When I finish, I rinse out the stall and wipe down all the fixtures. I put my bloody workout sweats in a garbage bag. I slip on my Darrel Fuller duds and go to work. I start by drawing a bucket of water, getting a sponge and some cleanser, and retracing my steps.

I want to get all the bloody smears and footprints I made in the kitchen. I'm not worried about my fingerprints—they were burned off in Jerome—but I've got this wild-hair idea that I can clear Charlie's name. These forensic guys are geniuses, but maybe I can throw them off the scent for awhile. I flush the wash water down the commode and throw the sponge and the paper towels in with my bloody sweats. Then I go back to the living room, plug the lamp back in, and have a look at Charlie.

His eyes are open too, so I close them. The teensy manicure scissors are still hooked over his big red thumb. I fold them up and zip them back into the manicure kit. Right beside him is the scrap of paper with the phone number. Dugan, was it? *Dupree,* that's it. I rinse it in the kitchen sink and see that the ink still reads. Then I turn Charlie over (no small task) and drag him facedown into the den. He's finished bleeding, but the rug still picks up enough to make the point. (EX-COP CRAWLS TO AVENGE WOUNDS.) I prop him up in the spot where I sat, and I fit his hands around the stock of the riot gun. (SLAYS INTRUDER, THEN DIES.) Give him some stature, I'm thinking. A little scenario for those dicks who thought he was a jerkoff.

I can't keep either weapon, or the scenario falls apart. But I take plenty—all my clothes and Charlie's down parka. The man said it was an *Alaska* area code. I go through the bathrooms and grab my toothbrush, my deodorant, and toilet stuff. I even take the hairbrushes that we probably shared. I keep our gambling stash—about five thousand dollars—and leave another two hundred dollars in Charlie's wallet on the dresser. *Robbery was not the motive.* I take some beer, a fifth of whiskey, and box of Oreo cookies. I lug it all down to the garage, along with the bloody trash, and put it in the trunk of Charlie's car. Then I sit behind the wheel for the longest time, walking myself through the whole house, seeing what the dicks would see. It won't fly, I'm thinking, not with that DNA analysis they've got. Maybe I should just torch it all. But no, I figure that's too cheap. They won't get on to me for a few days. Maybe Charlie would get a day's worth of hero headlines. I figure I owe him that.

Something else keeps me from leaving just yet: the realization that the stakes are raised, that I'm both a killer and a target now—one without many options. I will need a lot of luck to get through this, and I'd better find some fast. So I get a flashlight and walk around to Charlie's cactus garden. It's a small detail—sort of corny—but I do it, anyway. A golf ball can work like a rabbit's foot, I figure. It can serve as an object lesson about life in the real world.

Then I pull out into the cul-de-sac and motor down to the main gate. The guard with the spiky white hair is there, jawing away on the phone. Vigilance at minimum wage; you get what you pay for. I catch his eye and roll down the window. He winces like it's a colossal hemorrhoid for him to stop talking.

I just heard something that sounded like shots, I say. Over on Los Animas. From Charlie Cadeaux's place.

What? Shots?

Gunshots, I tell him. Maybe somebody should check it out.

We get kids with fireworks this time of year, he says.

I was in the DMZ when you were filling diapers, I tell him. I know gunshots when I hear them. Total bullshit, but it breaks his train of thought. As I pull away, I hear him telling his phone friend that he's got to call her back.

Chapter Five

◆

They tell me in Juneau that I'll be taking a commuter airline. I'm expecting a 737 or something, right? The kind of sawed-off jumbo jet they run between New York and Boston. So I grab my bag and my fishing rod and head out the door when some guy steers me over to a meat scale. Just step up here, sir. Your bag, too. I ask what's this about and he says it tells them how much fuel to carry. That should've tripped some bells, but I stroll out to the tarmac and another guy points me toward this relic standing on these huge pontoons. Single prop, made out of rivets and roofing tin. Last time I saw a plane like that, it was hanging in the Smithsonian.

What the hell is that? I ask the guy who grabs my duffel.

That's your flight, Mr. *Fuller.* That's a Beaver. They call it the Alaskan taxi.

I feel like telling him what we call a beaver in Newark, New Jersey. I bite my tongue and crawl up inside the little closet under the wing. There's about sixteen other people in there, grinning like maniacal fools. Well, maybe *five* guys, beefy bastards, all squished into the kind of metal bench seats they have in school buses. They're fishermen up from the lower forty-eight, holding their rod cases and tackle boxes; cracking all kinds of jokes about plane crashes and such. We're talking middle-aged frat boys here. The annual escape from the ball and chain. And I'm the fifth wheel because I don't know anyone, and because I'm dressed like Nanook of the North.

What do I know from Alaska? Glaciers. Igloos. Take my wife, please. I find out later that you don't see Eskimos south of Fairbanks, and you don't see snow in the southeast in August. I got all this war-surplus stuff in Seattle that I realize I won't be needing. Not the bombardier flight pants, not the mittens that cinch up at the elbow, not the ski mask right out of the slasher films. Some of the guys have stocking caps on, but nothing else heavier than a down vest. So much for my disguise. Maybe if my beard keeps coming in, I can hide behind that.

Since I'm half-sitting in the lap of the guy next to me, I decide to be friendly. Quite a plane, isn't it? I say. Who makes these Beavers, anyway?

Oh, they haven't built these things for nearly thirty years, he says.

I'm real sorry I asked that, so I switch the topic to fishing. I'll need to learn what I can in order to cover myself in Haida. Haida—I keep rolling that name around. That's where I traced the number that Charlie gave me. I used a reverse directory in Juneau to find Carl Dupree's new name. *Newton, Howard.* No street number, just *Haida.* I'm thinking they probably don't have streets in Haida. Judging by the skids on this jalopy, they don't have an airstrip, either. Poor little Carl Dupree. Alaska must be the bottom of the list. Witness Protection must save all those Caribbean jobs for the Sicilian capos. Major racketeers get Nassau. The burglars get Haida.

The pilot finally climbs in and says to the guy in the copilot seat, *You'd better buckle in, Mr. Schmudloch.* Which means the copilot is really just a passenger. Right there—amid all the sticks and yokes and stuff. I'm thinking, What if Schmudloch bumps the wrong button? What if the pilot has a coronary? Of course, none of my cozy seatmates is alarmed. They wouldn't care if

Schmudloch did the flying. So the pilot pulls the rope-start or whatever they do and the engine kicks in. It's like being inside a blender. My molars are clicking together and I look down to see my feet jouncing in a blur along the floor. I'm real glad at this point that I skipped breakfast. I'm glad I brought a ball to squeeze, to work off some anxiety. And I'm real glad I'm wearing the ski jacket, because wind is leaking in everywhere and we're only taxiing.

You get no intercom lectures, no little safety demonstration on a Beaver. The pilot glances back before lift-off—just making sure the doors are closed. He gets the green light and lays on the gas and we're lurching down the runway. And lurching. And lurching. I estimate that we're about three fishermen too fat to get off the ground. We're going to roll and roll until we smash into the big frosty mountain at the end of the runway. Still, nobody breaks a sweat except me. The pilot stares at that rock face like it's made out of vapor. I notice old Schmudloch has fallen silent, but behind me the party still rages. I'm thinking, They're going to die happy. I'm losing sphincter control and they're passing a flask of bourbon.

I close my eyes and feel some levitation. There is a teetering sensation that seems encouraging, but I'm not convinced. Then we get a giddy little dip and the nose points up. We're flying—but how far and how fast? I peek out and see nothing but mountain surface scrolling past the windshield. And scrolling. It looks like a lot more mountain than we have lift. It's like two lines coming together on a graph. I shut my eyes and try to breathe in some of these swirling winds inside the cabin. And then I get detached again. Just like that—so goddamn sudden. It hits like cocaine hits, like a long pull on a freebase pipe. One second I'm kissing my ass good-bye and suddenly there are no more seconds, no reason to mark time at all. And no fear. I know exactly how high we are, and what direction we're headed. And I'm so sure that we're going to make it. *Let it go,* something tells me. Enjoy the ride.

The pilot banks us away from Juneau. I look past my cozy friend, out the window at a channel. I can see fishing trawlers and different boats. The sunlight is on the water and it's all kind of nice. The plane levels out and I look out my window, to see Juneau all crowded along the base of these mountains, like the buildings are getting plowed into the bay. Somebody passes me the flask and I take a hit and pass it along. And I realize that for several minutes the guy on my right has been telling me how to fish. I only retain a snatch here and there above the engine sound.

He's pretty excited about plugs of some kind. Blue is the hot plug this summer for kings, whatever those are. And spinners. He whips something out of his pocket that is about the size of a motorcycle license plate. It's phosphorescent green on one side and kind of hologrammy-whammy on the other. Stare at it too long and your eyes cross. But salmon jump in the boat to get a look at these things. The guy puts away the voodoo plate and starts talking about halibut. Jigs are what drive the halibut crazy, he's saying. I don't touch that line; I don't even crack a smile. He opens his tackle box and pulls out something that looks like a mortar shell—pure lead, about six pounds of it. This jig has little rubber tentacle things and a hook bigger than my finger.

I miss most of his explanation, but it doesn't matter. I can't take my eyes off this weapon. The only fishing I ever did was in the Delaware River with a cane pole and worms. I'm trying to imagine a fish big enough to get his lips around that mortar shell. And the more I imagine it, the less I like this whole fishing idea. I'm thinking maybe salesman would be a better cover. Maybe I can go after smaller species.

And while we're admiring the guy's jig, somebody yells that he's seen a bear. The guys in the back are all lathered up and yelling that they want a better look. No, I'm thinking, we don't need to fly closer to any bear. But the pilot is just too happy to oblige, and so we bank down toward this ridge on some island. I look out and see where logging teams have cut out big patches of forest. There's some rock faces and white frothy streams and it's all kind of spectacular. And there, right beside one of the streams, is this raggedy-looking momma bear and two little brown cubs. The fishing expert is yammering about bears now.

You like that, you should hike into Pack Creek in the spring, he's saying. Bear City. Thicker than flies on shit.

I tell him this is as close as I want to get. The pilot banks the other way and we're past the ridge, but I keep glancing back. It really was amazing—the bear family just hanging out. No fences, no nothing. It occurs to me that I haven't been to a zoo in about thirty years. And I'm getting the idea that everything is big and bizarre and wild in Alaska. And rustic. You don't get stewardesses handing out nuts on your flight. No air-traffic controller talking you in.

The pilot makes a pass over Haida to wake up the mailman, and then it's down and onto the water. Once we're floating, he glides up to a dock and you step down into the real frontier. A quiet little bay with docks trailing down to the water from way up the bank. There's the dock where the Beaver lands and the mail is dropped. There's another dock with gas pumps for boats. And beyond that, a marina with the most ramshackle boat collection I've ever seen. I'm thinking ocean, right? Big waves and killer storms and you want something substantial. Guess again. Haida is where pleasure boats go to die. Any two-bit scow that could be patched and floated is sitting in one of the slips: waterskiing boats from the fifties, cabin cruisers reconverted to trawlers with big booms sticking out like feelers on a beetle, little toy tugboats with cabins like outhouses.

The buildings were all tucked into the tree line, about a hundred yards from the water. I guess that passes for a town out here—cabins with tin roofs. The bigger cabins with extra windows are the school, the hotel, the bar. They're surrounded by the biggest trees I've ever seen. And in the ragged limbs of those pines are half a dozen bald eagles. The national bird. They're scratching and sleeping and hanging out like vultures. I don't believe what I'm seeing until one of them drops off and soars out across the bay toward open water. Holy shit, I say to my pal from the plane. Those are bald eagles. Did you see that?

He's busy collecting his gear on the dock. He just shrugs and says, They're like pigeons up here, pal. Scavengers, really.

Pretty awesome pigeons, I'm thinking. This place is full of surprises.

Like our domicile, for instance. When I call ahead to reserve, they book me into the Haida Hotel for $175 a night. I'm not thinking private whirlpool, cable TV, or a trouser press. I'm thinking maybe a bed and a lock on the door, but even that is fantasy. The hotel is really a barracks room with a potbellied stove in the middle. My $175 buys me a stiff bunk directly under the Yukon Snoring Champion, heavyweight division. I got my own locker for rods and clothes and my own shelf in the walk-in freezer for all those fish I won't be catching. I do expect to take a chair at the poker table and hold up my end of the miniature bar in the corner.

That's really just for stand-up shots of tequila. You want a jukebox and conversation, you walk down the dirt road to Bill's. Bill serves Chinook beer on tap. He's got pinball and a satellite dish bringing in sports of the world. It's damn near cosmopolitan according to the fellow who checked us in. The hotel owner is a dark little butterball named Harlan. Harlan is quick to mention that he's Tlingit Indian, which is what the whole town of Haida was before fishing got popular. He tells me this while he's showing me my locker and turning down my bed. Harlan says everybody used to work at a sawmill until the sawmill burned down. Then everybody worked at a cannery, and that burned, too. Now everybody's a commercial fisherman or a guide. That's because the ocean is fireproof, I guess.

So who's your guide this week? Harlan asks me.

I haven't hired one, I tell him. I thought I'd get the feel of it first, have a look around.

Harlan stares up at me like I sprouted an eye from my forehead. Guides are booked a year in advance, he says. You got no guide, you got no idea where to fish.

Maybe I'll ask around, I say. You got all these commercial fishermen, right? Maybe I'll pick their brains.

White boy like you, they'll tell you shit, Harlan says. Every year, the catch gets smaller; the DNR makes the troll boats fish shorter seasons. Commercial boats barely make it, guy. Don't need the competition. They'll tell you shit, guy. Follow a trawler and he's liable to shoot at you. You need a guide out here.

Tell you the truth, I'm not that interested in the fish, I say. I figure just to hang loose, explore the island.

Harlan flashes his three remaining teeth and says, Quarter mile east to the point. Mouth of the channel. Two miles west to the other point. That's the whole island. Take you two hours to walk it. Then what you going to do?

Read a book, I say, thinking, *Get out of my face.* I heard about the pinball at Bill's. I came two thousand miles to play it. My money spends just fine, so what difference does it make to you?

I could ease up on Harlan a bit, but I'm tired from all the flying. Haida must be one gossipy little burgh, so I'm not about to drop Howie Newton's name. And playing Sam Spade down at Bill's won't get me anywhere, either. This is going to take some planning, a little finesse. I'll have to learn where Howie lives—presumably by wandering around. Get a fix on his routine, catch him alone, and make my pitch. He'll be real upset at getting spotted, so I'll have to play diplomat, too. The whole prospect makes me weary, so I hit my rack for a few hours.

I wake up and it's 10:00 P.M. and still bright as day outside. The huge guy sleeping above me has a snore like a broken chain saw. The other fishermen are playing cards at the table by the windows. Somebody just took a big pot on a bluff and they're all hooting and laughing like jackals. It smells like sweat and cigar smoke and vodka, and it makes me feel real hollow and sad. You can tell these guys are such tight chums, really cutting loose. I'm not like that with anyone now, not with Charlie out of the picture. I figure it will be a long time before my life is stable enough to yuk it up with some poker buddies. Maybe never. The idea gets me so depressed that I have to slip on a coat and get the hell out.

It's strange that it looks like day, but you can tell it's night outside. I don't hear birds, or see the eagles anymore. The water in the bay is flat, and there's about twenty more boats in at the marina. It rained while I was sleeping, and I'm walking around puddles in the wheel ruts of the road. I pass three or four mailboxes before I remember to start checking. *Newton, Howard.* How many can there be? I walk past Bill's and see half a dozen pickups parked out front. They've got trucks on this island to drive two miles, end to end. I guess they have to spend it on something. Sure as hell don't spend money on their boats.

I step down in the ditch to read one mailbox and come across these raspberries. They're big as a quarter, dark blue and red, and sweet as a peach. They're like nothing I've ever tasted, so pretty soon I'm berry picking. I start filling this discarded milk carton and I'm too engrossed to hear a truck pull up above me on the road. The driver honks and I turn, to see moon-faced Harlan and another Indian in the cab. Hey, guy—they call all of us white guys *guy*—he says. I got you a fishing guide!

That he did. His brother, Jonathon. It so happens that Jonathon is free this week and has a nice boat we can use. Jonathon has the same gap-toothed smile as Harlan, and they're masters of the hard sell. *I haven't got any of those spinners or plugs.* No problem, we got all the tackle. *I forgot to buy a fishing license.* They'll sell you one at Bill's. *How much does your brother charge?* You go out, give it a try, Harlan tells me. We'll talk about the money tomorrow.

So we stop at Bill's to buy the license. We stop at the cabin for my rod case and then Harlan drops us at the marina. Jonathon doesn't call me *guy,* doesn't call me anything when we're alone. He carries a bucket of salted herring and my rod case down to a late-model trawler. I get only grunts when I ask him if it isn't a little late to get started today. I don't get any answer when I ask how far he figures to go. Jonathon is short, like his brother, but thin and hard; the kid brother with a chip on his shoulder. Maybe he resents getting a client. Maybe he planned to take the week off. Judging by the size of the boat, I'm thinking he needs all the revenue he can get. After we climb aboard, I offer him a berry from my carton. Jonathon gets a real kick out of this. He shovels a handful into his mouth and casts off the lines.

I watch as Jonathon steps inside the cabin and starts the engine. He fusses with the throttle and steers us out toward the main channel. Then Jonathon turns and tells me to secure some line that's trailing off the stern. I figure the stern is behind us, and I find the line and start tugging it in. I'm looping it in my hand and watching the end jump around in our wake when I feel a cold nudge at the base of my skull. A voice follows right after, telling me, *Don't fuckin' move, pal.* It's a gun; it's some stowaway come up from behind. And while I'm contemplating how stupid I was not to see it, the guy with the gun at my head tells me to grab the boat and spread my legs. And not to turn around.

A big black hand is patting me down, turning out my pockets and giving me an extra thump at the groin. So much for my finesse. I try to keep a sense of humor.

Help yourself to the raspberries, I say. *Carl.*

Salmonberries, you stupid, wise-guy motherfucker, Carl says. He's holding my shoulder, bending me over the back of the boat like he wants me to finish puking.

Don't shoot him yet, Jonathon calls back from the cabin. We dump him out in the current. He'll carry farther.

That's one eager accomplice, I'm thinking. Good plan, Jonathon. But instead of hating him, instead of collapsing with the kind of fear I felt in the airplane, I have only annoyance. I'm getting boat-sick from looking over the side, but I don't feel like dead meat. Maybe Carl is radiating something through that gun and into my brain. Let it go. *Enjoy the ride.* He doesn't acknowledge Jonathon's suggestion. He's busy turning my wallet inside out.

Carl pops my tennis ball out of my jacket, tosses it over the side, and shoves me down into the fish slime and standing water. I skid across the deck and collide with a portable cooler. Jonathon has another suggestion: Hit him with the gaff hook, man. But Carl says, Shut up and steer the boat. Carl's really saying that he will kick my citified cracker ass without gaff hooks, thank you very much. I raise up to get my first look at him as he's dumping out my rod case.

One tall brother. He goes at least six five, with a mile of leg angling down into rubber boots. In his gray rain gear, he looks like a grain silo. Heavy brow, bald head, and a skimpy little Fu Manchu dribbling down over his lower lip. He tugs that lip in as he looks at my state-of-the–K-Mart fishing pole. The kiddie pole is so pathetic that I figure he might kill me just for that. But he lets it fall to the deck, takes the army-issue .45 from his armpit, and sits back on the gunwale.

Where's your gun? he finally says. Nothin' here; nothin' at the hotel. You s'posed to be Mister Karate or somethin'?

Not hardly, I tell him. You're going to be real disappointed.

How's that?

I didn't come here to kill you.

You just the advance man? Carl replies. Fly out to reconnoiter? Decide where to send the troops? You didn't come to do no fishin', Jack. You never wet a line in your life.

I boost myself up onto the cooler and try to wring out my pants. They're my new $160 cords, all caked with blood and fish scales. At least it's not *my* blood. But I sense it's time to get on his level, before Jonathon has another brainstorm.

What's this troops shit? Don't flatter yourself, I tell him. You talk like you burned off the Medellín cartel. Like you ratted out John Gotti. Your testimony didn't rock the underworld, I tell him. They probably forgot all about you.

Carl says, You didn't forget. But I can see it's had an effect. He's looked over his shoulder for so long that he's not going to let it go that easy.

I tell him, Fine, you're top song on the hit parade. They still want your head on a platter. I'm just saying that I don't have the contract. In fact, I'm on the hit parade, too.

Carl pats his chest with the pistol and watches the shore roll by. He finally says, That so? And the place you pick to hide your sorry ass is Haida? That's some coincidence, Jack. Just how the hell did you find me?

I tell him about the phone number and Charlie's DEA contacts without going into the whole Scottsdale shoot-out. But Carl's quicker than that.

So if I was to call my fed friends, this would all check out? They'd know your pal Charlie?

I'm sure they would, I say. Then I explain how Charlie's death has probably made him a celebrity. So if you think I'm a killer,

I guess you're right, I tell Carl. Three days ago, I blew away the sniper who killed my best friend. Nobody paid me and nobody cares. The world is full of Hector Lupinos.

Your world, Carl says. I been free of that scene for four years. And even if this phone number crap is true, who knows how many wankers are followin' *you*? Either way, my gig is blown. I should shoot your ass just for that.

Yeah, shoot his ass, Jonathon chirps.

Fuck you, you sawed-off, toothless little— I don't quite get it all out before Carl's sweeping boom of an arm cracks my head and sends me back into the fish slime. Then he's looming above me with the .45 in my face. That little monkey is behind him with the gaff hook, ready to brain me if I move. The boat is still at full throttle, turning in circles without a driver.

Give me two minutes with him, I tell Carl. Give me one clean punch and I die a happy man.

You got some stones, Carl says. And I don't give a rat's ass if you die happy. But you is certainly gonna die if you don't tell me what brought you here. Get the wheel, Jonathon.

I want a piece of this guy.

GET THE FUCKIN' WHEEL! he shouts. Then Carl turns back to me and says we're in the channel. Toss you out here and you float clear to Japan, if the orcas don't eat you first.

I came up to learn what I can about Tommy Delorme. Charlie found out that you were bunked with him in Carson City, I say. Tommy started this whole thing by jumping me when I was out laundering money. I'd like to feed his ass to the orcas. That's it, man. That's the whole program.

Carl's upper lip twitches a minute, and then cracks wide open across acres of teeth. He's got the teeth that Harlan and Jonathon are missing—plus a few dozen more. And this laugh wells up and rolls out across the water, echoes back from the pines. Carl lurches across the deck, head thrown back and laughing while he tucks the pistol into his pants.

Oh God, man, that's choice, he wheezes. That's a slice, man. That's a double slice. I *knew* it had to be somethin' like that.

Tommy Delorme. What a sorry-ass motherfucker. Tommy Fucking Delorme!

Yeah, I say, crawling back onto the cooler. But he's *my* sorry-ass motherfucker. Now, are you going help me or not?

Chapter Six

◆

Carl tells Jonathon to cut the engines and drift. Then he directs me through the little cupboard door into the boat's cabin. Don't worry, he says. I won't shoot your ass down here. Put a hole in my goddamn hull.

And all this time I thought we were on Jonathon's boat. But the cabin decor is too get-down funky for a Tlingit Indian. There is plenty of maritime junk—life jackets and lines and greasy engine parts stacked in shoe boxes. But there is also a framed picture of Magic Johnson ("To Carl, Best Wishes"), a Lakers pennant, and a boom box the size of a coffin. Carl's rack of CDs features everything Marvin Gaye ever did, some Natalie Cole, Temptations, Prince. There is red satin draped around like bunting, gathered by satin cords. The cushions are done in a leopard print and there is a black-light leopard mural on the wall. I'm looking at this and thinking, Elvis. Graceland. The jungle room where groupies lost their innocence.

Carl punches a button on the deck and Marvin croons into action. He slumps into the crook where the hull tapers to a V and says, I didn't get your real name, Jack.

Danny Castellano.

You done some time, haven't you, Danny? he says.

Quentin. Twenty-one months for possession, I say. Why, do I throw off a scent?

The way you got into Jonathon, he replies. It reminded me of two cons shoutin' in the cell block. I'll see your ass out in the yard, homes. I fuck you up good.

So how much time did you do? I ask. Carl glares back with a look that says, You're not off the hook yet, pal. You could still do that swim to Japan. Tell me about you and Tommy Delorme, he says.

About midway through the whole odyssey—after the hospital and before the shoot-out—Carl fetches his bag of herb from inside a life jacket. He has lots of trouble separating the rolling papers with his long, spidery fingers. I'm telling about killing Hector while Carl keeps spilling the joint on his chest. I skip the part about seeing through walls. And it's still real hard for me to talk about moving poor dead Charlie and propping him up with the gun. When Carl lights up and sucks it down, I get a sense of real gusto, of real fascination. It can't be the pot, that's too mundane. So it must be me. I'm the night's entertainment. I've spun Carl back into the scene where people get torched in cars and shot by snipers. Compared to the routine in Haida, I'm one exotic diversion.

That's some story, Carl gulps, still holding the smoke in his lungs. If you lyin', you right up in Tommy's league.

He passes me the stubby half joint and I take in some really awful toke, probably roots and stems. *Save the best for company, Carl?* Great shit, I tell him, handing it back. Got anything to drink?

He flicks the roach aside and sits up, darting one of those praying mantis fingers into my chest. I said it was a good story, man. I dint say I bought a fuckin' word of it, Carl shouts. Which means you ain't no charter client, man. *Got anything to drink.* Shee-it.

Well do you? I persist.

We pass that limbo kind of moment between orca bait and a

convict's respect. Then Carl shakes his head and says, I got beers. Warm as piss. Take it or leave it.

I'll take it.

He squeezes his huge self out of the cabin and comes back in a minute with a six-pack and my milk carton of berries. *Salmonberries.* He tosses me a beer, props the berries in his lap, and starts feeding his case of the munchies. My man out there asks me when we goin' to be finished, Carl says. Can't wait to see you bleed. Made yourself a real enemy, Danny.

I look out the hatch and see Jonathon sitting in the captain's chair, tying knots in some baskety-looking unit. He catches me watching and gives me his baddest scowl. You give me chills, Jonathon. I'm quakin' in my boots.

Looks like you made yourself some real friends, I tell Carl. Pilot your boat for you, tip you off when suspicious characters fly into town. Set up a little abduction. That's not SOP for Witness Protection. Looks to me like your gig was blown long before I got here.

Carl pours a fistful of berries into his mouth, starts talking while the juice spills down his chin. See that big number painted outside of this cabin? he asks. Numbers a foot high? That ain't registration. That's a commercial fishin' license. They don't issue them anymore, not for years. You get your daddy's license when he dies. You got to be Indian; you got to be related or you don't fish. But here we got a black man from California, motorin' into port with a nice big boat and a brand-new commercial license. You tell me how regular that sounds. You make some sense of *that.*

Awful peculiar, I agree. Must've set them tongues a-waggin'.

Bet your ass it did, Carl says. And it got worse when I didn't catch no fish, didn't make enough to cover fuel and tackle. How can the brother keep that boat? they wonder. How'd he manage to buy that house? The Indians just figure to wait me out, see how fast I can go broke. Don't nobody tell me how deep to fish, how to down-rig, how to run a hand gurney, how to catch halibut on a skate. We'll just smile and let the brother go bust. Maybe sugar his gas tank a little, drill a couple holes in his hull. Maybe he'll quit and go home. Maybe he'll die and leave us his license.

You're breaking my heart, I tell him. So cut to the chase, Carl. You're a regular kingpin now. How did you win them over?

We got four months of working, Carl says, eight months of winter. Man needs to occupy himself or else he just drinks.

You shoveled everybody's driveway for them? I say.

You want to hear this, or you want to swim? Carl replies. Reason I won their hearts and minds is *round ball,* man. Community hoops. Every town in the southeast has a basketball team, and we play all winter.

And you're the ringer to end all ringers, I add. You're the basketball messiah.

I get my points. Carl grins and drains off his beer.

Oh, I can picture this, I tell him. A whole league of little Jonathons and Harlans out there, trying to shut you down. I'll bet nobody else got a rebound the whole season.

Maybe one guy. Carl shrugs. I might've missed one or two. But that's what did it. After a season of hoops, I couldn't get enough advice about catchin' salmon. Guys loanin' me equipment, markin' their maps. Give me their wives if I asked, man. It's like everything I missed in stir has come back to me. I'm livin' right, Danny. I got it all except the sunshine here. Thing about Alaska is, you tend to lose your tan.

Carl pitches another one of his laughing fits and then cracks open another beer. I join him, and realize that my song and dance has had its effect. Gaff-hooking me is no longer a topic of discussion. If I can keep Jonathon away from my back, I might even make it to port. Carl announces that he's got to get fishing early, and so he takes the wheel and gets us under way. I have no idea how long we've talked, but the horizon indicates only dusk. Strange, strange hemisphere, I'm thinking as I take a seat in the stern. Endless days. Eagles for pigeons and bears for pets. I haven't slept in twenty-four hours, and I'm feeling a creeper buzz from the pot that goes tingling down to my wet socks.

There's my orcas! Carl shouts, lifting his hand from the throttle to point out at open water. I stand and follow the angle of his arm toward a commotion on the horizon. They leap in sequence, boom-boom-boom, so you're thinking it's only one killer whale. But there's at least four, buzzing the channel like a squadron of fighter planes. They're so distant and yet so clear—that sharp black dorsal fin must be as big as a house. Boom! The front one dives just as the trailing whale breaks out, shows his fin, and hits the water. And I thought momma bear was spectacular. This is unreal. They're so strong and fast and relentless out there, shooting past the island. In five minutes' time, they're completely gone. And I'm standing there rocking with the bounce of the hull and feeling like I've lived my life in a cave. For those few minutes, I don't care if I never catch Tommy Delorme, if I never climb out of the boat. Then I glance down at Jonathon's frowning pug and it all gets flushed away. You are what you are, *guy*. You play the hand you're dealt.

I walk back into the Hotel Haida and Harlan turns white as a sheet. He was so sure that I would turn up a floater that he emptied my locker and packed my bag. He goes scampering through the racks of sleeping fishermen to get me some dinner. Jonathon's a lousy guide, I tell him. We didn't catch anything.

Harlan just shoots me a look like I'm speaking Hebrew. These Tlingits got no sense of humor. I'm stowing my clothes again when I discover my plane ticket is gone. That's when I remember Carl's parting shot at the marina: I'm still callin' my man, check out your story, Danny. Don't even think about leavin'. Unless, of course, you like to swim.

I've still got about four thousand dollars in a money belt. But my guess is that it won't spend if I try to rent a boat. I'm shoveling in Harlan's fish stew and thinking that Carl had better be discreet. He gets too specific about Scottsdale, and bells could ring at the DEA. There's also the chance that Carl's Witness Protection buddy doesn't know shit. I imagine that program run by some glorified filing clerk with a bad sense of humor. Who else could book a soul brother into an Indian fishing village? They probably had a good long laugh about that one. Really delighted at the chance to stick the black fink burglar in the boonies. Joke's on those guys, I think as I'm climbing into the sack. Out here, Carl Dupree is bigger than Michael Jordan and badder than Captain Ahab. I drift off to sleep feeling a little high and very glad that I didn't back down on the boat. It was touch and go there for a moment. Still is.

And after what seems like ten minutes' sleep, I'm getting jostled around and seeing a light in my eyes. Am I dreaming about the hospital again? *Follow my finger, Mr. Delorme.* More jostling, and I peer around the flashlight beam and see Carl's shiny head poking out of that gray raincoat.

You want to talk to me, you come on the boat, he whispers. I be out all day.

And I'm thinking, Day? This is the first night I've seen in forty-eight hours. My watch says five-fucking-thirty and Carl is calling it day. Take it or leave it, he says. I be gone in ten minutes.

And I be going with you, I tell him, fighting out from under the blankets. I hear the door slam and wonder if the other guys heard Carl. But then I realize there are no other guys. Not a snore to be heard, because they're already on the water. Not my idea of a vacation, I'm thinking as I'm hopping around, trying to pull on a sock. But if you make your living in four months, you have to do your sleeping in December.

I walk out into a steady drizzle and follow the sound of voices and boat engines to the marina. There's a buying office for a cannery on the end of the main pier. It's a hangout for the commercial guys; they get a free cup of jack and a little conversation before heading out. I find Carl in back, filling his coolers with crushed ice. He's moving quicker now, all anxious to get a jump on the fish. We don't say anything as we load the ice into the stern of his boat. I notice for the first time that he has named it *Sanctuary*. He lashes the coolers against the hull and then we're up and out of the bay at full throttle.

The engines are too loud for much of anything except sign language. Carl motions me into the cabin and points out our position on a map. Then he drags his finger through a tangled series of islands and shoals. Must be his plan of attack. I brace myself inside the cabin and look out at the spookiest, lowest sky I've ever seen. The clouds come right at us on the water. Every now and again, some island rises up; some point with ragged trees pops into view. We spot the occasional running lights, but mostly we're out there alone. The engine vibes shake the cup of thermos coffee in my hand; they rattle my teeth and make Carl's rack of plugs and spinners jingle like sleigh bells. Hey, fish; Santa's coming.

He shuts it down in some arbitrary spot that must smell like salmon. Carl starts pulling those candy-colored plugs off the rack and rigging up lines. He climbs around the cabin and pulls down his two big booms that tip out the sides. The booms drag three lines each. There's three more trailing off the stern, all hooked to weights like little cannonballs. He's got so many hooks in the water that the fish don't have a prayer. When he fixes the last line, he tells me to take the wheel and throttle us up about a quarter. I do it, feeling the surge up through the controls. We've got a gentle wake behind and about three feet of visibility off the bow. Bastard will probably shoot me if we run aground. When I turn back to ask Carl about our direction, he's already pulling in the first fish.

We go like this for about four hours without conversation. When Carl isn't setting out lines or cleaning kelp from his hooks, he's gutting out fish on this gory little podium. He's so busy, it makes me wonder how he works without a driver. The rain breaks and the clouds lift a bit at midmorning. Carl directs me between all these hazy lumps of island, pointing and yelling *port* or *starboard.* (I'm glad he points, because I don't know the difference.) And he feels this duty to educate, so he'll hold up every new species. *That's a coho! That's a king! That's a silver!* Very nice, Carl. I nod and grin; humor the guy. He still hasn't mentioned if he made his call and cleared my story with the feds.

We don't talk until he breaks for lunch and leads me back into his jungle room. Punch up Aretha Franklin, open some beers, and chow down on baloney and cheese.

So what are we doing, Carl? I ask.

Workin', he says. You ain't allergic to work, are you?

I mean, are we friends here, or do I take a swim after you catch your limit? I say. He lets me wait a good long while as Aretha sings "Respect."

I figure it'll soak in sooner or later, he says. What I'm doin' out here is makin' a point.

That you can catch fish like the Indians?

That you can walk away from the life, Carl replies. It ain't the Fields of Ambrosia, Danny. Ain't no pot of gold. But it beats the shit out of dyin' facedown in some gutter, your brains blown out of your head. You black, you deal in the city and that's the way you die. You get one grandpa that makes it to forty-five, and three or four that get wasted at twenty. Had a prison counselor called it genocide. Self-genocide, 'cause it's brothers wastin' each other.

He takes a massive bite of sandwich and says, I know what you thinkin'. You thinkin', That don't confront me none; I ain't black, and I ain't headed for no gutter. Let 'em shoot the shit out of Oakland or D.C., long as I get *mine.*

I was thinkin' I'd have me another sandwich, I tell him. If I'm getting a sermon, at least I can get some dinner.

Carl crushes his beer can and tilts his slick head at an explain-me-this angle. You answer me straight—no bullshit now. Since you got into this launderin' gig—since you seen all that money, nice cars, nice clothes—did you ever once see yourself a workin' man? You ever see a single job you wanted—no matter what it pays? he asks.

I don't bother to respond. Carl's hotter than red chiles.

Fuckin'-a you didn't, he says. From where you sit, every man who works a straight day is dumber than dirt, just too goddamn stupid to make himself rich. I know it 'cause I lived it, homes. After three years of dealin', I wouldn't trade places with Lionel Ritchie. Maybe Magic Johnson—but I flunked my urine test in college, so that shit's out of the question.

What *is* the question? I ask. That I'm supposed to identify with your life? Your path to righteousness? I'm not even in the scene, Carl. I got retired, remember? I got a whole new nose; I got a patch of scalp that won't grow hair; I got these hands all coated with belly skin that look like they're dipped in acid. Maybe I will find me a real job. Maybe I'll be a professional gambler. But before I do anything else, I'm going to cut out the heart of Tommy Delorme and feed it to Luis Manzanaro.

Carl inhales a chunk of bread crust and shakes his head at me. You know, you remind me of that cocky motherfucker, he says. Tommy Delorme. Both of you on a big crusade. He's in search of the ultimate score and you're after his sorry ass.

And just what is that ultimate score? I ask. C'mon, Carl, tell me what you told the DA in Nevada.

Fuck you, he says, tossing his empty can at me. I got no time for a man can't learn from experience. Man thinks he's gonna live forever.

Carl works the lines for another hour before we get some slack time. He's gutting out a fish when I ask him what he means about living forever.

Lif' up the back of my raincoat, he says. Sweatshirt, too, he says.

He's got a knife in one hand, fish blood on his fingers, so I do it. I get through the layers of clothes to bare skin and see the wickedest knife scar—a spiral job starting at Carl's spine and curving up toward his armpit. I tug his coat back down and Carl digs into the fish again, saying, He marked us both, Danny. One way or 'nother.

Carl starts in on another salmon and tells me how Tommy got wise to his snitch status. They'd lived together about a month when Luis's attorney tipped Tommy off. Word about Carl leaked out of the DA's office and Tommy got wind of it. But Tommy's too smart—and too little—to try anything. He makes a few polite inquiries around the yard. He works his way up the ladder. There's people selling dope, people selling protection, and people selling hits. I'll take one of those, Tommy says. But he's one big kahuna.

Then there's no point in trying to wrestle the bastard, they tell Tommy. We'll jus' do the Roman candle. The bigger they are, the longer they burn.

So Carl tells me how Tommy eats saltpeter one night and earns a trip to the infirmary. So while he's off getting his stomach pumped, Carl wakes up smelling kerosene in the cell. The instant he smells it, he knows the drill. Grab both mattresses and head for the top bunk. Cover up and scream like a banshee. Maybe the guards will reach you before the flames do.

Is that what happened to your hair? I ask.

Very funny, Carl replies. All I lost was my *Sports Illustrated* Swimsuit Edition, my letters, my Nikes, and any faith I had in the DA's office. I told those bastards that I'd been *made.* I told them I'd have to kill Tommy on principle, and their big solution was to move me to another cell.

Dead meat in a fresh wrapper? I say.

Egg-fucking-zactly, Carl replies. Didn't another week go by before some Crip motherfucker did me with a sharpened spoon—make me look like a barber pole. Asshole never studied anatomy, else I'd still be bleedin'. Sixty-eight stitches, homes. The DA finally took the hint. I hyped up the conspiracy angle to get into Federal Witness Protection. They offered me a deli in Seattle, a construction job in Texas, and this. . . .

Looks like you chose right.

Destiny, Carl says. I actually got the *knack.*

After trying to rig lines all morning, I realize that I don't. The second beer nearly puts me under, so I figure to catch a few winks in the cabin. It's really kind of hypnotic there, with the rain on the roof and the engine throbbing. I probably sleep for six hours. I don't wake up until the trawler is docked in Haida and Carl is shouting at me. Hey, numb-nuts! he's saying. Get your ass up; got to show you somethin'. I wander out to the stern and see that all of his coolers are empty. He's already sold the day's catch and hosed down the decks. Some Indian kid is pumping gas in the tanks and Carl is way up the bank, walking toward the woods.

I don't catch up until he's nearly at Bill's. I can hear some sportscast rolling out of the place and smell burgers from an exhaust fan. Carl motions for me to follow him around back. We step around a rotting boat hull, through a stack of beer cases, and go in the rear door. Carl says hello to the fat grill chef (Bill?) and the pregnant waitress (Mrs. Bill?). He leads me past the sinks and through the kitchen to the little porthole where the cook lays the platters. From here, we can see out into the main room. It's full of smoke and fishermen. A real roadhouse café.

Check out that table by the window, Carl says. Four white guys. I peer out and see the bunch—three youngish yuppie-type jocks and an older guy. They're not talking, not working very hard on their pitcher of beer. Not even trying to blend.

Ever see them before? Carl asks.

No, but they're dicks, I say. Might as well carry a sign.

They're DEA, Carl says. Bush pilot told me. They had to show I.D. to get on the Beaver 'cause they're all packin' guns.

We step back from the counter and I say, You called your man, didn't you? That's some kind of turnaround. Better than Federal Express.

Carl shrugs and says, You do what you can to protect your gig. You don't trust nobody you don't have to.

I trust guys who do me favors, I tell him. You tipped me off, so now what? How do I get my ass off this rock without being spotted?

Carl figures the state ferry is my best plan. If I catch it at some other town, I can blend in with the tourists and ride it to Juneau. Carl meets me on the leeward side of Haida in an open boat that he borrowed from Jonathon. At midnight, we make the three-hour crossing to Tenakee Springs. I guess Tenakee is where everybody goes to bathe. Take the water, or whatever. It's got this Victorian hotel that looks like a false front on a movie set. Otherwise, it's just more cabins and the big pier for the ferry. Carl drops me there in the dark and tosses my bag out. I know he's not sentimental, but I wonder if that's all I'll get. He's standing with his back to me, running a huge hand over his head. He turns and walks over.

I could give a shit if you ever find Tommy Delorme, but I'll tell you where I'd look, he says.

Please do.

The man was always talkin' about downstream money, Carl says.

Downstream?

Downstream, yeah. Secondary shit. Comin' from the drug

trade but not from dealin'—like this money launderin', Carl explains. See, Tommy didn't want to be a two-timer—risk another possession bust. But he could still cut himself a slice.

A big slice, I mutter.

Just then, some fisherman steps onto the pier and starts untangling the lines on a crab trap. Carl backs me off to a corner, real clandestine-like, and says, Tommy wanted to export *chemicals*.

Chemicals?

Drug-refinin' chemicals, Carl replies. Ether was the big one he kept repeatin'. Said ether was the one they can't get in Colombia, but they gotta have it to process coke. Without ether, you jus' get that pasty shit that hopheads smoke like opium. Tommy said you don't get busted for possession of ether. Jus' be a little discreet. But you can make a thousand bucks on a drum of that shit that you buy for less than a hundred.

Ether, huh? I say. So where do they make this stuff? And how's he getting it to Colombia?

Submarine, man. How should I know? Carl says. But we both know how he's stakin' himself. He got his bankroll from you.

That's good for a deep belly laugh as Carl starts up his motor. *Watch yourself*, he shouts, and goes ripping off into the fog just as the ferry horn sounds from the other end of the channel.

The inside of that ferry at 6:00 A.M. looks like Jonestown after the Kool-Aid party. Bodies slumped everywhere—in the seats, in the aisles, on the tables in the cafeteria. Vagabond punks all coiled up together in sleeping bags; whole families tucked under a single ratty quilt. I walk from the front lounge through the mess hall and past acres of seats, seeing nothing but tourist faces tipped to the sky, showing me their tonsils and fillings. One thief could pick the whole boat clean—get all those seed caps with the souvenir pins, some binoculars, and about three hundred half-read copies of James Michener's *Alaska*.

I actually catch a guy reading his copy when I work my way back to the stern. He's in the smoking lounge, where the seats face each other, with that monster book on his knees. He's got a silvery beard and silvery hair and these reading glasses hanging off his nose. He's wearing the Eddie Bauer Starter Kit, all that coordinated wool and khaki. The professor on safari. But when he takes off the glasses to look at me, I get a whole different impression. This is no bookworm face—too square and sour and familiar. This is the fed that Carl pointed out through the kitchen at Bill's. And it just so happens that he's sitting with his preppie goons. And one of them just happens to block the aisle when I turn.

Let's not wake up the boat, Danny, the dick says. We can do this quietly.

So they lead me to the seat across from Eddie Bauer and cuff me to the armrest. And the boss polishes off another paragraph of *Alaska* while his lackey reads me my rights.

Part Two

◆

The Ethereal Body

When the heart weeps for what it has lost, the spirit laughs for what it has found.

—Sufi aphorism

Chapter Seven

◆

My best guess is that sawed-off gnome Jonathon tipped the feds to my escape on the ferry. I'm half-expecting the thumbscrews and the rubber hose when they get me to Juneau. The dicks don't quite follow arrest procedure when the ferry pulls in. They wait for the whole boat to empty before walking me down the gangway to this white van—not a police van but a rental with a Hertz bumper sticker. There are no seats in back, not even carpeting, so all of the agents and luggage are slung on the floor. The driver is wearing a business suit and talking into a portable cellular phone. Probably telling them, Charge up the cattle prod; we're on our way.

I'm lying against the wheel hub, my coat over the handcuffs, getting my ass bruised on every bump. When we turn, I keel over onto the agent next to me and he shoves me back into place. Turn the other way, I roll the other direction and get propped up again. The boss fed, the Michener reader, gets a smile out of this routine. He's been puffed up like a blowfish ever since my arrest; too busy gloating to care about bumpy rides in a cattle truck.

Gloat away, I'm thinking. *I know an attorney who will make you sweat bullets for every* Miranda *infraction.* But then I recall how the attorney is hooked into Luis. He used to defend poor little Hector Lupino about five times a year. He'd be pleased to hear from me—very pleased. No, this time it'll be a public defender. Law-clinic rejects, scum of the earth. I might as well use my one phone call on Dial-a-Prayer.

It is a long time before anyone mentions that free phone call. We pull out of traffic and into a garage under some building. Everybody piles out with their luggage and gets into an elevator. The only clue I get is a posting in the elevator advertising brunch at the Klondike Lounge. The lounge is on the tenth floor. We get off at nine. Two more agents meet us there to help with the luggage. It's a hotel all right, a Ramada or a Holiday Inn, judging by the puke pastels. They usher me into a group of connecting suites that look out on the harbor. So much for the torture chamber. Instead of the rack, I get to recline on a sectional sofa. Nobody's sharpening the bamboo shoots. The agents are all taking turns in the john or building themselves Dagwood sandwiches from a relish tray on the bar. Somebody passes me a can of soda. Then they empty my duffel on the table and root through the pile of damp, fishy laundry. I can smell it clear across the room. They're confounded by my kiddie fishing rod, thinking it's wired or something. When they don't find any drugs or bales of money, they start drifting away. I keep nodding at the phone, but they don't take the hint. Finally, I reach for the receiver, but the head fed moves it out of range.

Somebody orders coffee from room service. Somebody else sets a tape recorder in front of me. Eventually, everyone clusters within hearing range. The guy with the beard takes an easy chair and opens a nice thick file. I get it, I'm thinking. This is the good-cop part. Behind some door is Attila the Hun. He'll be out in a couple of hours.

I soon learn that the Bearded Avenger is going to play both good cop and Attila the Hun. He introduces himself as Special Agent Max Kohler. Before we get started, he says, I should tell you who we are and why we're interested in you.

Before we start, I tell him, I get my phone call and whatever passes for a public defender up here.

Kohler just rolls on like I never said anything. Our Phoenix branch has worked concert with a Treasury task force on money laundering, he says. They were interested in you long before your little shoot-out at Charlie Cadeaux's.

Was I dreaming, I ask him, or did somebody read me my rights? *Miranda* rights? I get blank stares all around. I might as well be in Teheran. I glance down, to see that the tape recorder isn't running. They're saving that for *my* speech.

Of course, the death of a DEA agent—even a disgraced one—gets lots of scrutiny, Kohler continues. You get different agencies reaching different conclusions based on the same evidence. (While he talks, he's passing me these glossy photos of the crime scene: Charlie with the shotgun and that gaping chest wound; Hector splayed out at the foot of the stairs, his silly grin gone flat with rigor mortis.) For instance, the local DA is ready to close the case. He doesn't even know you were there—nice shooting, by the way. (Kohler hands me a photo of the view out the stairwell, through the hole in the wall.)

Must've been some party, I say.

The DA doesn't know the half of it, Kohler says. He's rooting in a whole new file now, with a different set of pictures. He tosses them across the table at me, naming towns as he goes: Bakersfield, Kingman, Carson City. The pictures are taken by bank-lobby cameras. They're grainy as hell, but you can see that it's me. And clipped to each photo is the blown-up microfiche of each transaction—the teller's receipt and the cashier's check cleared through Luis's account in L.A. This is the deposit-reporting sting that Cadeaux warned me about. He also warned Luis Manzanaro. Luis could have closed the account and covered his tracks in time. He has lawyers diverting his money offshore; last I heard, it was in Netherlands Antilles. For Kohler and his task force, the paper chase probably stopped there. Box canyon, Kemosabe. That explains the interest in me, and the penthouse treatment I'm getting.

South-Central Bankshares has charted your whole itinerary,

Kohler says. We won't ask how you acquired all that cash you're flashing—not without your attorney present. So what if you won it at the dog track? You still have a real problem reconciling it with, say, your last five tax returns.

Before I can respond to that, Kohler has switched gears and dug out yet another file. He's a regular Rolodex. This one covers the Jerome accident. He's got pictures of the burned car, pictures of me in the hospital (that prick sheriff shot Polaroids while I was unconscious!), and one shot of the contents of Tommy Delorme's wallet—the planted clue that survived the fire.

Your laundering trip appears to have ended with another little party in Jerome, Arizona, Kohler says. Very interesting scenario constructed by someone who wanted to vanish. The sheriff says it was a body swap, and I'm inclined to believe him. By the way, I notice you're still wearing gloves. How are the grafts doing?

I don't respond; I don't look up because I'm staring at that shot of poor dead Charlie with the gun I placed in his hands. I'm thinking about how little he means to these assholes, to anyone but me. And I'm remembering his lecture about being given the gift of life, a life that will be painful to watch. Looks like the pain has come around. *How are the grafts doing?*

They throb all the time, I hear myself saying. I could use an aspirin and a fucking nap.

Get him an aspirin! Kohler shouts, then he turns back to me. You'll get your nap, and your phone call and your attorney, he says. But not until you get the speech. You'll want to stay awake for this.

Somebody hands me a little travel pack of aspirin and a fresh can of soda. I do the tablets while Kohler collects all of the pictures and sorts them back in their proper files. Then he takes off his reading glasses and gives me a pinchy grimace of a look that is probably supposed to stop my heart. Nobody else so much as clears his throat. The agents stand there with big hunks of sandwich stuck in their cheeks because they're afraid to chew. This is some kind of holy moment.

None of us joined the agency to be popular or to get rich, Kohler begins. We have no illusions about how hard it is to fight a cartel that can buy your whole division—can buy whole governments to get what it wants. What they can't buy, they kill. And when they can't kill you, they confound you with dummy corporations and laundering scams like the one you were running. You see the money flow into property and businesses and it almost seems benign. It seems cozy and remote and even glamorous. And when that happens, you get tempted. And when you get tempted, you get the kind of enforcement we had from Charlie Cadeaux. Well Charlie had his day; now we'll have ours.

Kohler passes a hand around the room, getting all paternal about his agents, his *people*. These men are very bright, very capable, and, most important, they're clean. It's no coincidence that they're young. You get close to a pension, get twenty years of riding a desk, and you just want to walk away without stopping a bullet. You get removed from the scourge, from the front lines and all of the little lessons. We've all kicked in plenty of doors, traded shots, and carried half-dead kids out of crack houses. We can all focus on the victim's faces when we meet slick-talking pricks like you.

Maybe you look in the mirror and see a guy just trying to get a stake, just playing the system, Kohler says. We look at you and see a chancre on the dick of humanity. You think you're smart enough to play the Smurf—just carry the money. We figure you're about as bright as the guy who mops the bathhouse floor after the queers have come and gone. But maybe, maybe you're just smart enough to save your own sorry ass. You follow? You still with me, Danny?

I nod, and press my temples to hold back what feels like a major migraine. The other agents are chewing again. They didn't want to miss the part about how bright they are.

Your *Miranda* rights don't concern us, Danny, Kohler says. Neither does your life. You're barely worth prosecuting, and it remains to be seen whether you're worth a trip to Alaska.

Don't tell me you're not having fun, I reply. You get to wear your little Eddie Bauer costume. You get to fly inside a giant Beaver. . . .

One of the agents likes this enough to choke on a piece of his sandwich. Kohler's little mouth clamps down until it vanishes behind his whiskery muff. The coughing agent leaves the room.

What I'm driving at is that you're real expendable, Danny, Kohler says.

Is this the part where you threaten me? I say. Why don't we turn on the tape recorder?

Kohler rolls on like he never heard a thing. You're also real expendable to whoever had you hit in Jerome. I'm guessing this Tommy Delorme is just as ambivalent as we are. Whatever his motive, it still serves our purposes. So here's your chance to be intelligent. We're giving you an offer that your attorney will never hear from us. You get one shot at it, and I suggest you take it. Because after we book you, after your lawyer arrives, we hum a different tune. *Capisce?*

So let's have the offer, I say.

Kohler takes a slurp of coffee and says, We want to know all about Covina Clockworks. You give us Luis Manzanaro's corporate flowchart—structure, distribution, schedules. You give us every name from yourself on up. And you walk us through the money trail—I don't care where it leads. Shelf corporations, wire transfers, offshore accounts.

I ask him what I get in return, and Kohler says, Your life.

I expected something smoother, I tell him. Either I flip for you guys or I wind up a floater in Juneau harbor. *Please.*

Oh, we're not going to kill you. Kohler smiles. Your old chums will handle that—assuming they've got someone smarter than Hector Lupino. No, Danny, we'll kill you just by pushing paper at a district judge in Phoenix. We'll give you the Barry Seal treatment. You've heard of him, haven't you?

Afraid not, I reply. Is he an agent, too?

Just a big, stupid pilot down in Louisiana, Kohler says. Made runs for the Ochoa clan, was very tight with Carlos Lehder Rivas. You've heard of him?

I don't let on, but anyone in the business has heard of Carlos. He started the Colombian airlift in the early eighties. He ran his own island in the Bahamas until he fucked over the gendarmes. He's the biggest player they ever extradited to the States. Got life without parole. That's what you get for being high-profile—even in Colombia.

Barry Seal got himself in deep shit, so he flipped and set up a whole string of arrests, Kohler continues. That was supposed to wipe his slate clean. But Barry wasn't contrite enough for this judge in Baton Rouge. Barry gave too many interviews; thumbed his nose a bit too much. Barry thought it was all just too damn funny. He expected to walk away with our eternal thanks for being a good snitch.

Wasn't that the deal? I ask.

Kohler sips his coffee, mops his mustache, and says, The deal was low-profile. The deal was Federal Witness Protection. But anonymity cramped Barry's style. He wanted out, and the judge gave it to him. Put him in a halfway house, required him to come and go at certain hours. Stripped him of his bodyguards. *Forbade* old Barry from associating with his armed buddies. Pretty much hung him out there with a sign on his back.

And he got hit, I say. And you're washing your hands like Pontius Pilate?

All we did was lay out the facts. Kohler shrugs. Push a little paper at the judge. The point is, if you throw yourself at the mercy of the court, you may not always get it. We book you down in Phoenix on tax evasion and federal currency violations, Danny, and we'll see it gets plenty of attention. The judge will set a nice low bail and maybe one of our dummy corporations will pay it. You'll be famous *and* back on the street.

Just like Barry Seal?

Just like Barry Seal. You've led a charmed life up to this point, Kohler tells me. Always one step ahead of the reaper. Hell, I'm surprised Carl Dupree didn't blow you away. Don't expect your luck to hold out forever, Danny. You saw them take out Charlie Cadeaux; next time, it'll be you. You talk to us now and the whole laundering rap disappears. You get Federal Witness Protection. You get to die real old, maybe even natural causes. But call your attorney, Danny, try to fight the charges, you get nothing. The laundering case is airtight. We won't even plea-bargain. That's the program, he says, and spreads his hands like a croupier. You can be real smart, or you can be on the next plane to Phoenix.

I suppose I started sinking halfway through the Barry Seal story. By the time Kohler finishes, I'm oozing between the sofa cushions like wet cement. The room has taken the kind of tilt you get after drinking lots of cheap champagne. I'm wishing I could leave my body again, find that other dimension, but I can't. I'm learning that it can't be induced. It's like grinding the ignition on a dead car—like flicking the wick on an empty lighter. I'm beginning to accept that Kohler is serious and that this is still America. This is how they're fighting the drug war—using bulldozers on crack houses and coercion on informants. And even as I'm hating them, hating the dilemma, I sense a change in myself. Before Alaska, before I went fishing with Carl Dupree, I couldn't care less if I lived. But you get out of the city, get out of your own skin and look at the orcas, and you think maybe your life *is* a gift. Maybe you can make some sense out of this. And maybe, just maybe, you can finish the job you started.

Can we do this later? I ask Kohler. It's a real long story and I'm real tired.

He's smiling now, that set-the-hook kind of grin. Sure, Danny, Kohler says. Catch some sleep. We'll start whenever you're ready.

Everybody stands like we've finished some cordial transaction. Grins popping out all around. Except one guy. This older agent with a three-day beard isn't amused. He's the one Kohler appoints to tuck me in. He's wearing a flannel shirt and these crisp new khaki pants and the obligatory shoulder holster. He's one of these neckless primates with a high forehead and a low-slung gut. He takes my arm and steers me into a bedroom, saying, Right this way, *Mr. Chancre.*

Real dry sense of humor. No smile, no eye contact. He dumps my fishy clothes on the luggage stand. He unlocks one wrist on the handcuffs but then locks it again to a rail on the headboard. Then he sits at the foot of the bed with a magazine. I thrash around to get comfortable—this whole bondage scene is new to me. After an hour or so, I peek up and see old scruffy-beard staring me down. It's not the curiosity the other agents had. This is pure malice. With Kohler, it was nothing personal, but this ape is another story. Not exactly relaxing. Try counting sheep when you're waiting to be smothered with a pillow.

And when I do close my eyes, I keep seeing that photo Kohler flashed me of Charlie dead against the wall of his den. *Next time, it'll be you,* Kohler said. That's the lullaby I get before finally nodding off.

Chapter Eight

◆

Strange how you integrate stuff into your dreams. I'm dreaming that I'm in that Beaver, that rickety airplane that we flew over to Haida. But instead of being in back with all the drunken fishermen, I'm the pilot. I'm real anxious about this—and not just because I don't know shit about flying. See, there's this real severe-looking drill sergeant–type guy sitting next to me. He's got one of those mouths you see on fifty-year smokers—all pinched down and apelike. That makes me anxious, that and this legal-looking form he has tacked to a clipboard. I'm bluffing, right? I'm pretending to check instruments and move throttles, and every time I do something, little pruneface makes a checkmark on this form. The only thing he says to me—he keeps repeating it—is, *When we're finished, you have to land on water.*

Fine, I tell him. But when I look out the window, I see endless desert. I see the kind of badlands you find between Barstow and Needles, California. No reservoirs, not even a canal. I tell him there's no lakes here, and the instructor guy says, You have to find water; it's part of the test.

But instead of popping off, instead of giving him a parachute and shoving him out the door, I just sweat more, fiddle with the controls, and look out at endless desert.

How about if we glide? I ask him. If we let the wind take us, it always blows to the ocean.

That seems really lame, and the instructor thinks so, too. He shakes his jar-head and makes another checkmark on his form.

I'm shutting down the engine, I tell him. We're going to glide to water.

You're the pilot, he says.

So I flick some button and we watch the propeller spin slower and slower until you can make out the blades. It slaps around one last time and then freezes, and we just have the wind rushing by. I can't let on that this idea is crazy, that I feel us dropping like a rock. Out of the corner of my eye, I can see Sergeant Rock has gotten to the bottom of his form. He's run out of items to check.

That should do it, he says, and he holds the clipboard out to me. Sign here.

I can't sign because I'm gripping the yoke, trying to hold the nose of the plane up. We're hurtling down, down into Death Valley, and he's not even fazed.

But I didn't find water, I tell him. We're not finished.

Sign, the guy says, end of discussion.

I want to reach for the pen, but I can't take my hand from the yoke. The nose of the plane is still dropping and I'm tugging back, trying to raise us and trying to get ahold of the clipboard. *I can't reach it!* I tell Mr. Monkeyface. And I'm lunging and jerking as the desert comes swimming up in a blur and then I'm yanking against the handcuffs that are attached to this hotel bed. And I'm finally awake and panting like an asthmatic.

I'm awake, but reality isn't any relief. I'm still a prisoner in Juneau, Alaska. My *Miranda* rights are being ignored by Nazi Max and his SS buddies. I steal a glance at my night nurse in the corner—a different agent with the same plaid shirt as the gorilla he replaced. He's picking his teeth with a cocktail straw and reading *USA Today*. The blinds are drawn and we're getting only faint neon through the window. More light is pouring under the door, from the room where I can hear grunts and curses and poker chips clacking together.

It's the second time in three days I'm lying in my rack eavesdropping on a poker game. And the sound of it, the rhythm of play, brings back another memory, one that is planted because of Carl's parting shot—his advice about Tommy. It has brought back a card game I walked into once, when I first learned about "downstream" action.

I first got recruited over a card game at La Cabaña Sport & Spa, Luis's club in Long Beach. I was brought in there by Alonzo Peña, who first bent my ear in Phoenix. *You ever come to L.A., my friend, and I'll introduce you around. You get sick of retail chickenshit, you give me a call.*

My "chickenshit" gig was serving as a bagman for an offtrack betting parlor. It worked like a floating crap game—in a warehouse one weekend, in some office basement the next. Guys drank our watered-down tippling-house booze and bet on the dogs and the horses. We got busted periodically, but the owners always got low bail and suspended sentences. We bought just enough favor with the vice dicks to operate three months at a time. I collected receipts every night and drove them out to the boss's house north of town.

The *patrone*'s name was Rahid. He was some disinherited Arab prince, got kicked out of Kuwait for dealing drugs. Rahid was also a music promoter, and so he always had babes—make that *vocalists*—mincing around the place, wearing swimsuits or one of his dress shirts. A real harem scene. I was never invited to dinner, not even drinks. I was just a drone in the hive. Rahid always took the bag and counted it out while I stood in the entry.

Except for one night. One night, Rahid introduces me to this real dapper Mexican guy. He looks like that tennis star, Pancho Gonzales—except with dyed hair. He wears the Rolex, the cuff links, the stickpin. His name is Alonzo Peña, and Rahid wants me to drive him down and show him the parlor. During the ride, Alonzo tells me what I already guessed: He's in town seeking a little juice in the Phoenix pot market. And since Alonzo needs to move inventory, our little den is a good place to start.

So we start offering loose joints to the clientele—then lids and the occasional kilo. The drugs raised the stakes enough for the feds to get interested. The last bust of the parlor netted enough dope to shut us down for good. I missed the dragnet because I was in Vegas. Rahid was never even arrested. And since his music business didn't need a bagman, I was on the street. I didn't even own a car. So I called Alonzo Peña and caught a flight to L.A.

The following night, I got led through La Cabaña, past all these naked beer-bellied Mexican mafiosi. Alongside the pool, we found four old Mexican men with towels in their laps dealing cards across a bench. They were all eating pistachio nuts and flicking the shells on the floor.

This is the guy I told you about who was bagman for that parlor in Phoenix, Peña announced.

The fattest of the four guys squinted over his cards for a second and spat a pistachio shell. Luis Manzanaro had polished that look, that sort of shrug with the eyes that cuts you off at the kneecaps. All the *patrones* have it: the knack for making people collapse like a used condom. They back it up with some casual threat, and Luis had one ready for me.

He wasn't the leak that got them busted, was he? Luis asked. You check that out?

Alonzo got ruffled enough about this to get my glands pumping, too. He cleared his throat and diddled his cuff link. We're still working on that, he said. But this ain't your guy.

Luis was convinced enough to give me a better look. It was hotter than hell, and I was sweating through my only satin shirt. Moisture rolling down to my socks. His fat Buddha buddies were really enjoying this. Finally, Luis turned back to his cards. He tossed a card on the pile and said, How much money you handle, Danny?

Now?

No, in Arizona. What you carry for Mr. Rahid?

Eight, ten thousand a night, I replied.

Smiles all around; stomachs jiggled as they laughed to themselves. Apparently, Rahid was small potatoes.

I'm out, Luis said, and he stood up, wrapping his towel under this vast goiter of a stomach. Take a sauna, he announced. He was headed toward this grotto of a locker room when he yelled over his shoulder, Bring him along, Alonzo.

Luis took about three tries to work his locker combination. (Why the lock? I wondered. Who would steal from him?) Then he reached inside to dig out his hairbrush, shampoo, and some car keys. He handed me the keys, and I noticed an Avis rental fob.

You got a car? he asked, slamming the locker door.

No.

Now you do. Right out back, he said. If you're used to ten thousand, that's where we start. Alonzo will take you to a guy named Hector Lupino. He'll give you the money. You take it up Highway One to the South-Central Bank in Santa Barbara. You ask for Mr. Durand. He'll open a teller window. He'll skim five hundred and give you a cashier's check made out to Covina Clockworks. Got that?

Got it.

You drive back down, give the check to Hector, Luis said. He gives you fifty thousand dollars, and you turn around and do it all over again. Okay?

Fine, I said. What's my cut here?

Fifty bucks on every thousand, plus expenses, plus a bonus every now and again, he replied. You'll see, Danny. I treat you good. I even get you a paycheck, cover your ass for taxes.

Then Luis stepped closer, narrowing his eyes until these black little pupils sucked the light right out of the room. He was so close, I could smell all of his vices: cigars and Chivas Regal and health-club sweat—his and mine.

I give everybody what they deserve, Luis said. You get lost up there, we find you, *cabrone*. You get detoured, you call up quick. We know how a man can be tempted. There's no such thing as AWOL, pal. This army shoots deserters. You run on me, Danny, and you look over your shoulder the rest of your life. The rest of your *short* life, *cabrone.*

That was my apprenticeship—two runs a week to Santa Barbara and back to Hector's place in Westwood. Hector had this terrific apartment on the crest of a hill above UCLA. Look out the front and you see acres of crosses in the Veteran's Cemetery. Out the back, from the balcony, you see the all the dorms and sororities for the college. Hector kept a telescope there so he could see a little better.

Even though Hector could pick the locale, he didn't have a clue about decor. His taste was stuck in the seventies—right down to bead curtains dividing rooms and those bug-eyed sad kids on the walls. I'd always find him sprawled on this huge red velour love seat unit that looked like a prop from a porno movie. He'd motion me inside, and take the checks while keeping an eye on the tube. Hector loved those chop-slaughter kung fu movies with Spanish subtitles. I'd sit in some beanbag chair while he entered the transaction in his book. More likely, I'd slip out to the balcony for a peep through the telescope.

One day, I strolled out through Hector's love beads to find somebody'd beat me to the goods. There was this preppie-looking guy with his glasses on his forehead, stargazing at the dorms. He wore Izod everything and had a sweater tied around his neck. (Tennis anyone?) Mr. Izod finally noticed me and offered his hand. I shook the limpest, dampest excuse for a hand and thought, since when did Hector swing both ways? Don't tell me this voyeur twit is a dusky.

We made introductions. His name was Eddie, and I'll never forget his job description: *free-lance chemist.* Every coke operation carries a guy like Eddie Izod on the payroll. They run a purity test on each new shipment. They decide just how much to step on the shit to break it down for the street.

Whoever Eddie was looking at pulled her curtains, so he gave up on the scope. He asked me about my job. I wasn't about to tip my hand to this guy, so I just said, I'm Hector's friend. (In California, nobody's related but everybody's friends. You tack it onto introductions: my lawyer friend, my dealer friend, Danny Castellano, my *Italian friend.*) This Eddie fellow, this preppie chemist, didn't care enough to pursue the matter—he'd rather light up a nice fat joint and tell me about his gig.

The pot was excellent, not domestic, but maybe Hawaiian. Turkish? *Jesus H.* It was much too good for me to hold my end of a conversation after three tokes or so. Eddie more than compensated. I figured he must have done some lines, too, because he wasn't falling over his tongue. Eddie jumped around in one of those director's chairs, giving me this litany of excuses about how he couldn't find a straight job (bullshit), how legit labs like Monsanto or Dow would pay him half as much as Luis did (probably true). But Eddie Izod's big rationale for being a dusky was that cocaine chemistry was so damn *interesting.*

Yeah? I managed. How so?

This launched Eddie on a long discourse on the refining process. He explained all these stages and techniques that I don't recall. I do remember that the coca leaves are dissolved in just about every acid, acetone, and poison you can name. And ether is the crowning step. Like Carl said, ether turns it from paste into executive powder.

Used to be the whole industry turned on cash, Eddie said. Sheltering all that money, moving it through the Caribbean. Seeing that all the officials get some grease, that the right people look the other way. When the money dried up, people got busted. But that's all changing now.

Yeah?

The infrastructure in Colombia has been in place for years, Eddie said. People have been bought off or killed for so long that the product moves pretty well. It's a society divided down cartel lines. The government is busting more labs, exerting more pressure—but they're still an annoyance. Interdiction isn't the problem. Neither is money.

What is? I asked.

Ether is the problem, Izod said. The DEA got wise, and now you can't export the shit. It's tougher to maintain supply, tough to keep the labs operating. So Luis decided to score some points with the cartel, help them out of a jam.

Buy them some ether? I said. I was following as well as I could through this dreamy cannabis haze.

Make them some ether, Eddie replied. Lots of it. Enough to refine every leaf in the fuckin' Andes.

I don't get it, I said. Luis has a chemical plant?

No, *I* have a chemical plant, Eddie replied. And Luis is affiliated with *me.*

All of a sudden, I got the take on this guy. Eddie was into the gangster fantasy, the whole Mario Puzo/Miami Vice, fuck-me-I'm-Sicilian syndrome. You could read him all the way back to grammar school: shaken down for lunch money, beaten up for sport. Choose up sides for stickball and Eddie was always last. Put a thumbtack on his chair, give him an underwear wedgie, tape a sign on his back that says KICK ME. Jeer him, harass him, and by all means exclude him. He was a pet, a grind, a *geek.*

But this geek was just smart enough to find a way into the criminal class. Eddie figured out that drug trade is Cigarette boats running the Coast Guard blockade; it's glitz and groupies and duffel bags of cash. It's all of those things, but it's also *pharmacology.* It's Chemistry 101. It's enough refining steps to make it *mysterious.* Anyone who can break down the compounds, who can heat up a beaker and pronounce purity, becomes a commodity himself. But the problem with guys like Eddie is that they're seduced by the idea of it. He was basically a cartel groupie. He bought the myth, and it hung on him like a bad suit. *Luis is affiliated with* me. Yeah, *right.* Luis is affiliated with the Colombians. The rest of us are just chained to an oar.

But Eddie was determined to convince me that he was a player. He ranted on about how he had an in with a shift foreman at a solvents plant in Louisiana. They made paint thinner, varnish, all that caustic shit. Eddie's persuasion (and Luis's money) got them to retool at midnight and make thousands of gallons of ether. We're still working out shipping logistics, Eddie said. I'm just on my way through from Carson City. I was up there on a little business. But when I get back, I expect to send our first big shipment out to Guatemala.

And that's all I got from Eddie Izod before Hector popped outside.

I see you got Eddie talkin' again, Hector said to me.

He does like to talk, I said.

Hector cut his eyes at Eddie, who was scrunched down into that canvas chair, his head bobbing around his chest. He ground out the roach on the sole of his loafer and flicked it off the deck. *Just business*, he muttered.

You don't talk business with anybody, Hector told me. You keep your end to yourself, you understand?

Eddie nodded and polished his glasses on the sweater tied around his neck. Sure, Hector. No problem.

Hector turned back to me. I expected more of the same, but he was back on track. Just got off the phone with Alonzo, Hector said. The Santa Barbara gig is falling through—bank's getting audited. We've got to move more money. Since you're such a righteous dusky, he wants you to go smurfing big-time.

Big time? I said.

Half a million. Got you a rental car, got some fake I.D. You drive to Nevada, Arizona, maybe New Mexico. Pass it any place you like, long as it's less than ten thousand.

Smurf patrol! Eddie said.

Big-time, I muttered.

My apprenticeship was over. From that day forth, I was a salaried "salesman" for Covina Clockworks. I even had a desk and a phone in the office in front of the plant. Of course, my butt never hit the chair. I just blew through long enough to give my expense vouchers to a bean counter there named Doreen Koontz. Doreen cut all the payroll checks and gave me traveling money. The real money, the duffel bag, was separate goods, inventory for dispersal. Perhaps Doreen found it strange that I got all this commission money without calling clients. I never got phone messages, never took anyone to lunch. She just figured my clients were out on the road, that I handled everything in person. Damn right. No cellular sales pitch from me. Nothing beats that personal touch.

Chapter Nine

◆

My baby-sitter agent looks up when he hears me shift. I tell him I need to tap a kidney and maybe take a shower. He goes to the door and shouts for an agent named Pierce. Pierce ambles in and I see that it's the older guy, the one who calls me Mr. Chancre. They uncuff me from the headboard and lead me into the john. They watch from the doorway while I do the whole routine. Pierce takes special note of my hands when I pull off my gloves to shower. *Enjoy the freak show, buddy,* I'm thinking. Next, we have short-arm inspection.

My other clothes are so gamy that I just keep wearing the stuff I slept in. Pierce ushers me out the door, where Kohler is waiting again. He's chased away all the cardplayers, leaving the chip rack, the cards, and a cloud of smoke over the banquet table. Two of the agents are finishing their cigars on the balcony. Tweedle-Dee and Tweedle-Dum loiter around the kitchenette. Kohler directs me back to the sectional sofa and hands me a room-service menu. The files are stacked up on the coffee table along with the tape recorder. Kohler's copy of *Alaska* is laying open-face on the arm of a chair. Judging by the spread of the pages, he's not making much progress.

Try the crab bisque, he tells me. It's the only thing they manage to deliver hot. He sits down and starts scraping out the bowl of this curvy briar pipe. *That fits*, I'm thinking. Just another part of the costume. It strikes me that Kohler's a real nervous guy—needs something to do with his hands. Type A all the way. Getting through that thick book must be torture for him. Probably reads the ending first.

I order crab bisque, a crab cocktail, a strip steak, and some boozy torte for dessert. (Your tax dollars at work.) Kohler orders a twelve-pack, some ice, and potato chips. He wanders into various rooms, delivering the stuff while I eat my dinner. Then Pierce clears the cart away—still looking daggers at me—and we settle in for the Big Revelation, the part where I'm supposed to flip like a dolphin. The recorder is rolling; Kohler is lighting his pipe and trying not to grin.

First off, I'm not Barry Seal and I don't work for the Medellín cartel, I tell Kohler. Luis Manzanaro has gone underground. I killed his best man in Scottsdale. So your whole rap about putting a target on my back doesn't chill my blood. Second, this Federal Witness Protection isn't exactly a carrot on a stick. I give you a billion-dollar bust and you give me a tract house in Omaha and a job stamping widgets with a drill press.

Beats a cell in Leavenworth, Kohler replies. And a job picking up soap in the shower while the cons play ringtoss with your rectum.

Touché, Eddie Bauer. He's not going to bluff, but he may go for my proposal—as long as it makes him look good.

It must be clear to you guys that I'm off the road, that I'm retired from the smurfing business, I say. And I sure as hell don't have any corporate loyalty. I hope the spic bastards all get two hundred years, and you can have the credit.

Reading upside down, I see Kohler write *spic bastards* on a tablet. I figured he would skip ahead of the story.

But before I get locked into testifying, before I vanish into Omaha, I've got a score to settle, I tell him. That's why I needed to see Carl Dupree, that's why I came to Alaska.

Would that score involve Tommy Delorme? Kohler asks. And your little mishap down in Jerome?

You said you like the cartel to do your killing for you—you should be ecstatic about this, I say. I was carrying three hundred and fifty K. Now Tommy Delorme has it all. He's going to finance something big enough to interest you guys. When I know what it is, I'll tell you all about it. *Capisce?*

Kohler blows out some pipe smoke before asking me, What is three hundred and fifty K compared to the billions you mentioned earlier? We ran the bio on Tommy Delorme. He's just a refried version of you. You're the bird in hand, Danny, he says. Puff. Puff.

You'll get the flowchart you wanted, I tell him. You'll get what I got. What I'm saying is that I don't need Federal Witness Protection, and you don't need my testimony. I've got an alias; I've even got a nest egg if you'll give back my money belt.

And what have we got? he wonders.

Covina Clockworks, I reply. An operation that moves five hundred pounds of coke a month—three tons a year, I say. Working the export trade out of Mexico with a manufacturing cover. It's not quite Fortune 500, but they're in the chamber of commerce. They employ about two hundred people and structure the thing so that only about thirty people know what they're really selling. It's so damn efficient, you'd think they were Japanese.

What's so efficient about it? Kohler asks.

That's as far as we go until I get some kind of assurance, I tell him. You get your bust, I get Delorme. That's five hundred pounds of blow, Kohler, and all I want is a free pass. You don't want me, anyway. You said yourself that I'm lower than frog shit and Delorme isn't worth the effort.

A free pass to where? Kohler asks, moving the pipe along the slot of his mouth.

That's up to Tommy Delorme, I say.

He laughs at this, then stands up, saying, I'll run this by my boss. Sit tight, Danny. Watch some television.

* * *

So I tune into another NFL preseason game and get to brooding about Charlie Cadeaux. This is the kind of night we'd be eating microwave cuisine and arguing about quarterbacks. But all I've got for company is six *really bright and honest* drug agents with necks like sumo wrestlers. You have to pity a guy whose lips move when he reads *USA Today*. I figure none of my keepers are worth cultivating. Probably under orders not to speak to Mr. Chancre. I'm thinking that the last stimulating conversation I had was on the boat with Carl Dupree. That man could turn a phrase—"do the dozens" is what they call it. And Carl's message was real similar to Charlie's. *You can walk away from the life.* I'm trying, Carl. One step at a time.

Kohler returns in about half an hour and tells me that he got a thumbs-down on my cover story. Of course they still want the Clockworks on a platter. Yes, I can walk away when the place is busted, but first I'll be arraigned in Phoenix on racketeering and tax-evasion charges. The court appearance will have no fanfare, and I'll be into Witness Protection the following day. The reason they want the indictment, Kohler says, is to keep you on a short leash. The DA is afraid of pressing the case without insider testimony.

He hasn't even *seen* the case! You'll get the whole enchilada, I tell him. I'll tell you exactly when to hit to find the shipment. I won't testify, Kohler. I'll plead the fucking Fifth.

Fine, Kohler replies. You've got a prior for possession and the laundering charge will jack you up to fifteen years. Like I said, we're happy to take the bird in hand. It's nothing you don't deserve.

So now it's me looking at the box canyon. We watch a few plays of the football game while I try to imagine any holes in Kohler's evidence. I know the media is tired of possession busts. Money and assets are the chic target, the kind of case that gets attention.

They need results before you get your vendetta, Kohler says. So tell us about the Clockworks, Danny. Start anywhere you want. Just be specific. I'm a stickler for detail.

* * *

So we're two days and a thousand dollars in room-service charges nailing down these details. If Kohler thinks the digital-clock scam is novel—or even plausible—he isn't letting on. But he wants to know Covina Clockworks inside out. So he has Los Angeles fax him some grid maps and makes me draw in the plant, the offices, the street exits. He orders up tagboard and I draw the flowchart with Luis at the top, Alonzo Peña below, and then the rest of us *cabrones*. I tell him how the coke pulls into the rail siding the third week of the month, usually a Monday. You can tell there's a dirty train in the lot, I say, because the loading docks are shut down. The portals where the clock parts go out to Chihuahua are locked and the crews sent home. It's also a good bet when both Luis's and Alonzo's cars are in the lot (his and hers BMWs with smoked windows).

I tell Kohler how a second shift comes in at six and unloads the containers with assembled clocks. These are all duskies who make a thousand dollars for the night. They take the clocks apart, remove the bags, and weigh them all again. They pour the shit into smaller bags, then Eddie Izod steps on it with a powdered laxative. After he's bumped up the volume by a third, they pack it all in boxes, load it in vans, and let the dealers take over. There's about twenty people preparing the load for the street. They work on lab tables in the molding department, and it usually takes all night. I tell Kohler which part of the plant where he can find this action, where the guards are posted, and what else I can remember about the room. Break in and you've got them, I say. Five hundred pounds is too much powder to be flushing down any toilet.

Kohler wants a lot more about the dealing end than I can provide. I never followed a load onto the street. I never talked to the dealers. Hector knew all of them and all their kids—but he's no good to us now. Kohler exhausts that topic and switches to the money trail. The best I can give him is some of Luis's other assets—a piece of La Cabaña Sport & Spa, some apartment buildings in Hollywood, a mansion in the valley. I have no idea where the cash goes after Luis deposits my checks, I tell Kohler. I heard talk about Netherlands Antilles, but don't quote me.

By the evening of the second day, Kohler has come back around to the clock factory. He's already had agents set up a stakeout in West Covina. They have someone go inside posing as an OSHA inspector. He verifies my floor plan and the location of the molding department. The fax is sending back grainy pictures of people coming and going at the factory for me to identify. I can help with about a tenth of them. I explain that I never spent much time in the office, that I watched the weigh-in process just once. But Kohler keeps at it. He's got the task force director on one phone, the L.A. DEA on the other. Another agent keeps walking me through fax pictures and mug books. The goon squad amuses themselves by cleaning their guns, by jogging in two-man shifts, and by shouting out letters on "Wheel of Fortune."

On Friday morning, I roll out and find Kohler still on the phone, but his bags are packed at the door. He hangs up and tells me he's flying down to coordinate the raid. We're coming up on the third week of August. He's got word from Mexico that a train has left the Chihuahua plant. It will reach L.A. Sunday night. If Luis and Alonzo are going to supervise, he wants them to be his collar. Can't let Treasury take all the credit.

You'll be plenty comfortable here, Kohler says. I'll leave Pierce in charge, and I've told him there's no harm in letting you get out—with an escort. No more handcuffs. Eat in a restaurant for a change. See the cancan show at the Ore House. I figure it's safe enough. You won't get far without I.D. and money. And of course they'll shoot to kill if you run. You've increased your equity, Kohler says. Just don't presume to be immortal, Danny. Until we get our half-ton bust, you're still the bird in hand.

So a couple of hours after he goes, I'm enjoying my first public stroll down souvenir alley. Franklin Street runs parallel to the cruise-ship dock. The road branches at Front Street and the sidewalks are clogged with tourists just off the boat. You can spot cruise-ship passengers because they wear stiff new Gore-Tex jackets and have camcorders impacted on the sides of their heads. They wander in mom-and-pop pairs, taping everything for posterity: taping the window displays, taping the other tourists eating, taping the Indian-looking guy in the hardware store giving them the finger.

And when they're not taping, they're buying drecky stuff with ivory attached—jewelry and letter openers and desk sets. Shops in Juneau all sell these Eskimo ulu knives—a kind of cleaver for idiots. Unless you strip lots of blubber off of whale skin, you won't get much use from an ulu. But everybody who goes to Alaska gets one—sort of like the Michener book. So I walk a few blocks, bumping into these cyclops-camcorder geeks and checking out the ulus. But instead of thinking about freedom or Tommy or maybe lunch, I'm thinking about Covina Clockworks.

I'm remembering my old friend from the accounting department, Doreen Koontz. Doreen takes her orders from Luis's comptroller, and I know she's an outsider all the way. She thinks I'm a traveling salesman out calling on electronics stores. Doreen is a widow, about fifty; probably makes twenty grand a year. And I love her like a son. She's always got a smile for people, and maybe some homemade candy on her desk. She also keeps a picture of her son in the service—an embassy guard for the marines. She's proud as hell of the kid; always giving me reports on where he's stationed. I can't pass through that office without getting a laugh out of Doreen.

And while I'm walking with my goons, I can't help imagining Kohler's bust. They'll hit the molding room at night. But you can bet they'll be back for the records the following morning. Maybe they'll drive a backhoe through the door and storm in with face paint and flak jackets. Make everybody hit the deck and lace their fingers behind their heads. Lots of weapons waving around; cops shouting *Shut-the-fuck-up!* That scene would be enough to kill poor Doreen. She'd get cuffed in a long string of people and led out to some van, lumped in with all the guilty shits who actually know the scam. Maybe show up on the network news. I couldn't give a shit for anybody else in that whole operation, but I'm grieving for poor Doreen. She doesn't know what her owners do, what she's implicated in. And the arrest will kill her. The shame will fold her up like a dry leaf.

So while I'm window-shopping, I get the notion that maybe I

can warn Doreen. Maybe I'm obligated to do it because I set up the damn bust. But phone calls are exactly the kind of thing my keepers are watching for. Even a rumor could warn off the delivery. Big, grim old Agent Pierce would probably ventilate me if he caught me on a phone. So I'll have to forget the whole idea, or get someplace private. That opportunity doesn't present itself during lunch, or over beers at the Red Dog Saloon. (The agents talk about offshore banks; I drink and watch fishermen shoot pool.) By the time we emerge, the two cruise ships in harbor have gone and we've got Franklin Street to ourselves.

I'm window-shopping when I come across something promising. This Mukluk Emporium has a stairway attached to the side. And at the foot of the stair is a sign directing clients up to the lair of some "Spiritual Counselor" named Indigo. *Perfect,* I'm thinking. I get privacy; I get time to talk. And unless Indigo communicates only through tea leaves, she might even have a phone.

How about it, guys? I ask. Let's all go up and get our futures read. Might be a pleasant surprise.

The younger agent named Tony turns to Pierce, and he just frowns. We're due back, he tells me. What the hell do you want with this?

It's probably the only bargain on the street, I say, giving them a chummy wink. What harm is it, man? You got something against astral projection? Spot me a sawbuck. I'll pay you back.

I don't want to listen to that crap, Pierce says.

Who says you have to? I tell him. I'm up and down—twenty minutes. It's my money, right?

Yeah, and it's our asses if you slip out the back, he replies. Go upstairs and look around; see if there's an exit, he tells Tony. Tony comes clomping back down in a few minutes and says the stairway is it. So Pierce gives me twenty dollars. Then he leaves Tony down in the street and walks me up to get my spirit counseled.

Chapter Ten

◆

Pierce leads me in the door to this little vestibule. There's a coffee table with magazines *(Reader's Digest, Backpacker, Game & Fish)* and a sofa and chairs right out of a dental office. Nothing about the room makes you think of a swami reading chicken guts and rattling bones at the sky. The walls are decorated with framed photos of channels and fjords—the Inside Passage I saw from Carl Dupree's boat. I'm admiring this one great shot of killer whales lolling on the surface when the other door opens and Indigo swaggers in.

She isn't quite what I expected, either. Real short, real cheery, and not indigo at all. If I had to guess at a race, I'd say Greek or Italian. She wears jeans and a Chinook beer T-shirt. Her earrings are turquoise and spangly, and she's got braided thongs in concentric circles around her neck. It is a neck worth lingering on—all of her exposed flesh is sort of translucent white. You want to touch it to see if it's real. Big smile, long lashes, black pupils. *Real* firm handshake. *What can I do for you fellas?* she wants to know.

I need some insight into relationships, I tell her. Pierce looks up from his magazine and snorts. Indigo's black eyes shoot over at him, wiping the grin from his face.

She says, Why don't you come inside? When Pierce drops the magazine and follows, she grabs his arm and says, One reading at a time. Care for a cup of tea? Maybe a beer?

Pierce glowers a minute and then shakes his huge head. He sits down on the secondhand couch while Indigo shuts the door behind me. Now we're in this studio space with a big slanting skylight. She's got six hundred varieties of fern growing in pots around the place. And amid this jungle are a few sticks of vagabond furniture: brick-and-board bookcases, director's chairs, and a packing-crate coffee table. Indigo strolls over to the kitchen, where I can hear a kettle whistling.

I CALL THIS THE FOG ROOM, she shouts. WE DON'T HAVE ENOUGH SUN TO CALL IT A SUN ROOM. I DIDN'T GET YOUR NAME . . .

Darrel Fuller, I lie. I'm just up from Phoenix for the fishing. Really a great apartment, I tell her. Not what I was expecting.

She's still shouting and rattling around with the tea: YOU WERE EXPECTING INCENSE AND BEAD CURTAINS. EVERYBODY SEEMS TO EQUATE SPIRITUALISM WITH TACKY DECOR. She hands me a mug of tea that I didn't ask for and says, I've got a black-light poster someplace if it would make you more comfortable, *Darrel.* Have a seat.

We park it in canvas chairs and face each other across the packing crate. I don't want to stare at her stark white fingers or those dark eyes. I catch her gaze when she passes me sugar, and she mostly looks amused. I fuss with my tea bag and look around for a phone.

So tell me something about yourself, Darrel, she says.

First off, I need to know what your rates are, I say.

She shrugs, looks real hard over the rim of her cup, and says, I charge ten dollars for aura readings. Chakra, meridians, the ethereal body . . . that's really my specialty.

I need to place a long-distance phone call, I tell her. To Los Angeles. I'll pay double your fee, but it has to be out of range of my friend out there.

Indigo's dark brows squeeze together and I sense that this bizarre request hasn't surprised her. She reaches behind her chair, lifts the phone up onto the packing crate, and says, It's your twenty dollars, *Darrel.*

I fork over the money. Then I pick up the phone and dial the switchboard of Covina Clockworks. I ask for Doreen and, when she picks up, I tell her it's Danny Castellano. She's all excited to hear from me. *We heard you had a bad accident,* she says. *We was worried about you, Danny.*

I tell her I wish I had time to chat but it's real important that she listen to me. Do you have any vacation coming? I ask. *A week,* Doreen replies. She's saving it for her son's Christmas leave, but I tell her to take two days. It's very important that you not show up for work Monday or Tuesday, I say. *Very* important.

Doreen's a little confounded by this, starts sputtering about practical jokes. I'm going to tell you something that you can't tell anyone, I interrupt. Not Alice, not Candy, and especially not your boss. If it leaks out, there will be lots of problems. I'm telling you this because I don't want you hurt. There is going to be a raid, a lot of arrests at the factory, I say. It will be very public and very ugly. It's better if they never know you worked there. Before you log off your computer tonight, pull up your personnel records and delete yourself. Pull anything that has your name and address. Take it all with you.

Are you *nuts*? she cries. I'll never get paid. I'll lose all my vacation, my sick leave—

I'm telling you this as a friend, Doreen. You've got to take my word for it, I say. If nothing happens, you can return the stuff on Wednesday. You can put yourself back on the system. It's no joke, honey. You're the only person I'm warning, and you're the only person who can know. *Capisce?*

What happens after Wednesday? she says. Will they reopen the plant?

Don't try to call the plant, I tell her. Just stay home, Doreen. Watch the news. Gotta go.

Danny, are you all right? Doreen says. Her voice is getting thick and I can tell she's scared. Did you really have an accident?

Take the vacation, Doreen, I tell her. Maybe I'll call you sometime.

I put down the receiver and Indigo sets the phone out of my reach like it's some kind of weapon. That was kind of you, she says. Anything you'd like to warn *me* about, *Danny*?

I should know better than to give a clairvoyant a phony name, I say. It's just that Doreen wouldn't know who Darrel is.

No, I'll bet she doesn't know who Danny is, either, Indigo says. But that's okay; my name isn't really Indigo. This business requires a little contrivance. Clients aren't going to be enticed by a medium named Kathy Karpolous. But enough about me. Tell me, how did you injure your hands?

That one comes in like a slap on the face. She knows it, too—the amused look is back.

Enough about me, too, I say, standing up. I appreciate the call, keep the—

Sit down. You don't have to tell me, Indigo says. You paid for the reading, you may as well get it. Besides, your friends will get suspicious if we don't take some time.

So now the little doe-eyed Greek is talking like an accomplice. Like it's real important I trust her. She's got her money in hand (well, in the hip pocket of very snug jeans) and plenty of cause to be suspicious. But she's not asking who's raiding which plant and why I know about it. She wants to know what's under the gloves. My friends will get suspicious. *Jesus H. Christ!* I slump back in the chair, and she says, Let me tell you how I know about your hands.

Have you ever heard about chakra, or the human aura? she asks. An aura is simply an energy field that surrounds the human body. This field is divided into seven centers, called chakra. The aura is like a halo, except that it tends to undulate and reflect various colors. I read auras, give impressions about what I see. I also get psychic impressions—entities, images related to your past. The quality of the reading—my ability to see—depends a great deal on the subject. If you're not receptive, if you're hiding elements of your life, it inhibits the process. It's like bad television reception.

And what are you getting from me? I ask. Static? A test pattern?

You're blocking more than any subject I can remember, she replies, blowing into her teacup.

How about if I climb up to the roof and turn the antenna? I say, and I'm instantly sorry. This is one serious Hellenic swami. And I'm doubly sorry, because she realizes that calling Doreen was a kind thing. Nobody ever accuses me of being kind. *I'm sorry,* I tell her. The truth is, I've just spent three days in a hotel room getting cross-examined. I'm a little defensive about personal questions.

I'm sorry, too, Indigo says. Because that's all I do. She puts down her cup and uncrosses her legs like she's ready to send me away. Back to cuddly Agent Pierce and Hotel Hell. Having my aura read is sounding more attractive by the minute.

You're right, we might as well try it, I say. Do I lie down? Do we dim the lights? I mean, how does this work?

That gets a big smile, a short cackle of laughter. I get the idea I'm making her day. No, no need to budge, she says. But like I said, if you're going to block off parts of yourself, we won't get much of a reading.

So how do I unblock?

You can start by telling me what you do for a living—that is, what *Danny* does, she replies.

What the hell, I figure. In for a penny, in for a pound. I tell her that I used to launder money. I used to exchange cash—*large* amounts of cash—for cashier's checks. That was last month. This month, I'm an informant for the DEA. Next month, I'll probably be stamping out widgets in Omaha.

She gives me another grin and says, I wish you could see the difference. It's like a curtain has lifted. Sit tight; I'll get my crayons.

Crayons! I'm thinking. What the hell. We're going to draw some pictures and maybe I'll even get a tattoo. Sure enough, she prances back with a Tupperware bowl full of every crayon color in the world. She's also got this mimeo sheet with an outline of a man's form. It's like a diagram from anatomy class, except that across the top is this letterhead that says READINGS BY INDIGO. She moves the teacups out of the way, bites her fat lower lip, and selects this bright red color. She says, Very nice, very vivid, Danny. I'm getting some impressions of entities, but let's get through recent history first.

I lean in as she outlines the figure's hands until they look like two red baseball gloves. The aura indicates red as an injury, blue as a healing color, Indigo says. She drops the red and colors over the hands with blue. You've injured your hands and now they're healing. It's the hottest spot in your aura—the first thing I noticed about you. Well, actually the second.

What was the first? I wonder.

She smiles and glances away like *I'm* getting too personal. Then she replies, You're ashamed of something and you're blocking it off, clouding your aura. Sometimes I'd construe that as an evil person, but I don't see evil in you.

Thanks, I say. But then, you heard the phone call.

Yes I did, she agrees, sounding annoyed. (Like Kohler, I'm jumping to conclusions.) Indigo is busy drawing angel's wings on the figure's back in the silver crayon. You've been protected or defended by a series of people in your life, she says. Lots of guardian angels around you. Her hand flies back into the bowl for a pinkish color. Your heart's been broken by a recent loss, she says, and makes this swirling blob where the figure's heart would be. Someone you had affection for but who also protected you. You're afraid you have no more protection now. That your angels have left.

What do you mean? I've got Pierce out there in the lounge, I tell her, but she doesn't look up.

Pierce is not related to you, and there is none of this affection, she says. His aura is clouded like yours was. And he's not a kind person.

I'm real pleased that I'm not lumped in with Pierce. Two months ago, I would've laughed Indigo and her crayons out of the room. But suddenly I want to suspend the moment, to keep her talking. It's strange, because she isn't even my type. I can't imagine her in a miniskirt—in any kind of skirt. And the more

I think about what's under the T-shirt, the more worried I am that she'll catch a whiff of those vibes and slap my face.

I glance back at the outline and see a pyramid forming in gold crayon above my head. You're a very concentrated person, Danny, she says, drawing away. The pyramid symbolizes concentrated energy. You have a very specific goal, am I right?

Yes, you could say that.

Her gold crayon leaps down to the feet of the man and she draws a rectangle under him, like he's standing on a doormat. Career confidence, she says. You are firmly rooted. You must be very skilled at this laundering job. You consider yourself one of the best. How am I doing so far?

Fine, I tell her. I *was* one of the best.

Indigo's looking amused again. She fishes out a green crayon, leans back in her chair, and says, Good. I want to gain some credibility before I go out on a limb. Danny, did you serve in the military?

I shake my head, and she leans back over the paper. Indigo begins drawing this figure of a guy in uniform, wearing a hat like some cadet at the Citadel. A brother maybe? Someone close to you serving in the army?

Not hardly, I say. I'm an only bastard child from a long line of conscientious objectors.

She shakes her head and starts filling in medals on this soldier's chest. Well you've got an entity here—a very persistent one. It may not be a literal soldier. It could symbolize something—some aspect of your character.

I'm thinking, There is that problem I've always had with authority—but I know better. I don't want to keep alienating this lady. In fact, I want her to keep talking, keep telling me that not all of my angels are gone. It's been awhile since anyone held out any hope to me. So what if it comes out of crayons and psychic visions? It's no worse than getting courage from Jack Daniel's and sensimilla.

I don't have a clue, I tell Indigo. Does it have to be part of my past? Maybe I'm *going to be* a soldier.

Absolutely, she replies. I mean, the part about it being a future image. I don't quite buy you in the military. You're much too selfish and rebellious for that.

And I suppose you're another Mother Teresa, I'm thinking, but I swallow that one, too. It's obvious that she's not going to keep stroking me just because I paid her double. But I want to make at least one play for her before things get downright insulting.

So if I were to ask you to have lunch with me, you'd think that was based on ulterior motives? I ask her.

Indigo shakes her head and starts collecting the teacups. No, not at all. But it wouldn't be very relaxing: You, me, and your little entourage. I'd feel like one of Elvis's babes. She nods at the drawing on the packing crate and adds, You may want to take that with you, Danny. Perhaps you can get some more insight if you look at it later.

She turns her back and makes a butt-twitching beeline for the kitchen. I fold up her little drawing, tuck it in my jacket pocket, and head for the door. But before I open the door, I think, One good play deserves another.

What if I manage to ditch the goon squad? I ask her. We could maybe have dinner. . . .

And she's way off in the alcove, shouting at me again: YOU'VE GOT SOME FASCINATING ENTITIES THERE, DANNY. BUT I STILL THINK YOU COULD BE REAL TROUBLE. Indigo takes a few steps my way, folds her arms, and adds, That's not a psychic impression. That's just a reaction. Take care of your hands. Try to visualize blue at night before you sleep. Blue is a good healing color.

I step into the alcove, to find Pierce working on his nails with a Swiss army knife. We're trooping back down the stairs when he asks me, So what's the prognosis, kid? You going to inherit a fortune?

I don't respond. I don't say anything on the walk back, but I look over my shoulder every few minutes in case she's right about that soldier. She was sure as hell right about everything else.

Chapter Eleven

On Monday morning, I finally talk the troops into letting me take a morning run. This room service lifestyle will put the flab back on if I don't get active. So Tony and the two other agents take me out about nine o'clock. Pierce stays behind, claiming he has to watch the phone and the fax machine. My guess is that he's going to need a wake-up beer and a double order of salmon Benedict. We leave him sitting on the sofa in his robe, the sports page in his lap, the TV remote in his hand. He's flicking between a slasher movie on cable and some infomercial about blenders. Who was it that said a superior intelligence can hold several ideas at once? I guess that makes Pierce a genius.

The boys lead me along the pier and we get a terrific view of another cruise ship pulling in. We work our way back up Franklin Street—partly at my suggestion. I'm wheezing pretty good by now, and it so happens that I decide to walk it off in front of the Mukluk Emporium. I look up the stair on the side of the building and I can see the shades are drawn in the door. The swami is out. Too early to deal with the ethereal body. And certainly too early for me. I'm remembering her parting shot about me being *real trouble*. Indigo's not the first girl to tell me that. Maybe they're all clairvoyant. And I'm acting like some love-struck punk cruising her house, waiting until the parents are gone. So what if she thinks you're kind underneath, if she says you give good entity? No still means no. I just want to thank her for the prescription. I think about blue all the time.

You'd be surprised at all of the places where blue pops up—in signs, in the hotel lobby, between the red stripes on Pierce's bathrobe. We come back from the run to find him waiting for us by the elevator. He's frowning even more than usual. He grabs me by the arm and drags me back in my bedroom. Pierce cuffs me back to the bed frame without so much as a hi-dee-ho. He rumbles off toward the door, and I get in a parting shot.

No kiss?

He stops in the doorway, and I'm instantly regretting the comment. I realize Pierce has more than a short fuse—he's got that blood lust that Hector Lupino had. But he manages to blow off whatever impulse I've inspired. He just snorts that bear-rutting snort of his and slams my door. Later on, I hear him muttering with the rest of Kohler's finest out on the balcony.

So I'm left there in my track shoes and sweats, trying to interpret this display of affection. The only thing I can figure is, they're getting ready to move me. They're planning to fly me to Phoenix for arraignment. For some reason, this makes Pierce go ballistic—maybe he wanted to be in L.A. for the bust. Maybe he hates Phoenix in the summer. I'm not going to lose any sleep over him. Sleep seems like a good idea, so I roll my head back and catch a few winks.

I wake up with some sheet of paper over my face, rattling every time I exhale. I pull it away with my free hand and see Pierce sitting in a chair by the window. He's dressed in his fisherman's costume again—the wool shirt, the down vest. I see a duffel packed next to the bed, and it isn't mine. Pierce stubs out a filterless cigarette and says, Tried to play both ends toward the middle, didn't you, Chancre Boy?

What's this? I ask him, holding the paper so it catches the light from the window.

Those are the phone records of a Kathy Karpolous—aka Indigo, Pierce replies. Your spiritual counselor. I've highlighted the call made yesterday from her place to Covina Clockworks, in L.A.

Pierce stands, shuffles toward the bed with this real weary, annoyed kind of expression. *Not this again.* All of the sudden, the air has gotten real tight in the room; Pierce's anger has filled in the corners, seeped under the bed, until I can hardly breathe. I can't breathe, and I can't think of anything to say that will change the subject.

And then Pierce reaches under his vest and lays the muzzle of his gun right between my eyes. He's right over me, with one knee on the bed, and the weight causes me to roll into him. He's breathing rancid tobacco fumes on me, mixed with the gun-oil, gunpowder smell of his revolver. He cocks the hammer and I watch the full cylinder click around and stop; Magnum hollow-points, most likely.

Where's that smart repartee, Mr. Chancre? he asks. You're not flying so high now, are you? You lost all your leverage when you ratted out your bosses. You lost your cozy patron cop when Kohler flew out of here. You don't even have the other agents watching your ass. They're packed up; they're all downstairs. Waitin' for the airport limo.

I'm supposed to go to Phoenix, I manage. They're charging me down there.

Kohler called while you were jogging, Pierce says. He's canceling that deal. You didn't hold up your end, he's not honoring his—

The fuck I didn't, I say, trying to rise now, trying to catch his eyes. But he presses me back down, hand on my throat, gun on my forehead. I tell him that the tip was solid. They checked out the factory. The train was coming from Mexico.

So it arrived, Pierce says. They got their coke bust. Kohler's probably having a press conference right now.

So I held up my end, right? What more did Kohler expect?

Bosses, Pierce whispers, pressing harder with the gun. You promised *patrones* and we found grunts—twenty guys with misdemeanor rap sheets and bogus green cards. You tipped off Luis Manzanaro and Alonzo Peña, and they didn't show. You promised the top of the flowchart. All we got was more powder.

Five hundred pounds of powder, I tell him. That doesn't count for anything?

I should waste your sorry guinea ass, Pierce says. He's puffing from the thrill, the prospect of it. I could, you know, he adds. See, there's no paperwork on this arrest. You were never even here. It would gratify me no end.

Why is that? I ask. (I'm feeling pretty futile now, pretty much history. I ask because I have nothing to lose.) If I'm Mr. Chancre to you, why risk your reputation? Because I copped a stupid phone call?

Because Charlie Cadeaux is in his fucking grave, Pierce replies. And you're not.

So there's my bolt of revelation, my moment of insight before getting whacked.

You knew Charlie?

That question has enough impact to lift the gun away from my face. Pierce slides off the bed and turns to face the window. Way back, he says. All the way back to Las Vegas. I used to help him spend a little of that grease you delivered at Caesar's. Charlie was a generous man. He was also very careful. The one time he fucked up is the time he sprang you from that hospital. His emotions got in the way.

Speaking of emotions, I'm thinking, but I keep it zipped. Pierce hasn't holstered his gun. He's still gripping it by his thigh, tapping himself with the muzzle. *Giddyap.* He turns, and I can see by his face that he'd still love to use it.

That was a different agency; those were different times, he says. Now it's exactly the way Kohler said: Nobody's got a hand in the till; none of us is dirty anymore. We focus on the victims. Charlie was a victim. That's why I could kill you without batting an eye, Chancre Boy. Because it's an eye for an eye out there, and you owe us a life.

Don't forget, I killed Hector Lupino, I tell him. First guy I ever killed in my life. But it won't be the last. You cut me loose now and I'll even it up. Charlie was my friend, and I miss him, too.

Pierce doesn't answer right away. He moves closer, until he's over me again, and then says, *Open your mouth.*

You can't get away with this, I say.

Open. Your. Mouth. Or I'll break your jaw, he tells me.

So this is it, I'm thinking. He wants it to look like a suicide. I open up, thinking I should say some Hail Marys; maybe start seeing that tunnel of light I've heard so much about. But instead of putting the gun inside, Pierce pops in something metal, something that clanks against my molars. He tugs my jaw back up and gives me a little make-sure slap on the cheek.

I won't spend the bullet, because you're as good as dead, Pierce tells me. Those guys at the clock plant are going to figure out who flipped on the operation. They've told their lawyers, and the lawyers sure as hell called Luis. They even know you're being held in Juneau. So you've got that target on your back now, Danny. Just like Barry Seal.

Pierce has a good chuckle over this as he lifts his duffel bag. But if you get tired of running, of ducking bullets and using up all nine of your lives—well . . .

Well what?

You could still walk through that valley and come out the other side, Pierce replies. Serve up Luis and Alonzo, and Kohler will reinstate the deal. Give us those *patrones* and you can have Federal Witness Protection. Remember, Danny, we're the only ones in the world who can take that target off your back.

And with that, Pierce lugs his bag out of the room and slams the door. I locate the metal chunk with my tongue and spit it out in my hand. It's not a bullet; it's the key to the handcuffs. It even fits. Hail Mary, Mother of God.

I suppose that when your life is spared, you should feel some kind of relief. You should feel that all your time is on loan, that you've got to atone or find Jesus or something. But I don't feel religious or grateful or even glad when Pierce waltzes out of that hotel suite. I feel like I've failed at everything—even failed as a snitch. The ordeal has given me nausea from too much adrenaline. This adrenaline is different from the buzz I got that night after killing Hector. This feels more like depression, like I'm spinning out of control. The truth is, I haven't had any sense of control since Tommy Delorme did his dance on my head. I have only this idea that if I live long enough I can kill the son of a bitch; kill him and steal back enough money to buy some distance, some way out of this purgatory life. Tommy's the pyramid that Indigo drew on my head. But she was wrong about the doormat below my feet. I no longer have a career, or a reason to feel "rooted." In fact, I have this nagging suspicion that my luck can't hold, that my number is up.

I feel that, and I feel incredibly alone. I feel this awful isolated sense that I haven't felt in years. I thought I had licked it back in New Jersey, long before Alonzo took me in, long before I turned my back on all those working stiffs that Carl Dupree described.

This isolation thing first dawned on me when I was about nineteen or so. That was when I got this premonition, this insight on how different my life was, how separate and frustrating it could be. I'll never forget the sensation, and I remember exactly what triggered it.

I was nineteen or twenty years old, ripping off houses for a living in New Jersey. I hit all the "fields"—Bloomfield, Westfield, Plainfield—and the resort towns along the coast. I wanted to be good—to be a second-story cat-burglar type who cracked wall safes or fenced original art. But there really wasn't any finesse to it: I'd get a couple of buddies and we'd drive the nice neighborhoods, smoking and pounding Johnnie Walker. We'd watch a house until people left, then go up and kick in the door. Toss all the drawers, rip out the stereo components, and lug it all to the car. If we found jewelry or guns or cash, we felt like we'd hit Fort Knox. Of course, the fence would maybe give us a dime on the dollar, but we didn't care. Easy come, easy go. We were working like hopheads, like smack addicts in withdrawal.

My moment of insight came when we get the notion to work the

Poconos. We decided to cross over into Pennsylvania and hit a bunch of vacation cabins. Some of them were real palaces—the A-frames, the cedar decks, the decor right out of Abercrombie & Fitch. Almost none of them had alarms, and we figured they were so remote that they didn't get drive-by patrols. We could work in broad daylight. Plenty of time to get in and out, plus a little fresh air and scenery.

So me and two pals drove all night and got up to the mountains on Labor Day morning. We cruised the forest roads until we spotted some monstrosity on a hill. It was a barn-shaped unit with big cathedral windows. It was really woodsy in there and we had no problem stashing the car and walking in. But when we got closer, we saw cars in the drive—not just any cars, but BMWs and Corvettes. My pals wanted to blow it off, but then I spotted some luggage near the door. These college-age kids started popping in and out, loading their stuff in the cars. It was obvious they were going to vacate, so we slipped around back to wait them out.

After watching them party on the rear deck for awhile, it became clear what was going on. This was a little weekend tryst for a bunch of rich preppies, three couples having a last blowout before they went back to college. Someone's daddy offered the cabin, along with the key to the liquor cabinet and—probably—the Corvette in the drive. They were all a little too fresh and giddy and WASPy for me to relate to. But I watched this bon voyage party for awhile and something else sunk in.

These kids were about my age. They were nineteen or so and their clothes were worth as much as the car I was driving. And it was not just the privilege, the class. They were all laughing because they were excited—excited about school, about life, about the great sex they'd had last night. And they were happy because they were good friends. I was lying on my stomach in the forest watching them through these bars, through this imaginary wall of friendship. They were not just happy because their future was all mapped out; they were happy because they were finishing off a whole summer of good times.

So I looked at them, and then I looked at myself and my prospects at age nineteen. Of course, I didn't have any friend with a cabin. And I didn't have a girlfriend to take to one. I wasn't in college, because I never finished high school—because I *chose to underachieve,* in the words of my probation officer. Instead of a college guidance counselor, I had a probation officer and a court date for grand larceny in three weeks. Instead of a job, I had a fence. And instead of friends, I had these two cronies that I hardly knew and didn't really trust. They were just two clowns named Hoagie and Mort that I met in a chop shop in Trenton. We were all fencing car stereos. A match made in Heck.

I know, you're not sympathizing at all; you're thinking I had what I deserved. But what I'm thinking is that *everyone,* even criminals, is supposed to have friends. You hear about the community of thieves, the brethren, the mob. It's supposed to be all fraternal and jolly and exciting. But what it really is is what I was—desperate, lonesome, isolated. It means wanting to have—more than any score, any status—exactly what I was looking at on that deck in the Poconos. A community. A life that isn't hand-to-mouth. A friend that won't stab you in the back.

I wanted it then, and I still want it now. So Carl Dupree called it wrong. Sure, the lifestyle seduces you. You do feel like you belong to something elite and beyond the law. But I'd trade every minute, every choice I ever made, to be one of those Pocono preppies, to live scenes out of some beer commercial, to sit on a deck with some sorority queen on my lap and my buddies crowded around.

Chapter Twelve

◆

Whatever Pierce leaves me with isn't exactly a new lease on life. I've got my Darrel Fuller I.D. and my money belt. I have the slimmest of leads on Tommy Delorme—and an even slimmer chance of finding him before Luis's men find me. I've also got the maid barging in the door, saying how she thought we had checked out. *We have,* I tell her. Just let me get my act together. While I'm showering, I'm thinking about my chances of evading a Mexican posse in an Alaskan tourist town. They could already be here, already be staking out the airport and the hotel lobby. *This army shoots deserters,* Luis promised me that day at the club. *You look over your shoulder the rest of your life.* The rest of my life starting now.

I'm packing my duffel when I realize that leaves me with two real specific options. I can run: I can climb back on that random, tilted circus ride and give it another spin. Running is just another way of spinning out of control. I'll have a life like one of those splatter paintings they do at the county fairs—hit the wall and hope something sticks. And even if I do it right, if I break clean and make some new life as Darrel Fuller, Luis still wins. He wins because the stress will kill me. He wins because I may have to settle for widgets in Omaha, and that would kill me, too.

The other option I'm left with involves a little running and a lot of thought. It means going back on the offensive against Luis and Alonzo. They're both reeling now from the bust in West Covina. I've forced them underground and they're running—at least for awhile. It could take them months to set up another import cover. The Colombians won't like the delay, won't want to warehouse the product. Times are tougher in Medellín, and that affects the whole cartel. And the cartel accepts the occasional bust as the cost of doing business. But big hits—like the clock plant—are interpreted as bad management. So Luis might be a little bit desperate, a little bit vulnerable. He's running, too, I tell myself; he's running, too.

As for Tommy Delorme, I can only guess where to begin. I realize that more than money, more than a good alias, I need some information. I need the kind of access and mobility that Charlie Cadeaux provided. But with him dead, and Kohler's troops now squeaky-clean, I'll have to improvise. I have to connect with someone in Alonzo's universe, from back in the smurf patrol. I need to get inside Luis's organization, and inside Tommy Delorme's head. I know that when I catch up with him, Tommy won't be standing on some roadside in his cowboy duds, holding my suitcase of cash. Getting Tommy and the money won't happen in one clean hit—it will be more like building a ship in a bottle. It will be intricate shit. But at least I know what I'm dealing with now, what the stakes are if I get careless. Agent Pierce was my wake-up call. Get smarter, get tougher, or get dead.

But all these battles—all this cloak-and-dagger shit—are just a means to an end. My plan isn't to hit and run and go back to smurfing or burglary. I'm not going to look over my shoulder, and I'm not going to live hand-to-mouth. Alone. The loneliness part scares me more than being hunted by Luis Manzanaro. I've come so far and seen so much, but I'm still back in the Poconos, still watching the party from the woods. Last week, I didn't care if I went back to jail, even if I died. Today, I want to live; I want to experience something better, something deeper, something more than just new towns, new restaurants, new billboards ticking by. I have seen the eagles and the killer whales. I have seen a crayon rendering of my ethereal body. What I want to see is if I can replace all those guardian angels that deserted me out in the desert.

I try to watch my own back as I stroll downtown to ring Indigo's bell. No answer. I figure instead of waiting, I'll do some clothes shopping. My next stop on the Vendetta Tour is going to be Eddie Izod's ether depot, somewhere in Louisiana. So I buy two hundred dollars' worth of jeans and cotton shirts—plus a visor to cover my face. I call the airport and reserve two seats to New Orleans—one for me, one for Indigo. In between, I leave a message on Indigo's phone. I empty out my duffel, and all of the blizzard wear I bought in Seattle goes into a dumpster in the alley. I'm working my way down Franklin Street, ducking into bars and shops to use the phone. Indigo still isn't picking up, so I get a fistful of quarters at the Red Dog and call L.A. information. I figure the news of the bust has hit the media. I'm in the mood for a pat on the back, so I call Doreen Koontz at home.

Of course, it's hysteria when I tell her who I am. Old Doreen sounds like she's won the lottery. She's gushing at me and wheezing between sentences; rambling on about how amazed she is that she worked for criminals. Scum. *You saved me; you saved my home,* she keeps repeating. She describes it just like I thought: The feds busting into the plant office, cuffing all the other clerks and typists and marching them outside for the cameras. Doreen tells me she wanted to post bond for a few friends but decided against it.

Good plan, I tell her. You keep clear. You never worked there; you never heard of the place.

I'm going to try to forget all of it, Doreen says. I had one of their clocks in my room—threw it out. To think that it used to have drugs stuffed inside! I'm going to forget everything except you. You're my *salvation,* she adds. If there's ever anything—

Now that you mention it, there is one thing, I tell her.

Name it, Danny. *Name it.*

I want you to think back to those expense-report vouchers, I tell her, the ones you processed for the "sales guys" like me.

Uh-huh?

Did you pay vouchers to a guy in Louisiana, maybe called himself Eddie—Ed?

All the time, Doreen replies. Eddie Moore. Expensive tastes—all the best restaurants. Wasn't frugal like you.

Right, right, I say. *Wasn't careful like me, either.* Eddie Moore lived in Louisiana. So tell me, do you remember what town you sent the checks to?

Eddie, Eddie . . . Doreen mutters. Geez, you stumped me there. I got all that stuff on a Rolodex. . . .

Which you left back at the office?

Pretty stupid, huh? I suppose he's all wrapped up in this, too, Doreen says. Are you planning to go down there?

Why not? I say. Eat some gumbo, little jambalaya, take the chill out of my bones.

Whatever works, Doreen says. You get to L.A., you give old Doreen a call. I can cook a green chile stew that will raise the dead.

Who could resist? I reply. I tell Doreen to watch her back and then hang up while she's still gushing about how great I am.

When I look back down Franklin Street, I see Indigo climbing her staircase beside the Mukluk Emporium. Tough to miss that wiggle, that bouncing black hair. Let her get inside, I'm thinking, listen to her phone messages. Give me time to look both ways before entering the field of fire.

I'm across Souvenir Alley in ten strides—out of whatever rifle sights are tracking my back. I pass through the waiting room and knock on her door. Indigo strolls across the greenhouse of hers and swings the door open without even looking up. She's wearing a white smock like a dental assistant's. It changes her look 100 percent—that and the orthopedic shoes. Apparently, she must work another job, some kind of straight life outside of hocus-pocus. She lets the effect register before turning and walking back into the room.

That's a new look for you, I say.

Likewise, she says. You look like a lumberjack in a gay bar. Indigo pivots on one squeaky heel and says, No, let me guess: You managed to ditch your entourage and now you're a fugitive from justice. I can tell by your voice on the tape.

I was going to suggest we have that dinner I promised. I should know better than to bluff a psychic, I say. I just need to talk. I need to tell you some things.

Indigo's chin dips down a few notches on that slender neck. She uncrosses her arms and marches over to grab the open door.

Please go, Danny, she says. I meant what I said about seeing trouble. You're hiding something right now. You're very dark. Are you carrying something you don't want me to see?

A torch? I tell her. The key to my heart. And my entity. Let's not forget him.

Indigo leans on the door for a minute, deciding whether to laugh or call the police.

I don't see your entity now, she finally says, drawing me in and closing the door. *Must've gone AWOL.* She picks up a water pitcher and hands it to me, saying, Maybe you can get started on the plants. I'm going to change clothes. Please don't call anyone.

So I get about ten of her ferns watered before she comes back in carrying two beers from the kitchen. She sets them on the packing crate and opens one—a sort of invitation to join her. Indigo wears a sweat suit now, with wool socks that taper into a moccasin unit. (Something from the Mukluk Emporium?) She quietly sips her beer while rocking in her director's chair and staring at the wall beside my head.

You work another job? I say. You were out all day.

I do home health care. Geriatric, she replies. I visit patients three days a week. I give baths, make beds, change dressings.

That must be—

I think we should get to the point here, Indigo interrupts. If you're running from someone, this isn't exactly a refuge. Your friends—the drug agents—must know you visited me.

They know, but they're long gone, I say. They flew out this morning. The people I'm concerned about have no reason to look here. But this isn't about a refuge. I'm sorry if I sounded desperate—it's just that . . .

Indigo puts her beer down to watch me fight back the emotion. Part of it is physical attraction—and the incredible relief of finding someone who really *listens.* My voice gets so thick that I have to start over a couple of times. When I get on track, I can see her eyes soften a little, like her aura has *unclouded.*

I nearly died a few weeks ago down in Arizona, I tell her. You could say it was something I deserved—the kind of risk that comes with the life. I'd been real cocky and lucky for a long time. Then my luck ran out. But starting in the hospital, and a few times since then, I've had this experience that I can't get my mind around.

A psychic experience? Indigo says. Visions?

I suppose there's visions involved, I reply. But mostly it's a *certainty;* it's a real secure feeling while I'm out floating someplace. I thought it was related to this assault, to my losing a piece of my soul . . . like it's out there and I can't get it back. I used to be able to summon it, you know? Get a jolt when I need it. Now it's gone. Am I making any sense?

Indigo takes a sip of her beer and does one of those silent, polite burps behind her hand that only women do. *You're almost certainly psychic, Danny,* she says. You've probably used the ability before; used it as a survival skill in your job. This assault you had, this brush with death, just raised your consciousness. Perhaps it made you value the power more. She puts down her beer and taps her forehead, saying, Your chakra indicates a growing awareness—an enlightenment, like an eye being opened. What do you mean by getting a jolt when you need it?

I tell her about shooting Hector through the wall, and about fearing for my life in the Beaver. Both times, I felt out of my body but totally in control. I throw in the story about watching my roommate die in the hospital. That was my first real jolt. The second time was when I knew I would never make it to the prison hospital. Hector was going to hit me before the transfer took place. Sometimes it's a real comforting vision; sometimes it scares you shitless.

That's because you're channeling that power solely into survival, Indigo says. It's like driving a Ferrari in first gear. It's hooked into instinct and nothing else.

What's it supposed to hook into? I wonder.

Everything, she whispers, leaning forward to tap my forehead. You let that eye open all the way, and your whole life can be a comfort. You can be certain about *everything*. We're not talking about a jolt you get from a crack pipe, Danny. This isn't a novelty, a gimmick. At least not for me. I couldn't take the tourists' money if I didn't feel I was helping people.

You are—I mean, you *did* help me, I say. Let me pay you again. I just want to get it back. I need to feel safe again.

Oh you'll get it back, Danny, she says. She's bundling her hair now while she talks, holding a rubber band in her lips that screws her pronunciation. *Yew geh buh, Thanny.* Then Indigo takes the band and hooks it onto her ponytail, saying, The question is whether it'll make you a better person or just torment you with random little insights—jolts every now and again. And I won't take your money, because I've already done your reading; your situation's very clear.

It is?

You either reconcile your lifestyle with your ability or die, she says. Throw out this whole concept of witchcraft and dark forces. Being psychic is just another dose of free will—a concentrated dose. You think your luck has run out: I couldn't agree more. Maybe that's too blunt, but there it is. I don't dilute my free advice.

I'm thinking how this is just more of what Charlie Cadeaux told me the night he died: It's going to be painful to watch. It will get lots worse before it gets better.

You're not married, Danny? she asks. *No.* No kids, no divorces? *No.* Any siblings, parents? *I lost track.* And now that you became an informant, I assume you'll give up this laundering business? I nod my head, and Indigo says, Which leaves you with what? What are your prospects?

Dim, I tell her. I just had a lecture from a guy out in Haida about the pleasures of a straight job. Tell you the truth, I say, sipping my beer, my only other skill is gambling. Sports book. Football pools, that sort of thing.

Is that what the pyramid is about? Indigo asks. This focus of your energies? A gambling career?

No, no . . . that's something else, I admit. That's something you would find pretty distressing. I'd rather not discuss it. What I'd like to do, Indigo, is buy you some dinner. You must be starved. I know a Chinese place that delivers; these agents called them—

You don't get it, do you? Indigo shakes her head. I can't be around this energy, this clandestine shit. You're an attractive man, Danny. You're probably intelligent. You have the potential to be kind. But you're so diffuse, and you're making the wrong choices. Indigo leans forward until I can feel her breath on my face, her heat, her aura. I can't open that eye for you, Danny, she says. I can't make you feel safe.

So I put down my beer and head for the door, still fighting the emotion. Suppose a guy wants to change his life, become a better person, I say. He can't do it overnight; it's not like getting baptized. Maybe he starts by helping the feds, getting his employer busted. And all that gets him is a lot more grief, a contract on his life.

Indigo is angry now, rising, shouting, It's *free will,* Danny! You can still choose! It's your actions that matter.

To who? I ask, still in the doorway. To you?

Sure, you could show me something, she replies, one fist cocked on her hip. Show me you really want to change. Surprise me. Surprise yourself.

I start back into the room, saying, You know, I wonder if turning your second sight into a concession is any better than what I do—using it to survive. I mean, we're both trading off something we can't take credit for. This baby gets blue eyes; this baby gets premonitions. You hang out a shingle and the tourists come—not because it will change them, make them choose a different path. They do it for the novelty, for the story to tell on the cruise back home. They pay to test you, to make you perform.

You can't tell me in your heart of hearts that your business is changing lives.

Indigo stares at me, pulls in her lower lip, and says nothing.

So your business is performing, and I'll bet it gets pretty routine, I say. You've seen every color in the rainbow, every kind of entity there is. But one day, a guy walks in with two real specific problems: He needs to rescue a friend and he needs to rescue himself. The first one is a phone call away, but the other one is complicated. He's blocking; he's got all his walls in place and you have to get through. What's more—you have to *want* to get through. Something makes you want to proceed. You could've taken your double fee and blown me off. So what was it, Indigo? Why did you make me stay? What did you find? What else did you see?

Indigo mutters something that I don't hear. I reach out, take her wrists, and make her repeat it.

I saw myself, she says.

So if I leave, I walk out that door and take part of you with me.

Don't go, she says. Not yet.

Indigo raises her eyes, and I see them move across me, beyond my silhouette. You should see your aura now, she says. The green is spiritual growth, empathy. The yellow fringe is wisdom, personal insight. It waxes and wanes a little, *but you're definitely getting warmer.*

Chapter Thirteen

We order up the Chinese food and sit at Indigo's kitchen counter. She opens the containers and dishes me a spoonful of everything; poking and sniffing and licking those incredible porcelain fingers. I get the idea that take-out Chinese is an adventure for Indigo. She's all winks and giggles, and I'm watching and remembering the last time I had dinner with a woman. It was in Las Vegas. Her name was Marie or Marcie and she ate exactly two bites of her lobster thermidor. She played keno while I finished eating, then got real miffed when I offered to buy her a set of those blinking earring lights that the cigarette girls wear. *Don't be ridiculous, Manny.* Danny. The name is Danny.

I want to avoid being ridiculous now. I want to forget every other date, every other Chinese meal I ever had. All the pretense about being a cocaine cowboy and a money man is out the window. This is a woman who is impressed—enthralled, actually—by little white cartons of stir-fry. Instead of satin and heels, I'm looking at slippers and a sweat suit. And instead of droning on about my cons and connections, I'm listening to Indigo. Between bites of moo shu and egg foo, she's revealing her path to enlightenment and commercial swamihood.

She tells me she grew up in Montana, working in a family restaurant slinging gyros and eggs. Indigo married one of her cowboy customers who talked her into his pickup and out of her virginity. (He was tall; I was desperate. Your typical Billings romance.) The only thing they had in common was a desire to leave home. So they sold their wedding presents, put a camper on the truck, and drove this brutal dirt highway up to Alaska during the pipeline boom. The plan was to get big-salary construction jobs, live out of the camper, and sock away a fortune.

And it damn near worked, Indigo says as she picks the celery out of her chow mein. We got the jobs, we got the salaries, but we also got sucked into the life. See, the contractor for the pipeline had everybody live in work camps—from Prudhoe Bay down to Valdez. They had this Spartan, puritanical mentality about promoting teamwork and prohibiting lust, she explains. That meant weeks on the job in some tundra station and separate domiciles—even for married couples.

That's pretty Spartan, I say. Not even conjugal visits?

Barely, Indigo replies. You get a little nip-and-tickle while everybody else is eating. But can you imagine a couple of newlywed hayseeds, twenty years old, trying to mix with all these welders and roughnecks? Everybody earning about twelve hundred a week and no place to spend it. You find ways, believe me, she says. *You find ways.*

Indigo describes this frontier pipeline economy that followed the work camps: liquor stores, drug dealers, and Winnebago brothels. There was this vice explosion mostly out of resentment toward management. And when workers got their off-weeks, they'd go on a bender in Anchorage or Valdez—buying house rounds, renting scores of hookers or throwing fistfuls of bills at the strippers. It was a good time to be young, drunk, and stupid, she recalls. It wasn't a good time to be married.

The work camps was the first time that I saw what a mean drunk Randy—my ex—was, Indigo says. Mean and jealous. I was an assistant to the surveyors, so I didn't exactly work with the dregs. But aside from RV hookers, I was the only "wool" in a hundred-mile radius. I got looks, I got leers, I got endless propositions, she recalls. Randy didn't see one-tenth of it, but he saw plenty.

Bust a few heads, did he?

More than a few, Indigo says. He was suspended twice for fighting before they finally canned his ass. And then they had to call the cops to haul him off, because I wouldn't quit and go with him. He was all set to drive back to Montana and he couldn't understand why I wanted to stay.

You were still socking it away? I ask. Still hanging on to the dream?

I thought if I could finish out the summer, we could buy some land and build, Indigo says. I wasn't crazy about the work camps, but I'd never seen money like that before—and I'm not just talking salary. Indigo sips her third beer and narrows her eyes with the memory, saying, People did things like bet their paycheck on the flip of a quarter. Heads, I take yours; tails, you take mine.

That's pretty macho, I say. You ever try it?

Indigo wipes her mouth and says that she made twenty grand in paycheck bets in a little over two months. I first tried it just to spite Randy, she says. Then you win a couple and you figure the worst you can do is break even. You keep winning and the word goes out that you're too hot to contend with, that you never lose. And then it becomes like initiation: Every new guy in camp has to go up against the master. Of course, I never equated it with psychic power. I just figured the quarter liked me.

Twenty grand would've given you a start on that dream house, I say.

It would have, Indigo replies, if I'd managed to save it. But I was supporting Randy down in Valdez, and he wasn't exactly frugal. He'd work a few days at the oil terminal and then empty our account in the bars. And I was using pretty heavily myself. See, alcohol could get you fired, but a few lines of coke just made you cheerful and poor. It tends to shrink the membranes around your wallet. So what if I got an occasional attack of paranoia? That pipeline job was a license to print money.

I dish myself some more MSG and think about the term *using.*

It has this sanctimonious flavor—using and chemical abuse. Most of us drink or smoke reefer or do a line. Only the walking wounded talk about *using*.

Randy's out of the picture, I say. And you're not living in that dream house, so I assume it ended badly.

She gives me the same glower I got when I first came in, then says, Bad as it gets. Like I said, Randy was crazy jealous. He'd work himself into a lather and just lay for me when I got my off-weeks. We'd be newlyweds again for a day or two and then he'd start in. Not being breadwinner was an incredible threat. He was old-fashioned in a lot of ways: He wanted me home, wanted me pregnant. We had some real marathons that wrecked the whole apartment.

Slap you around a little, did he? I ask.

Plenty, she replies. And I think the reason I took it was that I felt guilty about the coke. You know, like I must deserve this. Once Randy even tied me to the bed to keep me from reporting back to my job. That was pretty close to the end.

What was the end? I wonder. He get you fired?

Indigo stops eating, stops twirling bean sprouts around on her plate, and stares at the wall—just like she did during my aura reading. Her whole face goes flat and she says, This was before I knew what I had, what I could do with my powers. I didn't understand all the baggage we bring from past lives. We all have tapes instilled by our parents that define things for us—sometimes invalid things, like a woman obeys her husband.

Tapes? I ask.

That's just my word for your conscience, Indigo says. When I counsel, I try to define that for people. Most of us are getting some kind of message from our youth. Some of us get messages from past lives about what we fear, what we seek. My tapes were playing a whole litany of guilt about not loving Randy.

Then you had the wrong tapes, I tell her. Time to change the station.

If only it were that easy. No, I shut it all down with the drugs, Indigo says. That was my refuge. They called me the Snuff Lady because I carried a whole Skoal can full of blow. She lays a finger beside her nose and says, I burned a hole right through my septum trying to shut down my conscience.

But you're not the Snuff Lady, either, I say. You managed to break the cords?

I could never have done it myself, she replies. It took disaster and years of penance for me to get free. You know we've got lots of pilots up here—lots of *bad* ones, too. Randy had this friend with an old Cessna. They decided to fly up to Anchorage and look for jobs. And as long as they were up that way, why not have a look at the mountain?

The mountain?

McKinley, Indigo replies, chewing again. In Denali Park. Real scenic, real treacherous. The weather changes up there every half hour. On a clear day, you can see the peak from Anchorage, but a blizzard can develop in the time it takes to fly there—which is what happened to my husband. Plane crashed; big search effort. Civil Air Patrol can't fly, so they're lost for four days.

Four days of hell for you?

Not exactly, Indigo says. What I had was this incredible relief—like all the suffering was over for me, like my problems were solved. And I had lots of guilt about feeling that. But I made this pact, anyway. I prayed to whatever God was listening; asked him to please let Randy die swift and painless. But let him be truly gone. If he's dead, I'll live differently. I'll quit the cocaine, and I'll quit the pipeline job. I promised to devote my life to some kind of service and really be an example to people. You know the old saying, Be careful what you wish for? Because that's mostly what I got.

Mostly?

Randy lived, she replies. He broke his back, and he was frostbitten, but he lived. The pilot died, and Randy stripped the body and wore the guy's clothes. He had one candle to warm himself, and he held on until the climbers got there. So there I was with all my remorse and a paraplegic husband. I remember waiting while he was in surgery, thinking, Yeah, this is just. This makes sense, Kathy. No job, no social life, and no hope of having children. This is what comes of wishing someone dead.

I ask her how Randy handled it, and again she says, *Badly*. He was always self-centered and the disability only made him worse. More abusive, more belligerent—your typical rolling nightmare. Indigo finishes her beer and waves her hand as if to erase something in the air. You understand that all this is hindsight, she says. At the time, I could never call him that, because I was too caught up in guilt. Too busy trying to *atone*. Bedpans and sponge baths and tending this man was my new identity. I didn't realize that it was self-centered of me to cherish all that guilt. The redeeming part was that I managed to kick the drugs. I was dying as an individual, but my body was starting to heal.

But you're here. You didn't die, I say. How did you get free of this guy?

How did I get to home health care and spiritual counseling? She smiles. Strange mix, isn't it? Sort of like a plumber who does tax returns? And let's not forget the green thumb—I'm a grand champion fern cultivator. Ferns aplenty. Ferns R Us.

Indigo's eyes light up and she emits this throaty cackle. The three beers have had their effect, and I'm wondering if I will get the rest of the story.

Turns out I had perceived auras all my life—formed very rapid conclusions about people based on psychic energy, she says. My grandmother had this ability, too. She also married a drunk—don't ask me what the correlation is.

What conclusions have you made about me? I ask.

Like I said, you're intelligent; you have the potential to be kind, she replies. I see this tremendous fear of abandonment, and fear of being poor. I imagine you suffered from both those things as a child.

I don't rise to the challenge. Instead, I ask her why Randy didn't radiate bad vibes. Something about him should've warned you off, I say.

An aura is fluid, transitional, she replies. It's not like eye color, Danny. Sure, I recognized Randy's jealousy. I could smell danger. But you ignore that stuff because of what you're taught—those tapes I told you about.

And what about my entity? I ask. The mysterious soldier?

Have a little patience, Indigo says. But instead of elaborating, she heads for the kitchen with the dinner plates, and I follow. You wash, I'll wipe, she says, running a sinkful of water. I'm thinking that this is a deliberate test, but her back is turned and I can't see her face. I tell her I'd rather wipe the dishes. She turns around, looks at my gloves, and I see her cheeks flush. She takes my hands in hers, turning the palms up and running her thumbs over the leather.

I'm sorry, Danny, she says. You can't get them wet, can you?

Sure I can, I say. And I feel her fingers rolling back the gloves and stripping them down my fingers. Indigo keeps her eyes on mine and I feel—well, naked. Her thumbs are working my palms again, circular strokes moving out to my fingers. Finally, she looks down, and when her eyes come up they are all teary.

It didn't hurt when it happened, I whisper. I got thrown out of a car—

She brings her face up and kisses me so that my head is pressed back and I can taste the tears. She's still holding the kiss as she guides my hands down to her waist and then reaches up to cling to the back of my neck. When she breaks away, her head slides down my chest so I can't see her face. But I feel her breath through my shirt—heavy, fast, and my own breath is coming in gasps. And when I kiss her again, I feel like I'm not so aroused, not so calculating with this one. This woman is mostly making me warm, taking me someplace safe.

I can tell early on that this isn't going to be one of those gymnastic nights where you flail away at each other until you run out of lubrication. That's partly because Indigo's idea of foreplay is to work up from your feet with a hot-oil massage until you forget why you got naked in the first place. We agree that since she is so little, she can stay on top when she finishes rubbing. So that's where it begins and ends—real wet and slow and quiet together without any big theatrics.

Afterward, she looks at my hands again and I tell her about my therapy. Massage does wonders for your grip, she says, so I take the hint and start on her feet. And while I'm lathering on the oil,

Indigo wants to know why I'm so evasive about my pyramid. Why am I going to New Orleans?

Come with me, I tell her as I'm working my way up her calves. We can explore it together.

It's cruise season here, she replies, muttering into her pillow. That's when I get my walk-ins. Besides, I wouldn't go until I know what you're doing there. Are you carrying some more of that money?

I'm going after a guy who robbed me, I say. Splish-splash. Rub-rub.

To kill him? Indigo asks.

She really does get to the point, I'm thinking as I work the backs of her thighs. I tell her I used to think so. That was the original plan.

And now?

Now I just want everything over, I say. I want to get free of the life and start something else.

Mission accomplished, she says, laughing into the futon mattress. You sure as hell started something here.

She moans for awhile as I work on her shoulders, then she rolls over and flashes me another one of those black-eyed stares. Remember what I said about getting invalid things from your memory tapes? she asks. I'll bet your tapes are telling you that a man gets even. A man settles the score, eh? Eye for an eye—what do the Italians call it?

I'm holding her breasts, enjoying how the nipples lay like pupils between the eyelids of my fingers. Peekaboo. I see you.

Onore, I tell her. Honor. The Mexicans call it *cojones*.

It's all *merde* to me, she replies. That's antiquated thinking, Danny. It'll make you miserable.

I'm not miserable now, I tell her. See? *Feel.* I guide her hand down below, but she pulls back and rises onto her elbows.

She says, Don't get glib about this. I meant what I said about your luck, Danny. You can surprise me, but you can disappoint me, too.

I imagine other guys have disappointed you? I say. Guys since Randy.

Single women up here have a saying that the odds are good, but the goods are odd, she replies. You're not odd, but you're here and gone. Next week, you'll be giving a massage to one of those Louisiana babes—some voodoo priestess. (While she says this, her hand has migrated downward and she's playing a little peekaboo of her own.)

I was thinking more of a coed WASP from the University of Virginia, I say. I'll meet her out walking a beach at dawn. You get a low surf then, really gentle, carrying these little crests of foam. And when it pulls back, you feel the sand eroding at your feet. It caves under your heels and then slaps your calves on the next wave.

Oh it does. . . .

And just ahead of you, walking in the same surf, feeling the same sensations, is a girl, I say.

Of course, Indigo says, her hand turning jealous and abandoning me.

A girl with great posture . . .

Oh please! she cries.

No really! I say. Let me finish. I can remember the whole thing: She walks with her shoulders back, on her toes so her calves stay nice and tight.

Like mine?

Just like yours. And she's wearing one of those low-back one-piece suits that shows every notch in her spine. The suit is brand-new, and she's self-conscious about whether it covers her ass.

She should be!

She reaches back every few steps to tug it back when it rides up over one of her cheeks.

Indigo lies on her side, pulling her legs up from under me and frowning. It sounds like you've given this plenty of thought, she says. Girl in every port, right?

No, no, that's not my fantasy, I tell her. That's a routine from this guy who jumped me in Arizona. He's the weirdest bastard I ever met—living out this whole scenario in his head. Incredible, elaborate stuff.

Not your average criminal mind? Indigo asks.

Guess not.

And you don't have any criminal instincts at all, she says, smearing the oil on her stomach. I ask what makes her say that, and she says, *I just know.* You had to learn everything about your business, and you had to teach yourself to be cold. Your impulse is to do something good, and you're probably chasing someone who never had a good thought in his life.

I don't agree. I can't look at her, into those liquid eyes anymore. So I hunker down against her back, pretending to sleep. But I feel Indigo thinking—I can hear the little flutter of her eyelashes against the pillow. She starts telling me about the medium that got her free of Randy. She tells me how the woman hypnotized her, made her imagine breaking the cords, freeing herself and liking herself for doing it. But the act of telling him, the whole scene was so scary that she bolted with nothing but the clothes on her back and one Boston fern. Every plant in this room—every single one is grown out of cuttings from that fern, she tells me. It's actually *one plant.*

I think that's kind of symbolic, don't you? she asks. I think that says something about my decision.

I'm nodding, but I'm thinking that the only thing I've grown out of this adventure is scar tissue on my hands. I don't know if I'm any wiser. I don't know if I have second sight. I only know that this fog room, this fern sanctuary, is the only place I have found where the motion stops, where the ceiling doesn't spin.

Chapter Fourteen

◆

Indigo gets real quiet the next morning while I'm packing my bag. She takes a scissors and wanders around in her robe, snipping dead leaves off her ferns. I try to cheer her up, telling her she should join me. What the hell, we'll move there, I tell her. Get a real sun room; grow ferns and sensimilla. You can counsel tourists in the French Quarter and I can run an offtrack betting parlor. Call it Odds R Us.

Indigo isn't laughing. She won't even look at me. You're not going to keep house with me in the French Quarter, she says. If you're lucky enough to live through this, you'll just find some new scam that serves the dark side of your nature.

Oh, I have a dark side, eh? I mutter. I thought I was tending toward the greens and yellows.

Indigo turns away when I try to kiss her. She whispers, Don't trust your luck anymore. You've got to learn to think like he does, Danny. Or else you've got to be psychic like me.

You think I'm not? I ask.

While she's considering this, we hear the doorbell.

You probably are, she replies. But you can't live that way and still have me. I've got to get dressed. I've got customers.

I take her in my arms and I can feel her hand, the one with the scissors, moving up my back as we kiss. Indigo turns her fist and pricks me with the point—first gently, then hard. I step away and rub the welt under my shirt.

I realize this is my good-bye, because she's dropped the scissors and headed for her bedroom. There's nothing for me to do except lug my duffel through her lounge, past some grinning Gore-Tex people fresh off an ocean liner.

How was it? some tourist guy asks me. Is she any good?

I have to push Indigo out of my mind long enough to get through the airport. I've got my antennae up, got all the feelers working as I pass through Juneau's terminal. I figure that I'm halfway home when I get through the metal detector. If any of Alonzo's goons are beyond here, they'll have to kill me with karate.

I reserve a seat at the rear in order to board first. But when I get on, I sit at the front. This way, I can watch every face, every Moe that boards. I can look at their eyes and hope for one of my random jolts of insight—hope that somebody radiates assassin vibes. But there's not a single Mexican goon in the bunch. Just tourist families and business folk and the odd Indian or two. Nothing but homesick vibes, sales quotas, hope-they-don't-lose-my-luggage vibes. I can finally kick back and breathe when my plane rolls away from the gate. But just to be sure, I've booked myself into a layover in San Francisco. I'll get off the plane and go on standby to New Orleans. That should flush out anyone tailing me. Better safe than sorry.

I skip my meal on the flight out of California and try to rinse out my brain with music from the headset. But instead of getting a meditation buzz, I am haunted by Indigo's parting shot. *You have to learn to think like he does.* I know that means remembering what Tommy Delorme was like; recalling what he said during four days on the road. But what I'm really learning is how deep I've managed to bury that crap under lots of sweet malice. I've got this reflex of imagining his face and then shutting it down—next slide please. The kind of mind that dreams up Beach or Buffet is a world away from me. But if I really stretch, I can imagine the things he could do with the money, how he could set himself up.

The first image I'm getting is Don Juan, Prime Cock, Mr. Singles Bar. I figure anybody fresh out of the joint with a suitcase of cash is a walking testosterone bomb. Tommy's only human. The difference is that he's too good for hookers. In Vegas, he couldn't believe that I would go for the human sandwich; that a bubble bath with Marcie was worth two hundred bucks. Maybe he thought that they should pay *him*—or at least beg and pretend he was special. (It's not that he's high and holy; he wanted a recap of all Marcie's marvels.) No, Tommy's locked into that fantasy he cooked up in prison. He's out there chasing Quentin Quail down the beach. He wants bobby socks and saddle shoes and little girls gone bad.

But while I'm trashing his memory, the other half of me gets chills over Tommy. Indigo had it right: *Not your average criminal mind.* That Jerome hit was pretty intricate. Lots of things had to go right in order for it to work. He's not riding on good karma, so it must be a master plan. I'm banking that Eddie Izod has at least an inkling of Tommy's master plan. More likely, Eddie *is* Tommy's plan. I think back to our conversation, the one time I met him at Hector's apartment. If the DEA has shut down "precursor chemicals" like Eddie said, then Tommy can't have many options. That points the finger at Eddie; that, and his comment about having business in Carson City. The cartel world is too small for that coincidence. He was visiting Tommy in prison, getting a lecture on downstream action.

So Tommy has a talent for thinking things through, and he's sure got a talent for acting. I knew cons in prison who could plan scores, who could pull in the elements for a heist, but they always tipped their hand. They made sure everyone knew just how brilliant they were. But Tommy never tipped his hand—not to Luis and not to me. He plotted that exit with the body switch; didn't even want to rub it in Luis's face. How many guys could resist taking the credit? None that I can think of.

Indigo said, *You'd better learn to think like he does.* If that means cooking up fantasies, this will be harder than I thought. If it means thinking through every move, I'll do exactly that. And if it means sucking up your ego and forgetting about stuff like freedom and safety and Indigo—well, those are tapes, too. You can erase those as easily as tapes about *onore*. Carl Dupree said I reminded him of Tommy. We'll see about that. He's got foresight; I've got second sight. *You had to teach yourself to be cold,* Indigo said. *Your impulse is to do something good.* We'll see about that one, too.

Preparing to meet Eddie Izod means slipping back into my smurf identity. I know this is going to be easier than passing myself off as a fisherman in Haida. I've got the wardrobe (fresh off the racks in Juneau). I get my rental car at the airport (a Lincoln with cruise control and a tape player). All I'm missing is the cashier's checks and the duffel bag of cash. I'll have to think of a cover story if Eddie gets curious. He's got just enough yokel in him to ask for a peek at the goods. As I recall, scolding worked wonders on Eddie; Hector made him all contrite that one time we met. *You don't talk business with anybody,* Hector told him. *You keep your end to yourself.* Let's hope he hasn't learned that lesson.

But first I have to find Eddie Izod out in those Cajun swamps. Doreen got amnesia when I asked her which town. So I use directory assistance at the airport. There are some Eddie Moores in New Orleans, but I discount those because Doreen would've remembered New Orleans. I fish around in the 318 area until I flush him out of a Lafayette. He picks up, and I recognize the voice right away—drifting in a cannabis fog.

Danny. Dan Castellano . . . he mutters. We met at Hector's place?

I remind him of the telescope on the deck, of the toxic reefer we did while discussing his export gig.

Oh, okay, *that's* why I'm a little hazy, Eddie says. You're the supersmurf. Manage to work your way into bayou country?

I got the time if you got the banks, I say. Figured I'd give a professional courtesy, take my colleague to dinner. After all, I'm on an expense account. Got to spend it *somewhere.*

For true, for true, Eddie replies. Let me give you some directions. . . .

I drive across delta flatlands, straight through Lafayette's junk-food strip and then north into the boonies. It's dark when I finally get there. Eddie's house is at the end of a long drive with runty trees on either side. It's clapboard, very white trash from the looks of it; couple of outbuildings for hogs or chickens now gone dark and derelict. Damn shame. Anybody with a paint roller and a domestic notion could turn the place into a postcard. But I can see Eddie bought it for proximity. Beyond a field to the west is a factory complex all lit up like Christmas. That would be the solvents plant, Eddie's ether scam.

I figure to be better safe than sorry, so I park on the main road and cut through the weeds and the elephant grass to the back of the place. I want to make sure there's no extra vehicles with California plates stowed in the garage. All I find is a satellite dish, a bunch of ratty patio furniture, and Eddie's Miata convertible with one of those black car condoms on the front. Leave it to Eddie to pick the perfect stud-yuppie ride. And no doubt the satellite dish is hooked to some big-screen, eight-hundred-channel system. Exactly what you need to watch Australian rules football or Pakistani election returns.

I'm not sure what Eddie is watching, but it takes five minutes of banging the screen door to tear him away. He shuffles to the door in a bathrobe straight out of *The Honeymooners.* He's a little more jowly than I remember; unshaven, hair unkempt, and glasses on the end of his nose—Polo designer horn-rims with tape securing one of the bows. So much for the gangster mystique. This is white trash with cash, a dusky gone to seed.

Danny? What you doin' at the back door? Somebody following you? he wonders.

Can't be too careful, I tell Eddie as I walk past him into what smells like the kitchen. Hit some lights, Eddie. This place is like a tomb.

He flicks a switch, and I see the kind of havoc a guy can create with lots of money and no maid. Every gimmicky French gadget you can name is stacked along the counters. The slicers, dicers, and juicers are all spattered by various shades of processed slop, and so are the cupboards and the floor. Dishes, kettles, and colanders are piled in a sink that has gone gray from some mildewy creeping fungus. A two-lane highway of ants marches out from under this sink rubble, down the cupboard, and out the door.

Yeah, we got ants, Eddie says with this amused tone, like he was saying, Yeah, we got kids—aren't they *precious*?

No roaches, though, he adds. 'Cause I keep a few geckos. Lizards are the newest organic exterminator.

Just then I see this reptile herky-jerky his way out of the shadows of the table. *An organic exterminator.* The newest, the latest. Eddie wouldn't bother with an *old* solution, like a sponge and a bucket of cleanser.

Eddie hands me a beer out of his also-grayish refrigerator and says, C'mon, I'll give you the tour.

I'm dreading this, but I follow him down a corridor, flicking light switches as I go. I'm pleased to find that it gets better, more coherent in the dining and living rooms. Unlike Hector Lupino, Eddie has passable taste. The furniture has a vague colonial/baronial theme, with an actual antique here and there—a sideboard with leaded glass doors, a butter churn in the corner, a musket hanging on the wall. Nothing whorehousey or headshoppy here—except for the coffee table.

Apparently, Eddie passes most of his time on the sofa facing the TV (a monster, just as I predicted). There's a whole radius of bachelor clutter here—plates with sandwich crusts, newspapers and *Playboy* magazines, CDs spilled out of their boxes, unread junk mail, and science fiction videocassettes *(Highlander, Star Trek V, Deathstalker III)*. And in front of this command center, this base of operations, is a chemistry set on the coffee table. There's a Bunsen burner, some stands and beakers, and a rack of test tubes. Eddie's got various powders separated on petri dishes and a propane lighter for heating crack. He's got pipes and candles and eyedroppers and one of those kitchen fire extinguishers just in case he torches the place.

Quite an arsenal, I say, nodding at the paraphernalia.

Oh, that's just where I dabble, Eddie says. The big stuff is in the basement.

The *big* stuff? I thought you said this ether was processed at a factory? I say. The one on yonder hill . . .

Oh it is, it is, Eddie says. He tosses some papers aside and parks himself on the couch. All that involves is checking inventory and paying them off, he adds. That's got nothing to do with *science*.

I was hoping to hear about your science projects, I say, taking a long draw of beer. Now suppose you put on your tomcattin' clothes and we go find us a roadhouse that serves up that killer jambalaya. . . .

Eddie isn't the killer jambalaya type, so we wind up at a yuppie fern bar—the kind of place where guys make phone calls out of their briefcases and women stow their Reeboks under their chairs. Everybody looks like Madison Avenue and talks like gator bait. Armani suits and Cajun drawls—it doesn't work for me. But Eddie is in his element, drinking scotch and reading a menu tacked onto a cutting board. He's so engrossed that I can study his features in the brighter light.

We were both stoned the only other time we met, so my perspective is rather dim. But it's clear that drugs have aged Eddie Izod, drawn his skin tighter over that chipmunk face and weighted the lids of his eyes. He's got a lopsided grin that he flashes whether the topic is funny or not. His fingers are twitchy, very nervous, like he has to fight to keep that gram in his pocket and out of his nose. He still wears the Izod sweater tied around his neck, but the cuffs are frayed and his golf shirt has a few stains on the front. I guess this is what comes of being stranded in the provinces. Too many chemicals and not enough friends. Too many channels on TV.

So how much has Hector got you carrying these days? Eddie asks, through with the menu.

Quarter mil, I lie.

Hector isn't giving any more orders, and all I've got in the rental car is luggage and empty soda cans. But I pitch some shoptalk bull about how I have to make more stops, turn lower amounts because some Treasury task force is on the case. They're linking deposits with surveillance cameras. They're nailing smurfs all over the country. It's getting so a man can't make an honest living.

You look like you're doing okay, Eddie says. Hector always said you were the one they didn't have to worry about. You could travel three months with half a million and account for every nickel.

The waitress arrives just as Eddie says *half a million* and doesn't bat an eye. Eddie orders the chili and corn bread, and I get a salad because I'm still working off some room-service pounds from my stay in Juneau.

Eddie's casual tone seems to indicate that he hasn't tried to call Hector recently. I tell him that being reliable is how you stay employed. That's how you stay alive.

Gets pretty routine though, doesn't it? Eddie says. He drains off his drink and asks me if I ever feel like getting off the road, working a different side of the game.

Which side do you have in mind?

All I know is what I read in the papers, Eddie begins, picking his way around the edge of his napkin with his nervous, spidery fingers. But don't the big cartels use lots of wire transfers, shelf corporations based in the Caribbean and offshore bank accounts?

Sure, there's plenty of that going on, I agree. I hear Luis and Alonzo do some business in Netherlands Antilles. So what's your point? That I should run a shelf corporation? That I should wire the money around?

Exactly! Eddie exclaims, so loudly it turns heads at the next table. That's exactly what you should be doing. The weather's nicer; the hours are better. You get twice the money for half the risk.

Twice the money from who? I ask him. All that clandestine financial shit is like a house of cards. Alonzo talks with lawyers and accountants all day. The contracts run for pages! They screw up one little clause and customs can take it all. That's a long way from smurfing, Eddie. Alonzo isn't going to send me to the Bahamas just because I can be trusted.

Who says it has to be Alonzo—or even Luis? Eddie asks while the waitress delivers our food. He mashes crackers into his chili while I ruminate. Eddie tucks a hunk of corn bread in his cheek and starts up again. I mean, you said yourself that Treasury is clamping down on smurfs. Pretty soon it's going to get too precarious to make any sense. When that happens, and they take you off the road, what's your next gig going to be?

I munch on a bread stick and tell him that I'll worry about that when it happens. After all, they know I'm a righteous dusky. They'll make a place for me.

Probably a *lateral* place, Eddie says. A lateral move. I mean, Hector is in for life—he's comptroller, cashier, whatever. You don't move up until he dies.

Hector is dead, I'm thinking. And they're not about to offer me his job. I hold my tongue; I just nod and dig into my salad while Eddie orders another drink. Then he stares me down with those drug-sunken eyes and cuts to the chase.

Suppose you could create a position that combines all of the stuff that Alonzo and Hector do for Luis?

Suppose the Cubs won the World Series, I say. And if pigs had wings, they'd fly rings around the moon.

I'm *serious,* Eddie says. I'm offering you exactly that kind of position. I want you to work for me.

Chapter Fifteen

I should've seen it coming, should've been ahead of the conversation, but I'm jet-lagged and drinking on an empty stomach. I'm still on Alaska time. What Eddie is saying is a logical extension of the conversation we'd had in L.A. Back then, he projected this sort of giddy wonderment at being ushered into the fold. And you have to figure that nothing is going to match his fantasy—certainly not working for Luis. Give him two years of baby-sitting a chemical plant and the fantasy gets pretty stale. Nobody's kissing his ring, or offering to have his enemies killed. He hasn't met any Central American dictators or been hit on by slinky chicks like Michelle Pfeiffer in *Scarface*. No, Eddie's been stuck in Cracker Hell, Louisiana. And out of all this isolation, this home-synthesized, self-medicated stupor comes the notion that he can be a player. It's the same kind of fantasy that Tommy Delorme cooked up in prison. Eddie cooked his up on a coffee table while watching *Deathstalker III*.

Laundering *your* money? I ask. Since when are you so liquid, Eddie, that you could send me to the Caribbean?

Since I got smart and started diverting some of that ether from

Luis's pipeline, Eddie says. That and my science project in the basement will be enough to launch us, Danny.

And just what is the science project?

Crystal meth, Eddie says as he wolfs the rest of his corn bread. I let him chew while I try to recall what I heard about methamphetamines. I've never done the stuff, but I know it's an upper with a sustained kick. It enjoyed a few months of legality while the feds scrambled to declare it a controlled substance. It was part of a designer-drug wave that never interested Luis. The coke market is presold, he would say. We don't need to jump on every gimmick that comes down the pike.

Apparently, Eddie Izod sees more money in this gimmick than Luis did.

Is there a lot of science to it? I ask Eddie. I mean, compared to refining coke?

You've got to hit coca leaves with nine different compounds before you add the ether, Eddie replies. And it takes seventeen liters of ether for each kilo of coke. Crystal meth, on the other hand, is just three ingredients—ephedrine, red phosphorus, and hydriodic acid. My unit cost is one-tenth what the Colombians spend for a pound of blow. And I don't have to fly it across the Caribbean or mule it through El Salvador.

Yeah—I sigh—but meth isn't blow, Eddie. Never will be.

But for blue-collar hopheads, it's close enough, Eddie replies. And ten bucks' worth will get a college student through a week of final exams.

I don't see it catching on at the dorms, but I don't want to burst Eddie's bubble. I've got him talking now, and I want to hear about the other dimensions of his scam.

And Luis doesn't suspect that you're shorting him on that ether inventory? I wonder.

Danny, try to understand that this chemical plant is a blank-check operation, Eddie says, condescending as hell. Nobody's around to whack my knuckles with a ruler. I've conditioned them to expect a fluctuating supply. I tell Luis that what we produce depends on what level of management heat we get on any given week. In fact, management is bought and paid for; they're only too happy to play a little double-entry bookkeeping. Skimming here isn't like skimming cash on a smurfing trip. As far as Luis is concerned, all them barrels never existed.

Okay, so you've got a nice stockpile going, I say. You're fighting the same embargo that Luis is. You've got to connect with the refining labs in Colombia.

Guatemala, Eddie corrects me. The Cali cartel has moved its operation north. In Colombia, the Medellín gang kept losing labs because Big Brother spotted them by satellite. So the Cali boys ship their leaves from Peru to northern Guatemala. They set up in the jungle, same as in Colombia, only with less scrutiny. As for connecting—they hear you've got ether to sell and the cartel connects with *you.*

I gnaw some more greens before popping another question: All these logistics and payoffs take lots of capital, Eddie. Been saving your allowance?

I've got some help with the distribution end, he replies. We'll break even on the first load or two, then it's *pure profit.*

How much profit?

Eddie flashes me that lopsided grin and gets real conspiratorial. He leans across the table and whispers, Each year, Fabio Ochoa of the Medellín cartel makes the *Fortune* magazine list of the richest men in the world. He came up from dirt, and now he's worth billions. Right up there with the Gettys, with Rupert Murdoch and all them Japanese. We expect to be there, too, Danny. We don't stop until we make the list, and that's why we're going to need every tax-shelter shell game in the book. That's why we're going to need *you.*

I haven't been recruited in a long time and it's sort of flattering. It's also kind of bizarre and pathetic, how Eddie & Co expect to amass billions from ether and crystal meth. Maybe the fantasy gets bigger than that; maybe Eddie's going to concoct the next coke hybrid in his basement and turn the tide away from crack. Maybe he's going to buy *Fortune* magazine and put himself on the cover. This I'm thinking while we're digesting dinner and driving back to Eddie's cracker box. *Billions,* he says. I'm thinking about this dream scheme, and two other thoughts intrude.

First, that being a financial wizard in the Caribbean would suit me fine—the kind of job you do on the phone, on the veranda of some plantation estate. Yes, it would certainly appeal, and it also makes Indigo look like a genius. She warned me that I'd find some new scam that appeals to the dark side of my nature. This certainly qualifies.

And second, I have to wonder how much room there is in the marketplace for chemical kingpins. Luis is running ether to the cartel in exchange for cash and coke. After Kohler & Co closed down his clock plant, that ether pipeline is more precious than ever. Now Eddie wants to supply the Cali cartel. And if Carl Dupree is right, Tommy Delorme also wants into the ether scene, this "downstream action." That's a lot of guns in Dodge City, a lot of competing interest. This could be the first drug war that's not about drugs. And I'd put Eddie Izod dead last in that altercation.

That depends, of course, on Eddie's affiliations; this "distribution help" he's bragging about. I'll want to hear more about that, but I don't want to trip any flags. If I can get Eddie stoned or a little drunker, he'll tell me whatever I want to hear.

We never get to that point, in fact, we don't do any talking at all after Eddie plays back his phone messages. He walks down the corridor while I fetch two beers from his dingy fridge. I stroll into the dining room, to find Eddie leaning over this phone machine on the sideboard. And out of the little phone machine speaker comes the voice of Alonzo Peña.

Eddie, he says, Alonzo here, got some interesting news. Call me when you get in.

Eddie waits out the *beep,* some static, and then Alonzo leaves a second message. Call me, *tonight.*

Alonzo was pretty impatient, because we hear a third *beep* and he comes on to say, Eddie, it looks like we got a rogue smurf out there, and I want you to keep an eye out. Danny Castellano killed Hector down in Phoenix. We got a report that he's headed for

Louisiana. He calls, you give us a call. Watch yourself, Eddie. That Danny's one *loco* fucking—

I don't hear the rest because Eddie's got his hand in a drawer of the sideboard, and he's pulling a gun—a *lot* of gun. It's one of the Israeli 9-mm cannons, a real gangster-fantasy pistol. It's a good thing, too, because anything smaller and I wouldn't have had time to cross the room and jump him. I hit him high, a flying tackle with the crook of my arm at his throat. Eddie flails backward like the twit that he is, and I figure this is going to be a one-punch affair, until I get harpooned in the side.

We're falling together along the wall and all of a sudden I get this shock to my ribs that knocks me back the other direction. For a second, I wonder if I am shot, if Eddie managed to squeeze one off on the way down. But I look up and see that I've hit the goddamn antique butter churn. It's got this handle sticking up that caught me as I fell. It's like falling on a sword. And all I can do is grip my side and roll away, wheezing and gasping for breath.

Eddie lands a lot softer than I do. I know he's going to get up a lot quicker, too. My best plan is to get something—a wall, a door, some furniture—between me and the muzzle of that bazooka. So I get up on one knee and pitch myself under the dining room table, then I roll for the opposite side. The slightest move shoots pain through my rib cage, but I know I don't have a choice. Somehow I've got to make it into the hall, where I've got darkness to cover me. Eddie should be shooting by now, but I roll again and reach the hall without hearing anything but my scuffling feet and Eddie grunting and huffing across the room. I rise up on one knee and take a look back.

Eddie isn't shooting because he is trying to work the slide on the pistol to chamber a shell. He's standing with his butt against the wall, hunched over the gun, which he's gripping between his thighs. The slide ain't coming, but he ain't giving up. Eddie's eyes have gone squinty with the effort, and I can stand up and hobble up to him without even registering. I kick for his groin and get both his balls and the pistol. The blow hurts me damn near as much, and we both collapse backward—Eddie with his hands on his crotch and me gripping my ribs. We writhe on the floor for awhile, then I shuffle back to my feet as Eddie gropes for the gun. I kick this time with my other foot, and it doesn't hurt nearly as much. My heel catches Eddie in the side of the head and pretty much ends the discussion. He rolls onto his back, with his mouth flopped open.

I rip off a lamp cord and tie Eddie's hands just in case he wakes up. I have to stop in the middle of this, lean back on my heels, and catch my breath. My ribs hurt like hell. But I don't have time to convalesce. I need to toss the house and search for clues about this "distribution help" Eddie mentioned. I don't find any promising leads on the bulletin board near the kitchen phone. (Pizza delivery, liquor delivery, outcall massage.) Next, I check Eddie's bedroom upstairs—a real fraternity dive. Eddie hangs most of his clothes on a StairMaster machine—which tells you how much use it gets. I find what passes for his office in a spare bedroom. Eddie has a rolltop desk heaped with spools of adding-machine tape, receipts and brochures, and crap. I pull up a chair and wade in, thinking that if I don't find something quick, I might have to take it all with me in a sack. I find Eddie's day planner in a pigeonhole.

I sit in a chair draped with more of Eddie's clothes and study it through. None of the names listed here rings a bell; none of them are even in Central or South America. But I keep paging back to the *C*'s. There is a brochure stuck in the page, which makes the day planner fall open. But there is also a corporation in the listings that stops me cold: Cencor Technologies, Ltd. No address, no names underneath. Just a series of cities and phone numbers, scratched out in sequence. Apparently, Cencor was first based in Minneapolis, then St. Louis, Memphis, and, finally, Port Arthur, Texas. But like I said, the numbers are scratched out, like they got obsolete.

I mull that over while I'm thumbing the brochure stuck in the page. It's promoting a singles resort in Mexico, on a place called Isla Mujeres. Island of Women. The brochure is bilingual, and the English part describes how the island sits just off of Cancún.

Now I didn't go to college, but even I'm hip enough to catch the meaning of that. It harks back to Tommy Delorme's fantasy game, Beach or Buffet. We're talking spring break. All those nubile coeds flock to Fort Lauderdale, Daytona, and Miami. But the ones with money—with daddy's Visa card—fly off to Cancún, where everyone speaks English and nobody checks your I.D. Island of Women. Mexico, where the import restrictions on things like ether are—well, *casual*. String bikinis and Corona beer. Even a geek like Eddie could score in a place like that.

I keep paging through the day planner and find a key in a little plastic bag, stapled to the page. It looks very familiar. It looks like a luggage key, so I go to work on all the closets, rooting for a matching suitcase. I find a gym bag, a camping duffel, and a briefcase that doesn't fit the key. I try the attic—*nada*. Just a bed frame, one of those tailor's torsos, and the box for the giant TV.

But something about the sewing dummy catches my attention. Dust lies thick and gray on its fabric shoulders, a quarter inch at least. But along the rib cage, or where the ribs would be, are handprints, fingermarks in the dust. And not just one set but several. They're fresh, as distinct as a palm on a mirror. Now, either Eddie has been dancing with this dummy or he moved it very recently. I look at the floorboards, and I can see a path worn in the dust there, too, back and forth from the stairs. So he walks upstairs, fondles the dummy, and then leaves? *No*. He *moves* the dummy. I step over and check the floorboards under the dummy stand, and, sure enough, three of them are dust-free. The nails are pulled loose, too.

I move the dummy, hook a fingernail under a board, and lift it free. I stick my foot in the slot and pull out two more boards, exposing Eddie's secret stashing place. I'm about to peer down into the gap when I remember that it's pretty common for dealers to guard their stashes with snakes—rattlers, cobras, viper of the week. Since Eddie keeps geckos, I figure he won't be squeamish about something more lethal.

I search the kitchen for a flashlight but find only candles and matches. When I get back to the attic, the snake is already poking its head out of the hole—a huge jet black head. He spots me and rears back, showing fangs and a bright white mouth. It doesn't rattle at me, doesn't even hiss; no warning to anyone groping under those boards in the dark. Cute, Eddie. Got yourself another organic exterminator. The snake gets halfway out of the stash hole before I blast it with Eddie's pistol. Thank God for overkill.

Downstairs, I find that the shooting didn't rouse Eddie at all. In the kitchen, I dig some newspapers out of the trash. I fashion the papers into a bouquet and light the top of it off a burner on the stove. I'm going to use this makeshift torch to check out that stash hole. There could be a whole nest of snakes, and I'm not taking any chances. So I go in first with a broom handle to draw any strikes. Then I lean over and give the hole a good look, with the newspaper blazing away. I don't spot any more snakes. But what I do find is enough of a shock to make me burn my hand while I'm standing there staring at it.

It's not body parts; it's not kilos of drugs. It's not even illicit weapons. It's just a garden-variety Samsonite suitcase in an imitation deerskin suede. You see ones like it on carousels in every airport in the country. But this suitcase stops my heart because it used to be mine. It was mine right up to the moment Tommy Delorme swiped it from the trunk of that rental Lincoln in Jerome, Arizona. I know it because it's got a telltale L.A. Raiders sticker, and a pair of latches I had custom-installed, latches that fit the key in the little plastic bag.

I mash out the burning newspaper and fish out the suitcase with the broom handle. I notice it still has a tag with one of my aliases—Tony Granato. One latch is pried loose, the other still opens with the key. It pops, and I step back and aim the pistol. The suitcase doesn't have much heft, but enough to contain another snake or two. I use the broom handle to toss it open. Nothing hisses; nothing slithers or moves. And of course I don't see all those neat rows of twenty-dollar money packs; those two-thousand-dollar bundles that Hector Lupino packed into my suitcase after running them through his autocounter. There were 175 of them when Tommy stole the case. Now there are two, and some loose twenties—about five grand.

I find the money, and an unsealed manila envelope that contains a stack of photographs and some documents. I'm almost afraid to look at the pictures. I mean, what could be so secret to

Eddie that he guards it with a poisonous snake? So I've braced myself for orgy scenes, but what I find is pretty mundane. I step into the middle of the room, under the lone naked bulb, to examine the stuff. For some reason, Eddie shot a whole roll of film of a freighter in dry dock somewhere: side angle, bow, stern, three-quarter left, three-quarter right, etc., etc. In some shots, you can see workmen chipping at barnacles on the hull while other guys repaint the thing. And in with the photos, I find a clipping from the classified ads. It describes a German-built freighter for sale or lease, with registry in Port Arthur, Texas. They don't name a price, but it's clear to me where at least some of that 350K was spent.

The papers are invoices to Cencor Technologies, Ltd., for purchase of various amounts of ether. There are no signatures or names, so I don't get a lead on Tommy Delorme. I'll give them a closer look later. I do notice, however, that the envelope has a return address for Cencor. It is a P.O. box in Nassau, Bahamas. I think back to dinner, when Eddie played naïve about shelf corporations and Caribbean banks. *All I know is what I read in the papers. . . .* Yeah, *right.*

I can't get consumed with this stuff, because I want to split while Eddie's still unconscious. I take the brochure and the day planner page with all the scratched-out numbers. I take what money is left in the suitcase, along with the Cencor envelope. I leave the pistol, but I take Eddie's car keys and a steak knife from the pile of dishes in the kitchen. I rip the phone jacks out of the walls on my way out the door. I load everything into the Lincoln. Then I puncture all four tires on Eddie's Miata with the crusty steak knife. At least he will have a nice long walk to the phone. Short of killing Eddie, this is the best I can do at buying some getaway time.

Chapter Sixteen

I canvass the airlines and learn that I can't leave for Cancún until morning. The delay feels like a death sentence. I've got the same fears that I had in Juneau, that I've got that target on my back and they know where I'm traveling. I know that Eddie's going to have to walk to a phone whenever he wakes up. He'll call Alonzo and they'll probably put some goons on the next plane out of L.A. They would hit the New Orleans terminal about the time I leave. That's crowding my comfort zone. I don't want to be in the same state with those clowns, much less the same airport. Indigo warned me before I left: *You think your luck has run out. I couldn't agree more. Maybe that's too blunt, but there it is.*

Maybe, but better safe than sorry. I book a flight to Miami that leaves in twenty minutes. They have better fares to the Yucatán from Florida, and the layover won't give me an ulcer. Once the plane is up, I can exhale again and tend to business. The short flight over the Gulf Coast gives me a chance to sort out some recent revelations.

First off, it's clear that Tommy and Eddie Izod have been tight since Tommy's prison days—and probably before that. Prison, after all, was where Tommy was all pumped up about downstream action. And judging by those numbers in Eddie's directory, Tommy stayed on the road after he robbed me. Strange itinerary; Minnesota, Missouri, Tennessee, Texas. But it gets more relevant when I match the stops Tommy made with those invoices to Cencor Technologies. The invoices are all chemical companies, billing for ether deliveries—located in Minneapolis, St. Louis, and Memphis. I don't find transport costs, so unless they were factored in, Tommy took delivery in each city.

On a hunch, I pull the airline magazine out of the seat pouch. I page to the map where they illustrate the routes on the continent. Connect the dots. When you connect Minneapolis, St. Louis, and Memphis, you see they're all river towns, convenient stops if you're pushing a bargeload of barrels to New Orleans. A Huck Finn kind of scam; collect ether in discreet amounts and keep rolling downstream. Pick up those stray gallons they embezzled from Luis in Louisiana. Then they load it onto that freighter they leased in Port Arthur, Texas. From there, it's a milk run to Cancún and Guatemala.

Very nice, very efficient. Since you're not getting greedy with a single source, you're not attracting DEA. You're not going into Colombia, so customs leaves you alone. People on the barge, at the warehouses, and on the docks would need a cut. But Luis would have already seen to that. I look at my Louisiana map and see that Port Arthur is a short hop from Lafayette. My guess is that the ether that Eddie produced for Luis went out of Port Arthur, too. So Eddie and Tommy probably rode those coattails, used the same distribution without having to spend any grease of their own.

So *that*'s Tommy's downstream gig, I'm thinking as I pop a couple of the airline's aspirin. My side is still throbbing from that fight with Eddie, from that fucking butter churn. I'm guessing I've cracked some ribs. I'll probably roll over in my sleep and puncture a lung. Assuming I *can* sleep. I should've tossed Eddie's cabinets for some Valium, some Darvon, or even morphine. What a pharmacy! Tip that house upside down and pills would fly from every window. I imagine Eddie's curing his headache right now with a little home remedy.

I'm thinking about Eddie's house, about how much it would interest Max Kohler. Hitting a crystal meth lab would be another feather in his cap. Cracking that ether scam would be icing on the cake. That would shut down Luis on two fronts, keep him occupied and keep him running. Yeah, I'm thinking, I could just about bury Luis with a call to the DEA. But then I remember sucking Agent Pierce's gun while he called me Mr. Chancre. I remember handing them a five-hundred-pound bust and getting the bum's rush for my trouble. Fucking ingrates.

I decide to call the bastard, anyway—not because I want to make his day but because I need some information. I need to find out how Alonzo knew I was in Louisiana. I'm convinced I didn't have a tail down from Seattle. That means somebody talked, and there are only two somebodys in a position to know. I told Doreen, and I told Indigo—which troubles me indeed. If Doreen tipped them off, that means I'm a lousy judge of character. It means that she was connected in ways I never imagined. If Indigo tipped them off, it could mean Luis put the screws to her. I don't even want to imagine what *that* could mean, but I call her as soon as I reach the concourse in Miami.

I'm fine, Indigo tells me when she picks up.

You haven't had any visitors? I ask. You don't get the feeling you're being followed?

Of course not, she replies. Danny, are you in some kind of trouble—already?

No, not yet, I tell her. Listen, the real reason I called was to change your itinerary. . . .

My itinerary?

Yeah, you won't be keeping house with me in New Orleans, after all, I say.

Like this is news to me?

No, I thought you'd enjoy something sunnier, a bit more tropical, I say. How does Cancún strike you? Mexican Riviera. Mariachis, tequila, endless beach. Montezuma's revenge.

Danny, Danny . . .

Don't answer—don't say anything, I tell her. Give it a couple of days. Next time you look out that skylight, imagine what the sun looks like. Imagine what it could do for your aura, your epidermis. . . .

Are you trying to hustle a hustler, Danny?

Let's just say that I'm willing to forgive that scissor in the back, I tell her. Tell me this, what's it doing there now? What's the weather like?

It's raining, Indigo says.

Your ticket will be at the United counter under your name, I tell her. Layover in Miami, and on to Cancún. I'll be at the the El Presidente. Gotta run. See you in a couple of days.

I hang up while she is protesting, but I do hear the part about *In your dreams!*

I walk on to the main terminal and use Eddie's cash to buy three tickets, the two for Indigo and then my own to Cancún. Then I find another phone and ask information for the number of the Los Angeles DEA. I call the number, get some agent, and ask for Max Kohler. He asks who am I, what do I want, and I tell the guy that Max will want to talk to me. The agent takes the pay phone's number and says he'll look into it. Five minutes later, it rings, and Max Kohler says, Is this the man with nine lives?

Very funny, I tell him. As long as I'm still breathing, I'm still in a position to help you.

Maybe, Kohler says. What did you have in mind?

Anytime you make a distribution bust—no matter how big—you're just slicing off the tail of the snake, I say. Just giving middle management some heat. They found ten tons in L.A. in '89 and the street price of coke *didn't budge*. The retail market hardly flinched. That's because there's plenty of labs pumping out product. This snake dies from the head. To make an impact, you need to bust labs. And in order to bust labs, you need to find them.

We're hitting the labs, Kohler says, his voice getting all pouty. But you have to work with foreign governments. That got stickier after we invaded Panama.

I'll give you labs that produce a ton a month, I tell him. Unless you guys are squeamish about the jungle—malaria can be a real bitch.

We can handle the jungle, Kohler says. (I figure he's got an Eddie Bauer costume for guerrilla war.) This would all be more plausible if I thought you were anything but a foot soldier. You expect me to believe that you've done field inspections in South America?

Central America, I tell him. The labs are in northern Guatemala—and no, I've never seen them. But I know you can track them, because you've done it before. You track their ether shipments.

I figure I'm getting through because I can hear Kohler hammering his pipe in the ashtray, *ticka-ticka-ticka.*

Charlie Cadeaux once told me how you busted a lab in Colombia, I say. You can tack a beeper on cargo containers and follow it with satellites. Tell me I'm not lying.

Kohler sighs, says, Nice sting, but it's obsolete. We've sealed off the exports, Danny. Nobody's getting American ether—legal or otherwise.

I tell him about Luis bankrolling the production in Lafayette. I describe how it is probably trucked from there to Port Arthur, Texas. And then from Texas to Guatemala. I give him Eddie's name and address, adding that if he hits the place in the next two days he will get a crystal meth lab in the bargain. I was good for the clock factory, Kohler, and I'm good for this one, too. Fire up the satellite, I tell him. That cargo will take you straight to Coke Central.

You get a charitable streak? he wonders. I'm waiting for the list of demands.

I need to know what you said at your press conference, after you busted the clock plant, I say. How much information you leaked to the media.

Zip, Kohler replies. Absolutely *nada.*

You're kidding!

There was no press conference, Kohler replies. See, we got plenty of leads about Luis's street-level distribution. Since we missed the *patrones,* we figured to milk the initial bust for all it was worth. So it's hush-hush for at least another week while the L.A. narcs kick in some doors.

Thanks, Kohler, I tell him, my mind spinning off from the conversation. You have fun in the jungle—

Suppose we have some follow-up, he blurts. How can we reach you?

Dial one–eight hundred-CHANCRE, I tell him, then I hang up the phone.

I turn to walk across the terminal and damn near get nailed by one of those courtesy carts. The skycap is honking at me and I don't hear him because I'm not in Miami. I'm back in Juneau on the phone, hearing Doreen Koontz say, *I had one of their clocks in my room—threw it out. To think that it used to have drugs stuffed inside!* Yeah, Doreen, imagine that. Doreen Koontz. The one person I tipped off prior to the bust. The person who tipped off Luis. All three of them skipped the bust—Doreen, Luis, and Alonzo. And then Doreen gives them a bonus shot at killing me in Louisiana. I'm thinking that my intuition really failed me there. I wish I had read her aura. But Indigo said those colors are fluid. They can change. So can mine, Doreen, so can mine.

I've got another hour on layover, so I decide to catch some lunch and ruminate. I'm not certain where to go, because I forgot my Spanish dictionary. This was still America last time I checked—excuse me: Los Estados Unidos. *Bienvenidos* a Florida. You could fire a cannon through Miami International and not hit an Anglo's ass. Of course, the shell would take out thirty-six trendy little boutique restaurants that serve yogurt and blintzes and papaya boats filled with asparagus mousse. Airports stopped selling real food when they found out people would pay six bucks for a cucumber sandwich. I'd kill for a chili dog and they're offering Tofutti on a stick. Of course, you can't buy Cuban food, either, so I guess there's some justice in that.

I have to use sign language to order a giant pretzel and a cappuccino. (Coffee? *No comprende.*) Ordinarily, I'd let this stuff roll off my back, but today it's feeding on this gloomy sense I've had since the fight with Eddie Izod. I know that I should be glad I didn't take a bullet, or get bitten by his stash viper. And the information I found has pretty much handed me Tommy's scam on a platter. I also reclaimed five grand of the money Tommy stole. But I gather from the receipts and my near-empty suitcase that the other $345,000 was reinvested in the operation. Tommy bought ether; Tommy bought a ship. He's traveled and lived like an Arab prince—hitting buffets at every hotel from Minnesota to Cancún. And he's not living the pauper's life on Isla Mujeres. So I can forget about reclaiming the balance when I do catch up with him. I envisioned that money as a kind of pension, an alternative to Witness Protection. It could set me free, and set me up in legitimate business. But unless my business is ether exports, I'll have to settle for killing Tommy.

Unless . . .

What's the point of collecting all of this ether, of forming Cencor in the Bahamas, of using Luis and Eddie and me if not to make money? If Tommy can get chemicals to the labs, then he will be turning millions. Cash. It's a transaction as basic as any drug deal, and Tommy will confront the same problems. How do you move it, invest it, launder it? How do you keep it safe? All of a sudden, Tommy exposes himself to the kind of hit he made on me. The problem with an expanded operation is an expanded chain of command. You recruit people; you confide in people. I know it because I lived it. And somewhere down Tommy's chain, I'll be watching and waiting. But I sure as hell don't want to be waiting alone.

Part Three

◆

Island of Women

Utopian voyages turn inward rather than outward; they do not escape from this world but concern themselves with it.

—William Nelson, *Twentieth Century Interpretations of Utopia*

Chapter Seventeen

◆

The novelty of sun, the weirdness of daylight, strikes me as I'm walking across the tarmac at Cancún Airport. I've lived in fog, indoors, and in airplanes as far back as I can remember. It was chilly in Lafayette, and I never went outside in Miami, so the heat is another shock—the heat, and that aftertaste in the air of salt spray and ocean swells. And the Caribbean sure doesn't smell like the beach in L.A., or the Gulf Coast at New Orleans. I check into my hotel and step on the deck to check the vista. It is a beach straight out of Tommy Delorme's mind games. A beach with a human buffet.

Apparently, fall semester hasn't begun back in the States, because there's plenty of college students here. You can spot them by the noise they make (boom boxes, donkey laughter, chicken fights in the pool), and by the not-so-casual strolling. I watch guys walk three miles, past dozens of hotels, just to cruise chicks. I suppose I'd do the same. You fly all the way from Michigan Tech and you're going to get your money's worth.

I heard that the beach along the Zona Hotelera got sucked up by Hurricane David. From the tenth floor, I can see the white sand running under a couple feet of water, out two hundred yards or more. I'm not sure if this is the new coast or just high tide. But it's gorgeous water—smooth and turquoise in a crescent bay that is sheltered from heavy seas by Isla Mujeres. The bellhop pointed out Isla Mujeres when he opened my shades. It is a low rock—relatively undeveloped and unimpressive. Maybe Tommy intends to buy it after he makes the *Fortune* list. Build a high rise with a heliport on the roof.

I'm not quite ready to explore it yet—plenty of time for that later. First, I've got to address the problem of recruitment. I know I will need someone to watch my back if I'm going to hit Tommy's operation. And I don't mean just a bodyguard; I mean a real personal dusky. A stand-up guy who can help formulate a plan. I'm talking more than a wheelman here, more than you could meet over beer at a taverna. I want a guy I have some kind of history with, someone like Charlie Cadeaux. But even if Charlie had lived, I doubt if my offer would hold any appeal. One of the prerequisites here is to relish the challenge. And it won't hurt to have an ax to grind against Tommy Delorme.

That pretty much narrows the field to the Basketball Messiah, the man with a knife scar courtesy of his prison roommate in Carson City. But Carl Dupree isn't going to leave his cozy little island just to risk his neck for me. He might even want to forget that Tommy almost had him killed. No, the way to get Carl is to play up the intrigue, the James Bond angle. I can recall that night in the cabin of Carl's trawler, see him smoking his lousy reefer and hanging on my every word. It was like his life was on that boat but his heart was in my story. So I'll give him a chance to jump in without sounding desperate. He'll figure out that he can help me here, *after* he helps me in L.A.

It takes me three calls to Haida at various times of the day to get Carl to pick up. He never mentions if I disrupted his sleep.

This is a blast from your past, I tell Carl. Just another sorry-ass motherfucker checkin' in.

Carl sounds almost happy to hear my voice. My guess is that, being undercover and all, he doesn't get many calls. He tells me he's been at sea the last forty-eight hours, catching halibut on a skate—whatever the hell that is. He's home for a shower and a nap. Then he's going to overhaul the engine in his boat.

Jonathon tells me them cops arrested you on the ferry, Carl says, letting out one of his belly laughs. Guess you made the wrong enemy, homes. Where you callin' from—jail?

I give him the ten-cent summary, explaining my arrest but leaving out the liaison with Indigo and the visit with Eddie.

So you flipped and they didn't do shit for you. Carl laughs again. Danny, you gotta get you a lawyer—or some better information.

Well, that's the reason I'm calling, I say. I got a few too many balls in the air. I need an operative. I wondered if you know anybody in L.A. who is willing to do something quick and dirty?

How dirty? Carl says.

You must know some homeboys from Oakland, I say. Maybe somebody you trust from prison.

How dirty?

Break-in. Two-bit burglary. Residential apartment—I think. Nothing to it, man. In and out.

Nothing to it, Carl says. Second-biggest lie on the planet. Prison's full of nothing-to-it guys. Piece-of-cake stickups. Candy-store banks. What the hell's a burglary got to do with findin' Tommy Delorme? Ain't *his* apartment, is it?

Just a middle-aged lady name of Doreen Koontz, I say. Used to work at the clock plant the DEA busted. I don't know her address, never seen her place, but I know she's in the phone book. She's an accountant. She lives alone. How tough can it be? I wouldn't ask your friend to do anything I wouldn't do myself.

So why ain't you doin' it yourself? Carl asks.

I give him some rap about logistics and my needing to be available down here in case some contacts call. But I'll cover expenses, make it worth the man's time. I know she keeps cash around the place, I tell Carl. Jewelry, maybe a gun. Your man can take it all, take the furniture for all I care. I just want paperwork.

Paperwork?

Correspondence, check stubs, credit-card bills, and—most important—itemized long-distance phone records. Have your man mail me anything like that and I'll throw in a bonus.

I can tell Carl is writing some of this down, because he keeps stopping me and making me repeat. When he gets the spelling of Doreen Koontz, he asks, And this is going to help you nail Tommy?

It's going to help get my ass out of the frying pan. It'll help clarify stuff, I say. Remember, phone bills are the whole enchilada. I want them as far back as he can find.

This Doreen is *connected,* isn't she? Carl says. She's got some influence around town. . . .

Probably, Carl, probably.

Then it's not just a two-bit job, Carl says. Man should know that goin' in.

Yes, he should, I say, listening to him breathe and wondering if he'll stiff me.

And where would this homeboy contact you? Carl asks. After the thing goes down?

I'm a moving target, I tell him. You be intermediary. Leave a message at the El Presidente, and I'll tell you where your man can send the stuff. Then I get one parting shot before he hangs up the phone. So tell me, I ask, what's the first-biggest lie on the planet? I gots to know.

I'm doin' it with *her,* but I'm thinkin' 'bout *you,* baby, Carl replies. Them other girls don't mean nothin' to me.

That's cold, all right, I say. You could burn in hell for that one.

You got it, homes. He laughs and hangs up.

After I finish with Carl, I put on some cotton slacks, stuff a few bucks in the pocket of my Hawaiian shirt, and head out. I figure to catch dinner at the cabana restaurant while the sun goes down. But I only get as far as the elevators before I have this incredible sense of foreboding again. I'm *way* outside of myself here, bouncing around the hall like a volleyball. This isn't the safe feeling, the comforting sense that all will be well. This is the five-alarm fire. I am in danger again. I'm about to turn and head back to my room when I get another jolt. Something is wrong with my room—it is negative space. It is tainted. And while I'm letting that wash over me, the elevator doors open—two sets at once.

I step inside the one in front of me as two guys file out of the other. They don't see me, so I can hold the DOOR OPEN button and check them out. They are college age, dressed like half the dudes on the beach—T-shirts and gaudy shorts and sandals, plenty of mousse on top, and one of them sporting this teensy braided ponytail down the back. I watch while they walk straight to my room and knock on the door. That's when I release the DOOR OPEN button. Before the doors sweep shut on me, I can see that the guys have lumps under their shirts, guns tucked in their waistbands.

I have ten floors to contemplate exactly what this is about. They're not DEA, because Kohler & Co don't care if I live or die. They're not affiliated with Luis—unless he started a new Anglo hiring policy. Luis is too hung up on appearances to recruit beach-bum frat boys. I discount the notion that they were mistaken, got sent to the wrong room. That's not what my instinct says, my "random jolt." The whole surfers with guns concept really smacks of Tommy Delorme—a very connected, very efficient Tommy Delorme. Even though Eddie tipped him off to my arrival, he didn't have my flight plan, or my Darrel Fuller alias. But he must've had a picture, a composite sketch, something to spread around the hotels. A clerk or a concierge tipped him off, and the goon squad arrives *muy rapido.*

So Eddie Izod wakes up in Lafayette, checks his attic, and discovers that I'm on to Tommy's plan. If he's smart, he'll torch his laboratory and skip town. If he's not, he'll get stoned and wait for the DEA. But Eddie is the least of my problems now. I have to get off the Zona Hotelera; I have to duck these beach boys and find a disguise—all without a wallet or a passport. Things have gotten relevant here in a real hurry, and I'll need to think this through. I'll need a plan of action for when I hit the hotel lobby. What if the elevators open and Tommy has posted another goon squad in the lobby? At the very least they have a car and a wheelman standing watch out front.

Best avoid the lobby, I'm thinking as I stop the elevator at two.

I get out on this mezzanine level with shops and a restaurant facing the ocean. The idea is to give the beach people access—off the sand, up a staircase for lunch. Down that staircase, onto the beach, and I'm clear—except for the two surly beach bums loitering by the pool. They definitely fit the profile of the point men upstairs. The only way I can be sure they are part of the gang is to hang out my face and see if they jump. Right now, they're busy hitting on a cabana girl, the ones who sell sun block and pass out towels. A gringa with half a mile of legs. They're preoccupied enough for me to reach the bottom of the stair and lurk behind some potted yucca. And from there, I can see that my best option is just to show them my back and head for the ocean. Out on the beach, I can fall into the grand promenade and disappear.

But just as I'm about to break for it, the cabana babe gets a signal from some patron on a chaise lounge. She's off and running and her surly friends shove off and head in my direction. They're just mounting the steps beside me when they pull up and wait. I am behind and below them, making like a potted plant. I look up at the restaurant and see the two guys from my room at the top of the stair. Their leader is a blond guy with a Fu Manchu mustache that hides a Kewpie-doll face. If it wasn't for his arms, his facial hair, you'd think he was nine years old. So Fu Manchu starts giving orders, directing the troops. One of them heads back inside. The two on the steps confer for a minute, then backtrack and stroll toward the rows of beach chairs down on the sand. Fu Manchu remains at the head of the stairs, talking into a cellular phone. He turns his back to the beach and I take my chance. Keep it casual. Try to saunter, to *mosey*. Look like every other undergrad making the bikini circuit.

Being casual means not glancing back until I am well beyond the hotel. I carry my shoes, letting the waves lap my pants cuffs while I move steadily north. Finally, I turn, surveying the cabanas and the beach chairs until I spot the goons. Fu Manchu is down on the beach, talking to two cronies. He is agitated. I see him smack one of the guys in the back of the head with an open hand. Then he turns, points directly at me with one hand while talking into his phone with the other. I turn away and pick up the pace a little. In the time it takes this guy to call reinforcements, I will need to formulate Plan B. I will need to find a cop, find a gun, steal a helicopter.

But even if I should somehow ditch these guys, time is on their side. They know what I look like; they know where I'm staying—*was* staying. Going back to my room would be suicide. They have separated me from my money, my passport, and most of my clothes. All I've got is my beach togs, my Ray-Bans, eight dollars, and my lucky golf ball. This must be what Charlie Cadeaux meant about being *painful to watch.*

I walk another two hundred yards, and, when I turn again, I see that Fu Manchu and his cronies have fallen in step behind me. They are walking four abreast, hands in the pockets of their gaudy shorts, their shoes tucked in their armpits. They are like a flying wedge parting the humid air. That air gets pushed ahead of them, out far enough to strike me in the back. I am being prodded along by their smirking disdain, their punkish conceit. It's the look I remember from high school, from faces of guys I fought. Somebody gets dis'ed and he tells his buddies. The home-boys assemble; they thump their chests and get primitive. Joe Cool After School. *West Side Story.* Only we're not going to rumble over this turf. They're simply going to present arms and ventilate my ass. Here, on this gorgeous Mexican beach in front of drunken frat boys and gawking dudettes. Here, within hailing distance of Tommy Delorme.

I am trying to swagger, trying to wade in the gentle surf without collapsing. I tell myself, *This is not my fate.* I did not survive what I have, learned all I know just to get whacked like a lamb, like Kohler's friend Barry Seal. I will escape by force of will. I will improvise; I will prevail. Just let it be dignified.

Of course, that is exactly what my escape is not—dignified. I wish I could say that I stole some cop's gun and blew my assassins away. I wish some speedboat had veered out of control and killed them all. But what I end up doing is bribing some guy to haul me away on a floating banana.

I'd never seen this contraption before, but I guess banana-boat rides are a real institution. Every year, it's something new; parasailing, Boogie boards, paddleball—and now this guy on a Jet Ski, trailing this inflatable obscenity and charging people to ride on it. I see him shoot by and head to the shore, about thirty yards in front of me. The thing I notice, besides the absurdity of it, is how *fast* he moves. Fast enough to put lots of space between me and my entourage. And so before I can stop myself, before I can worry about how it looks, I go sprinting down the beach and into the surf where this wiry Jamaican guy is sitting, revving his whiny engine.

How much? I'm asking—panting, *gasping*.

Ten bucks for twenty minutes, he replies. Give you a full circuit of the bay.

I don't need a full circuit; I need one-way. Will five bucks get me off the Zona Hotelera?

Got no *meter*, he says. Ain't no taxicab, mon.

I glance back and see that the four beach bums have taken their shoes from their armpits and begun jogging our way.

Take me as far as five bucks goes, I say. Then I straddle his huge rubber toy. The pilot kicks up his throttle and we go lurching out, away from shore and into the fading light. I hunch over a hand strap, not looking up until the water beyond our wake turns darker, until we pass the shallow bottom and the likely range of the four *pistoleros* on shore. They don't shoot; they don't even pull their guns. When I finally look back, I see that Fu Manchu is back on his phone, but the others are just standing in the water watching me flee aboard a giant floating banana. I improvised and I prevailed. The only problem is, now I have three dollars and no I.D., no credit cards, and no other clothes. I don't know a living soul in Mexico. And I've been spotted by Tommy in Cancún, in the kill zone, so to speak. This must be what Indigo meant about running out of luck.

Chapter Eighteen

I'm trying to blend in, trying to do the beach-bum, Moondoggie act, and I picked the wrong place to do it. I had to get away from Cancún because I'm a marked man on the streets and beaches. So I hitchhike down the coast to a town called Playa del Carmen. There is no Zona Hotelera here, no nightclub strip or theme parky malls like Cancún has. It looks like Playa del Carmen evolved from a fishing village to a tourist town in the last five years. Siesta would nearly shut down the place if it wasn't for the pier action.

Most of the local commerce involves fleecing the touristas who catch the ferry or the hydrofoil to the island of Cozumel. They pile off of buses and taxis and pile back on a boat. Carmen's merchants and hucksters get about fifteen minutes to sink their hooks. These bony, thin-faced Mexican boys taunt the procession as it moves toward the pier: "Come in, come in, we make a price." And the tourists who get derailed seem to go for the straw beach mats, the straw hats, the straw anything. The tavernas prosper in those parched, lazy minutes between boat dockings, pushing the *cerveza* and daring people to try these white-hot nuclear chile peppers called *habaneros*. Get a gringo to bite a *habanero* and you've just doubled your liquor tab.

There are a couple of small hotels and some bungalow units fronting the beach. The residents swim, but almost nobody else does. Pity, because I found it nicer than Cancún—no frat boys with boom boxes; the swells are perfect for bodysurfing. And since I can't afford to do much else, I kill an afternoon dozing on the beach. No jets roar overhead; no hit men threaten my life. It is possible for me, in my woozy, semiconscious state, to imagine that things are fine; that my cover isn't blown; that I am not indigent, dead meat. A street person with a price on his head. A chancre on the dick of humanity. No, there is something in the sun, in the tropical breeze that lets me deny all that. The Mexican term is *mañana*. I will solve this *mañana*. They will kill me *mañana*. Today, I will sleep it off.

When *mañana* actually comes, the new day finds me bundled under a sailboat that one of the hotels rents to its guests. I'm fighting off a surprising chill, wishing I'd done the proper transient thing and slept in a cardboard box. I can't fight the elements dressed like this, I'm thinking as I stumble to a fountain and rinse my face. I'm going to have to rob someone and steal their sweater, their serape, their bathrobe. . . . And why not some money while I'm at it? Yes, I'm thinking, I flew this far and lived this long to become a purse snatcher. *This* is the scam that Indigo thought would appeal to my darkest nature. She lectured me on how I don't have criminal instincts, how I'm overmatched against Tommy Delorme. But rather than dwell upon Indigo, I park it on the beach, gaze at Cozumel on the horizon, and consider what Tommy Delorme might do in my position.

If Tommy were trapped in Mañanaland with no money, what would he do? Tommy with no money is tough to imagine, but my best guess is that he'd play gigolo. Tommy would latch on to some tender wench, a meal ticket in skirts. I'll bet he would trade off looks for a gullible groupie mentality. And I'll bet he could score big in Cancún, maybe even in Playa del Carmen.

I am more inclined to go retail, sell straw hats or coconut carvings at a whopping markup. And like a lot of the locals, I would get off the streets and work the beach, moving among the towels and *turistas*. I see guys roaming with Polaroid cameras, taking photos and selling them. There are weavers making hats to order out of palm fronds. Another guy is hawking Frisbees and paddleball and hula hoops. There are women who will cornrow your hair, do braids for two bucks a pop. All kinds of beachfront, towelside commerce; all kinds of novelty scams. And after ruminating for an hour or two, I hatch a novelty scam of my own.

It comes out of sun block I applied to my face before I left my room yesterday. It was a twenty-power or so, real industrial strength. Apparently, I smeared some on my leg, because I see this white patch forming above my knee as I lie on the beach at Playa. Not just a white patch but a sort of rosette design, a fluke straight out of Ripley's. And the more sun I get, the better it looks. So I think to myself, *That* is at least as interesting as cornrows. Like a temporary tattoo. And it negates all the fears people have about dirty tattoo needles and excessive sun exposure. A compromise for the nineties.

So I stroll back into town and blow my net worth on a fine-point brush. And while the clerk is distracted, I shoplift some colored sunblock. Sorting through all these art supplies takes me back to high school, to art class in tenth grade. Art was the only subject I wasn't failing at the point when I dropped out. I liked art because I was good at it, and because most of the time nobody was lecturing you, giving pop quizzes or reading your essays out loud. You could talk to chicks in art class. The teacher liked rock 'n' roll, and he let us play the radio or even bring records. But I mostly liked art because I could paint and draw—and not just copying pictures. I could pull images out of my head. And as I'm carrying the stuff back through Playa del Carmen to the beach, I'm thinking, I'll bet Tommy Delorme can't draw a circle with a compass; I'll bet he can't even trace his own hand.

My pitch is a little shaky at first. The object is not to sound like a lecher while offering to do body paintings on perfect strangers. It would also help if I had a shave or a clean shirt, but eventually I get it down. I walk up to two or three coeds lying on towels and ask if they need sun block. *We've got plenty*, they say, and I open my shirt and tell them, Maybe, but not like this. I've done this parrot design from my collarbone down to my sterum. It looks good for an upside-down creation; maybe a little owlish in the head. But it gets people's attention, gets them talking, and pretty soon they're willing to have a fifty-cent rosebud done on their shoulder, maybe a dollar for a skull and bones. *Shower that off, and you'll have a nice silhouette,* I tell them. I'll do touch-ups for half price tomorrow.

I cover my overhead by noon, and the rest of the day is profit; an anchor on the chest of a sailor, a Batman symbol on a little boy's hand. A daisy here, a lizard there. I even do some cleavage and buttock work, but mostly it's shoulders and arms. By the time dusk settles in, I've made enough for a decent meal, or perhaps for a flophouse room. I'm debating how to spend it as I'm doing my last design of the day, a two-color toucan on the shoulder of a girl named Monica from South Dakota.

The big, elaborate toucan is consistent with Monica's taste. She wears the skimpiest, loudest neon bikini on the beach. She's got sunglasses with neon loops, got those braided ankle bracelets and about six holes punched in each ear, with gaudy hoops and parakeets dangling there. The friend who shares Monica's blanket and beer cooler is a shade less flamboyant. She is a broad-shouldered farm-girl type named Rita. Rita wears her one-piece suit very high on the hip, but a lot less hardware on the ears. She is quite leery of this unshaven Italian and his sun-block scam, this artiste who wears bicycle gloves. While Monica jabbers about her life and times, Rita turns away and studies me out of the sides of her Vaurnets.

Monica offers me a beer when I finish painting, because she isn't quite finished with me. She is telling me how she and Rita both work at a screen-door factory back home. Monica does moldings; Rita installs latches. Back home, they also play slow-pitch softball, watch rodeos, and sing along with *Karaoke* machines in shit-kicker cowboy bars. Monica tells me that *Karaoke* is what launched them on their trip. Rita entered a contest, sang along with some Travis Tritt "your cheatin' heart" kind of song, and won third place, a hundred dollars. We put that straight into our vacation fund, Monica says. It pushed us over the top; and here we are.

Rita interrupts long enough to correct Monica on the name of the song. Then she looks at me over the tops of her sunglasses and asks how long I've been in Mexico.

Few months, I lie. I pretty much bounce around the Caribbean. All's I need is a beach and a vacation clientele to practice my trade.

So you've been here long enough to meet the locals, get *connected,* Rita continues.

I'm not certain where this is leading, whether she wants me to recommend a restaurant or get her parking tickets fixed. So I take a sip of their beer and tell them I'm as connected as I want to be.

Then perhaps you can score us some blow, Rita says, and I nearly spray them with a mouthful of beer. You chase the dragon, don't you, Danny?

I could really use a toot, Monica adds. All this beer is making me sleepy.

Chase the dragon? A toot? Last time I heard those expressions, I was stepping in dinosaur shit. I feel like answering, No, I'm into reefer madness. But I'm not thinking clearly. This coke proposition is the first thing they've said that truly shocks me.

It's exactly what I need to get this vacation rolling, Rita continues. And since you're almost a native, I thought maybe you could show us the ropes.

The two of them start talking about their last—and perhaps only—coke experience while I try to figure a way to exploit this opportunity. It's been apparent since I first chatted them up that they were glad to see me. They haven't exactly fought off the guys since landing in the Yucatán. Perhaps I'm the first guy they've talked to who isn't a waiter or a hotel clerk. How would Tommy Delorme handle this? Go with the flow, I imagine. Set the hook and reel them in.

I can get you plenty of blow, I tell them. You give me some cash and I'll set it up. The less you guys know, the better.

How much cash? Monica whispers.

Hundred bucks should do it, I say.

Hundred! Why so much—this is Mexico, isn't it? Rita says.

That's precisely why, I tell her, droll as hell. You're going to trust some clown selling blow for twenty dollars a gram? I wince; I shake my head. I'm so hip, so connected. The girls roll together on their blanket and confer for a minute. Then Monica pulls on her shirt and begins packing her bag while Rita closes the deal.

We've got the cash in a lockbox at the hotel, she says.

So go, I say. I'll wait.

It's over on Cozumel, she replies. Maybe we can meet back here tomorrow. . . .

I'm movin' on tomorrow, I say. Who knows, maybe I'll work Cozumel. In fact, that's where my best contact is. . . .

Then come across with us! Monica says—before Rita jams her with an elbow. She's taking this one step at a time. I haven't exactly won her confidence.

You're saying this deal would go down on Cozumel? she demands.

Why not? I say. Dealers go where the big money is. I can score over there in half an hour.

Rita takes off her sunglasses and gives me a very calculating stare. Does she read auras? I'm thinking. What color am I now?

Why not? she finally says. If we don't get rolling, we'll miss the boat.

During the channel crossing, I try to formulate a plan for ripping off Monica and Rita. My thoughts are distracted by Monica's recitation of their entire vacation to date. They have toured the Mayan ruins at Tulum. They took wind-surfing lessons. They snorkeled on Cozumel and partied in Cancún but got weary of "high school twerps" in the bars there. Apparently, "I have a condom" is a popular pickup line. Rita interjects that real men are few and far between. Judging by their attention to me, I guess I qualify. I suppose if I had cowboy boots and a rodeo buckle, they'd be fighting me out of my clothes. That's how it goes with gigolo roulette.

The plan when we hit the island is to "freshen up" before exploring the nightlife of greater San Miguel. We cab over to the Mayan Plaza Hotel so that Rita can *soak the salt out of all her crevasses*. Monica says she doesn't care if she ever sees another beach. She wants to find a bar with country and western on the jukebox, someplace that checks I.D.s so the high school gringos stay the hell out. *Amen to that,* Rita says. The implication is that I am invited. Perhaps their plan is to toss a coin over me—loser has to sleep on the beach. My plan, of course, is to fleece them for the coke money and anything else I can get. If they get drunk over the course of the evening, so much the better. Drink enough and you lose your judgment. And when that happens, I win.

I get them started down that road by fetching a six-pack after we reach the hotel. It's a good moment to make myself scarce, what with Rita soaking those crevasses and Monica catching some Zs. I get back with the beer and find the room all humid from shower steam and reeking of hygienic potions. Since the girls have an escort tonight, they're taking extra long in the bathroom. I can hear them squabbling over the curling iron, the mascara, you name it. Occasionally, one of them darts out of the bathroom, and the other one yells for her to close the door. Like I've never seen women's underwear; like I'm even *interested*. Besides, I'm busy rifling Monica's purse. She was careless enough to leave it on the minibar. She has about ten dollars in cash and a bunch of Mexican coins. She's got traveler's checks and credit cards—which I don't want to mess with. But before I put it back, I page through the photo slots. There's a "friends for life" shot of Monica with Rita—probably taken on a different vacation. There's a group shot of women who must be the gang at the screen-door plant. But the first one on the stack, the one that throws me, is this portrait shot of a grinning kid about five years old with mommy Monica and some bearded guy wearing a real cheap suit. *Married?* No, must be divorced. But definitely a mom. I snap the purse shut and put it back, thinking, Indigo is right. Maybe I don't have the stomach for this. Maybe I am out of my depth. But I saw lots of family pictures when I ripped off houses back in New Jersey. I managed to forget those, and I'll forget Monica's, too.

Chapter Nineteen

◆

I must admit, I like the effect that Monica and Rita achieve from all their bathing and preening. They're both wearing backless sundresses and tottering on those elevated sandals with the laces that crisscross their ankles. Monica still overdoes the jewelry, with Zulu beads and bracelets stacked to her elbows. She explains where she bought every damn piece while Rita gets into her lockbox at the front desk. Later, in the back of a taxi on the way into town, she counts five twenties into my hand. The driver watches this in the mirror, then rubbernecks at me and grins. Two women, this gringo has, and they're paying *him.* And he damn near has a coronary when I let Monica pay his fare. I guess he's never seen a gigolo work before. *Pay attention, Pancho.*

I have a simple plan for when we part company in town. They wait, and I vanish like Jimmy Hoffa. If Rita is stupid enough to set me loose with her money, then she deserves to get burned. They can cast their fortunes with some other stud and I'll get on with my quest in Cancún. Until Rita hit on this coke scheme, I found them entertaining, in a ragged kind of way. Monica is a little too fond of talking about "back home." Rita has a mouth like a sewer, but they *mean well.* All they're after is a walk on the wild side, which I'm supposed to provide. Fine. You walk on the wild side, girls, and I'll just keep walking.

So that's the plan; that's my intention until I drop them off at a taverna near the public square. I'm on my way out the door to connect with my mythical "man" when Monica grabs my elbow. Perhaps she sensed something; perhaps she got vibes—who can say? But she lays the perfect guilt trip on me, saying, Try not to spend the whole hundred, Danny. We'll take the change and have a nice dinner when you get back.

Right. Thanks. Gotta go. And by the time I'm halfway across the square, I know that I'm not going to split. I'm not going to be the guy who screws their perceptions of men. I won't be the guy who leaves them dining alone, cursing every swinging dick on the planet. I am walking down a street of darkened shops, thinking how Monica told me they had saved for this vacation for two years. I finger the twenties in my pocket and keep flashing on the face in those wallet photos. Rita even broke down and said how she was glad I "rescued" them from the sailors and the frat boys and the geeks. No problem, Rita. Just doing my job. It's just that I don't have the stomach for it. Never really did.

So Plan B for me is to score the components for a synthetic burn—artificial sweetener, talcum powder, aspirin, or laxative. Maybe all of the above. I can deliver the goods and retain my self-respect. Give them what they think they want. It will be their *big adventure story:* the night we blew coke on Cozumel with the sun-block body painter. And unless I've misjudged my clients completely, the buzz won't even matter. Luis was always so obsessed with quality. He didn't realize that you can step on it six hundred times and still sell it to gringa touristas.

After walking several blocks, I find a souvenir shop with a miniature *farmicia.* I buy baby powder and a roll of film. I beg some packets of Sweet 'n Low off a waitress in the café next door. Then I duck behind a dumpster. I mix the two kinds of powder in the plastic film canister and shake them together. I have to keep sweetening it to cover the baby smell. I'm so preoccupied with this taste-and-tamper routine that I don't notice the two *policía* with their German Shepherd sniffing around the dumpster.

They aren't sure what I'm doing there, but it's clear that I'm not window-shopping. My unshaven, rumpled appearance doesn't help my cause. The dog snarls while its pudgy, bearded handler tugs it back and glowers at me. His partner, a gangly, hawk-faced cop gestures for me to stand and begins the interrogation. I leave the bogus drug canister behind, hoping it blends with the alley trash. Hawk Face speaks perfect English, and the first thing he wants is my I.D. and passport.

I tell him I left these at my hotel in Cancún—the first true thing I've said in days. Of course, the cop doesn't buy it. *Where are you staying on Cozumel?* I don't want to draw anyone else into this, so I say I tell them I figured I would sleep on the beach.

That is illegal, he says. You could be arrested for vagrancy.

But I have money, I explain as the dog bolts behind me and begins sniffing around my bogus makings. The pudgy cop ducks in right behind him while I'm muttering about how I won't sleep on the beach again. I was looking for a youth hostel, I say.

You are not a youth, the thin cop tells me. You are a dirty gringo hustler who was seen in the company of two gringas earlier tonight. We had a report from a taxi driver that they paid you for sex, he adds.

Say what?

He explains that I match the description they got of a gringo hustler who received cash from two Americans. (Pancho was paying attention, all right.) And while the one cop is explaining this, I turn and see that the dog is lapping at the contents of the film canister. The bearded cop snatches it away and presents it to his partner. Hawk Face sniffs at it, licks his finger, and gives it a taste. His partner is grinning and pulling handcuffs from his belt. And the dog gets all lathered at the sound of the jingling handcuff chain. *Hubba-hubba, woof-woof.* Obviously, my case has been heard and rejected. I'm on my way to jail.

You know, I say as I reach in my pants pocket, I noticed the fountain in the square wasn't running. I realize how important image is to a tourist community.

You do?

Absolutely, so I wondered if you might be willing to take a contribution toward its repair, I say. I pull out the wad—my wad, my body-painting money—and palm it toward the cop.

Hawk Face is still mulling over the various flavors he tasted in the film canister. He looks at the money—thirty-some dollars, all ones—and sneers. Then he takes my wad and spends what feels like an eternity reshuffling and straightening the bills. He's stalling, expecting me to cough up some more. He's going to throw it back in my face. The dog sniffs at it and glares at me—like he can actually count.

The cabdriver said there were twenties, Hawk Face says. Several twenty-dollar bills. . . .

I spent that on the coke, I say. I got burned. As you can see, it was bogus.

The cop regards his partner, rolls his eyes up at me, and tosses the film canister in the dumpster. Then he shoves me against the wall, kicks my feet apart, and starts emptying pockets until he finds the hundred dollars. He counts this stack; does the same routine to get all the Jeffersons facing the right direction. Then he nods to his *compadre* and they start to walk away.

How am I supposed to get off the island? I demand. I need boat fare. . . .

Hawk Face turns, peels several grubby ones from the stack in his hand, and throws them on the ground. Have a nice trip, señor, he says. And don't let us catch you sleeping on the beach. We consider vagrancy a very serious offense. Image is very important to a tourist community.

That gives them plenty to laugh about as they meander out of the alley and onto the street. And I'm left to scoop up the littered bills and proceed with Plan C.

I wind up sleeping on the beach, anyway. Some clown with a metal drum wakes me up just after dawn; I guess he's supposed to walk the beach and scare off the gulls or something. He scares me plenty, too, and I shuffle stiffly up to the main boulevard and follow it into town. I imagine what I might say if Monica and Rita happen by. *I got mugged; I got arrested.* I OD'd on your stash, okay? Stick to screen doors and *Karaoke,* you'll live longer.

At the pier, I find out that the first boat doesn't arrive for another hour. There are no cab runners, no free-lance bellhops, no fruit sellers out yet. It's just me and some filthy-looking pelicans. I'm looking out on this great flat azure ocean and thinking, *You don't have any criminal instincts at all. Your impulse is to do something good.* Thanks a lot, Indigo. Don't you get tired of being right?

My first customer, somebody says, and I turn around and see a lady setting up a card table. She's gypsy all the way down to her gold lamé slippers; got the saffrony skirt, the clunky bracelets, the melanoma tan. The leathery tone makes her features ageless, her hawk nose more prominent. And above her flat forehead is this white mane flowing back, gathered with a gaudy scarf. On closer examination, I figure her for a mestiza, probably descended from pirates. She's unfolded her second chair, the one she pats with a big brown hand as if to say, Let's get started.

Isn't it a little early to be contemplating your fate? I ask, walking over.

She shakes her head so her earrings rattle. Her chapped lips pucker to make this *tsk* sound. *I give better readings in the morning. Better rates, too.* Sit, Mr. Early Bird. For three dollars, I will look into your soul.

I'll bet you will, I say, paying up and sitting down in her rickety chair. I pay her partly because I have the time—and because I'm lonesome, missing the only other sage in my life a continent away. And I do it because there's something fascinating about this woman's hands. They're huge and gnarly and square—farm hands without calluses. I do it because I want to see her reaction when I peel off my gloves.

She doesn't flinch, doesn't skip a beat. She just leans over this table with the old-fashioned embossed checkerboard and gathers up my pink skin in those tan paws of hers.

You are right-handed?

I nod.

She turns my palm to the light rising over the water and *tsk*'s a couple of times. *Psychic mind, psychic fingers,* she says.

Where do you see that?

In the shape, she replies, guiding her thumb over my index finger. See how the knuckles curve—like hourglass. There are seven basic hand shapes. Yours is psychic. Which is strange, because you have such conflict with fate. You must embrace it—trust fate in your life.

Where do you see that?

The fate line, here, divides the palm vertically, the reader says. Yours is deep, distinct, until it collides with the head line. That's conflict, denial. Let me see the left.

I strip off the other glove and show her the left. She peers again, then raises these green watery eyes to me and says, Other readers would look at your scars and describe an accident. I will show you where it happened in the lines.

She taps me just below my index finger, then slides her finger around the base of my thumb. Your lifeline: Begins here; you die down here. Yours breaks once, she says. And continues. The burns, they happened then.

I almost died, I tell her.

You will be tested often in your life, she tells me. Not like the accident, not necessarily danger. Your Saturn finger shows intelligence. Your Mount of Venus is passion, empathy. And you have stars—

What are they?

The points where lines converge, she says. See? They almost always mean good fortune.

She points out the little clefts that look like asterisks. I'm relieved enough to get specific—get my three dollars' worth.

So what conclusions do you draw about me, about my character? I ask. Who would you say that I am?

The reader studies my right again, brushing a finger over my palm as if smearing in some lotion. Then she raises her eyes and says, If you're not very rich, you should at least be very wise. The wealth comes from good fortune; the wisdom comes from surviving death. However, a psychic man who spurns his own fate will never be happy.

She offers to deal the tarot for another buck, but I thank her and walk away. I leave the gloves there, on the ground, because I figure I'm finished healing.

Chapter Twenty

◆

Now that I've surrendered myself to fate, I find hitchhiking works like a charm. It took me five rides to get down the coast to Playa. It takes me one to get back to Cancún—a cabdriver rolling back empty. He drops me at the Zona Hotelera, and I head straight for the deck chairs along the seawall. People who stake out a chaise lounge usually leave some article of clothing. In the course of an hour, I manage to steal a Panama hat, a safari-type shirt with epaulets on the shoulders, and a canvas bag full of towels and flip-flops. Put all of this on and I am transformed into Wally Weekend. I'm gambling that this ensemble will save my life. I don't know how big Tommy's entourage is, how many beach boys are chasing the price on my head. But if I keep my old shirt and hang my face out there, I could find out in a hurry.

With my boosted disguise in place, I'm tempted to return to the hotel and check my old room. If for some reason the boys failed to rip me off, I'd be back in business. Six thousand dollars, my I.D., and my passport is a tough sacrifice. But I always trust my gut, and it says that there's some punk in the lobby just praying I'll come drifting back. I call instead, checking for messages in the name of Darrel Fuller. I am told to call a Miss Kathy Karpoulis in room 925.

I am a little dazed by this revelation—I had hoped against hope. But did she come because she wants me, or because the Juneau climate drove her away? The only way to find out is to call, so I do. Indigo answers and uses the same flat, impersonal voice she used on her phone machine. All that's missing is the sitar mood music. We get through the how-was-your-flight discussion and she finally says, Nice of you to check in again. I've been ringing your room since I got in. I even knocked a couple of times—

Don't go near my room, I tell her. You don't want to knock on that door.

Where are you calling from? she says. Where have you been?

I tell her I'll explain it all but that we have to meet somewhere else. I pick a club on Kulkulkan Boulevard called Señor Froggi's—real crowded and loud and impersonal. Not much for romance, but I figure a college hangout is the last place they would look for me. It's only teenage wasteland. Of course, Indigo has no trouble spotting me amid all the moussed-up hair and sunburned baby fat. I'm the only guy in the place who isn't bobbing his head in time with the Dolby backbeat. But I catch myself leering like a pimpled freshman when Indigo starts across the room toward my table.

I guess this qualifies as our first real date, and Indigo is taking it seriously. She's wearing a short, gauzy black skirt and heels—enough to stop traffic alone—with a green shimmery silk blouse that drops off of one shoulder. I notice that bare shoulder is delectably brown; in fact, Indigo's arms, her bare legs, and her amused-looking face are all a shade and a half darker than I remember. She has been here less than two days and she is already into earth tones. And as I help her with her chair, I can't help thinking how effortless the effect is, how *impulsive*. Indigo has this incredible thrown-together, sultry look—no makeup, no jewelry, no pretense. Monica and Rita could toil for hours and not get the same effect. Actually, Indigo could teach them a few tricks. Less is more. Knowledge is power. Travis Tritt sucks.

I suppose I should say something like *buenas noches,* Indigo says. I'm still gripping the back of her chair, and I lean over as she puts her clutch purse on the table and give her a hello kiss. She's not impressed. Maybe it's the public-display-of-affection crap, but I suspect it's something else. I settle back into my chair and try to keep the pimply freshman within me at bay. I don't want my aura to project anything obscene.

Interesting restaurant is her next comment, spoken with the kind of irony that demands an explanation. She'll get it, but I'll get mine first.

So, Danny, I say, it's nice to see you're still alive. Thanks for the plane ticket.

She gropes across the table for my hand, squeezes it, and says, Danny, I really am glad to see you. Thank you for the plane ticket.

Then she follows her hand with her eyes, and I can see her phrase the obvious question—and then stop herself. *Why aren't you wearing your gloves?*

Dropped a few bad habits since Juneau, I say. Lying, stealing, hiding my faults. Wearing the gloves just called attention to the scars.

Indigo strokes my palm in silent agreement, then flags the waitress and orders a piña colada. Do they serve food here? she wonders.

We don't need to eat here, I say. We don't need to eat until later.

I put the kind of inflection on *later* that I had not intended. Lust has a way of intruding like that—involuntary, subliminal. It's just that I never wanted a woman so badly—or needed a friend so much. But this friend is keeping her distance, *blocking,* as it were.

So where have you been? Indigo asks. I thought we agreed on the El Presidente. . . .

I tell her the short answer is that I am a lamster; I have a price on my head. The whole story is a personal odyssey, a kind of pilgrimage.

Indigo tastes her drink and says she knew I was on the lam

before she reached Cancún. A Special Agent Pierce visited just before she left to ask if she knew my whereabouts.

Pierce *released* me in Juneau; they don't give a damn—

Please let me finish, Indigo says. She sips again, wipes away some colada froth, and says, You're wanted for questioning in connection with a homicide in Lafayette, Louisiana.

Eddie . . .

Eddie Moore, she says. According to Pierce, he was murdered and his house was torched—a house that was also a production lab for amphetamines. They said it looked like a deal gone sour—double cross, vendetta. Sound familiar?

I don't deny I was there—

Good, because if you did I would walk out right now, Indigo says. They knew you were there because you told them to investigate the place the day after—

Indigo, I didn't kill Eddie, I say. Am I stupid enough to call the feds in on my own murder scene, run a flag up a pole that says ARREST ME? You're supposed to discern this stuff, right? You're so intuitive—what do you think? Am I lying? Am I blocking now?

You ever heard about a persecution complex? she says. Criminals who beg to be caught? You said yourself that you're looking for a way out of the life. Prison is one solution.

Not mine, I say. Do you want to hear it? Do you want to know my side of it? Or do we part company—say *vaya con Dios*, thanks for the plane ticket . . . ?

Okay, I believe you didn't kill him, Indigo says. I came down here because I didn't believe it, and because I hate to be wrong. I hate having my perceptions of people shattered. I hate being a one-night stand for a pathological liar.

And fugitive, I say. Don't forget the lamster part.

Fugitive from God knows what, Indigo says. She's avoiding my eyes, but I detect the subtlest twinge of a smile. When it does come, it warms her face, warms the room. This is not a lost cause, I'm thinking as I stand up and take her hand.

C'mon, I say. There's tables outside. We need someplace quiet to talk.

* * *

We sit under the stars, overlooking the lagoon, and I tell Indigo that I think Eddie Izod was killed by Alonzo's goons. He was killed because he was skimming, and he was launching a crystal meth business without rendering unto Caesar. He was also working with Tommy Delorme to sell ether to the cocaine labs. Alonzo's boys probably beat that information out of him. In fact, they might know as much as I do, and we might see them down here, too.

And how much do you know? Indigo asks.

I tell her about finding my old suitcase, the invoices, and Tommy's progressive phone numbers that indicate an ether-smurfing strategy. I suspect I will find Tommy on Isla Mujeres, I say. I hope I can locate that freighter he leased before it sails to Guatemala.

That's your plan? Indigo wonders. Find the cargo and steal it back?

Who would I sell it to—Luis? I say. No, I'm after Tommy's money courier, his financial officer, his smurf. I want to be close enough to the transaction to hit him like he hit me.

You don't want to kill him?

I used to, I admit. But not anymore.

What changed your mind?

You, I say. And that personal odyssey I mentioned. It's hard to describe. . . .

Try, Indigo insists, so I do.

I run through my failed gigolo scenario, the shakedown by the *policía*. The Cozumel trip was such a rolling fiasco, such a *waste* . . . but I explain that the real lesson was being humiliated, becoming a street person and a grifter. And the Night of the Bogus Coke was very instructive. I've been around plenty of drugs, around stoned people and partied like the fall of Rome, but it took these two hayseeds, these *novices*, to show me how cocaine could conquer Colombia, the Caribbean, and the whole economy of south Florida. The drug didn't do it alone; it was marketing. It's the gram of glamour, the shared ideal, the after-hours club that everyone talks about but no one invites you to.

Coke is the Big Consolation, the not-so-exclusive club for all of the Monicas and Ritas of the world.

So if that's your revelation, Indigo asks, how does it apply to your life?

You told me that all my resources, all my powers, are keyed to survival, I tell her. The plan is to change that. Stop living hand-to-mouth. I know it won't happen overnight, but it will happen. I feel it starting already.

How? What's different now?

I had a friend tell me awhile back that career criminals can't get free, can't get out of the life, because they despise straight jobs, I tell Indigo. They actually pity the working class. Well, I'm finding that I've got the *opposite* reaction. Every straight job looks good to me; *every* lifestyle other than mine is appealing. I tip the bellman two bucks for turning on my air conditioning, but I'd trade places with him in a heartbeat. The clerk who rings up my purchases, the waiter, the parking valet—I envy them all! I envy them because they can *choose*. They can walk away anytime and be free. They won't be killed for changing careers. They don't have warrants and indictments and audits hounding them. Maybe the paycheck doesn't stretch far enough; maybe they can't find true love, but, Indigo, at least they're *legit*. They've got a *life*.

You sound like you want to be worthy of me, Indigo finally says. Like I represent some moral standard. I've thought about you a lot since you left, and, believe me, I wasn't thinking about how I would change you, overhaul you like a car. All that stuff I said about clairvoyance and free will is like . . . like *icing*, Danny. It's one of life's perks. It's also something we have in common, something we could share.

But I don't understand, I tell her. How am I supposed to use this? What's the payoff here?

I get this long pause where I gaze out at the lights winking off the flat lagoon water. Then Indigo says, Projecting in the short term. Setting short-term goals is a start. Worry about remaking yourself after you meet some basic needs. I mean food, shelter, clothing.

Love? I add.

Let's talk clothing first, Indigo persists. Now what's with this safari shirt? You look like Marlin Perkins.

It's part of a disguise, spur-of-the-moment stuff.

And as for shelter—you're avoiding the hotel because Tommy knows you're in town? Indigo asks.

I explain to her about the banana-boat escape, which she finds hilarious. And when Indigo recovers, she takes a swig of my beer and says, Tommy doesn't know what I look like. Why don't you give me your key; I'll let myself into your room and we can at least tell if you've been robbed.

No, that'll look too suspicious. . . .

I'm *staying* there, she persists. I've been coming and going for two days. Nobody's going to get suspicious. C'mon. I'll find a rest room and you pay the bill, then I'll drive us over there and take a look.

You've got wheels? I ask.

Well, I figured since you sprang for airfare, I could contribute, Indigo replies, collecting her purse and standing up. Besides, I needed a fast getaway in case you turned out to be Ted Bundy.

I have big problems with this scheme to liberate my luggage. If those goons did break in, they could easily have planted someone in my room to shoot whatever comes through the door. Indigo blows this off, saying her intuition would tell her if there was danger inside. Yeah, *right.* You read auras through walls?

You did, Indigo replies, reminding me about the shoot-out with Hector in Scottsdale.

We pull up in front of the hotel and I tell her I'd feel a lot better if she went upstairs with a guard. Tell them you're having trouble with your key, I say.

Let me take a reading, she replies. If the vibes are bad, I'll be back.

So I give Indigo my room key. Before she leaves, I warn her not to answer the phone in the room. They could be calling from the lobby, I say. Maybe another room down the hall.

Danny, get a grip, she says. It's only luggage.

So I watch from the car as the bellhops hold the door for Indigo, as they take a long second look at her butt when she strolls inside. Then I'm left to worry about what could happen, what could be waiting in the room. I don't have to dwell on that for long. The reality gets a lot more vivid, a lot more immediate. Indigo is inside for maybe three minutes when a shiny new Range Rover pulls into the drive and parks at the opposite curb. I notice the car because it is both very ugly and very expensive. It gets even uglier when the doors pop open and out jump my beach buddies from the other day. Baby Face with the Fu Manchu is riding shotgun. Three others are in the back, but I hardly notice them because I see that their driver is Tommy Delorme.

Chapter Twenty-one

Tommy's a lot tanner than I remember—a little heavier, too. He still wears the mustache, but his hair is slicked back with industrial gel. And he's got a doorknob ponytail—none of those teensy braids for him. Got the diamond stud in one ear, the Rolex on his wrist; cotton blazer, cotton slacks, and cowboy boots—the only remnant of his smurf costume. He leads his beach boys right past Indigo's car, walking with this sort of rolling swagger that takes me straight back to the last walk I took with him, when we went sight-seeing in Jerome, Arizona. The same thrust of his bony chin, same tilt to the head as he speaks to his scampering minions. One of them rushes to hold the door. Another one remains outside to watch his back until Tommy is inside the lobby.

This promenade takes all of thirty seconds, but it stops time in the way that bad news stops time, like something horrible lapping at your mind in waves, something so sharp and cruel that it can't be digested whole. I have to remind myself that Tommy is not bigger than life—in fact, he's not big at all. Good posture props up his height a bit, but any one of those goons could break him in two. He's just the wannabe leader of a new cartel, the same scruffy ex-con that I found in the desert, just dressed up and reinvented. But the fact of his presence, the fear and rage and helplessness of the moment—all converge on my brain. I could not anticipate how I would feel, how I would react when I actually found the bastard. And the purity of that reaction, the *essence* of it, is washed away by a fresh and numbing fear. He didn't come to the hotel for dinner. They're not hanging out in the bar. Tommy and his entourage are headed for my old room, the room where Indigo is packing my socks and shirts and sniffing the air for "vibes."

I can't dwell on the prospect of them finding her. I have precious few seconds to consider my options for staging a rescue. The obvious one, the immediate plan, is to get on a house phone. Call my room and warn her off before Tommy's posse arrives. So I bolt from the car and through the lobby, not even caring if Tommy left a lookout below. Let him spot me. I'll be the diversion. But nobody spots me in the time it takes to snatch up a house phone and dial. It rings, and nobody picks up. No! No! No! I'm remembering the last instruction I gave Indigo: *Don't answer the phone.* She took me at my word, and I listen to endless ringing. I listen and think, Vibe on this, Indigo. It's me. Now pick up the phone or die.

Time for Plan B. I could rush upstairs (ten floors!), present myself, and let them chase me down the fire escape. That would be suicidal—but effective. Problem is, they're probably at the room by now. They might be inside. They would keep Indigo as a hostage. Tommy would watch her while the goons chased me. Even if I escape, Indigo doesn't. That leaves the final option of a frontal assault. Also suicidal—especially since I don't have a weapon.

I'm standing just off the lobby, doing a stationary jig near the phones, when another option appears. An armed security guard strolls out of the gift shop eating a candy bar. He's a stocky, burly little guy with a Sam Browne belt and a paunch. I'm on him in three seconds, jabbering about a robbery in my room while coaxing him toward the elevators. He nibbles his chocolate and squints at me for a minute, looking mostly annoyed. I pause long enough to let him respond, and all I get is, *Como? No entiendo, señor.*

Just my luck. *Monolingual.* Everybody in Cancún speaks English except him. So I launch into my *mercado* Spanish and we still don't connect. The guy keeps shrugging and pointing toward the reception desk. No, it's you I need to talk to, I'm thinking. You're the one with the *gun.* And as I glance around in frustration, I look up at the atrium and see Tommy leading his boys along the railing on the eleventh floor. Enough, I'm thinking. No time to talk. Time to act.

I've managed to usher the guard over near the fire escape. I open the door to the stairwell and coax him inside with sign language, repeating, *Aquí, señor!* And when he steps inside, when the door swings shut, I spin around from a half crouch and hit the guard as hard as I can with an elbow to the jaw. I really swing for the fences, and it hardly has an effect. The guy's head snaps back, but he doesn't even stagger. He pivots and comes back with his nightstick drawn, cursing under his breath in Spanish. So from the get-go I realize this will not be like fighting Eddie Izod. This guy is more like Roberto Duran—with lots of weapons.

I catch a couple of nightstick blows, then I duck under his arms and drive him into a wall. He jams the club handle into my back while he pumps at my body with his knees. Wrestling like this, holding his chest, I can feel the strength, the brute force of the guy. I can smell his candy breath and feel him wheezing as I compress his ribs. I'm thinking, Bad idea, Danny. But it's not like I can call time-out. I have to hurt him before he can draw his gun and cancel my ticket.

I grope down to his belt while he's busy ramming my back with the stick. *Boom!* I catch a blow and sink down. *Thump!* His knee raises me up again. We have about four rounds of this before I can pop his Mace canister out of its holster and climb up his shirt to his face. He knocks me down once, but I finally press his chin back with the heel of one hand while I point the canister with the other. I start squirting just as he goes for his gun—the eyes, nose, mouth. The rest is reflexes—the guard crying out and rubbing his eyes. That distracts him and allows me to drive home a couple knees of my own. When he collapses, I mace him again and then go for the handcuffs in his belt. I lock one end to his wrist, the other to the handrail.

Now I figure the guard is subdued enough so I can step over him and take his gun. He's blind from the macing and half-conscious from a shot at the groin. But while I'm freeing the pistol from his holster, I find he has enough fight left to reach out with his free hand and grab my balls. I know I could never do that to another man, but this guard isn't shy at all. His short, thick fingers close on my jewels and I feel these daggers of pain radiate from my crotch. The whole world goes dark for a moment, and I sink down as he pulls me, steers me with his grip. But I have the gun free now, and, with my last gasp before falling unconscious, I swing it butt end first and catch the guard in the temple. His head rolls, and this time it doesn't snap back. His hand goes slack and we both collapse at the foot of the stairs.

I lie there for moment, staring up at a security camera, wondering who witnessed this whole ordeal. If somebody was on the monitor, I'm going to have company real soon. How much time do I have? How long were we fighting? *Too long,* Danny. Long enough to sap any strength I have for a fight with Tommy's boys. Too long for me even to consider walking up the stairs. So I shuffle to my feet, stow the gun in my pants, and try to smooth my clothes. Then I do a little side step out the fire escape door to disguise my limp. I wait with a bunch of German couples for an elevator, then ride up with them, stopping at four other floors before I make it to ten.

I'm still walking funny as I follow the rail around toward my old room. I've got one hand on the gun under my shirt—a revolver, a .357 by the heft of it. I will have six shots to stop five guys, assuming I get my chance. I will need more ammo if I have to face other guards. The thought of the guard reminds me to look over the rail—down to the fire escape door—to see if there is any commotion. No problem there. But while I'm watching, the elevator opens in the lobby and Indigo steps out with Tommy and his friends. They're smiling and talking and he's carrying her bag—my bag—as they walk toward the door.

It doesn't even look like a kidnapping. Nobody has a hand in a jacket pocket, or a hand on Indigo. Tommy is grinning and jabbering away about something as a beach boy holds the door and they walk right out of the hotel. Go figure. Live long enough and you get to see everything. But what I need to see is whether or not they leave together. So I'm hitting the DOWN button on the elevator and trying to compose myself. Of course I don't get an elevator, so I have to hobble to the fire escape and stumble down ten floors to the lobby. I reach the landing, to find the security guard up and alert, groping in his pocket for his handcuff key. I slap it out of his hand on my way by, and the key goes skipping down toward the basement. Then I'm out the door and gimping my way across the lobby—bathed in sweat, looking rumpled as hell, but nobody seems to notice. Outside, I see Tommy's Range Rover turning onto the street.

I'm about to flag a cab when I notice that Indigo is in her car, at the wheel, waving to me. She hits the horn and grins. *Beep-beep.* A bellman opens the car door, then loiters for his tip. I climb inside and Indigo points at the street, says, You see that guy driving the Range Rover? That's your man, isn't it? That's Tommy Delorme.

Yeah, I groan. That was him.

Let's go then, Indigo says, tromping the accelerator. They've got a lead, but I think I can catch them. She glances over, her dark eyes all wide with excitement, her mouth going a mile a minute. I *knew* it! I just knew it was him! I was in the room packing and they came to the door, wanted to know who I was, what I was doing there. I bluffed them, Danny, said I had only been in a day, said I was moving on to Isla Mujeres. Made it look like I was on my way out—walked right by them. He's *suave*, this Tommy guy. Hit on me all the way down the elevator. *Insisted* on carrying my bag. Wanted to set me up with a new hotel, give me a lift in his van. . . .

I hoist myself in the seat so I can see the road. I'm a little sick, I say. Do you have to drive like this?

He'll get away! Indigo replies. I mean, you've tracked him this far, at least find out where he lives.

So we go speeding along a lighted strip of the boulevard and Indigo finally takes a long look at me.

Danny, your aura looks like fireworks. You tore your shirt. What happened to you? she says.

I look down and notice for the first time that my left sleeve is hanging by threads at the armpit. The shirt is drenched with sweat and I bear a lingering odor of Mace. I draw the .357 out of my belt and show it to Indigo.

I jumped a security guard and took his gun, I say. We fought in the fire escape.

What for? she demands.

He didn't speak English, I say.

Well of course, then he had it coming—

Because I watched Tommy walk into the building, watched him head upstairs to my room. I called; you didn't pick up—

You told me—

I know, I say. But I didn't have a weapon, didn't have a lot of options. I figured they would kill you. . . .

Indigo takes her hand from the wheel, strokes my face, and smiles. It's a patronizing gesture, but I'm too wasted to fight about it. She spins the wheel and we go careening around a corner. The car rights itself, but my head keeps spinning. *Very distinctive taillights,* easy to follow, Indigo mutters to herself. Remembering me, she nods her head toward the backseat, says, Did you notice? I got it—your bags, your clothes, your money belt.

I noticed. I'm delighted, I say. But I think I'm also going to be sick.

Tommy heads north, along Mujeres Bay, past the isthmus part of Cancún, beyond the town, and up the coast to Puerto Juárez. The area is much poorer, more residential. It's not exactly shantytown, but there are no theme malls or gringo clubs or high-rise hotels. There *are* plenty of tavernas, tapas houses, and businesses that serve the locals who serve the gringos. There is also a port here, with docks and slips occupied by the fishing trawlers and the charter catamarans. Tommy steers his Range Rover past this district, beyond the fish-processing plants, and into a shipyard with cargo docks for freighters. This is not a traffic area—especially at night. I tell Indigo to pull up and let Tommy get out of sight. We're too conspicuous when we're the only other headlights around.

I can drive without headlights, Indigo suggests.

No, park it. I'll walk in from here, I tell her. (*Limp* is more like it.) I figure I've endangered Indigo too much already. It's a miracle she made it out of the hotel.

I'll hit the horn if I see anything, Indigo says.

You do that, I say, then I'm out and hiking along a concrete pier where I last saw Tommy's taillights. I find his vehicle parked near a manager's shack, where a staircase leads down to the water. A freighter is moored along the length of the pier. From my vantage behind the shack, I can see light leaking out of a doorway under the ship's bridge. Tommy and his pals are standing in this circle of light, hands in their pockets, mulling over the night's events. I watch Tommy shake Fu Manchu's hand—a soul-brother-type handshake—then walk over to the side and skip down a staircase along the ship's hull. The beach boys duck into the door, and I hear the clatter of their feet on a metal stair. With them out of sight, I can crouch at the edge of the pier and watch Tommy. I draw the gun and follow him from above.

He jumps off the staircase onto a narrow strip of floating dock. Normally, a crew would use this to scrape barnacles or paint off the hull. But Tommy's crew has parked four Jet Skis there, linked together by a chain. I watch Tommy skip past these toys and step into the stern of a midsized cabin cruiser named the *Quintana Roo*. The boat is old but nothing pretentious—Carl Dupree's rig in Alaska is twice as long. Guess Tommy blew his wad on the freighter. The *Quintana Roo* is pure utility. He casts off his lines, cranks the inboard engine, and flicks on some running lights. He makes enough noise to cover the sound of gunshots. I'm directly above him, maybe twenty feet—a good percentage shot. But I don't even raise the pistol. It's not because

I can forgive, or even pity, the bastard. I don't shoot because I can't look him in the eye—and I couldn't face Indigo afterward. Killing is no longer the object here, at least not the primary one. Tommy dies and the ether deal dies with him. That happens, and I never recoup a dime.

So I watch Tommy steer his cruiser out from between the ship and pier and throttle it up. In five minutes, he's just a light on the water, buzzing off toward another low string of lights that is Isla Mujeres.

I can hear rock music blaring out of the doorway on the freighter. I assume it comes from crew's quarters—the live-in security guards for Tommy's ether stash. I'll want to investigate the cargo sometime, but first I'll need to know where to find it. So I climb down to the floating staircase, creep forward to the stern, and read the ship's name and registry: *OCHO RIOS*, PORT ARTHUR, TEXAS.

Chapter Twenty-two

◆

Indigo drives me south, past the Zona Hotelera, and we book a bungalow at Club Med. I want someplace where I can slip in and out without getting eyeballed by staff. My friends at the El Presidente could broadcast a description. And Tommy might also have contacts on the lookout. So I hide in the car while Indigo checks us in. It's nearly dawn by the time we confront that awkward moment of a shared silence, a honeymoon suite, and that pulsating aura of mine. Later on, Indigo will check out of the El Presidente and collect her stuff. But for now, it is just us and our half an acre of bed.

Indigo sits in a wicker chair, grinning as I bounce on the edge, testing the mattress (very firm, very theraputic). I hold out a scarred pink hand and she steps out of her shoes and walks over to stand between my knees. Her energy, her aura, is swept aside as I press my face into her. Indigo lifts that shimmery blouse so I can nuzzle her tight brown stomach, so that I can be warmed and enveloped by her. This is something much more familiar than her scent, her heat, her vitality that seeps directly through my eggshell skull. This is pure absolution. This is home. It has a life and a rhythm of its own, this sanctuary we create. It begins with Indigo's gentle swaying, shifting her weight from one leg to the other in time with my roving hands. They rove higher; she loses the skirt, the blouse. We lose everything and fall backward onto this tumbling mat of a bed, this Posturepedic playground.

I'm trying to keep the rhythm going, trying to cover all of the bases, when Indigo calls a halt. She doesn't blow a whistle, but it has the same effect. *You're trembling*, she says, and presses up with her hand at my shoulder. I rise out and away from her, breaking this precious seal of musk, sending all of these vaporous molecules into the air. We can get them back, I'm thinking as I rest on one elbow. Plenty more where those came from.

Indigo lies beside me for a minute, running her fingers along my arm. Is there some urgency I should know about? she asks. I mean, we're not renting this room by the *hour*.

I can take it slower, I say. It's just that it's so great to see you—

I didn't say anything the first time we made love, Indigo continues, but I got the feeling you didn't want the massage. *This* is what you wanted.

Isn't this what everyone wants? I ask, returning her caress.

Certainly, she replies. *Eventually*. But have you ever just held someone? Just touched for the sake of touching?

I can see what this is driving at, what's missing for her. I thought it went fine last time, I say. It *felt* like you had fun.

Of course I had fun, Danny, she says, brushing my hair away from my eyes. But it was the touch—the being held—as much as anything. You're a fine lover; you're *thorough*. But you work around my body like . . .

Like I'm watching the clock, I say. And then I turn away because I know she will read the rest of it in my eyes.

That's it? That's all you've known? she says—*demands*.

Not all of it, I whisper. But when I wasn't paying for it, it seems like I was in some girl's parents' house, humping in the TV room. You never know when mom is going to pop in; maybe kid brother will shoot your ass with a dart gun. . . .

Indigo laughs at that image, then cuddles against my back. She says, You might not believe this, but we all reach a point where touch is all that matters. When I do home health care, I work with shut-ins who don't have anyone else. They thrive on the contact. They love having someone rub their feet, scrub them, shampoo their hair. They purr like kittens. For an hour or so, they get pampered, then it's back to the walker or the wheelchair, back to needlepoint and soap operas.

Yeah, touching is nice, I agree. But there's got to be a *point* to it, right? You can't touch someone forever.

Why not? Because she'll charge you extra? Indigo asks. Not me, Danny. It's all one price. And nobody's parents are barging in on us. Listen—put on a condom. . . .

Now?

Indigo tugs my shoulder, pulls me around to face her back, so that her high rump with its fresh tan lines is bumping my navel.

Put on a condom and come inside, she says. We'll make spoons and go to sleep.

Sleep? I say. Maybe *you* can!

You can, too, Indigo says, ripping the Trojan package with her teeth. You might surprise yourself. This is exactly what you need to relax you, Danny. Take the pressure off performing for me.

Okay, I say. But what if I come?

What if *I* do? Indigo laughs, then she cocks her leg, pulling one knee to her chest as I assume the position. Spoons it is. Into perpetuity. My new therapy.

She is right about the relaxation. I feel my pulse drop steadily down, down into the rhythm of Indigo's breathing until we really are one pulse beat, one mechanism—not colliding forces. And when I finally sleep, I go way down, beyond flesh and sensation and anything remotely erotic. I am drifting deep down in those ocean trenches where the fish have running lights and giant eyes so they can see well enough to eat one another. And deeper still, out of sonar range, there is a radiant, volcanic warmth from the core of the earth. That's where we are drifting, Indigo and I, warm and weightless. Prehistoric sleep. Nautical spoons.

But since this is bliss, not death, I have to climb back out again. I muster up just enough consciousness to open an eye and see that the room is dark. We have spooned the day away. We have become nocturnal. Indigo hasn't budged from her fetal crouch, except to toss an arm back across my hip. It is a surprisingly heavy arm as I lift it, return it to her, and slip out and away from her back. Now we have two different pulse beats, two mechanisms, and mine is hungry, thirsty, and keenly alert. I realize I haven't slept like that since the night I shared Indigo's bed in Juneau. And thoughts of Alaska give rise to thoughts of Carl Dupree. Before yesterday, before Indigo robbed my room and drove the getaway car, I had recruited a conspirator. I gave Carl an excuse to leave his cushy exile and join the cocaine wars. Time has come for me to check his progress, to see if he called my bluff.

I trail the phone into the bathroom and wait out the inevitable hit or miss to get an overseas operator. When the lady finally dials up Carl Dupree's number, my old buddy Jonathon answers. Last guy on the planet I want to talk to, right? He's almost friendly, saying he's watching the place for Carl.

Where did Carl go? I ask, already sensing the answer.

He's in Mexico, Jonathon replies. He said if you call, you should meet him at the Tarpon Marina, in some lagoon. They got lagoons down there, guy?

Yeah *guy,* I say. We got lagoons all over the place.

I forget which lagoon. . . .

I can figure it out, I tell him. He calls, you tell him I'm on my way.

I hang up and sneak back into the bedroom. I dig out the visitor's guide and page to a map of Cancún. I find the big lagoon, Nichupte, and the smaller one, Bojorquez. They are chopped up with little peninsulas and an island or two. There is a channel to the ocean north of Nichupte, but no marinas are marked on the map. I am looking up Tarpon Marina in the phone book when Indigo's sleepy hand meanders down my back.

I hope you're ordering take-out, she whispers. I kept dreaming about Chinese food.

I turn, kiss Indigo's slackened mouth, and tell her that I dreamed about swimming to the center of the earth.

What did you think of the spoons? she says, yawning.

Miraculous, I reply. Just what the doctor ordered. And I'll be happy to order any kind of food you want.

I hear they actually have some good restaurants here, Indigo says. Even a Hard Rock Café. And I want to hit at least a couple nightclubs. You know the one with all the neon—

I stop her with a finger to her lips, saying, We need to talk about this. About the two of us in Cancún. Restaurants make me very nervous. Barhopping isn't such a great idea. Being seen with *me* isn't such a great idea. . . .

Danny, you insisted I come down here, she replies.

Yeah, but that was before Tommy sniffed me out, I say. Before I had a price on my head. I don't want you to miss all the sun and fun. You might like Cozumel. Listen, I want you here more than anything in the world—

I don't get to finish, because Indigo is out of the bed and bounding into the bathroom. She locks the door. I jiggle the knob; I knock. *Don't do this,* I say. Please let me in.

Nature calls, Indigo replies. Talk through the door.

Do you understand this isn't all about me? I say. About revenge? It's about keeping you safe.

Bullshit, Danny, Indigo says. You like running. You like running from me!

Then the door flies open and Indigo strides past me in all her naked glory, starts following the spiral of clothes that we spun off in a kind of lusty dervish. I was wrong about the persecution complex, she says as she's unwinding the lacy little swatch that was her panties. You're in denial, Danny. Avoidance behavior. You see, I didn't come this far to be someone's *two*-night stand.

So where are you going?

Back to the El Presidente, Indigo replies. I never checked out, remember? I've got four more days in Cancún, and I'm going to enjoy them.

I grab her by the arms as she's wriggling into her skirt, asking, What would you do if you were me? Just tell me what you want!

She lets out this extended sigh, sinks backward onto the bed, and finally looks up at me. *I want to help,* she whispers. I feel like I should help you here. I can't love you, Danny. I can't have you in my life until you finish this fucking quest. And you certainly can't expect to do it alone—

I don't. I'm not, I say.

You've got help? she wonders.

I think so, I say. But I can always use more. I just never expected it from you. That whole chase last night surprised the hell out of me.

Surprised me, too, Indigo says. But I enjoyed it.

There's going to be stuff you won't enjoy, I say.

Like killing?

I hope not, I say. Not unless something goes terribly wrong. But this isn't *you*, Indigo. You don't have any ax to grind; you don't have anything to gain.

I just told you, she says, pulling on her blouse. I have *you* to gain. And I have plenty of axes to grind.

Indigo tugs me down beside her on the bed and digs into her purse. She pulls out a picture she clipped from a magazine about the coke lords of Colombia. It's this Fabio Ochoa, the guy Eddie said was so rich. He's a real human zeppelin, goes 350 easy. In the picture, he's riding one of his prize stallions—a horse about half his size. Indigo says, I blew nearly fifty thousand dollars up my nose when I worked on the Trans-Alaska pipeline. Only reason I never freebased is that nobody was doing it back then. All that cash, all that work, and I look at this fat fuck and think, He's got it. There's my life's savings, in that creep's pocket. In his airplanes and cars and in his vulgar house. Paying off his bodyguards, his lawyers, his politicians. Of course, he's got it because *I* gave it to him, but that doesn't make it okay; it doesn't make us *even*. See, Danny, I look at this vulgar cartel pig and think, I want it back. Not even the money so much as the time, the misspent youth. I want what cocaine took from me.

Me, too, I say. Me, too.

So how do you know this Dupree guy? Indigo asks me the following morning as we're driving to Tarpon Marina. I wrote directions on a scrap of phone book paper, and I'm trying to answer her and read my own writing.

You'll like him, I say. He's an Alaskan by way of Federal Witness Protection.

Like him? Indigo says. I probably *dated* him!

We find the marina on a peninsula near the channel that cuts through Playa Tortugas to the ocean. I give the attendant my name and he rummages his desk for a message. He finds a smudgy note on the bulletin board, turns it this way and that like some hologram. The attendant makes enough sense of it to march Indigo and I down the steps and out to the end of a dock where all these cruisers are moored. He stops at a cabin cruiser named *Angeline.* There's nobody on deck, but the engine compartment is open in the stern. There's tools spilled around the hatch, along with rolls of tape and some greasy pieces of hose. And there's cabin junk stacked on the dock at our feet—moldy seat cushions, soggy life jackets, paperback books that got wet and then dried with their pages puffed up like tissue paper.

We hear some clunking under the deck, and the attendant calls out, Hey, man! I think we found your guy!

Carl Dupree pokes his shiny head out of the engine compartment, grins at me with those two thousand teeth of his, and says, Yeah, that's him. Thanks, Pablo.

Pablo walks away and Carl leans his chin on the rim of the hold and cuts a clean piece of hose to length with some clippers. He doesn't look up, just eyeballs that hose and says, So what you say, Danny? You want any of that stuff?

I gather he's talking about the stacked junk at our feet.

Why would I want this? I say, trying to catch the rhythm.

No reason, 'cept you own it, Carl replies. See, we bought this boat yesterday for five thousand dollars.

Chapter Twenty-three

◆

This one, I didn't date. I would've remembered, Indigo whispers as we stand on the dock in front of the *Angeline*—our *Angeline.*

Carl, say hello to Indigo, I say. She lives in Juneau—at least last week she did.

Carl laughs, strips off some tape, and cuts it, saying, Don't tell me; she did a burglary for you, too? You the Pied Piper, Danny? Turn aroun', I'm liable to find ol' Jonathon here. . . .

No you're not, I reply. Feed that little prick to the orcas, for all I care. Now what's this about buying a boat?

Best I could do on short notice, Carl replies. I been in Cancún two days now, and I spen' most of it replacin' belts and hoses.

What for?

So we don't break down at sea! Carl replies. I figure by the time you fetch us some beer, I'll have this can runnin'. I ain't used to this climate. So thirsty, I can barely talk. And believe me, you gonna want to hear what I foun' at Doreen's place.

You found? You hit Doreen's apartment?

Get the beer, homeboy, Carl says. Mayhaps the young lady would like a tour of the boat while you're gone. She bein' a limited partner and all. . . .

Indigo gives me a Say-what? look, and I just shrug and tell her I'll be back. Carl mops his hand with a rag and then offers it to Indigo. Carl's horizontal boom of an arm hangs a moment before Indigo clutches two fingers and steps over the gunnel. I'm turning away, but I hear Carl ask Indigo if she ever sailed the Inside Passage. Just the ferry, she replies, and he says, Then you in for a *treat!* They duck inside the cabin like two old fishing buddies, and I'm off to the nearest bottle shop to quench the captain's thirst.

Carl is true to his word and we shove off as soon as I get back with the *cerveza.* He pops a Dos Equis while we motor out of the slip and along a row of cruisers, yachts, and Cigarette boats. We pass the back sides of high-rise hotels, running parallel to Kulkulkan Boulevard and the beach beyond. This is a different kick than cruising the Inside Passage, but just as gratifying. Beats the hell out of the vagrant life. I've jumped into fate with both feet. So far, so great. Indigo seems to think so, too. Whatever was said in my absence seems to have broken the ice. Of course I want her to like him. It's been a long time since I won something as unconditional as the friendship of this black Ahab, this expatriate homeboy. I can't stop grinning, just watching Carl grin through our shakedown cruise.

New-toy fever. Carl stands at the wheel, at least two heads higher than the windshield, peering out from behind these blue sunglasses. Carl's wearing luminous biker shorts and a neon green tennis shirt (I think we shopped at the same place in Juneau). In between swigs of beer, Carl delivers a rambling explanation of why he's helping me.

Every time I look at my scar, I think about how I shoulda done the world a favor and killed Tommy Delorme in prison, Carl says. Thought about it real hard after you left. And that call you made about needin' a favor was real opportune. Salmon season's over; won't fish halibut again for a month. I ain't been out of Haida in six months—ain't been south in two years. And I broke into enough houses when I was a kid to know my way aroun'.

I was hoping you'd do it, I tell him. But it wasn't polite to ask.

It *was* a house, by the way, Carl continues, fluttering the throttle and listening to the engine respond. Stucco row house with a little-bitty kidney pool in the back. Watched it from midnight to damn near dawn. Jumped the fence, went in through the patio doors.

Carl interrupts this story to explain that he bought the *Angeline* because its hull was solid and the cabin didn't have much wear. Lotta neglect on that engine, he says, taking a deep pull on his beer.

It's real fun to be out floating with the nouveau riche, I tell him. But that doesn't explain why you wanted a boat in the first place.

Heard about the fishin' down here—bonefish, tarpon. Great scuba, too. Always wanted to give it a try. Never had the money. Now I got the money. And I ain't used to sittin' in traffic, waitin' for lights to change, Carl replies. All this bathtub water, gentle surf, I couldn't resist. But before we take this rig outta the lagoon, you'd best look at the goods.

So Carl throttles back and drops anchor among a bunch of sailboats. He ducks into the cabin and comes out with a gym bag. He lays the bag on the floor, unzips it, and walks us through the take from Doreen's.

We'll save the best for last, Carl says, squatting over the bag, beer in hand. Lots of loose papers and jumbled files are strewn in the bag. Carl sifts the stuff until he locates a wall calendar, something from an insurance company, turned to the month of September.

Foun' that in her kitchen. That's your first big clue that the lady's *connected,* he says, running his finger back a week to a citation under last Saturday. It reads: Flt. 1520, 8:00 A.M.

When I flew out to Miami, I made inquiries at the airport 'bout that, Carl says. It's a Pan Am flight, to Panama City, continuin' on to . . .

Medellín?

Close—Bogotá, he replies. Course, they wouldn't say if the Dragon Lady was aboard, but I *deduced* it.

How so?

No luggage in the closets, no toothbrush in the rack, Carl says.

She's got cat food, cat dishes, cat shit in the box, but no kitty in the house. Carl pops a fresh beer while I page forward on the calendar. Nothing else is marked for several weeks, just a reminder note to "Call about Chichen." (*Chicken,* perhaps? Planning a dinner party, Doreen?)

I know what you're thinkin', no return flight, right? Maybe she skip the country. Carl waits for a loud waterskiing boat to pass before adding, But she didn't leave forever, Dan-my-man, not without *this.*

Carl unrolls a plastic garbage bag from a pocket in the suitcase. He lets the contents drop on the deck without even flinching. It's money packs—my former stock-in-trade—six of them. Twenties, bundled in stacks of one hundred. Interesting coincidence, I'm thinking. Just like the bricks I found in Eddie's attic; just the way Hector used to bundle cash for my smurfing trips. Could Doreen have skimmed some from him? Could she have been smurfing for Luis, too?

I whistle appreciatively, thumb one of the stacks, and ask Carl if this was the whole take.

I wouldn't hold out on ya, homes, Carl replies. I paid five thousand dollars cash for the boat, plane ticket, few incidentals. Took my commission. Lady made us *liquid,* Danny.

Where did she hide it?

Hollow lamp on the coffee table, Carl says. Shook it and out they come.

You have done a few houses, haven't you? Find any jewelry in the lingerie?

No, but I got her phone bill, Carl says. Couldn't find it in the desk, the mail rack, the kitchen. Lucky I checked the mailbox on my way out. He passes it to me, unopened, and says, You got lots of shit to decipher here. But nothin' near as interestin' as *this.*

He shifts the papers aside and pulls out a portrait in a frame—the kind people set on the mantel. Only this one is from Doreen's desk at the Covina Clockworks. It's the photo of her grunt son in dress blues, the one who worked at embassies. The one she gushed about all the time.

It's lucky for you that I did this gig, Carl says. 'Nother man would've passed this over.

I've seen it, I say. Doreen kept this in her office. It's her stupid grunt son.

Look at the fuckin' guy! Carl says, turning the picture to keep the sunlight off the glass.

I study it for awhile before it hits me, rolls over me like a runaway truck. Nothing else in the face is familiar, and I've got to fill in the hair and mustache. But it's all there, in the eyes. Cockiest expression you'll ever see. Smug mouth, trace of dimples. Tommy. Tommy Delorme.

It's your entity, Indigo says. The man in uniform, the one I saw during your aura reading.

This is incredible; this is amazing, I keep repeating as I lean back to steady myself on the bench. Nice work, Carl.

You think he's really her son? Carl wonders as he's putting the money back in the bag.

Oh yes, I say. That fits. That helps explain a lot of coincidences—like why these are the same packs of twenties that Tommy stole off me in Arizona. And it explains how Tommy could set up this Bahamian company while he was running a chemical barge down the Mississippi.

Come again? Carl says.

I explain my discoveries at Eddie Izod's, how the Cencor invoices and the Isla Mujeres brochures led us here. I describe how we made our narrow escape from Tommy, and trailed him to the shipyard and the *Ocho Rios*.

You figure that's his chemical stash? Carl asks. Waitin' to ship out?

Gotta be, I reply. He must plan to make round-trips with that boat—if he hasn't already. I'll need some time to sort through the rest of these papers, but from the looks of it Doreen's his chief financial officer. She's doing all the stuff that Eddie Izod tried to recruit me to do—wire transfers, shelf corporations, smurfing the cash.

A *secretary* is doing all this? Indigo says.

She was actually more of an accountant at the clock plant, I say. Who the hell knows what Doreen was before Tommy got her hired on as his personal spy. See, Tommy's in prison serving time for a bust that Luis handed the DEA. He's mad about it, and so's Ma Barker—Doreen. But Tommy's smart—and patient. He plays dusky, not letting on that he's pissed. And he plants Doreen in the front office, where nobody suspects that she knows the real scam. Doreen tracks the smurfs and tracks the clock shipments. And she knows all about Eddie Izod and his chemical scam in Louisiana. She's in a perfect position to feed Tommy whatever he needs to know about Luis's operation.

She'd visit him up in stir, Carl recalls. At least once a month.

He ever get visits from a guy named Eddie? I ask. Dapper little preppie geek?

Name rings a bell, Carl muses. Could be, could be.

Count on it, I say. Tommy had Eddie in his pocket before he ever got out. Doreen was the intermediary. She probably opened channels for him in Colombia, too. So by August, all they needed was seed money, and that's where I entered the picture.

The robbery in Arizona? Indigo says.

Doreen would know how much I carried and where I was headed with it, I say.

Well, if he's got as much ether on that ship as you say, Carl says, Tommy's going to have to carry some cash of his own.

All we have to find out is when and where, I say. Find Doreen Koontz, and we find the money.

I heard that, Carl replies as he pulls up the anchor—*our* anchor.

So I retreat to my new office on one of *Angeline*'s fold-down bunks. Before I start sorting through Doreen's papers, however, I close my eyes and try to get a mental picture of her. This is as close to psychic trance as I want to get. I'm not trying to be mystic, just accurate. So I place myself back in June, waltzing by her desk and tossing the receipts from a road trip into her basket. She's rattling away on the calculator portion of her keyboard, putting figures into her terminal. Doreen spins around in her chair (with one of those ergonomic back cushions) and smiles, saying, Where you been, sugar?

This is about as kind a face as you'll ever see: round cheeks appled up with some rouge; straight teeth and a small mouth formed into this Betty Boop sort of *O*. I can see some of Tommy in her eyes—nothing sinister, just a family resemblance. Doreen wears her hair curled and permed, with one of those auburn tint jobs that never looks quite natural. Bangs just touching high eyebrows. Polyester blouse with ruffles on the collar. Big pendant around her neck. A Seiko watch; no rings. It's like she took a page from my smurfing book: Dress down; avoid flash and pretense. Be neutral, vanilla, invisible. If you register anything, make it maternal. Talk up your son, the hero marine. Pump the smurfs—make that salesmen—for information. But don't let on that you care.

Where *you* been, sugar?

Of course, I'm too happy to park it on the edge of Doreen's desk and tell her about every town I hit, about every hayseed motel. Did the information help her? Did it help Tommy? Look at the scars on your hands, Danny. There's your answer, *sugar.*

It is almost noon when I go topside to brief Carl and Indigo on the take from the house. We convene again on the cushions in the stern, Indigo with my visor on, her brown legs tucked up beside her; Carl with his shades up on his slick, sweaty head, holding his umpteenth beer in the loop of his finger, hefting it to his mouth like a cider jug. I strip off my shirt and begin with the phone bill.

Doreen's long-distance charges seem to correlate everything else, I say. She called Lafayette; she called Port Arthur, Texas, and a number on Isla Mujeres that I expect will match up with that resort brochure I found. But that's not the half of it, I add. That's just keeping tabs on Tommy. The other calls went out to places like Cali and Bogotá, Colombia, Nassau, Bahamas, and Netherlands Antilles.

Where the hell's that? Carl wonders.

Couldn't tell you without a map, I reply. But I remember it

from hearing Alonzo Peña talk about tax-refuge finance. And it pops up again in this. . . .

I pull out a sheaf of papers from a file marked "Antilles." I explain how it documents a loan made by the World Bank of the Netherlands, based in Willemstad, Netherlands Antilles, to Cencor back in Nassau. A Bahamian attorney signed most of the documents, along with Doreen. There's the stub from the bank, and a photocopy of the check: two hundred thousand dollars.

So what's it for? Carl wonders. Office equipment?

A boat, I tell him.

The *Ocho Rios*?

That was my guess, I reply. But I was wrong. The loan was used to buy a cabin cruiser called the *Quintana Roo.*

The one Tommy used on the night we followed him, Indigo replies.

Exactly. And if I hadn't seen the boat, I wouldn't think anything of it, I say. But the *Quintana Roo* was a rust bucket—not half the boat that this is. If the *Angeline* is worth five grand, the *Roo* is worth maybe two. Tommy's car is worth a lot more than that boat.

So why would he borrow for a hundred times the value? Indigo says. They can't skim the balance, because the bank would need a bill of sale.

But you have to consider the source, I reply. Some banks are less meticulous than others. No, what we're looking at here is a thing that Alonzo Peña called a "Dutch Sandwich."

Come again?

It's a money-laundering method perfected in Netherlands Antilles, I tell them. The bank is basically loaning Tommy his own money in a give-back scheme. Sandwiches usually involve a trust company—like the one in Nassau—and a branch operation that cuts the actual check—*this* check, I say, holding up the photocopy.

And that check can go anywhere in the world without getting flagged by the feds, Carl adds.

Anywhere, I agree. But in Tommy's case, it went down the Mississippi with him, buying precursor chemicals. Two hundred grand is a small sandwich in the cartel scheme of things. My guess is that Doreen was just setting up, opening channels for a bigger score this month. That's the good news: I'm willing to bet we're still ahead of the transaction.

What's the bad news?

I've read everything here, I say, and nothing points to the where and the when. If Doreen is in Colombia making deals, she'll probably fly out with the client. They could come here, or they could meet on any island in the hemisphere. They could be doing the deal right now.

The deal is for the cargo of the *Ocho Rios*, right? Carl asks. Man's spendin' good money, wants to *see* the goods. Long as that ship is moored here, we got to expect the man. Jus' takes a little recon, Danny. Little confidence game. Say I meet these Jet Ski college boys, win they confidence. That ship ain't gonna disappear with Uncle Carl on the case.

I suppose you'll also need somebody to watch Tommy Delorme, Indigo says. And since both of you are sworn enemies, I suppose that someone is *me*.

Chapter Twenty-four

Lady's got a point, Carl says while I mull over Indigo's offer. Much as I like the notion of an Island of Women, we can't be hangin' our bare faces roun' Tommy's turf.

I'm not certain that she can, either, I mutter. After all, he caught Indigo in *my* room.

I swear he bought the story, Indigo protests. They were just casing the hotel on a long shot. Tommy expected that you would switch hotels when your life was endangered.

Indigo jumps off her seat in the stern and slides onto the cushion next to me, saying, I even set up my cover. I told him I was moving to Isla Mujeres. So what if he spots me? I'm supposed to be staying there!

Did you tell him you were from Juneau? I ask.

No. Why?

Doreen knows I was up there, I reply. That's pretty coincidental—you being in my room and being from Juneau. It would raise some flags. *If* we put you on Isla Mujeres—and it's a big *if*—you've got to find a new hometown.

Name it, Indigo replies, taking a swig of *cerveza*. Anyplace but Butte, Montana.

Or Carson City, Carl chimes in. Don't want them thinkin' she's a fed.

I take a long look at Indigo, see how pumped she is. Part of it is beer on an empty stomach, giving her all kinds of fake bravado. Immortality vibes.

Plenty hot out here on the water, I say. Carl, why don't you take off your shirt?

Why don't you polish my knob? he replies. Like I need to work on my *tan*?

This isn't about sunshine, I say. It's about educating Indigo. She needs to see what we're dealing with. Take it off and show her the scar.

Carl glowers for a minute and then rolls his empty beer bottle into the cabin. He hoists his golf shirt to his armpits and turns away to look at the water. It looks worse to me now in the sunlight than it did in the Alaskan fog. It's exactly like Carl said: The man didn't know his anatomy. But he sure made his mark.

That'll be twenty-five cents, Carl quips as he pulls the shirt back down. Nobody laughs. When Indigo finally speaks, it is anger directed at me.

So what's the point of that? she demands.

The point is that it's not too late to catch a flight back to the States, I reply. I'd miss you, but I sure wouldn't blame you if you left.

I'd miss you, too. Carl grins. Need three to crew for a bone-fishin' trip.

Then I guess I *have* to stay, Indigo says. She gives me a level gaze and says, Let's play out the string for a couple of days. I'll let you know if it gets too intense.

Carl has really keyed on the notion that Tommy's goons are partial to Jet Skis. He figures he might have to rent one just to get familiar. And he doesn't elaborate on what *familiar* means. All I figure we need is a man with binoculars near the pier; sound a general alarm if the *Ocho Rios* puts out to sea. But apparently that's not close enough for Carl. He wants to know all there is to know about this floating dormitory. So we drop him at a marine outfitters and proceed with Operation Isla Mujeres.

We agree that I will keep the pistol that I stole from the hotel guard. I will also commandeer the *Angeline.* My object is to cover Indigo, remain within hailing distance without getting spotted. It would be chancy at best if I checked into any of the island hotels. We agree that a floating mobile command center is a perfect cover. I can put in at the nearest marina and let Indigo come to me. But being a command center means being wired for sound. So I go searching for a cellular-phone company while Indigo checks out of the El Presidente.

This phone quest takes the entire afternoon. Nobody rents, so I have to buy the unit outright for an arm and a leg. And the electronics shop has no affiliation with Telefónica Mexico. I learn that I need a license, for which there is a waiting list. But after I peel half an inch from one of our reclaimed money packs, I jump to the head of the list. Of course, since I don't have a mailing address, I have to fork over a deposit. Two thousand dollars later, I am hooked to a central cellular command that issues *beaucoup* white noise and static, no extra charge.

I am still working out the bugs on the *Angeline*'s transmission when I swing by the El Presidente. They have a dock at the rear, trailing into the lagoon. Indigo waits there with her luggage while I swing by once, realign, and try again. The engine kills five feet short and Indigo has to pull me in with an oar. But from then on, it's smooth cruising—through the channel and beyond the Zona toward Isla Mujeres. We're half a mile out when Indigo spots this gnatlike object in pursuit. It's a Jet Ski, and I'm thinking that somebody spotted me during my phone errands. I'm holding the .357 at my thigh while Indigo scans the guy with our brand-new binoculars. She passes them to me, saying, It's one of ours.

It's Carl with another case of new-toy fever, doing a flyby on his personal watercraft. He salutes; he waves. He stands up on the seat and hits our wake and goes flying ass over teakettle into the water. By the time I can come about to lend a hand, Carl is mounted and roaring again. He pulls up close enough for a quick hello, then guns the throttle, and he's off to Puerto Juárez, leaving us to explore Tommy's little sanctuary on the Mexican Riviera.

Indigo reads to me from the guidebook as we motor toward Isla Mujeres. Judging by the low skyline, the island escaped all this rampaging coastal development that makes Cancún look like Waikiki. Isla Mujeres is shaped like a dagger, with the main village and commerce all jammed into the butt end of the handle. This north knob of the island supports a fishing port, the ferry dock, and even a destroyer base for the Mexican navy. The Allies built an airstrip along the dagger handle to launch their U-boat scout planes in World War II. Indigo reads on, describing the ruins of a huge estate that a slave raider named Mundaca built for his favorite wench.

Did they live happily ever after? I ask.

No. She jilted him, Indigo says, checking the text. Left him for some commoner.

Figures. They should call it Island of Fallen Women. . . .

Oh, and listen to this! Indigo says, the guidebook an inch from her nose. Isla Mujeres is famous for the Cave of the Sleeping Sharks.

Say what?

It's a dive site, she continues. See, they used to believe that sharks don't sleep; that they have to swim; have to force water through their gills or they die. But apparently there's this grotto here where the sharks come to catch a nap. A natural spring keeps the water moving, and they just *snooze*.

Imagine that. . . .

And you can swim in and pet them, cuddle up—

With sharks! Who would want to—

I would! Indigo says. It sounds fascinating.

Well, you go right ahead, I tell her. I'll keep my distance.

The brochure I swiped from Eddie Izod describes this swinging singles resort called Club Caracol near the dagger point of the island. Caracol and another El Presidente are the only four-star resorts on the rock. I reserved Indigo a bungalow before we came over. The clerk at Club Caracol also gave me a lead on a marina in Makax Lagoon, just below the town. We arrive around dusk, steering past a little pirate theme park on a piece of rock jutting out of the bay. Things are winding down on Treasure Island, all the kiddies getting packed off in cabs to the ferry pier. As we throttle *Angeline* along the boat slips, Indigo watches with her binoculars for any sign of the *Quintana Roo.* She spots it in a slip nestled between a huge trawler and a sailing yacht.

I don't see any life on the deck, Indigo says, still scanning Tommy's boat. If you're worried about getting spotted, we can put in somewhere else.

No, I say. Let's park it here. Tommy doesn't know anything about the *Angeline.* As long as we're not too close, I can watch him come and go.

So we rent a berth for the week from the harbormaster, and he calls Indigo a cab. I've already warned her about being aggressive with Tommy, being anything but furniture. If he approaches you—fine. Be *civil,* I say. Indigo is more concerned about me, wondering if I'm okay camping out on the boat. She says that if she spots Tommy in his bungalow, that means I'm clear to get out on the town, go to a restaurant or a beach. *We'll see,* I tell her, thinking that I don't want to stray from the phone. Indigo doesn't say much as we stand in the drive with her luggage stacked around. But if I could read her aura, I suppose it would register fear. I hold her for a moment, then we spot the headlights and the taxi pulls alongside.

Call early and often, I tell her. And you might want to make a conjugal visit now and again.

Count on it, she says. I pull her back for a last long kiss. Then she's in the cab and off down the coast to her new digs at the tip of the dagger.

The canned hash in the galley has a dubious expiration date, but I fry it up anyway. I take my dinner and two fingers of scotch in a coffee cup out to the prow. I've just settled back against the cabin windows when I get my first call. I rush back to the stern to pick up and hear Indigo's staticy hello. She cuts out periodically, but the gist of it is that she spent nearly an hour at a check-in interview where the staff surveyed her "needs and expectations." *Do you play water polo? Do you need a wake-up call? Do you need to get laid?* Indigo's voice cuts out when she is describing her room. She fades back in during the meal dissertation. It is lavish, infinitely varied foods served buffet style.

That fits; that's perfect, I say. Tommy cultivated a buffet fetish in prison. Speaking of—

Have I seen him? Indigo says. Oh yes.

Of course, the phone picks that time to cut out, and I get snatches of Spanish conversation that sound like air-traffic control. Indigo's signal returns as she's describing the premier suites overlooking the pool. Tommy's bungalow is the best of these. Apparently, her room affords an excellent vantage on Tommy's balcony. She tells me that he spent most of the evening sitting in a deck chair writing on a laptop computer. We cut out again, and I have to ask her three times if anyone was with him.

So far, I'd say he's kind of a recluse, she replies. Doesn't like to join in any reindeer games. . . .

Too busy writing his memoirs?

We'll see, Indigo replies. He might be a day person. Got a full slate of activities tomorrow; I expect he'll be at that bikini egg-tossing contest, or maybe the coed sack race.

Maybe, I reply. We exchange some endearments before the reception gets too dim to tolerate. Then Indigo is over and out, back to this unchaperoned, fabricated gaiety—buffet style. And I'm back to botulism du jour. I get to sleep on plastic cushions in a wool blanket that smells like harbor sludge. But I console myself with the notion that it could be worse. I could still be a street person, mugging tourists in Playa del Carmen. I could be entertaining Monica and Rita—living in gigolo hell. Or I could be in the Maricopa County Jail, waiting to be tried for every currency violation on the books. Yeah, there's worse fates than this, I'm thinking. Compared to the last month or so of my life, this almost feels like control.

I don't get to savor this for long. I wake up out of a dreamless sleep just before midnight because I sense there is someone else on the boat. Sense it—hell, I *know* it. My survival vibes are hitting the general alarm, which has primed my adrenals and scorched my mouth like a *habanero* pepper. Luckily, I am sleeping with the pistol and a dim flashlight at hand. I gather these, toss aside the rancid blanket, and go padding to the cabin door. The instant I touch the handle, I know there is someone on the other side. I don't hear breathing, don't hear any sound but the waves lapping the hull. But this is like the time I shot Hector through a wall—I have the measure of a human form standing in the stern of the boat, perhaps measuring me. I have the choice of calling out, opening the door, and taking a look or just shooting like I did with Hector. The wood is like a peach crate, and a .357 bullet would make a hole plenty big enough to peep through.

Danny? a low voice whispers just as I'm cocking the pistol.

Carl? That you?

Yeah, man. Open the fuckin' door, he says. He doesn't say, Don't shoot; spare my life. Sorry I scared you senseless. And he doesn't give me the chance to read him the riot act when I flick the latch and let him in.

We gotta get over to Puerto Juárez—now, he says. No time to lose, Danny.

Why, what's up? I ask, still reeling from my adrenaline buzz.

Everybody's dead on the *Ocho Rios,* Carl replies. You gots to see it to believe it.

Carl insists we take his Jet Ski because we would be able to evade the cops, should they get interested.

What about Indigo? I say, tugging on my jeans. She might call; she might have an emergency.

Leave her a note, Carl replies. We won't be long, just over and back.

Then he's vaulting the gunnel to mount his watercraft. So I scrawl a note and climb on behind, gripping Carl's waist as he throttles past the NO WAKE marker and then kicks in the afterburners.

The trip across Mujeres Bay would be a lot of fun under different circumstances. The Jet Ski wallows a bit under our combined weight, but I still get a sensation of a cavalry charge, of Hell's Angels on Waves. The bay is empty, and the shipyard and pier deserted except for the freighters and ferries moored there. Carl glides as quietly as the engine will allow, passing under a long pier and between the log supports. When we emerge, we are facing the stern of the *Ocho Rios,* at the dock where I watched Tommy climb into his cruiser. We shut down and pull the sled onto the floating dock. Then Carl stands listening a moment before he signals that he wants the gun. I fork it over, and he starts up the stairs alongside the crusty hull, the .357 leading the way.

We take another look-and-listen at the top before stepping onto the deck. There is no motion on the adjacent piers, no vehicles, and hardly any lights. Easy to imagine lots of shooting going unreported here. The deck light on the freighter still burns, mounted just below the bridge. Carl pops this bulb with the gun butt on his way by. (I couldn't reach it without a ladder.) So now we move across the deck in darkness, toward the door where I saw the beach boys enter during my last visit. As I expected, it opens onto a steep metal staircase. Carl heads down first, creeping and listening. At the bottom, he surveys both directions of a hall, then signals for me to follow. When I climb down, I find Carl in the doorway of one of the crew cabins, the gun tucked in the waistband of his shorts. The ceiling is almost low enough to make me duck. Carl is bent at the waist, his shoulder hunched and his head nodding—nodding as an indication of direction. I notice this, and then I notice the first victim.

Chapter Twenty-five

◆

There is a dead beach boy on the floor of the hall. His surfer shirt is pocked with burned-looking bullet holes—enough to suggest a burst of full auto. He was apparently shot from behind, pitched forward while carrying a pizza. His tan hands still clutch the box, but the pie has slid out, making a round island in a pool of blood. Looking past him, down the corridor, I see a second guy, who died in a fetal crouch in a doorway of one of the rooms. He managed to draw a gun that is still in his fist. He was turning to fire when the hose sprayed him, and the door, and the wall. There are enough bullet holes in the walls to account for two or more shooters. That would also explain why the other two victims never returned fire.

Carl directs me past pizza boy to the doorway of a crew cabin where my buddy Fu Manchu and one of his cronies died. They were watching television when the fireworks started. Only Fu Manchu managed to stand up. He was blown backward over a stack of stereo components. The other one, a blond guy with some design clipped into his hair, was pinned to a ratty couch. Stuffing blew out of the sofa cushions and has settled around the room like fairy dust. Of all the corpses, only blondie has an expression approximating surprise. Just getting into "Wheel of Fortune" when the lights went out.

I turn at the sound of Carl's voice, find him craning his neck into the room. Flooded out my engine in the channel, he says. On purpose, right? Figured I'd use mechanical trouble as a foot in the door. So I walked up the stair, kept yellin', Anybody home? They was home all right. Home for *keeps*.

I step out in the hall and have another look at those bodies as I recreate the hit in my mind.

Pretty close quarters, I say. Tough to get the drop without being spotted. You think the shooters followed the guy with the pizza down the stairs?

Shooters *delivered* the pizza, Carl replies. Took they money, maybe a tip, and as soon as the customer turns his back, out come the Mac-Tens. Guaranteed to kill you in thirty minutes or the next one's free. . . . You think Tommy was cleanin' house?

Oh no, no, Tommy needed to keep this shipment secure, keep things quiet around the docks, I say. If he had done the hit, he would've cleaned up and put some other goons in position. No, this one smacks of Luis Manzanaro. They worked over Eddie Izod before he died and he handed them the *Ocho Rios*. That means they'll be homing in on Tommy, too. And unless I'm way off the mark, we'd better shag it out of here, because this boat is going to sail. Luis is going to want his cargo back.

This boat is goin' nowhere, Carl announces, stepping over the corpse in the hall. You are talkin' to an ace saboteur.

That so?

That is right as rain, Carl says, stooping his way toward an air-lock door beyond the staircase. Have a look-see, he says, tugging on the iron wheel to draw open the door.

I don't know, Carl, I say. All these dead frat boys are giving me the—

Them killers are long gone. You chased this cargo four thousand miles, Carl says. At least see what all the fuss is about. . . .

So we go through the air lock and step onto a catwalk over the hold. The smell hits me first—a resiny pine tar sort of smell that turns out to be the sealant on the barrels. The compartment we enter is vast, with hundreds of barrels of ether here, stacked in pallets three deep. And while I'm contemplating all the blow that this could refine, the vast Saharan dunes of cocaine, Carl is climbing down from the catwalk on a metal ladder.

I've seen it, I tell him. Let's go.

Not yet, Carl says. Show you what I did to the engine.

He's off the ladder and through another air lock before I can follow. When I finally work my way to the engine compartment, I find Carl standing beside the huge diesel power plant with this quizzical expression. He is facing a huge chain-driven set of flywheels attached to the motor. The chain, however, has been broken and stripped off the gears. There are also a couple of other belts lying in pieces on the floor. A toolbox is open at Carl's feet, and a full set of wrenches is unrolled from its case, ready for use.

Don't *that* beat all, Carl whispers.

What?

I took them belts apart with a fire ax and a pry bar, he says. Somebody brought down them tools, tryin' to fix the whole mess. . . .

Somebody was here, I say, while you were making the round-trip to Isla Mujeres?

Looks like. . . .

We're leaving. *Now,* I command, but even as I'm saying it I hear footfalls on the deck three floors above. I hear muffled, Spanish conversation and the clatter of feet on a metal stair. Whoever it is is already in the hallway with the dead beach boys when Carl whispers, *No place to hide in here. We got to get to the hold.*

Then he's off and leading again with the gun drawn, ducking out the air lock and past the first stack of barrels just as we hear the door hinges creak on the catwalk above. Light plays into the hold as we duck into a narrow aisle between the pallets. Judging by the footsteps on the catwalk, it sounds like at least three guys are mounting the ladder and climbing down. I don't dare peek because the light would catch me, and because we're sitting ducks trapped with one exit and one pistol. I have no idea what their business is in the hold; I'm hoping it's not a search of the premises. If they spotted an extra Jet Ski parked on the dock, we could be in for a firefight. I peer over at Carl, and he makes a lever motion with his hand—a hand turning a wrench.

Carl's theory is that the phantom mechanic is back. And sure enough, the footsteps ring past our hiding spot and trail back through the air lock into the engine room. I hear more Spanish emanate from there—Spanish curses, *chinga la* this, and *chinga la* that. There is a second, more subdued voice that strikes me as instantly familiar. I can't make out words, but the tone is formal enough—using the *usted* form—that it resonates. Alonzo Peña always spoke to his *cabrones* that way—formal and aloof and always *usted* and never *tu*. That and the monotone voice tip me off. It makes sense that Luis would tap Alonzo for something this big. And Alonzo would want to inspect anything that looked like sabotage.

I can catch enough from the conversation to conclude that Alonzo is being briefed on the damage. It would appear that Carl's handiwork is beyond a short-term repair. They are vexed. They are pissed. The *Ocho Rios es muerto*. But Alonzo isn't buying it, isn't going to wait for whatever delay the mechanic has proposed. He probably promised Luis he would have the cargo in Colombia yesterday. So Alonzo tosses back a few curses of his own and stalks past, out of the compartment. I can hazard a peek as he mounts the ladder, knowing he will be facing the wall. Sure enough, I think as I watch him climb, that's the guy I first met years ago when I was bagman for Rahid in Phoenix. The man who recruited me out of podunk; the man who also ordered my death. Just a stocky, dapper little guy with a silver pompadour. Not very comfortable on a ladder, not a happy camper. He's probably going to call Luis and give him more bad news.

The two other guys follow Alonzo out of the hold, carrying the broken drive chain and chopped-up belts. When they pass through the air lock, I can hear lots of activity around the crew quarters. Alonzo is giving orders there, and I figure it involves the disposal of corpses. Someone is hugging and clanking their way up the stairs to the deck, lugging bodies to toss over the side. The sound offers plenty of cover for me to fill Carl in on what just transpired. When I finish, Carl says, They gonna need parts. Special order is my guess. This tub ain't goin' nowhere, homes. Guess *we're* not, either.

But he's hardly finished speaking when we hear a guttural, rumbling sound from out on the water, beyond the prow. I'm thinking another freighter is being launched, but Carl yanks my sleeve and whispers, *Tugboat.*

That would explain why Alonzo pulled the mechanics off the job. First priority is to pirate the ether, take possession of the goods. They'll worry about fixing the engine another day. I ask Carl how far they can get towing the *Ocho Rios,* and he says, Far enough to screw up Tommy's gig. Maybe put in at Belize and sell it to somebody else.

Belize?

Maybe farther, Carl says. Depends on fuel, winds, how many bribes. . . .

Interesting, I say. But I'm not riding this scow to Colombia. Not with Indigo at Club Caracol. So I guess we swim for it, right? We got another exit?

Carl shrugs, steps out from the aisle, and ducks along the inside of the hold. While he's exploring, I climb up to the catwalk again to eavesdrop at the air lock. There is plenty of strolling topside, and more conversation in the crew cabins. Somebody is operating a mop wringer, no doubt sopping up all the gore. Other guys are trooping back and forth from the cabins, plundering anything of value. I'm listening to them march up the stairs when I feel the ship drift laterally. There is a jerk that coincides with a louder rumble from the tugboat beyond the prow. Somebody yells something—*salir,* which I figure is an evacuation order. Then everybody mounts the stairs and goes clomping over the deck, across the hold covers, and off the ship. The next drift I feel is unmistakably forward. We are under way.

I meet Carl at the bottom of the ladder, and the prognosis isn't good. Bolted hatches is all we got, he says. Right at the waterline. Even if we did get out, waves'd wash back inside and sink the boat.

We may not have to resort to that, I say. I think our friends upstairs vacated. I heard them stampeding across the deck.

S'pose they want to be able to cut the ship loose, Carl muses, in case they get stopped by the navy. We better start looking for a lifeboat. It's a long swim to Isla Mujeres.

I follow Carl to the air lock and hold the gun while he pops the seal. He tugs the door open and we peer together into the hall. I can see the two bodies are gone, along with the blood and the pizza. The only sounds are the wake against the hull, the sea breeze filtering down the stairwell, and the rumble of the tugboat engine. Carl leans against the wall at the bottom of the stair while I take a quick look in the crew cabins. There is still blood in Fu Manchu's berth, but the television and all of the stereo equipment are gone. Alonzo's goons left the Sex Wax surfer posters on the wall—out of reverence, I guess. There is nothing in the cabins that a guy could use to float back to terra firma. Our next stop is topside, where a half-moon provides enough light for us to search the deck.

Here, we discover that somewhere between Texas and Cancún, the lifeboats disappeared. That leaves the other cabins, storage rooms, and the bridge. We have to break through one door with a fire ax, work another with a pry bar. We find plenty of beer, lots of food in the galley, and a treasure trove of XXX videotapes in the lounge. We find the janitorial supplies, the charts and maps, the volleyball set, and—finally—an inflatable raft with dinky plastic paddles. It inflates with two Co_2 charges, activated by pulling a cord. Carl gives it a yank, and only one chamber of the raft fills. The other sprouts a leak. We are left with a raft in a kind of horseshoe shape. The paddles will be useless; we will have to ride a rubber horseshoe to land.

Fortunately, the moonlight gives us a nice take on our position. We are southbound in the middle of Mujeres Bay, less than two miles from land. The sea is a bit rougher than I would prefer, swimming with half a life raft, but it's not as if we have a choice. Carl lugs the raft around to the stern and pulls off his deck shoes.

I'll jump first; you follow, he says.

I'm looking forward along the darkened, rolling deck of the *Ocho Rios* when Carl reads my mind.

Kiss that fortune good-bye, he says. Next time you see this boat, it be headin' the other way full o' worl'-class blow. At least it won't be linin' Tommy's pockets. . . .

Yeah, but it'll put Luis back on his feet, I say. It'll be like that bust back in Covina never happened.

Unless . . .

Unless what? We get on the radio and send an SOS? They wouldn't get busted, anyway, I say. This cargo is legal.

No, we could hurt 'em lots worse than that, Carl says, rubbing a hand over his sleek head, grinning down at me. We could fix all them motherfuckers if we had the time.

Time?

See, we open them hatches I tol' you about, the ship sinks like a rock, Carl replies.

I like it, I say. I like that a lot.

Problem is, we're damn near out of the bay already. Take awhile to work them hatches. We'll be in open water.

Fuck it. Let's sink it, I say. I can swim.

Can you swim all night and all day? Carl asks. Got no fresh water, Danny. Nothin' to keep off the sharks.

The sharks sleep in caves around here, I tell Carl. Indigo read it, so it must be true. Let's do the hatches and swim for it, Carl. We'll shoot the sharks if we have to.

Carl gives one of his great guffawing belly laughs, says, We'll drown before the sharks ever find us, but I like your style, Danny. *I like your style.*

So back down the stairs we go, into the hold. Carl takes the wrenches that the mechanics left, along with a flashlight and a big maul-type hammer. We work our way forward to the first hatch. Carl sets the flashlight on a barrel so it shines on the hatch. He fits the box end of a wrench to this two-inch bolt, braces himself, and shows me where to swing the maul. *BOOM!* I hit the wrench. It budges—barely. *BOOM!* again, and I'm wondering how far that resonance carries, because we're going to be doing lots of hammering tonight. We fall into a silent, efficient routine, working the rusted nuts on the hatch covers. One by one, they turn and loosen; one by one, the hatches drop. Waves usually lap in before we get the last bolt, and a torrent follows when the hatch drops to the floor. *BOOM!* We keep swinging and working our way along until six hatches are flowing and I'm in water up to my chest. Carl, of course, has a ways to go before he's submerged.

How many do we have to do? I ask.

Gotta sink it *fast,* Carl says. They get wind o' this and they could come down and close 'em up.

So we work our way toward the stern. Six hatches later, we are in water too deep for me to stand. I can't plant my feet to swing the hammer. The ship has taken an obvious list. The *Ocho Rios* probably weighs twice as much as it did when they towed it from port. If they haven't caught on yet, Carl says, they will in a minute.

So we run up the catwalk and out of the hold for the last time. The deck is tilting with every wave, and I know we're cutting it close. I can see a thick black smoke trail from the stack of the tug as it contends with all that new ballast, all of that water weight. A spotlight rakes across the bridge and rigging, but we're already off the stern and into the ocean before the tug pilot stops his boat. Deep troughs lift us as we surge to the surface, sputtering and laughing. It is the first ship I ever sunk, and I'm thinking how great it feels to be an ace saboteur—or at least the ace's apprentice.

I swim over a couple of swells to reach Carl and our half raft. I'm just getting a hold on the thing when Carl says, *Look at the bow drop!*

I turn, looking up at the stern of the ship as it kicks up with a wave and just keeps rising, higher, higher against the night sky. There is a muffled metallic creaking noise that rumbles up from below us, from below the ship as the stern angles damn near vertical. Then we hear a hissing, sloshing sort of groan as the ship knifes down, as the wake spreads away and the rudder, propeller and nameplate of the *Ocho Rios* slide under the waves.

JESUS CHRIST! DID YOU SEE THAT? DID YOU SEE THAT? I'm yelling at Carl, sputtering as waves slap me in the face and I come up hooting and screaming. I come up a third time and find Carl's broad, flat palm over my mouth, his hand closing over my face.

Shut up, now, he hisses. Quit yellin'. The motherfuckers are lookin' for us!

Chapter Twenty-six

◆

The tugboat has indeed come about, still belching heavy smoke as it churns toward the spot where the *Ocho Rios* vanished. A spotlight plays down from the conning tower, sweeping over the peaks of waves and catching bits of ship debris—rubber thongs and plastic jugs and clothing. During a wave trough, I glance at Carl and he's looking more annoyed than scared. Of course, his head blends with the surface better than mine. Hit me with a searchlight and I light up like a marker buoy. As the tug rumbles ever closer, I realize that the orange Day-Glo raft is a liability, too. Carl is thinking the same thing, because he cups a hand to my ear and says, *Ditch the raft! We'll meet up again after they gone.*

That's a scary command for a guy who's never swum in open water. I swam in L.A., and I swam in hotel pools—but mostly where I could touch bottom. But since I'm the one who insisted we sink the ship, who is so gung ho about swimming, I can't start whining now. I splash away as we rise with a swell and the searchlight finds the raft. I see the wave crest illuminated, see the orange rubber catch the light, and I dive, kicking and thrashing under the next wave set. It is funny how safe this feels, how tranquil. I'm only about three feet down, and I break surface on the next wave trough and take a long, sucking breath. I hear the tugboat engine both above and below the surface, every piston fire, every clattering nub on the crankshaft. When the sea boosts me again, I get a side view of the tug—the high prow and long red gunnels with tires draped on the sides. I dip with the wave before I can tell how many men are aboard. I have to assume there are plenty, and that they are armed.

I have no idea where Carl is, but I see the searchlight swinging around, so I dive again. This time I'm down longer, holding position with crawl-type strokes until my lungs call a halt. When I surface again, I find the light has homed in on the raft. The tug pilot has throttled down and they are drifting in for a closer look. I don't dare stroke, don't dare break the surface with my hands, so I try to keep my head clear by kicking. My legs are only good for five minutes of this, so I suck wind and let myself sink again. While I am under, I hear shots—two, three. Shit, they spotted *Carl*! I'm thinking. Found that black head in all this black water!

I don't care if they hear me thrash; I'm determined to ride a wave crest to get a look. But all I see is the stern view of the tug as it accelerates away. Whatever they shot at is gone, because they're not sticking around. The engine sound covers my strokes as I do a steady crawl toward the point where I figure the searchlight stopped. If Carl is hit, I need to reach him fast. And as I'm treading toward the raft I feel an acute sense of death, of the gamble we have undertaken. I think of Charlie, and how I never wanted to lead another friend into this. And all of this gets manifest in anger, so much that I have to suck wind and cry out—the war cry, the rage of the wounded. And then to my complete shock and relief, I get an answering cry.

OVER HERE! Carl calls, and I turn left, dip with three or four wave sets before I see Carl clinging to what remains of our raft.

I come wheezing, splashing up to the raft and ask, You're not hit, are you?

Hell no, Carl replies. Assholes shot the *raft*. Jus' for spite. Lucky the bastards only hit it once. Two holes right here, he says, holding up a section of rubber gathered in his fist. Carl is maintaining a seal by the force of his grip.

Better grab ahold, he says. This baby's all we got.

You can't hold that seal forever, I say, gripping the raft.

I figure we'll trade off, Carl says, ducking his head into a wave crest. One can hold the seal, the other guy kicks.

Kick where? I ask. Which way?

Dawn's about an hour away, Carl replies. We'll be able to spot land by then. Best jus' hang on and rest. You'll need your strength.

What strength? I say.

Pretty sight, that ship goin' down, Carl says. But next time, let's do it closer to land.

Do me a favor, I tell Carl. Next time you stumble on the scene of a contract hit, call the police.

Carl laughs, splashes me with his free hand, and says, You wouldn't miss this ride for the worl'. Sight o' that ship keelin' over, Danny, that's a memory you take to the grave.

My *early* grave, thanks to you!

So where's a banana boat when you need one? Or a Coast Guard cutter, or better still a Windjammer Barefoot Cruise frigate with cold beer flowing from the taps, shrimp cocktails in the galley, topless babes on the quarterdeck. We figure if we're going to get rescued at sea, we might as well do it in style. So Carl and I pass the morning hours with a kind of modified Beach or Buffet. It's a guy thing, this rescue scenario, pandering to every cliché you can name, most of them involving alcohol and cleavage. It's funny how, in our dehydrated euphoria, we start craving all of those faggoty tropical drinks with the umbrellas and swizzles sticking out. Anything involving crushed ice and a blender would suit me fine. In fact, keep the blender, hold the booze, and just bring me—

What's *that*? Carl interrupts.

It is our third watercraft sighting of the day, the pilot tower of a shrimp boat. Unlike the other two—a distant freighter and a fishing launch—this one appears headed for the same landfall we are, on roughly the same track. With a little luck, he'll pass within hearing distance. We are in desperate need of luck, because our raft is damn near flat, leaking from the bullet holes despite our best efforts to maintain a seal. We're both cramping up and dehydrated. But at least the sharks have stayed in their grotto. No dorsal fins circling us yet.

The shrimp boat veers on its approach and looks to be passing north, out of shouting range. He's not trailing his net, so he's making good time. We have all of two minutes to scream our throats raw, to wave like idiots. My last desperate act as the boat runs parallel is to draw the .357. I tip it upside down to drain the barrel, then fire a couple of rounds. The gun fires close enough to Carl's ear to piss him off. But while he's railing at me about it, I notice the shrimper change course and head our way. In another minute, he's close enough to wave at us from the tower. Carl and I exchange that we-cheated-the-reaper look and begin hugging and hooting and partying in the water. We're so happy that we forget the raft, and the last of the Co_2 leaks out. It sinks by the time the shrimp boat pulls alongside and a deckhand named Felipe catches my arm and saves my life.

Eduardo, the captain, and Felipe, his net man, speak no English. Carl is left with handshakes and body English while I spout ungrammatical, effusive thanks. I can't talk long without water, which I get from a dipper out of what was probably an old ether drum. What conversation we manage between gulps of tepid water involves our position relative to shore. Eduardo manages to impart that we are roughly three miles out, and bound for Puerto Morelos. I recall from my short hiatus that Puerto Morelos is about halfway between Cancún and Playa del Carmen. Carl estimates that it took us about twenty nautical miles to open the hatches on the *Ocho Rios*. I can't get an answer out of Eduardo about the approximate depth where the ship lies.

Don't sweat it, Carl tells me as he wrings out his shirt. That ship is *history*. Some diver'll find it ten years from now, get writ up in *National Geographic*.

Right, a memorial to the war on drugs. . . .

If Eduardo thinks we're a couple of cartel goons, he isn't letting on. He's so blasé about rescuing us that you'd think he found pistol-waving castaways every day. He doesn't think to offer us beer or food—but he also refuses my attempt to pay for our ride with soggy pesos. Good thing, too. For after we part company on the fishing wharf, we are faced with transporting ourselves back up the peninsula. We're exactly the kind of dog and pony show that could not thumb a ride in a million years. Frankly, I wouldn't pick us up, either—with our beard stubble and our wet clothes and our concealed weapon. So that leaves cabs (astronomical), rental cars (beyond our means), or the municipal bus.

I think beard stubble and concealed weapons are mandatory on the municipal bus. And it doesn't hurt to follow a black man down the aisle who is six feet six and surly-looking. The overflow crowd parts on reflex, climbing onto seated passengers to get out of Carl's way. When we reach the very back of this rattletrap bus, two young brothers double up and give us seats. And after we sit, every passenger—the field hands in Panama hats, the street hustlers, the grandmas with kids in their laps—all turn on command like some Hispanic hydra and stare at us with their black Mayan eyes.

Most of the reaction is sparked by Carl; but we are likely the only Americans they have ever seen on a public bus. And if they dismiss the notion that we are tourists—where is our luggage? Our tennis toys and snorkel gear?—then we can only be some kind of expatriate banditos, hijackers or soldiers of fortune. (Guilty, on all counts.) They expect the *federales* to pull us over, roust us out, and arrest us any minute. But the only rousting is conducted by adolescent hucksters who work the aisle between stops, hawking icons and popsicles and *tortas buenas*. Most of the vendors are girls in bright satin dresses, with anklets and patent leather shoes; they're like little dolls that float out of the squalid villages, out of stucco ruins and stick huts to work the buses. Most of them stop short of Carl, turn on their heels, and head back up the aisle.

Shit, I don't *bite,* Carl says. This outlaw mystique is getting on his nerves.

The vendors are getting on my nerves, along with the sardine conditions and glacial pace that we ride up the coast. I am worried about Indigo, recalling how we planned to meet up in the morning. I tried calling her room, but the operator wouldn't do collect or credit-card calls. We needed our pesos for bus fare, so I have to grit my teeth and wait until we can reach Cancún.

We don't reach it until early evening. I'm for scamming our way onto the ferry, but Carl insists we head back over to the freight pier and check on his personal watercraft. I'm shocked to find it still there, still parked beside the units that belonged to Tommy's goons. If the dead boys ended up in the bay, they floated out with the tide, because all we see at the pier are dead fish and garbage. There is also no sign of police or an investigation. Apparently, nobody reported the loss of a Texas freighter with all hands on board.

Carl puts the sled in the water, throttles it up, and I hop on for the brisk, bouncing ride to the marina on Isla Mujeres.

Other yachts are just pulling into Makax Bay as we motor in past Treasure Island. Deckhands are wrapping sails and looping lines while the passengers enjoy a nightcap. What light that remains is a hazy pink. It strikes all of the white boat hulls in the marina with a rosy tint. It's all so serene and tropical and lazy that you'd think nothing in the world is wrong. But that's all dispelled when we board the *Angeline* and find Indigo cowering in the cabin—her eyes puffed up and her voice so shaken and stuttery that it takes half an hour to piece it all into a coherent story.

Carl stokes up the stove and opens some cans while I wrap Indigo in the blanket and talk her through the ordeal. The gist of it is that she spent most of the day hostage in her own bungalow, being tormented by Tommy Delorme. She insists she didn't blow her cover, that Tommy never guessed she was connected to Carl and me. But the whole thing progressed out of a dinner they shared at the Club Caracol buffet.

He was fine, he was suave, he was very much the guy I met at the El Presidente, Indigo says. Came waltzing along with his food tray, recognized me, and sat down. *Real* attentive. Hung on every word, laughed at my jokes. Fetched me stuff from the buffet. Wanted to know all about my vacation, my itinerary, my impressions of Mexico. Pretty much your typical soft-sell seduction, Indigo says. It was going on all around us, at every table—that's the theme of the place. Tommy Delorme is just more polished than most. He at least pretended to care about my life, my work, my hometown.

Which was? I ask as Carl serves up hot tea all around.

Home health care, she replies. I tried to tell as few lies as possible. He thinks I'm Kathy from Butte, Montana. Called me Montana. When he was rational. When he wasn't, he called me bitch and cunt.

I get furious all over again, but I don't press the issue. I figure Indigo will get to that part soon enough. She describes her impressions of his aura; dark and blotchy and broken by occasional bursts of color—like flak exploding around a B-17. Tommy has cords leading away from his heart that Indigo says indicate all sorts of unresolved conflict. Grudges harbored. Unpaid debts. *(Surprise.)* And according to Indigo, he also has an entity. Unlike my marine, Tommy's is "nebulous," free-form, and mostly a "presence." This entity/cloud is just unfocused gloom, projecting despair and fear of failure.

It is the aura of a school-yard bully, Indigo concludes. All bluster and swagger, hiding lots of personal demons.

He won't be swaggerin' long, Carl interjects. His demons jus' caught up with him.

So what about later? I ask. Did the seduction get more obvious?

We had drinks, watched a game of water polo in the pool, Indigo says. He was still being low-key—except that he wanted to order champagne and I vetoed the idea. I finally got us off the subject of me—which was harder than you would imagine. He's the first con artist I ever met who isn't totally self-absorbed.

Oh, he might not be talkin' 'bout himself, Carl says, from in front of the stove. But you can bet he's *thinkin'* 'bout Tommy Delorme. Jus' watch the man's eyes.

Yeah, he avoids eye contact, Indigo agrees. But he compensates by *touching* a lot.

Groping, you mean?

No, just lots of pats on the wrist, maybe the knee now and then, Indigo says. She sees the anger welling up in me and gives me a reassuring pat, as well. Danny, she says, this wasn't sexual; he didn't force himself on me. That was the implicit threat, but he never followed through.

So let's get to the threatening part, I say. He came to your bunglow and forced his way in?

Carl breaks in for a moment to serve us mugs of chicken soup. Indigo mashes crackers into hers and then proceeds.

This all relates back to his purported career, she says. See, he's like me in that he tells half-truths. He uses his real name, and he told me that he's exporting chemicals—but they're supposedly used in the rubber plantations in Brazil. He even admitted that he's got a freighter load parked at Puerto Juárez.

Not anymore. . . .

Oh you heard, Indigo says between sips of broth. I didn't pry that out of him for a couple of hours—somewhere between his breakdown and his delusional phase. It's scary to watch someone's facade collapse, see their self-image disintegrate.

Back up. Back up, I tell her. When did all these hysterics begin?

He walked me to my bungalow. Indigo sighs. And he left without a struggle—no kiss, no pressure. I went to sleep and Tommy woke me up at six A.M., banging on my door. We're talking Gomorrah at Club Caracol, right? He had to be the only living soul awake at that hour. I opened up and he barged in. It was clear that he hadn't slept a wink. His eyes were wild—pupils dilated. His aura was like looking through cheesecloth.

What did he want?

Someone to fulminate at, Indigo replies. Walls to bounce off of. But this tirade was nonspecific, right? It was all about the world's injustices, the forces that prey on guys who want to make an honest buck. He talked about bribes, saying, *You think you've greased everyone that can fuck you, but there's not that much money in the world. What it takes is* muscle.

Even muscle ain't no match for an ace saboteur, Carl says, grinning.

What are you talking about? Indigo asks. And just where have you two been?

Oh, you know, I say. Sunk a ship. Ducked a few bullets. Got rescued at sea. Just another day at the office.

Indigo doesn't find our "day at the office" very amusing. She listens to the recitation, drinks down the last of her soup, and then berates us for not calling the cops.

Why didn't you? I ask. Tommy was being abusive, holding you against your will. . . .

Like I said, the threat was more implicit. He never told me I couldn't leave, Indigo said.

I'm glad you didn't report him, I say. We can get to him easier if he's not in jail. I'd say the sooner, the better. I'll just put on some dry clothes, then Carl and I will go explain to him the facts of life.

You'll have to take a number, Indigo says.

Come again?

Long as I was hiding out here, she says, I figured I could watch Tommy's boat, the *Quintana Roo.* Just before you guys arrived, I saw two Mexican guys looking it over. They called out, made sure nobody was aboard. Then one guy stood watch while the other one broke into the cabin. They're both inside right now, lying in ambush, I suppose.

Chapter Twenty-seven

◆

Ice is meltin' under his feet, Carl says, issuing a low whistle. Jus' about close the book on Tommy Delorme.

Yeah, his past has caught up with him, I say. But that still doesn't make us even. We let him die, and we walk away with nothing.

Aren't you the guy who told me how much you admire the straight life, how you yearn for a salary job? Indigo chides.

Yeah, and aren't you the gal who wanted into this score, wanted to take back what cocaine took away?

Still do, Indigo says.

So you're still in?

I said I'd let you know when things got too intense, she adds. This is intense, but I'm not bailing out yet.

Carl pipes up: Me, too, homes. Sinkin' that ship was half the battle. We don't win until we find the money.

Indigo divines my next question before I can speak it.

I didn't get anything from him about an impending transaction, she says. When he told me his ship was hijacked, I tried to hint around about what that would mean. He ranted about blowing this lucrative deal, chance of a lifetime and all that. I didn't dare bring up his mother or he would've smelled a rat.

We *have* to be close, I say. Nobody can sit on that much product for very long. Tommy would lead us straight to the money if it weren't for fucking Luis. Follow Tommy, and all we get is another scene like the *Ocho Rios*. They're probably delivering a pizza to his bungalow right now.

Occurs to me that the man might like a way out, Carl muses. Other than gettin' whacked. I'll bet he can smell that ambush comin'. And Doreen ain't exactly home free. She number two on the hit list.

Carl's right, Indigo says. He's confronted his own mortality. Tommy's pretty vulnerable now.

Grab him and squeeze, Carl says. If he don't play ball, you can always drop him back at his boat.

Or call Domino's. . . .

We arrange the kidnapping just like Carl did when he set me up with his Indian buddies on Haida. Indigo claims they parted on good enough terms that she can play the Judas. The only question is how to steer Tommy past his own boat and onto ours. Indigo strikes upon the idea of a cruise sanctioned by Club Caracol—just another singles-mixer event on their singles itinerary. The only difference is that this one is "off the books," special invitation only. Tommy gets an invitation on stationery that Indigo swipes from the concierge. She slips it under his door. Indigo spots him on his terrace, shouts up to ask if he's going. *Wouldn't miss it,* he replies. No reference, of course, to his tirade the day before. Now he's the model of composure. Back on the seduction track. A little sea air, a little Greek Gidget are exactly what the doctor ordered.

Carl plays our monosyllabic Jamaican captain, trading on the stereotype that all black men—even six feet six jailbirds—look alike. He hedges his bets with a scarf on his head, sunglasses, and a stoic manner. We figure it's a minor risk—Tommy making Carl. All we need is to get him aboard, and Indigo manages to do that just after breakfast. She's wearing the same ensemble that turned my head back at Señor Froggi's. I'm only catching glimpses through the slats of the cabin door, trying to control my breathing. I watch as Carl casts off and the "private singles mixer" departs. Of course, there is that last pesky line trailing off the stern, dancing in the *Angeline*'s wake. Tommy is only too glad to fetch it, lean out of the boat and loop it up for the captain.

And he feels exactly the same dread rush of certainty that I felt when that gun muzzle prodded the base of my skull. He's thinking that the line in his hand, the frothy wake, and the blue water beyond are the last things he will ever see. He's thinking that the flash will come next; he will never hear the shot. Maybe he'll see that tunnel of light that everyone talks about. Maybe he'll see Jesus or Satan. But he's pretty sure he won't be seeing Kathy Montana's smiling face—or even that sulky Jamaican captain.

Qué pasa, motherfucker, I whisper, pressing down on Tommy with the gun.

The expression on Tommy's face when he gets his first look at me is damn near worth the whole ordeal—damn near. Every notion I had about bailing out, about involving Indigo and Carl, is washed away by the clarity of that moment, by his complete stupefaction. For he's not just facing down his death; he's confronting his own failings. Carl and I are the resurrected, the intangibles in Tommy's scheme, the loosest of loose ends. More than the loss of his ether load, more than the death of his goons, we are that fog that encircles him, that nebulous entity. It finally has a face for him, all that vaporous fear. It has a gun stuck just below his doorknob ponytail while its many hands pat him down and shove him to the deck. Indigo steers us out of the bay toward open water while Carl and I settle onto the benches and savor the image.

Tommy is packing a small-frame Baretta that Carl tucks into his shorts. I sort through his wallet and find that in addition to his own driver's license, Tommy still carries some of my old bogus credit cards—Tony Granato from Trenton, New Jersey. He's got three hundred-dollar bills, some account cards from Caribbean banks, and, of course, a condom. No phone numbers, no memo notes or leads on Doreen Koontz. I keep the money and the license and toss the wallet in the ocean, saying, I'll credit this against the balance. I got five grand at Eddie Moore's house. Carl found another twenty K in a lamp at your mother's place. So let's round it off and say you still owe me three hundred and twenty-five thousand dollars. And an apology. You harassed my woman, called her a bitch and a cunt yesterday. I'm willing to forget about your torching my car and leaving me for dead. That was business. This is personal.

If any of this registered, Tommy isn't letting on. He's slumped in a corner, with his knees drawn up and his hands clutching a seat cushion. One sandal has jarred off his foot, and most of the color is washed out of his tan face, leaving just the highlights—a red nose, rosy cheeks. Tommy looks like a corpse wearing makeup. He looks puffy and tired and—well, *feminine*. I see nothing of my old cowboy accomplice, of the rooster strut he had when those beach boys were watching his back. But even in his fallen state, Tommy can still muster some *cojones*. He looks back and forth between Carl and me and says, What's this supposed to be? A society of all the guys I fucked over on my way to the top?

Don't suppose we'd all fit on one boat, Carl says. We're jus' the ones at the head of the line.

And what about her? Tommy asks, nodding toward Indigo. Lemme guess: She's some hooker along for the ride, hoping to make a percentage—

I'm on him before he can raise his guard. I land two or three good punches and then Tommy does a turtle, drawing his head down to his chest, shielding his face between his elbows. Carl grabs me as I rip at Tommy's Hawaiian shirt, tug it out of his pants and over his head with one hand while I swing with the other. Carl bundles my arms and heaves me back until Tommy's shirt begins to rip and I can't reach him anymore. It is a gratifying few seconds, though, seeing him cower and recoil from me. I'm yelling about what a pussy Tommy is when he doesn't have a tire iron or a bunch of goons around. Indigo is shouting for me to stop and Carl is just wheezing with the effort of wrestling me out of range.

And as for Tommy, the attack just spurs him on. Carl has no sooner gotten me clear than Tommy pops out of his turtle pose and says, You got quick hands, Danny. *Ugly* hands, but you throw a decent—

He doesn't finish that one, either, because Carl has him by the throat. What follows is one of the most astonishing feats of strength I have ever seen. Carl crouches down, emits a groan, and picks Tommy up off the deck by his throat, all the way up until his feet dangle in the air. Carl holds him just long enough to make the point before heaving him off the stern and into the sea. I think the stunt even surprises Carl, but he isn't going to let the comment go about my ugly hands. We are a hundred yards beyond Tommy before Carl reclaims the *Angeline*'s controls, motioning Indigo aside. *Man overboard,* he mutters as he throttles back and spins the prow around.

We double back to find Tommy looking belligerent as ever and plenty content to tread water on the gentle swells. His doorknob has pulled loose and he has hair in his face, but otherwise he is fine. Carl pulls within shouting distance and slips the *Angeline* into neutral. He flips up one of the seat benches and lifts a five-gallon pail from the storage bin. The scent from the pail hits me before I can look inside: fish heads, filleted carcasses, entrails, and scraps. Carl hefts the bucket so Tommy can see it, then says, You'd best listen up. This here's five gallons o' chum. Bought it three days ago at the processing plant, so she's plenty ripe. You can probably smell it from where you're at. Shark can smell it from five miles away. . . .

Carl hands me the bucket and says, Start dumpin' when I start to move.

He steps to the wheel, revs the engine, and tells Tommy, We gonna work this chum in big spiral. Sharks'll work their way to the center. I figure you got ten, fifteen minutes to get your head right before they start carvin' yo' ass!

He kicks in the motor, and I step to the stern as Indigo grabs my elbow. This is a little *intense* for me, she says. The plan was not to kill him.

This is a bluff, I tell her. Remember? All the sharks are asleep around here.

So I start dumping as Carl charts the spiral course. We're about fifty yards out when I empty the bucket. Then Carl cuts the motor and we drift, gazing at the dark speck of Tommy's head. Carl serves up beers all around, pulls the kerchief from his head, and stretches out on the bench. I am finished with my beer, smearing a little sun block on my nose when Indigo—standing like an ornament on the prow—shouts, THERE!

It is indeed a dorsal fin, up from the grotto, an insomniac with a nose for chum.

I thought you said he was kidding! Indigo cries.

Carl props up on one elbow long enough to spot the shark, then he sinks back and starts laughing. Jus' like ringin' a dinner bell, he says. Thing is, they *communal*—like mice. You never got jus' one shark.

He has no sooner spoken this than a second fin appears. It is big—bigger than the first dorsal fin and plenty big enough to make the point. I can tell by Tommy's sudden agitation that he has spotted them, too. He's kicking to boost himself over the swells, trying to keep both sharks in sight. They are cruising in a pattern that roughly correlates the spiral of chum. While the lead sharks tighten their loop toward Tommy, a third fin appears farther out.

This is enough! Indigo shouts. We're not going to watch him get *eaten*. I won't be a party to—

It's Tommy's choice, Carl tells her. Don't nobody want him decapitated. But he's got to get his head right. Got to come down a peg, humble himself a bit. He's got to realize we're his only friends in the worl'.

Some friends! Tommy shouts. What the fuck do you want from me?

We've been over this, I reply. You need to apologize to the lady, and you owe me three hundred and twenty-five K.

Like I'm gonna' pull that out of my pocket? he calls. Out of thin air?

You can start with the apology, Carl shouts. We'll talk about the money. Or you can wait 'til they start bumpin' your ass. Sharks always bump before they bite.

You can kiss my white cracker ass, Tommy jeers. There's plenty of boat traffic out here. I'll signal one of them.

Can't signal without any arms, Carl says, lifting another seat cushion. Lookey here! he exclaims, hoisting out another pail of entrails. A whole 'nother bucket o' chum! We gonna have a *convention* out here.

I got *bumped!* Tommy calls. SOMETHING BUMPED MY FOOT!

Danny! Indigo snatches my shoulders and spins me around. You have to bring him in.

It's not my show, I say. I didn't even know Carl was going to do this!

STILL WAITIN' FOR THAT APOLOGY! Carl shouts. Them sharks bump only once, maybe twice. Then it's feedin' frenzy. . . .

I'M SORRY. I'M SORRY, HONEST. ANYTHING I SAID TO OFFEND YOU, HONEY, I TAKE IT ALL BACK! Tommy crows.

And with that, Carl circles the boat so Tommy can grab the gaff pole and heave himself over the side. He flounders down the bench and collapses on the engine cover. Now even the sunburn color has drained from his cheeks, and he looks gaunt and defeated. Tommy is lucky to still have legs—and he knows it. Carl heaves the second bucket of chum off the stern and in less than a minute we have four sharks knifing behind the boat in a mad search for wounded prey. Carl watches them a moment, then addresses Indigo.

You satisfied with the man's apology?

Oh yes, Indigo says. Everything's jake.

Maybe you can watch topside while we go below? Carl asks. Indigo nods. He shuts off the engine and we drift amid the chummy waters. Carl and I each take an elbow and slide Tommy headfirst down the steps and into the cabin. I keep my gun in hand, and frisk Tommy another time just to be sure. I keep expecting him to conjure a tire iron and start hacking again. But the swim—and Carl's menacing style—has taken the fight out of Tommy. He crab-walks back against the door to the hold and wraps himself in the blanket. The sight of him so deflated, so humbled should be more gratifying than it feels. Perhaps it's because we haven't gained anything yet in playing the heavy. Maybe you have to be a sadist—like Tommy—to enjoy this kind of scene.

I don't suppose you'd believe me if I told you I spent all the money, Tommy says.

We know that, I say. We've tracked the deposits. We found Doreen's records, Tommy. You loaned it back to yourself in a Dutch Sandwich and used it to stock the *Ocho Rios.*

Yeah, and yesterday my men were all killed and the goddamn ship was hijacked—

Sunk, Carl corrects him. Midway between here and Puerto Morelos. All that cargo weight, sumbitch dropped like a rock.

Tommy studies us for a moment, hoping to discern a bluff.

Your men were killed by a pizza boy, I say. I describe how we found the crime scene, and how we got trapped in the hold during the hijacking. We describe enough about the layout, the cargo, and our sabotage to make our case.

If that's true, he says, you just blew more than two million bucks. Not counting the cost of the ship. That was all my equity, guys. And that was your only chance to score a profit off of me.

If I believed that, I say, I would've killed you when you climbed on the boat. At the very least, we would've let the sharks take a bite or two. Then you could know how it feels to be mutilated—

Oh spare me! Tommy shouts. You just can't accept that Luis beat you again, that you'll never be a player. Wake up and smell the fucking tequila. You want to get even—shoot me. But you're too late to get rich on this one, Danny. The money went down with the ship.

Carl looks up from his examination of the confiscated Baretta.

It is tiny, a toy in his giant hands. No, Tommy, he says, the *product* went down with the ship. The money is still comin' in from Colombia.

What makes you think so?

If we had missed the drop, we would've missed the ship, too, I say. And instead of loitering around Club Coitus, you would be out with Doreen celebrating your first big score. *Certainly* driving a newer boat. One with an alarm system. Indigo—aka Kathy—reports that you have some uninvited guests on the *Quintana Roo*. It's Luis's boys, tying up all the loose ends. They found the ship, they could sure as hell find you. That's what Carl means when he says we're the only friends you've got. We saved your life just by keeping you away from your boat.

Watching Tommy consider this news, seeing him weigh all of the implications, I get a flashback to the man I met on the road in Nevada. He's a great poker face, a real showdown gambler. Now that the immediate threat is past, with the panic over, he can maneuver again; he can reshuffle and stall.

How do you expect me to get that money when I've got no product to sell? he asks. Man brings his money to the table, he's gonna want to see the goods. I'm supposed to give him scuba gear and point him toward the horizon?

Obviously losing the *Ocho Rios* complicates the scenario, I tell him. But you don't have to worry about getting the money. That's your *mother*'s problem.

How do you figure?

Doreen's your emissary with the Colombians, I say. She's your chief financial officer and—most important—she's the only person on the planet who values your life. If she's half as resourceful as I think she is, she'll pay to see you again. Now either you tell us where we can find her or else you go for another swim.

Chapter Twenty-eight

◆

I'm surprised at you, Danny, Tommy Delorme says. All the scores in the world and this is what you settle for—a kidnapping shakedown?

We could've hijacked your ether load, I reply. But you're easier to transport.

And jus' as valuable, Carl adds. Unless yo' momma don't love you. Guess we'll find that out soon enough.

Tommy ruminates for a few minutes, and when he raises his face I can see that the bile has welled up inside; the dense cloud of failure is suffocating him. Those cords that Indigo saw in his aura would be tangled now, maybe tied in knots. He absently strokes the hair from his face, tucks it behind his ears. But out of this blue funk, this darkest hour, I can see him clutch at a straw. He shrugs his head, indicating topside of the *Angeline*, and says, You won't kill me in front of her. That's why you pulled me out. You murder me in cold blood and that chick'll never speak to you again.

I borrow a page from Max Kohler's threat book, saying, She doesn't have to watch, doesn't have to know when it happens.

See, Tommy, all we have to do is hang you out for Luis's boys. We could drop you at the marina and wash our hands of the whole affair. You think we're kidding about those guys on board the *Quintana Roo*? Call our bluff. We'll go back to your boat right now and you can knock on the cabin door.

He doesn't take that dare. He doesn't say anything for almost five minutes, then mutters, Mom pays and I walk? How do I know you won't kill us both?

Best I can offer is a running start—get you away from Luis's goons, I reply. Like I said before, if this was about killing, you'd already be dead. Now where can we find your mom?

Chichén Itzá, Tommy mutters again.

The Mayan city, I say, remembering it from the airline magazine on the flight down. Suddenly, it also springs out at me from Doreen's papers—an entry in her calendar. "Call about Chichen." Not a misspelling, after all.

They have an airstrip there, and a few hotels around the ancient city, Tommy continues. She's flying in tonight with a guy from the Cali cartel named Enrique Lorca. They're checking into some villas nearby. He'll have the money, but he'll bring muscle, too.

You're expected to meet them?

Tomorrow night, Tommy replies. Lorca's never seen the ruins; he's going to tour around. I'm expected at dinner, probably stay the night. Then we were going to drive up to Puerto Juárez the next morning and have a look at the goods. The money changes hands. Lorca flies out and his goons ride the freighter to Guatemala City. At least, that was the plan.

How much muscle? Carl wants to know.

More than you idiots can handle, Tommy replies. With your pistols and your shark bait.

How much money? I ask.

I told you, the ether is worth two million five, he says. We were going to negotiate some kind of deposit on the ship—they would return it empty. So I imagine Lorca's carrying just under three mil.

I smile at Carl, a look that says, Didn't I tell you?

Go ahead and gloat, Tommy says. But he's not about to hand it over just because my ass is in a sling.

Interior roads of the Yucatán are like plumb lines drawn through scrub jungle. No reason to build them in curves, because the only obstacles are scrawny dogs and the occasional Mayan city. Indigo would love to see all of those ancient cities, but we agree that we've embarked on the "intense" phase of the operation. (She told me, I don't care if you come back with all that money. Just come back.) And Indigo's not interested in schlepping Tommy Delorme around "like a bunch of Shiites in West Beirut." I remind her that Shiites stow hostages in the trunk—we let Tommy drive the car. Can't have Amnesty International on our asses for giving him heat stroke, I explain. So Carl handcuffs one of Tommy's wrists to the steering wheel and I ride up front with a gun in my lap.

Carl bought the handcuffs—four pair—during a shopping spree of spy regalia. We spent the previous night aboard *Angeline* plotting strategy. Tommy gave us enough of the logistics of the El Castillo Hotel to draft a plan that includes—among other things—a room-service uniform (Carl bought the pants, tie, shirt, and shoes; we had to scam the jacket off a waiter for a whopping $200), a sawed-off shotgun (because Tommy scoffed at our firepower), a canister of Mace (to back up the shotgun), and a set of walkie-talkies that occupy Carl for most of the drive—installing batteries, tuning and squelching and deciphering the manual. New-toy fever strikes again.

I really miss not having Indigo to read aloud from the guidebooks, describing all these lost civilizations and jilted slave raiders. Tommy, of course, wants to pass the miles with another of his mind games. We've covered all the relevant topics, things like what happened after I survived the car crash, and what happened to Eddie Moore. I don't tell him where I found Carl and Indigo; don't want Tommy haunting us after the score. I ask about Doreen, how it came to pass that she was his eyes and ears at Covina Clockworks.

It was the only way I was ever going to keep a promise I made to her, Tommy says.

For a job? I ask.

No, for a better life, a better world, Tommy replies. Instead of elaborating, he starts to reminisce about his boyhood. He says his parents moved around a lot because their chosen vocation was a loan-brokering scam. They took front money from credit losers and pushed lots of paper around. They'd work a town for three months or so and then skip before the feds got wise. He claims he lived in twenty states before he finished high school. It was worse than being an army brat, but he learned lots about creative finance.

The way Tommy describes it, Doreen was the brains of the outfit. When the law finally caught up with them, it was Tommy's dad who took the fall. Everything was in his name. He was front man for all the transactions.

And while the old man did time in Texas, Tommy contracted spinal meningitis. He was in and out of hospitals for three years. Tommy's mother had to work the loan scam during the day and waitress at night.

She'd get home at eleven, I'd rub her feet, and then she'd help me do my weight therapy, he recalls. By the time I woke up, she was already at her office, fleecing some poor bastard. Meanwhile, his father read case law and got smarter in prison—figured out that he'd been conned. So he beat up Doreen after he got out, then left them both for good.

After I got better, Tommy recalls, after I could work, I promised her that I would buy her a house someday—a fucking palace. And not in America—not where she had to move every few weeks and live out of a suitcase. A palace someplace where they leave you alone.

Where did Luis and Alonzo figure in? I ask. How did Doreen get to Covina Clockworks?

I got into it when I was carrying eight-balls for some dealer in East L.A., Tommy replies. They used me because I didn't have the kind of face the cops would shake down just for spite. The gringos, they left alone. Anyway, Alonzo Peña was at the top of that food chain, and I made him a pitch. Pretty soon, I was carrying all over the country. I thought I'd caught the brass ring until Luis set me up on an informant bust in Lake Tahoe, Tommy says. Hung me out to dry. So I'm talking to mom one day during visiting hours, and I tell her, If I'm going to buy you that dream house, you're going to have to help. I need you to take a job at Covina Clockworks and learn everything you can.

Then Tommy shuts up for awhile, probably thinking about what he's led his mom into now. We've got only Spanish crooners on the radio, so he proposes another mind game. Tommy hasn't changed a lick from this summer, from his prison imagination. This one is called Utopia. The premise is that you become dictator of a sovereign island nation. What kind of nation would you create? You make all the laws—edicts and proclamations and shit. You call the shots.

While I'm mulling the prospect, Tommy goes first. He says that he would create a tax haven of entrepreneurs. Taxes would be low because his society would not have this vast safety net that throws America's budget out of whack. America's in debt, Tommy says, because all of these federal agencies coddle people who are too stupid to work their own scams. If you're rich, he figures, you don't need Social Security. And his Utopia would exclude by net worth.

Sort of like Monaco, I say.

Except that Monaco has laws and police and zoning bullshit, Tommy replies. My island can't be bothered with all that.

No police?

Tommy says that the rich don't need laws and police because nobody would commit robberies or assaults. Those crimes occur *way* down the food chain, where cousins marry and people still walk on their knuckles. And why should Utopians have to worry about parking tickets?

Rich people commit other crimes, I reply. Securities fraud, insider trading, embezzlement. . . .

We're talking a *haven* here. Tommy smiles. Those things are *credentials* on my island.

Drug abuse? Domestic violence? Incest? I ask.

Strictly private, Tommy says. People are free to settle their own family squabbles.

Okay, but suppose some feuding couple shoots an innocent bystander? I wonder.

Bad marksmanship; bad luck, Tommy says.

Hey, homes! I say toward the backseat, where Carl sits with his knees scrunched into his chest reading the walkie-talkie manual. How about you? You want to live on an island where people do whatever the hell they please? No laws, no cops, no morals?

I already do, Carl replies. And after this score, I'll be able to buy the whole goddamn place and elect myself sheriff, mayor, and king.

Tommy laughs, then checks Carl's expression in the rearview mirror and realizes he isn't kidding.

We reach Pisté, the town near Chichén Itzá, just before Lorca's plane is due to land. Tommy explains that Lorca chose this tourist airstrip in the boonies because he needs to avoid customs. All the top brass in the cartel have been indicted in the United States. He would risk arrest and extradition at an international terminal like the one at Cancún. They don't see many corporate propjets here, so we won't have a problem spotting him.

First thing I notice when Tommy steers us past the runway is the El Castillo pyramid above the trees to the west. According to the books, this is the center of Chichén Itzá. Other ruins and roads spread out in the jungle for miles in every direction. I want to see that ballcourt where they played soccer around the clock until everybody dropped dead. Or the well that Indigo told me about, the Sacred Cenote, where they threw gold and sacrificed virgins. No time to gawk, however. We've got to get into position at the airport and get Tommy into the trunk.

The *trunk*! he complains. I'm cuffed to the wheel. Where am I going to go?

Carl unlocks him and leads him to the back of the sedan as he explains that we can't have him honking the horn or driving onto the runway. It's time he started acting like a hostage instead of master of ceremonies. Before Carl slams the trunk lid, he promises to tell Tommy if we see anything interesting. I can hear everything you say anyway, Tommy calls.

Our object is first to get a head count, then watch to see where their bungalows are located on the hotel grounds. We sit in the airport lot testing the walkie-talkies and eating pistachio nuts until sunset. Then somebody switches on the lights in the little cinder-block terminal building. The runway lights come on next, just before we get our first look at Enrique Lorca's propjet. It's a beauty, a sleek little white fuselage mounted between thunderous engines. Carl and I watch through binoculars as it skates in perfectly level and touches down on three wheels at once. I guess if you can afford the plane, you don't scrimp on the pilot. I ask Carl how many runs he thinks it has made to secret airstrips in the Carolinas.

Not likely, he replies. Those babies need endless runway. Naw, this plane is *recreation.* Probably got a bed in there. Maybe ol' Doreen joined the Mile High Club—

I heard that! Tommy calls from the trunk. But we're too busy watching Doreen climb out of the plane to respond. She follows the pilot down this fold-out stair, tottering a little on heels. She's a short, waistless woman with a wide face and thin ankles. Doreen wears a beige suit and a scarf on her head. She is carrying a briefcase. That's a new look for you, I'm thinking—jet-set smurf. Beats the hell out of crunching numbers at Covina Clockworks, eh, Doreen?

Two bodyguards emerge next, empty-handed. They're not schlepping luggage in order to free their hands. Enrique Lorca follows them. I notice two things—that he is taller and older than I imagined, and that he is empty-handed. If Lorca isn't carrying the money case, who is? Certainly not Doreen. My answer comes in the last guy off the plane—the single biggest Hispanic person I have ever seen. This guy is Colombian by way of Samoa. A South American sumo wrestler.

Holy shit, Carl whispers, and I concur. And in this Odd Job's hammy hand is the aluminum camera case, *the* aluminum camera case. The goon's bulk makes it look like a lunch pail. Watching him squeeze through that tiny fuselage door is like witnessing birth. Holy shit is right. Three bodyguards. Four, if you're factoring size. The Three Million Dollar Question that Carl and I are asking ourselves is, How many baby-sit the money?

Tommy said that Lorca would bring some muscle, I say.

Shotgun, *shit,* Carl mutters. Gonna need a bazooka.

They caravan back to the El Castillo—goons and luggage in taxicabs and Doreen and Lorca in a rented jeep. I get a better look at him when they pull up at his bungalow. Lorca is reed-thin and white-haired; tailored suit, Italian shoes. He's the kind of thug who lets the clerks on Rodeo Drive dress him from head to toe. It looks like his bodyguards use the same tailor—even Mr. Sumo. Score one for the Cali boys in the Colombian style war. Medellín thugs like Pablo Escobar dress like cigar makers on holiday.

The men all move into a bungalow on the north end of the hotel compound. Lorca's place is straight out the back of the hotel, past the pool and a cabana bar. Directly behind Lorca's unit is a tennis court, and beyond that, jungle. Doreen's bungalow is alongside the road to Chichén Itzá. Most of the tourists walk this route from Pisté to the ancient city. Carl and I agree there will be no need to shadow them tonight. They will likely have dinner in the hotel restaurant and retire early.

And now that it's dark, we can smuggle Tommy into the bungalow we rented at a resort down the road. We keep him in the trunk while we scope out our unit. The beds are flimsy, there are no doors on the closet, and the furniture is sticks. Carl and I agree that the only secure place to handcuff Tommy is the toilet, which pretty much ruins his day. But that's nothing compared to the next indignity, when Carl holds down his legs and I whip out the Swiss army knife.

Souvenir time, I explain, while Tommy thrashes beside the commode.

What the fuck is this about? he demands. I thought this was *business*! I thought we had an *understanding*!

Our business is scaring the shit out of Doreen, I explain. She's gotta know that we're serious.

And afterward, when the shock has subsided, we can still hear Tommy mewing and cursing in the john. Samson humiliated. But

Carl and I manage to tune him out. We're sitting at the card table, drawing diagrams of the bungalow compound. We agree that the setup at Lorca's unit is perfect. Doreen's is more of a problem. It's in full view of the hotel, and lots of pedestrians passing by. But the plan will turn on two things—how many goons Lorca leaves with the money and whether or not he will go for a catered dinner in Doreen's bungalow. We don't want to attempt this score in the hotel restaurant.

Got to be room service, Carl repeats. If not, we shitcan the plan.

Just let me work Doreen, I tell Carl. She'll stand on her head for us after she sees the souvenir.

Chapter Twenty-nine

◆

I get my chance to "work" Doreen the following morning. Carl is on early watch in the jungle behind the tennis court. I am watching Tommy eat his breakfast, the room-service tray resting on the toilet lid. (Of course, everything's wrong now—the eggs are stiff; the coffee's cold. After our minor surgery, Tommy is not a happy camper.) Carl rings me on the walkie-talkie and says Lorca has departed with the not-so-gentle giant. It appears they're off to the ancient city, video camera and all. That leaves two mutts still in the bungalow baby-sitting *the* aluminum camera case.

What about Doreen? I ask.

She's sitting on the porch behind her unit, Carl replies. Room-service grapefruit and café con leche. Readin' the *New York Times,* catchin' some rays.

Both goons are still at Lorca's? I ask.

Far as I know, Carl replies. Coast is clear, amigo.

Then you come on back and I'll go set the hook, I tell him.

The shrubs around Doreen's bungalow provide enough cover for me to get in between her and the patio door. She sees my shadow fall over the newspaper and turns just as I put the .357 to her ear and close my other hand on her mouth. She manages a quiet gasp and then stiffens, shaking under me. If she could turn, could see it was me, she might relax. But under the circumstances, she holds up well.

Let's go inside, I tell her. Don't do anything to make me shoot.

Doreen pushes away from the table and stands, turns to face me, and goes another shade of pale.

Danny . . .

That's right, I'm not dead yet, I say. No thanks to you—*sugar*. Time for us to have a talk.

Doreen squints at me for a few seconds, scrunching up her brow and turning her rosebud mouth into a sneer. She still has to process the shock of it before she can follow orders. And like Tommy, her first visceral response is to bluff a little.

You know I'm not alone here, she says. I've got some friends in the compound. They're coming by any minute.

We'll talk about that, too, I say. Because if we get any visitors, you're going to cover for me.

She mulls this over while leading me into the sitting room of her bungalow. The place is done in low-rent Hawaiian, and I notice a huge fruit basket on the bar. I'm guessing that the card reads, "Love, Tommy." I direct her to a hard-back chair, telling her to keep her hands in her lap. I give the room a quick once-over, looking for guns. Nothing in the drawers, nothing in the sofa cushions. So I sit opposite Doreen and reach under my shirt for a little gift-wrapped box that I leave on the coffee table. Doreen is pretty wary of this; probably figures that it's a bomb.

A little remembrance, I say. A keepsake from our days together at Covina Clockworks. Open it. Now.

She draws off the bow, then lifts the lid, holding it at arm's length. Nothing goes *Boom!* or jumps out at her, so she moves the tissue aside. Doreen squints again—an annoying expression—when she sees the contents.

Hair? She says. You're giving me hair?

Very special hair, I reply. Take it out; have a look.

She lifts the hank out with her thumb and forefinger, pinky

extended. She is holding a brown curly shock that is formed in a crude knot.

Don't recognize it? I say. That's your son's doorknob ponytail. I always hated them, but he was—well, *attached* to it. His driver's license is in there, too.

Suddenly, the hair has acquired more appeal, become something worth examining. Doreen cradles it in her palm as she examines Tommy's license. She places both items back in the box, emits a long sigh, and then levels a gaze at me.

How did you know he was my son?

Same way that you knew I wasn't a sales rep for Covina Clockworks. Deduction, I say. Research.

And I'm supposed to believe he's still alive?

We'll call him in a minute, I reply. But first we need to talk about our heavy date. You, me, dinner. Tonight. *Here,* if at all possible.

That would be swell, she says, but I already have plans. I've got these clients from Colombia—

Oh, they're most cordially invited, I say. As many as we can get. See, I know everything worth knowing about this dinner, about this whole ether deal. I know that Enrique Lorca wants to abscond with the *Ocho Rios* and leave behind a suitcase of cash. Around three million dollars, by Tommy's estimate. I know that Tommy is expected for dinner tonight. Lorca wants a look at this upstart smuggler, and Tommy wants to formalize a relationship. Since all of your equity is riding on this, it's an important meeting. If Tommy doesn't show, it reflects badly on you.

Doreen fingers the hair again and asks how would it reflect if I crashed the party.

It wouldn't be crashing, I tell her. See, I'm impersonating your son.

Doreen cradles her head in her hands while I explain that Lorca's never met Tommy before, never spoken to him on the phone. That's how I can pass myself off as Tommy, I say. But there's two elements here that I can't control, that are entirely up to you.

Doreen looks up again, asks, Such as?

The con is dependent on how you act, on how well you sell me as your son, I tell her. Lorca gets a whiff of something wrong, and we're both dead.

That's for sure, she agrees.

And second, you need to persuade Lorca to do a room-service dinner here, in your bungalow, I add.

Why's that?

Because something about armed robbery doesn't lend itself to the dining room of the El Castillo. We plan to use Mace and gags and handcuffs, I say. It's kind of an intimate scene, if you catch my drift. You do catch my drift?

You're holding Tommy hostage in order to force me to help you rob Enrique Lorca? she says.

Very good.

And supposing Lorca does have all this money; we're not doing the deal tonight. He won't bring it with him.

We thought of that, too, I reply. It stays back at his bungalow with what we hope is *one* guard. You can help there, too, Doreen, by making sure everyone's invited.

And once they're here, you're going to burst in with guns, and mace people and handcuff them?

Probably in some kind of daisy chain, I say, around the commode. That's where Tommy is now. I'm sure you're wondering if this is all a bluff, so why don't we say hello?

I grab the phone and dial our room. Carl answers and I tell him to put Tommy on. Then I pass the phone to Doreen and her voice breaks as she says, *Baby? That you?* Then she's asking if he's all right and blubbering about how such terrible things could happen. If you didn't know the players, didn't know what both were capable of, it would damn near break your heart. Apparently Tommy reassures Doreen, gets her settled enough to listen. She keeps nodding and uh-huhing before saying good-bye. She sets the phone on the cradle and keeps her head down, hiding the emotion behind all that tinted hair. When she looks up, I see the fire again, the family bravado.

He says we're all screwed anyway because our ship got hijacked and sunk, she says.

Lorca doesn't need to know that, I say. Unless you're foolish enough to tell him.

And Tommy says not to do a fucking thing you say, because you're never going to kill him, Doreen says.

That so?

He says you've got some lady love who would dump you if you did. He says you realized you couldn't kill him, so you cooked up this robbery scheme. . . .

Okay, suppose that's true, I say. Did Tommy mention the man baby-sitting him? You ever heard the name Carl Dupree?

I can tell by the shift of Doreen's eyes that she has. She heard all about him during those prison visits in Nevada.

That's my partner, I say, and I give her the ten-cent summary of how we met. I describe Carl's knife wound in some detail. Then I explain that Carl has no lady love holding him back, no emotions other than pure loathing for Tommy Delorme. It was my idea to cut the doorknob, I say. Carl wanted to take something more *substantial.* And he'll kill Tommy without batting an eye if you do anything to queer the deal.

Doreen takes a few moments to consider this, to get her mind around it all. Perhaps the most repugnant part for her is acting like she loves *me.* I'm thinking she could lay on the charm when she was a spy in the office. If she can charm a snake like Alonzo Peña, she can charm Lorca, too.

But why can't Tommy show up for dinner? she wonders. He knows all the history here, all of the negotiation. What do you know about our sources, about the pipeline—

I know enough.

It won't play!

It has to, I say, standing up and tucking the gun into my pants. All we need to do is get everyone in and seated. Carl will come in the patio door that you leave open. We subdue everyone, collect weapons, and then hit Lorca's bungalow. It'll be over before the salad course. And after we get the money, you and Tommy are free to go. Now I'll call you by six to confirm. If Lorca doesn't go for the room-service dinner—well, we'd best not think about that. I'll slap on the Aramis and bring the wine. Hell, I'll even pick up the check.

Doreen follows me toward the door, beseeching. How do I know you won't whack us all when you get the money?

Don't you remember? I say. I'm pussy-whipped; I don't have the stomach for it.

And Carl . . .

A *maniac.* So don't do anything to anger him—like spilling this to Lorca. We're watching his bungalow, I lie. If Lorca takes off in a hurry, so do we. And you can kiss Tommy good-bye.

I find the "maniac" back at our bungalow rehearsing with the shotgun. He has ordered room service and told the kid to leave the cart—for a $100 tip. Then Carl removes the food warmer underneath and fashions a sling for the shotgun. Spread the tablecloth, and you can't see a thing. Carl gets it down to a fluid motion, sweeping the cloth aside, pulling the scattergun. And the candles are still standin'! he brags as he trains the muzzle on imaginary targets.

Very nice, I tell him as I get us both a beer from the minibar. I think you've got a second career there. . . .

They'll nail your black ass to the wall, Tommy jeers from the bathroom. They'll chase you to the ends of the earth!

Let 'em, Carl jeers back. 'Cause I got a million-dollar head start. Get me a jet like Lorca's and fly to the friggin' moon.

They'll find you there, Tommy mutters. They'll find us all.

Carl and I move out of Tommy's hearing range and I brief him on my chat with Doreen, saying how I feel like the hook is set. I hyped up your temper, your blood lust, I say. Sinking the *Ocho Rios* helped us, too—gives her less reason to rat us out because the deal's gone belly-up. All she wants is her baby back, maybe her old job at the Clockworks. It was a revelation for her—having me walk out of the jungle and sabotage her life.

Felt good, though?

Better than sex, I reply.

Now don't go exaggeratin', Carl says. Gots to keep perspective on this. It ain't the money . . .

It's what the money can buy, I say, and we high-five it loud enough for Tommy to hear.

When I call Doreen at six o'clock, she gives me a very terse thumbs-up. Lorca likes the private dinner idea. Seven-thirty; casual dress. Lorca has ordered up a VCR. After dinner, we're supposed to watch the tape he and Goliath made today of his Chichén Itzá expedition.

Damn shame you be missin' *that,* Carl says.

We can always steal the tape, I reply. I'm checking my cotton suit in the mirror, thinking that all I need is the hat to look like a plantation boss. Tommy glowers at me from the bathroom floor, saying that my clothes are off the rack, very *gauche,* very *plebian.* He'd never meet a cartel boss in anything less than . . . Carl finally shuts him up by popping a lime into his mouth and sealing it up with duct tape. I tell him Doreen will be by in an hour or so to free his plebian ass. You better hope nothing goes wrong, I add. could be weeks before they find you.

MMMMMBBBBFFFF! Tommy says. Always the last word.

Carl and I take one last look at the diagram I drew of Doreen's unit. Before I lug my knapsack out the door, before I do what can't be undone, I give Carl a reality check. Still plenty of time to abort, I tell him. I mean, we made our point. We can still walk away smilin'.

Smilin' and *poor,* Carl replies. This is the only chance I'll ever have to be rich. Wouldn't take that chance with nobody else, homeboy.

That's as close to a compliment as I'll get from Carl, and I carry it with me across the compound to Doreen's patio door. She must wonder why I'm so relaxed, so blithe about it all. Doreen wears a sundress, a necklace of huge plastic beads, and little painted parrot earrings. It's the bon voyage, tour-group look, very festive. But behind all this color, behind bright lipstick and rouge, is a lot of grief. Doreen looks shrunken to me, a head shorter than the woman who emerged from the plane yesterday. And her hand shakes when she works the latch on the patio door.

We didn't talk about after, she says, by way of greeting. Where am I supposed to find Tommy?

I hand her a key to our bungalow and describe its general location. As soon as everyone is bound and gagged, I say, you're free to go. You want to stick around, we might even skim you some expense money.

I don't want it, Doreen says. When they come after me, I want to be able to say I didn't take a dime.

Suit yourself, I reply as I'm stowing the knapsack underneath the sofa. Inside are handcuffs, Mace, and duct tape. I give the walkie-talkie a test, and Carl answers, clear as a bell. He's loading the room-service table into the car. He will park within sight of Lorca's bungalow and wait for them to leave. He will give me two *clicks* on the call button just before he hits Doreen's place. That is my signal to draw the gun that I am taping underneath the table.

You asked everyone to join us? I say as I'm crawling between the chairs. All of Lorca's merry men?

I tried, but he'll bring whoever he pleases, Doreen replies.

I walk over to where she is hovering by the wet bar and take her hand, but she shrinks away.

You should touch me occasionally, I say. Pat my head, put your hands on my shoulders when you walk behind my chair. I'm the golden boy, right? Pride and joy? Lorca will notice if we're not affectionate.

Doreen sighs through puckered lips, asks, *Anything else?*

You know that I was staying at Club Caracol on Isla Mujeres, I say. I drive a Range Rover. I own a broken-down cabin cruiser called the *Quintana Roo*. By the way, what does that mean?

It's a *state* on the peninsula, Doreen replies. Yucatán, Campeche, Quintana Roo.

Catchy. Anyway, I met someone at the resort, I say. Someone I want you to meet.

Bullshit, Doreen says. I never meet Tommy's women.

I pass on the oedipal shadings of that and go on to relevant business. As far as Lorca knows, Eddie Moore is still alive, still getting the product to Port Arthur, I say.

I didn't know he was dead, Doreen mutters.

You still don't, I say. I own a laptop computer. I work on it every day. What am I writing?

How should I—

Make something up! I demand. Is it schedules? Tables? The Great American—

Utopia, Doreen whispers.

Come again?

It's this Utopian society that Tommy's obsessed with, she explains. He thinks that someday he's going to run an island—a country. He's got this whole flowchart, this model—

A heavy knock at the door interrupts her.

Show time, *Mom.*

Chapter Thirty

◆

I can't say precisely when I knew that things had gone terribly wrong. All this dread, this foreboding, and the ethereal sense of floating out of myself is a cumulative thing. I don't know when it started, but by the time the waiters arrive with our entrées I've long since departed my body and I'm coping with a heightened awareness, an expanded sense of motion and space. If anyone notices the change, if they see my body deflate and sag in the chair while my soul wafts around, they don't comment on it. Maybe Colombians see that Santaria-voodoo shit all the time. But you can bet that Doreen notices.

We are two courses and about an hour beyond our launch window. I am waiting for *clicks* on the walkie-talkie that I have tucked in the back of my pants. They don't come. They don't come after the platters are cleared and the café con leche is prepared. I couldn't even tell you what I ordered, or what I ate. The food entered a body that I have vacated out of fear. It occupies a chair; it looks conscious and acts cordial, but it is a human husk. The rest of me is off in the compound searching for Carl—or what's left of him. Because when he is late, when he forces Doreen and me to ad-lib and stall, it can be for only two reasons: Carl is dead, or else Carl hit Lorca's bungalow by himself, stole the money, and split. He is sailing down the road with a song on his lips and three million dollars in the trunk. He took his one chance to be rich and made himself even richer.

Of course, I prefer the first theory—which is why I am consumed with dread. If Carl got caught by Lorca's men, we will know about it shortly. Lorca left two goons with the money, bringing only Odd Job to dinner. The bodyguard, named Manolo, is not talking, not eating, and not letting his hand stray from his lapel—under which he has bulge about the size of a submachine gun. Manolo does not sit at the table, instead parking his considerable bulk on a stool at the wet bar.

After he enters and takes that position, I start calculating the odds: Manolo can see the patio from there. He can see everything. He could hose Carl before he got through the door. I am going to have to shoot that bastard in order to pull off this score. So I am faced with violating Indigo's trust or losing my only other friend. But that dilemma is negated by Carl's AWOL status. I excuse myself, go to the bathroom, and try the walkie-talkie. Earth to Carl Dupree. Nothing.

Somehow we manage to bluff and kill the time. Enrique Lorca tells me right away that he's in a great mood. Because of the extradition threat, he and his *compadres* don't get out much anymore. They can't tour, can't shop, can't *hang out* without worrying about the DEA. When you already own anything worth buying in Colombia, life can get pretty stale. Lorca used to buy suits on Savile Row; now he has to mail-order. (Poor baby!) So a weekend blowout with the cartel jet is Lorca's chance to howl. And it helps that he and Doreen have been catting around Cali for a week. She can talk about all of these discos and bistros and guys in Lorca's organization.

And Doreen makes an effort to touch me—bless her heart. She actually squeezes my waist when she introduces me (and damn near activates the walkie-talkie!). She strokes my neck when she walks by my chair, and I can feel her fingers tremble. The wait is taking its toll. I pour Lorca more wine and get him talking about the ruins. He's nuts about this observatory the Mayans built that looks like the ones of today. It's like the architect came from the future, he says, a direct link to modern astronomy. You *really* must tour the park and see it, he says.

Why don't we watch your videotape? Doreen chirps. After you went to all the trouble of getting the VCR . . .

Sounds delightful, I say, standing up. While you're cuing up that tape, I wonder if you'll excuse me—

Son, that wouldn't be polite, Doreen warns, failing to keep the malice out of her voice. She is actually saying, You can't stiff me now. We had a deal.

I was going to say, I continue, that I've arranged a special dessert for the occasion. To celebrate our alliance. I want to check on arrangements. I'll only be a minute.

By all means, go, Lorca says as he taps his umpteenth Gauloise on his cigarette case. And Manny, you go with him.

Manny slides off the bar stool and rumbles toward the door, like he expected the order.

No, no, really—stay put, I say. Start the tape. I'll be back in a jiffy.

Manny's seen the tape, Lorca says, adding in a voice that won't allow contradiction, You go; Manny goes. You should have someone watching your back.

Manny is holding the door, Doreen is glowering, and I am fresh out of excuses. So out we go into the humid night, leaving Lorca on his knees in front of the VCR, hooking up the cables. Leaving Doreen to keep stalling or else collapse from the stress. Leaving my bondage kit and my gun behind—stuff I may never get to use. Manny shambles along behind me as I make for the hotel. I glance back to see if he has read my panic, but nothing registers in this giant's eyes. They are brown and flat and not at all amused with me. There may not be evil lurking there, but there isn't any charity, either. So I lead Manny the long way around to the back entrance while I try to think. The best I can come up with is to walk him through the dining room and try to ditch through the kitchen.

I'm mounting the steps up from the pool area when I hear this *ooof!* sound of expelled air—lots of it. This is followed by the sound of Manny collapsing onto the granite steps. He takes awhile to fall, and I have turned and absorbed the whole scene before his head strikes hardest—and last. Carl Dupree stands above him, holding the shotgun by the muzzle. The shoulder stock broke off with the force of the blow. The broken piece clatters down the steps as Carl heaves a sigh and lowers the gun.

Had to bring the big one, dint ya? Carl says.

He grabs Manny's MAC-10 out of a shoulder holster and tosses it to me. Then we are scrambling back out of the lights, into the gardens around the pool, when I ask him where the hell he's been.

Tommy escaped, Carl says. Musta picked the handcuff lock. He was out and runnin' jus' after I talked to you. I never even got into position at the bungalow.

I tried to raise you! I cry as we duck behind a trellis.

Dropped my fuckin' radio. Carl sighs.

You still could've hit the bungalow!

With Tommy roamin' the woods? Carl says. He coulda called Doreen and queered the whole deal!

But my ass is twistin' in the wind for more than an hour! I say. Manny's got one finger on the trigger—

Not anymore. Carl grins. Forget about Tommy. Let's go jump Lorca, and then let's get that money.

So Carl leads us back along a hedge and around to the patio of Doreen's bungalow. First off, I notice the patio door is wide open. I can see straight inside; no sign of Doreen or Lorca. This could be bad, bad indeed. Carl covers me as I creep through the little kitchenette and into the main room. Carl checks the bedroom and bath. Doreen is long gone, but Lorca is there—lying on top of the television, shot through the back of the head. He died exactly as I left him, on his knees tinkering with wires. Doreen drew the gun I had taped under the table and whacked him after I left.

I explain this to Carl, and he says, At least she waited till after you was gone. If that goon hadn't been here with a machine gun, she mighta done you and Lorca both.

And while I consider the killing I missed, another one is going down. Shots are ringing out in the compound, coming from beyond the pool. It is muffled semiautomatic fire. Steady shooting, not an exchange. I don't have to guess the source, and Carl knows, too, because he leads us in a mad sprint past the pool cabana toward Lorca's bungalow. We hurdle a flower bed and break from some trees in time to see Tommy and Doreen careen out of the lot in Lorca's jeep. I start toward the bungalow, but Carl snags my arm.

No point lookin' in there, he says. The money jus' went thataway.

Carl leads me back to our rental car parked out on the main road. I snatch the keys from his hand, saying, I'll drive. You shoot their tires. We can still take them alive.

It is clear that Tommy doesn't know where he is going. They have turned east on the airport road, a dead end at the terminal. Sure enough, we make the last turn toward the airport and here comes the jeep, westbound and throttle down. I fishtail the sedan across both lanes of the road, and Tommy veers into the ditch. Carl can't get a shot at the tires, but I get a good look at them as they bounce on by. Doreen grips the camera case with one hand, the roll bar with the other. *Buckle up, baby*, I'm thinking. You're in for a three-million-dollar ride.

We get westbound and come up fast on the jeep's tail. Carl hooks an arm out the window with the MAC-10. Tommy spots him before he can fire and veers into the oncoming lane. There are headlights coming, a delivery truck of some kind. I pull back as Tommy tromps it, forcing the truck to lock up and skid sideways.

Comin' at ya, Carl says, instead of screaming.

I shoot to the ditch and evade the truck but not the terrain. We bottom out and lurch up a few times, and two of our hubcaps fly ahead of us down the road. We get out of the ditch and just catch sight of the jeep pulling into the jungle.

Goin' off-road, Carl says. Can't catch him there.

That's not off-road, I say, hitting the accelerator. That's Chichén Itzá. They're headed into the park.

Tommy has steered them through a gate that was open because

of the light show. Tourists sit on folding chairs and watch colored lights hit the temples and ruins. We go careening right through the middle of this, ripping up the turf and gunning engines over the sound of some narrator. People scream and scatter away from the path of these maniac drivers. But it doesn't faze Tommy and it doesn't stop me from gaining space on the even ground. We are out of the restored city in a flash, rolling down a corridor of trees, with the occasional granite wall zinging by. There are no colored lights here, no indication of where Tommy is leading us. I know the cleared ground doesn't run forever. Pretty soon we will hit jungle.

And just as that thought strikes me, I see the taillights of the jeep disappear. Instantly. Now you see them; now you don't. Would Tommy be driving dark to screw us up?

Where'd he go? Carl says. And before he can finish, I'm hitting the skids, ripping up fifty yards of sod and gravel until the sedan sways to and fro and finally stops. We are half a car length from the rim of the huge Mayan well, the Sacred Cenote that Indigo told me about. Two hundred feet wide and sixty feet straight down. And down is a freshwater spring that probably runs to the core of the earth. All that Carl and I see when we look over the rim is the rings spooling out from some gigantic splash. Rings, and a few duplicate moons that break across the reflected surface. No jeep, no swimmers, no suitcase of cash. All sacrificed; all accepted.

And behind us, the convergence of sirens and headlights heralds the arrival of the park police.

Toss in your guns, I tell Carl. All of them, *quickly*.

He tosses his pistol and the MAC-10 while I fetch the riot gun from the car. If the *policía* see any of this, they don't mention it. They're too upset about the missing persons, and the damage to the groomed lawns. The gringos in their cars are an abomination, an insult to the ancient ones. It's an offense severe enough to hold us for two nights, until Indigo can arrive with our stash from the *Angeline* and buy our freedom again.

* * *

When we get out of jail, we all drive back to Chichén Itzá together and walk to the Sacred Cenote. I can't help but think about Tommy Delorme as I look at the ancient city—the Group of the Thousand Columns and El Castillo. This place functioned as a kind of Utopia for hundreds of years. But come to what—jungle rot that was reclaimed and restored for the tourists? Whatever empire Tommy could make would have come to this, too: Behold; the vulgar castle where the coke lord once ruled.

Indigo stops to read a placard describing how the shadow of a snake descends the steps of El Castillo during the equinox. Our shadows fall into our own wheel ruts as we approach the Sacred Cenote. A construction crane is still in place at the rim, but the jeep and the bodies have long since been removed. Word is that below the waterline is silt—enough to swallow the jeep before Doreen and Tommy could work their seat belts. They found the bodies impacted in scum, and still in their seats. But nobody found the camera case. The gods kept that for themselves.

The water below the scalloped levels of granite is broken with patches of green-gray algae. It looks malignant, every bit the life-taker that it was back in 900 A.D.

Can't jus' leave it there, Carl says as we gaze down at our muddled reflections.

A waste, Indigo agrees. Even the gods can't be that greedy.

But the gods aren't going to help us bring it up, I say. So who's for a swim?

Not on your *life*.

Not for three million dollars?

We could spend that much jus' gettin' it back, Carl says.

They say you can't take it with you. Indigo sighs. But it looks like Tommy beat us, after all.

So we wander out of Chichén Itzá, out of Cancún and the Yucatán with our collective chins on our chests. But unlike Carl and Indigo, I'm not letting Tommy have the last laugh. I'm not cutting any losses here, because I have a Plan C. I have a magazine stowed in my suitcase that represents that proverbial kernel of hope. It's one of those in-flights I picked up between New

Orleans and Miami. I kept it because of an article about this alarming trend in dental-floss bikinis. They have passed ordinances to keep this fashion scourge off the streets of Palm Beach, Key Biscayne, and so on. Plenty of photos accompany the text. Just the kind of political think piece I like to read at night, alone in a hotel room while listening to Jay Leno.

But the magazine also happens to contain a story about oceanic archaeology. It talks about limited partners that create these consortiums that finance guys like Bud Sadler. And when Bud Sadler's crew found the wreck of the *Sevilla,* the consortium was instantly rich. Doubloon City. Sadler was the first, the most famous of all, but there are plenty of others. This remote video-technology, computer-enhancement shit has made exploration a snap. And if they can find the *Sevilla,* the *Titanic,* and the *Bismarck,* then they can sure as hell find an aluminum suitcase in the bottom of a Mayan well. *Somebody* can. It's just a question of recruiting the talent, greasing the Mexican authorities, and defying the Mayan gods.

Key West is as good a place to defy the gods as any. It is the absolute end of the road for Rainbow Family rejects, born-again Christian bikers, and panhandling one-man bands. Key West is the last stop on the subway platform performance tour. If you're a tone-deaf musician with a tenor sax, you open your case on Duval Street and wait for change to fall from the sky. If you're an acrobat tired of the carnival scene, you can always play Mallory Square at sunset. You just have to be freakier, geekier, and more flamboyant than the fire-eating contortionist or the hermaphrodite who dances on broken glass. I'm talking the fringe freaks who used to work Coney Island, Asbury Park, or the boardwalk in Atlantic City. It's like some virus flushed them them all down the American intestine to this little appendix called Key West.

Carl likes the Keys because he can go bonefishing every day. Indigo likes the "diffusion of anger" here, which the rest of us call "tropical mellow." She claims to feel a pervasive, shrouding sort of antidote to hostility and fear. I feel it, too; two parts psychic energy and one part Puerto Rican rum. Stir in some ganja and singles-bar sex, and you begin to levitate. That's where the tourists get that Key West strut—from moving in a thicker atmosphere, a foot or two off the ground. They float in and out of bars, trying all of these funky drinks called Hurricane this and Typhoon that. They buy T-shirts. They eat conch fritters, conch burgers, and conch on a stick. And they buy tickets to the Bud Sadler Maritime Museum, where they display all of Sadler's spoils and pirate booty.

I'm not that interested in Bud Sadler's shrine to his own expeditions. But I am *very* interested in Bud Sadler's expedition company. I learn, for instance, that Sadler hires divers, technicians, and crew by the score. He operates more than fifty boats on various expeditions in the Caribbean and the Atlantic. Some of them hit paydirt. Others just cruise in endless sweeps, tinkering with sonar and computers. But win or lose, the crews all draw a salary—a pretty good one. And that is enough to attract every swab jockey with a PADI certificate and every free-lance maritime gadgeteer to Uncle Bud's door. Some of them are even qualified. And one of them is bound to be interested in slime-diving for a suitcase of cash.

We pick our man out of a crew that puts in at the boat slips reserved for Sadler's boats. I chat up one of the roustabout lackeys and learn that they have been chasing the ghost of a treasure frigate near the Turks and Caicos. Three months of drifting over shallow reefs, hoping to turn up an anchor, a rusted cannon. But all they got is tanner and hairier, by the looks of them. Even the guys who shouldn't try to grow beards have gone scraggy and leather-skinned. I settle on one of the scraggier, darker crewmen because he appears to be in charge. The guy is tall and very wiry. He looks like a biathlete or a marathoner. I first spot him helping some technician tinker with a giant air-compressor unit. It is clear as we watch this guy roam among the divers, support crew, and volunteers that he is some kind of generalist—or supervisor. Indigo agrees. She stands with me on the marina dock, sipping an Evian and watching them come and go. When the scraggy biathlete saunters by, she tips her head ever so discreetly and says, *Him.*

I take my chance to buttonhole the guy as he saunters back

from the equipment truck. I fall into step beside him, saying something trite like, You guys carry lots of equipment, eh?

He shrugs, looks down at me from behind these sunglasses with the side flaps like horse blinders. Not exactly congenial.

Listen, I know you're busy now, so I'll be brief, I say. Name's Darrel, Darrel Fuller. (I don't offer my hand, because I know he won't take it.) I represent a consortium of investors who are need of some expertise.

That so? He grunts. Diving expertise?

Exactly, I reply, skip-hopping to match his long stride. I, uh, didn't get your name . . . ?

I didn't give it, the fellow replies. Honestly, pal, I'd love to—

We're talking six figures for one quick job, I say. Cash.

That stops him dead. He turns, looks down at me, and pulls off his sunglasses for a better look. I leave mine on—air of mystery and all. I peer up at a very narrow face, ageless in its simplicity, in its creaseless vitality. But the eyes are set well back and very flat. It's as if he still has sunglasses on—a hard, dismissive look.

What is this? he finally says.

Pay or play, I tell him. Quick and dirty. I don't have time to win your confidence, to give you a song and dance. This isn't about archaeology or navigation. This is about money. If you're interested, we can talk down at Jimmy Buffet's place on Duval. I'll be there around dusk with the rest of the investors. I still didn't get your name. . . .

I still didn't give it, the lanky dude says. Then he puts his shades back on and ambles back down to the boat slip where his crew is stacking their gear.

Mr. Congenial shows up well after dark. He comes ambling down the sidewalk and through the bar without making eye contact. I direct him to a chair beside Indigo, but he sits at a table adjacent to ours, laying a tan bony ankle over his knobby knee. Wants to keep up appearances, avoid fraternizing, I guess. Anyway, I break the ice by ordering *cerveza* and introducing Indigo and Carl. The guy squeezes lime wedges down the neck of his beer bottle and drinks without looking at us. His Adam's apple bobs in a mesmerizing rhythm. Indigo looks at me and shrugs. I can tell from Carl's expression that he would like to throttle him. *Pompous ass.* But with his throat finally lubricated, our man becomes a regular chatterbox.

Name's Dwight, he says. And you sure as hell don't look like any consortium of investors that I've ever seen.

Let's just say we've invested some sweat equity, I say.

And we're that close to cashing in, Carl says, holding his finger and thumb a fraction apart.

Drug boat? Dwight asks, wiping his mouth with his hand. Went down in a storm? Tell you right now, I won't risk the lives of my crew to salvage your soggy kilos of skag.

Nobody's asking you to risk your life, Indigo interjects. We're just saying look it over and give us an estimate—like any contractor would do.

And it ain't skag down there, Carl adds. So get that notion outta your head.

Money? Dwight says after another pull of beer.

I told you up front that this was about money, I say.

How much?

Equal shares of three million dollars, I reply.

But it isn't equal risk, is it? Dwight says. And whereabouts might this be?

I tell him, and Dwight drains his bottle as he mulls it over. We've got a month of shore leave; I could fly there tomorrow, he says. Finders keepers. I can't think of a reason to cut you in at all.

That's as much as Carl can take, and he's out of his chair, grabbing a fistful of Dwight's curly hair and tipping his head back so far that his chair almost slips from under him. Indigo shouts and grabs his arm, but Carl is on autopilot.

We already put our lives on the line, motherfucker, Carl says. We chased this score halfway aroun' the worl'—and I'm willin' to chase you twice as far. You take a dime of our money outta that hole and you never sleep another night as long as you live!

Carl lets Dwight tilt back forward and contemplate the new

balance of power. I let it simmer a good long while before giving the rest of my pitch.

Dwight, I'm sure you can appreciate the perils of transporting large amounts of cash, I say. Anyone who experiences a *windfall,* shall we say, confronts a new world order. You don't carry it through customs; you don't explain it away. Instant wealth is like nuclear waste—it makes people crazy and it glows in the dark. People have meters to sniff you out, and all of a sudden it becomes common knowledge; it becomes a curse. Laundering that kind of money requires a particular skill that I—we—possess. You have your expertise; we have ours. Believe me, we need each other.

Dwight hunches over the table where his upturned bottle lies. I flag the waiter, who is wary about serving a potential brawl. But he brings Dwight a fresh beer with more lime. Dwight fusses with the lime wedges for a moment, then he turns and shrugs over his shoulder at Carl. You get him the fuck away from me and we can talk about making a deal, Dwight says.

I'm not about to tell Carl to take a hike, but he understands the bad-cop dynamic enough to know when his part is over. He fades back into the room and parks himself under the television. Dwight waits until Carl is seated, then speaks directly to Indigo.

I don't need to estimate this job, he says. Crews have gone into those Mayan holes for the last sixty years. It's no picnic; logistics are a bitch. The silt forces you to go with surface air; compressor and hoses and regulating hardware to keep us at a consistent ninety pounds of pressure. That's a crew of four—diver, tender, timekeeper, and topside supervisor. To move the silt, you need motor-driven airlift and some seining gear. That's five more people. You want people to move cable and run the generator.

Ouch, Indigo says. Lots of fingers in the pie.

This isn't reef diving, Dwight says. Can't see your hand down there, even with massive lights. Diving in silt is like swimming in chocolate mousse.

We were thinking something smaller, I say. Truth is, we were thinking just *you*. . . .

Dwight laughs out loud at this, takes another swig of his beer, and stands. He pushes his chair in, still shaking his head, when Indigo grabs his arm.

What's the fewest, the least you can use? she demands. Every man you cut doubles your share.

Dwight spreads his palms over the table, leans forward, and sighs. He sights down the neck of his beer bottle and asks, What are we talking about—loose bills, suitcase?

Camera case, I say. Aluminum.

We forget the airlift, all the other hardware, Dwight says. We go with a jackstay and a radius of line. The timekeeper can suit up, double as tender. Three. Three people. Three million dollars split six ways: Take it or leave it.

We'll take it, Indigo says, and she stands up and shakes the tan hand of our newest conspirator.

A jackstay turns out to be a concrete weight that Dwight drops in the center of the hole. It anchors a line with a surface buoy. And on that vertical line is a rope with a slipknot, rotating on the horizontal. The plan is for Dwight to follow the jackstay line to the bottom, grab the radius line, and step out three feet. From there he does a 360—or at least his estimation of one. He gropes the murk until he's made a complete circuit. Then he ties a knot in the rope to mark progress, moves out another three feet, and rotates again. At two knots out—six feet from center—Dwight finds a jerrican of gasoline from the jeep. At twenty feet, he finds Carl's sawed-off shotgun.

We don't see these discoveries because they are working at night, operating off of a platform on the water sixty feet below. Carl, who is also entrusted with the generator, gets periodic word by walkie-talkie. We have bribed our way into the park, and although Dwight thinks we're clear of all constables and brass, we still can't risk using lights. Dwight's supervisor—a big Swede named Olav—checks his gauges with a penlight. We can see it play over the rumbling equipment while the white buoy jerks in whatever direction Dwight is moving. After about an hour, the buoy stops jerking. I proceed to panic until I hear Dwight break the surface, see his black slimy arm raise up the case that reflects the sliver of moon.

Later, up topside, we inspect the goods and make plans to meet for the split at a bungalow at El Castillo. But for now, it all gets very quiet. We have had plenty of war whoops and backslapping—especially after Dwight opened the case. But now that Dwight has shed his gear, after the compressor is quiet and the generator is off, it doesn't feel festive at all. We will meet for breakfast, at which time I will explain the Dutch Sandwich and Caribbean finance. That's when we can fantasize and act like nouveau riche. But now it falls to Indigo to do the benediction.

It's terrible karma to take from the spirits like this, Indigo says. We already violated the park, the sacred grounds, and all of the spirits here.

We're not just plundering here, she whispers. We're *better* than that. We need to offer something in return, something with spiritual weight.

Carl looks at the ground. Dwight and his team just stand there shuffling, kicking stones over the *cenote*'s rim.

What did you have in mind? Dwight asks.

An heirloom, Indigo replies. A talisman.

What about some of the money? Carl says. We never did cut in poor Doreen. Give it up for her.

Doreen got what she deserved, I say. She's not the issue. You want an object with personal significance, right? I ask Indigo. Something that squares us with the gods?

Indigo nods, and I reach in my pocket and pull out the golf ball—the lucky ball that I retrieved from Charlie Cadeaux's cactus patch, the talisman I carried to remind me about the price of vengeance. I don't know if it saved my life, but it always kept me focused. And when I toss it into the Sacred Cenote, it certainly feels spiritual; it makes me feel like I have broken some cords, chased away the entities.

But Indigo won't leave it alone, won't let me sleep that night without exercising my "ethereal sight." What is the point of being incredibly rich, she wonders, if you can't make enlightened choices? This is no longer about survival, we're not living hand-to-mouth.

That's for sure, I gloat, rolling away from her in the vast bed of a honeymoon suite. Indigo chases me, pulls back the comforter, and shakes me by the shoulders.

Look, I made lots of choices over the past four months, I say. At least *some* of them were enlightened. I chose you, didn't I?

THAT'S NOT THE POINT! Indigo shouts.

Sssshhh! You'll wake Carl, I tell her. (He's sleeping in an adjoining suite, perhaps dreaming of all the bonefish he will catch on his new yacht—the *Angeline II.*) The point is that I have you now, I say. You can read all of the auras and tell me what they say.

You can read them, too, Indigo insists. You've come so far, the rest is *easy*.

Then she tosses back the covers and goes bounding over to a curtain that serves as a closet door. The curtain is black. Indigo, of course, is luminous white—an intentional contrast.

Try, she says. Maybe tonight's the night.

She wants me to look beyond her image, her frank and compelling nudity, and see her aura. She insists that if I focus on the space she occupies, the black curtain will display colors. The air will softly undulate in the negative space.

I peer, I squint, and I rove over her while banishing lust from my mind. I look away, then back. But no matter what I try, I see only human light, only positive space, only the secrets I was meant to see.